CRAZY SORROW

SUSAN BOWES

CRAZY SORROW

SUSAN BOWES

POLESTAR
BOOK PUBLISHERS

Polestar Book Publishers acknowledges the support from the publishing
programs of the Canada Council, the British Columbia Ministry of Small
Business, Tourism and Culture, and the Department of Canadian Heritage.

Cover photograph by Susan Bowes
Cover design by Jim Brennan
Editing by Suzanne Bastedo and Brenda Brooks
Author photograph by Marilyn Bowlby
Printed in Canada by Best Book Manufacturers

This is a work of fiction. While some of the people and places in this story
do exist or have lived, their presence in this book is purely imaginative.

The author is grateful for permission to reprint lines from "Mr. Tambourine
Man" by Bob Dylan. Copyright © 1964, 1965 by Warner Bros. Inc. Renewed
1992 by Special Rider Music. Used by permission. All rights reserved.

Special thanks, as well, to the singers and songwriters whose phrases are
lovingly reprinted here and for which the copyrights had lapsed or
permission was not required.

CANADIAN CATALOGUING IN PUBLICATION DATA
Bowes, Susan L.
     Crazy sorrow
ISBN 1-896095-19-4
     I. Title.
PS8553.094C72 1996   C813'.54   C96-910416-2
PR9199.3.B637C72 1996

POLESTAR BOOK PUBLISHERS
1011 COMMERCIAL DRIVE, SECOND FLOOR
VANCOUVER, BRITISH COLUMBIA
CANADA   V5L 3X1
(604) 251-9718

5   4   3   2   1

For
Marilyn and her Mum

❖

"When shadows creep, when I'm asleep, to lands of hope I stray."
There's a car hurtling through the darkness. And a woman inside, singing a duet with the headlights. She would have sung with the moon, if the moon had even a single pair of jingles. But the moon has only a soft, stained head, stretched tightly across a tiny black hole in the sky. She'll take her chances with the headlights, which at least are a pair of steely-eyed choristers.

"Happiness, you seem so near me. Happiness, come forth and cheer me."

There's a navy blue datebook lying on the front seat, next to an empty silver clasp. It's filled with reminders about this year's meetings and appointments; about which mission of mercy she's embarked on now. But it's also filled with echoes — of secret embraces, secret denials, secret assignations with cowardice and deceit. The years of relentless activity haven't worked. She can't escape the weight of the pages. She can only press down on the pedal and sing even louder.

"I'm forever blowing bubbles. Pretty bubbles in the air."

Back from the road, there's the towering silence of the forest. But closer to the shoulder, there's something more sympathetic. Trees that have turned into telephone poles. A twist of fate and they might have been hymn-books or murder mysteries, mastheads or steeples, ladders or hockey sticks or hardwood floors.

"They fly so high. Nearly reach the sky. Then like my dreams, they fade and die."

At first, the poles are just a blur. But then she adjusts to the darkness and speed and they turn into frets. And their wires into strings. She hasn't played the guitar before; only the piano, where the strings are all hidden inside. But she bets she can. The frets are very far apart. And sorrow has that long a reach.

"Fortune's always hiding. I've looked everywhere. I'm forever..."

Suddenly, there's a big black crow in front of the car. An ugly black sorrow, waiting to peck at the carcass of her dreams and expectations. She doesn't care if it's a mirage this time. Even mirages make sickening explosions of blood and bones and feathers.

"Pretty bubbles in the..."

There's a moment of astounding clarity, when she realizes what she and the car must finally do. It's that clarity which makes her swerve to miss the ugly black sorrow; that clarity which makes her crash headlong into the telephone pole.

"Aaaaair."

Afterwards, there's a certain harmony to the images. To the tangle of metal. To the lifeless body. To the bits of stained glass twinkling up from the cuckooflowers. But there's no resolution. The headlights are still beaming. The big black crow is still waiting. The navy blue datebook is still lying on the front seat, next to an empty silver clasp.

2

Brian slips his hand into the box of Bugles he keeps by the bed.

"Not as sweet," murmurs Rebecca, as she pulls the covers over her shoulder.

"What isn't?" he chuckles. "Rebecca? Are you awake?" He lifts one of the tiny yellow instruments to his lips and blows a tender reveille into her ear.

"Not as sweet," she murmurs again.

He drops the Bugle back into the box. "Not sweet at all, if you ask me."

It's early Sunday morning. There may be salt on Brian's fingers but the air itself smells like red licorice. Not as sweet as last night, perhaps, when the M & A Candy Company on Ewen Road was making a batch of pink bubble gum, but sweet enough.

Rebecca slides down one of the long red twists into the past. There's green licorice, too. And licorice Allsorts. But she likes the soft black pipes the best. With those smooth black curves in their stems. And those bright red dots on their ends, to make them look like they're lit.

"The red ropes are fake," she murmurs. "Only the black ones are real."

"Whatever you say," smiles Brian. He leans over and kisses her on the cheek.

"When we were five," she murmurs.

"What?"

Artie Dixon's younger brother Ernie kissed her on the cheek. In Marion's garage. When they were five.

"And then we pulled each other's pants down."

"That's nice." Brian kisses her again.

And Alan Rawding, too. When they were eleven. At the movies in Middleton. Very proper. But on the lips.

"Don't."

Brian strokes her hair. "Rebecca? Wake up, sweetheart."

Her eyes flutter open.

"Are you awake?" he asks gently.

"Yes."

"Wide awake?"

"Well, how wide do you want?"

Brian laughs. "Well, wide enough for..." He tries to take her in his arms but she rolls away from him. "What's the matter?" he sighs.

"Nothing."

"Great." He flops back down on the pillow. "You won't make love and you won't talk. So what else is new?"

She closes her eyes again. The long red twist is still dangling there.

Her Mum doesn't keep the Baby Book. Her Aunt Marion keeps it. Her Aunt Marion jots down every new word or phrase she learns. "Da" at seven months. "Mum, Mum", "Bye, Bye", "No, No" at eight months. Kisses and patty-cakes and "See, See" at nine months. "Don't" at ten months. Whole sentences at...

"Rebecca Peterson!" Miss Hamilton pinches her on the arm. "How many times have I told you not to talk in class?" She stands her up on the desk. "Maybe that'll teach you not to be so..."

"Rebecca Peterson!" Mr. Armstrong throws a piece of chalk at her. "Do you think we can get through a single morning without your yippy-yappy, yippy-yappy, yippy...?"

"Rebecca Peterson!"

"What!" She shinnies back up the long red twist.

"That's been your problem from the beginning, you know."

"What beginning?"

"Us. Since I met you. You never talk."

"I talk."

"No, you don't. Well, at least you never initiate the conversations. And you never really respond when I do. Jesus! Sometimes I wonder how you got to be so...repressed."

"Sorry. It's just the way I am."

"It's just the way I am," he mimics. "Ha! Cold, unfeeling, unresponsive...And when you do talk, it's never about nice, sweet, happy things. Only awful things. Jesus! You're the most pessimistic person I..."

"Look! First, you make me talk. Then you don't like the way I talk. Jesus!" She yanks at the covers. "I'm too tired for this."

"Yes, well...maybe because you never think of anything but work. You never do anything but work. You have to learn to delegate, you know."

You have to. You have to. You have to.

"You can't do everyone else's job for them." He jams his hand into the box of Bugles. And the world won't come to a complete standstill if you spend a little more time with..."

"Maybe I'd feel like spending a little more time with you if you didn't criticize every single thing I..."

"Jesus!"

"What?"

"I spilled the god-damned...!"

Rebecca sits up. There are tiny yellow instruments all over the covers.

"Ha!" She pops one into her mouth. "At least they're better than Fluffs."

"Fluffs? What are Fluffs?"

She springs out of bed. "I have to get ready for work."

"OK, but..." Brian scoops up the Bugles. "Don't forget to look in on the kids before you..."

The shower is already running.

"Do you want mustard or mayonnaise on your sandwich?" he shouts at her.

"Mustard!" she hollers back.

Rebecca frowns as she sweeps the Miracle Brush across her white cotton pants. It isn't going to work. She isn't going to be able to get rid of every single one of those little black balls of lint. She could kill Brian. He should know better than to wash the darks with the whites.

Meanwhile, there's a steady stream of muttering coming from the bathroom. "She never, ever changes the toilet paper roll. She never, ever shuts the door to the medicine cabinet. She never, ever..." Brian could kill her, too.

Rebecca smiles.

He doesn't lead a charmed life. Looking after the house. Looking after the kids. Writing his pithy little columns on movies and music for the *Hamilton Spectator*. But then the only charmed life is the oblivious life.

She brushes even harder.

The boys are still all right, however, even if they have turned out to be funny little crosses between Wimpy and Mighty Mouse. All they know of life is what they see beneath the manhole covers, where their Teenage Mutant Ninja Turtles do battle with cartoon copies of evil and deceit.

"Kawabunga, dude!" they suddenly shout, from the next room.

"Yabba dabba dooooooo!" she bellows back.

"What?"

"What did you say, Mum?"

"Nothing." She flings the Miracle Brush onto the dresser.

"I think she's lost it," they whisper.

Rebecca is standing in the parking lot across from Stewart Webb Memorial Arena. There are hundreds of gulls swooping low over the pavement, diving down for the scraps of last night's merriment. They don't care that the Macho Man came without Elizabeth. That the Legion of Doom got disqualified. That one of the Nasty Boys hurt his back. They just want the leftovers. The splashes of beer. The traces of chocolate. The popcorn, the wieners, the licorice, the buns.

You're a long way from home, thinks Rebecca, as she leans against the door of her car.

There are hundreds of piercing cries.

They aren't cries of loneliness and sorrow, however. They're cries of annoyance. The gulls don't miss the waves, the weirs, the terrifying beauty of the sea. And there are thousands more scraps here, in the parking lot, than on the beach after those measly old bonfires. They just want her to leave, so they can get back to their scavenging in peace.

"And so am I, thank God." She strides across the street and into the arena.

"Is it fixed?"

"No, it's not fixed."

Rebecca peeks between the curtains. The scoreboard clock has been lowered to the floor.

"Well, which side is it?"

"The home team."

"Jesus! I can't understand it. It was working OK for the wrestling."

"Yeah, well, fuck it. I can't see that we'll need it for the monster trucks anyway."

Rebecca strolls toward the escalator.

"Calm and concise. Calm and concise," she repeats to herself, as she approaches the door to the Box Office. And then she laughs.

Everyone there must think she's Nancy Drew or something. They're always talking about how cool and composed and practical she is. An infallible judge of character. With an amazing memory for detail.

"Ha! I wish."

And the ability to reduce crooks to jelly, of course. And to give eminently reasonable explanations for things which seem puzzling or complicated or downright spooky.

She reaches for the panel of buttons above the doorknob.

But she never had much luck being Nancy when she was little. And now she feels a little more like Olive Oyl. Drab, ugly and inept. Only with a mean streak. *They're all idiots.* And a sad streak. *Nothing ever turns out right.* And a wild streak. *The dirty yellow hula hoop twirls faster and faster and...*

She punches in the numbered code and slips inside.

"How many Will Call and how many Sales?" One of the part-time clerks dumps a bag of white plastic letters onto the table.

"Jesus," mutters Angela Hunter. "We seem to be running short of vowels."

"And punctuation, too," sighs Glenda Macoritti. "Remind me to order some..."

Grind, clank. Grind, clank. Click, click, click, click. Riiiiiiing!

For a moment, Rebecca just stands there, listening, with her hands on her hips, and her long, dark brown hair flickering beneath a ceiling full of faulty fluorescent lights.

"Twenty-two dollars, please."

"It's up the escalator and to your left, sir."

"For tonight's event?"

When she was little, there was never anything in particular she wanted to be. There were some things she definitely didn't want to be. Like a nurse, because she didn't want to carry bedpans around all day. And a vet, because she'd feel too sorry for the animals. But there was never anything special. And she certainly never imagined she'd end up being the Box Office Manager for three entertainment and convention facilities in Hamilton, Ontario — for this ugly, noisy, yellow world she's standing in now.

"Will that be cash or charge, ma'am?"

"No, the tax is included."

"Have a good time!"

Still, she has to admit there's something comforting about that constant hum of voices and machines. Or at least numbing. It's a protection against the unconscious. Against most of the conscious, too, as long as she can ignore the flashing rows of diamonds on those constantly ringing telephones.

"Will someone please get that?"

"None of the bloody staplers have any staples in them!"

"Oh, wait a minute! She's just come in!" Angela presses the Hold button. "It's for you. A customer. He says he thought he was buying...Anyway, he wants a refund. Oh, and...just so you know...the bloody printers aren't cutting properly, so you'll have to...And the people from Ebony called. They're accusing us of racism because we won't..."

"I'll take it in the office," says Rebecca calmly.

Rebecca is sitting at her desk, gazing up at the rows of dots in the panels on the ceiling.

"*To dance beneath the diamond sky,*" she hums derisively, "*with one hand waving...*"

"Hello? Yes! I'm fine! What are you doing here on a...? Yes, I'll hold." Dots are just as difficult to count as stars. "Yes, I'm still here...Oh, you are?" And even more difficult to group into anything light and lovely and harmonious. "Well, then, maybe I'd better come down and..."

"What's *he* want?" Dorian Donaldson pokes his head through the doorway, just as she lowers the receiver.

This is my sky, she thinks. An ugly yellow twinkle and a blur of meaningless dots.

"Rebecca?"

She lowers her eyes. "He wants to cancel the Gift Certificates."

"What did *you* say?"

"Not much. I just told him to think of the implications."

"As if he knows what those are."

"Yes, well..." She pushes herself up from the chair. "I'd better go down and make sure he thinks of the right ones."

"Who threw paper towel down the toilet?"

"The house seats have all been released, sir."

"Well, if you can wear spandex, I don't see why I can't wear..."

The Chief Executive Officer is in way over his head — apart from his pathological disgust with alcohol and his penchant for paying off his barber and painter with complimentary tickets. But then who isn't? thinks Rebecca, as she strolls past the empty offices in the administrative wing. The Publicist has just issued a memo reminding receptionists at the arena, the convention centre and Burrows Place theatre that they must "at all times keep their facial hair trimmed."

"Calm and concise," she repeats to herself. "Calm and concise."

"I have an extra ticket."

"Well, I'm afraid we don't give refunds, sir."

"I don't want a refund. I want you to give it away to someone. Anyone. As long as they have skin like mine. I don't want to be sitting next to a..."

"Who stole the last piece of pineapple pizza?"

"Well, it started almost an hour ago, sir."

"Can we close now?"

"Dammit! I'm fifty cents short!"

"Have you run the journal yet?"

There haven't been any major problems tonight. No duplicate seats. No customers whose tickets turned black when they left them in their pockets and ironed them. No maintenance workers who hooked the hot water lines up to the toilets. But the phones are still ringing off the hook.

Rebecca pushes the buttons which activate the taped message, then sets the alarm and leaves.

Rebecca leans against the door of her car.

There's a huge stained-glass window in the south wall of Canadian Martyrs Church on Emerson Street, right across from her house. In the daylight, it isn't very impressive. In fact, it looks like cracked pottery, with no discernible colours or designs. But at night, it's a different story. At night, with the lights in the sanctuary glowing through it from behind, it's gorgeous.

She doesn't think much of Jesus in general. And she's a little disgusted by how wide the one in the window has thrown his arms.

But she has to admit he's a knockout.

Suddenly, there's the sound of ringing from inside the house. "Now what?" she laughs, as she sprints up the steps. She hopes the mice haven't set off the alarm in the vault again.

"It's Vivian," mouths Brian, as he hands her the receiver. She rolls her eyes. "Hi, Mum. Who's died now?"

3

"Great," murmurs Rebecca. "I can't see a damned thing."

Her bright red Miata is inching through the fog along the Saint John River, like a drop of blood might inch through the steam in a slaughterhouse.

"I'll never get there at this rate."

At first, there'd been sunshine. And miles and miles of crests and hollows. And a swarm of gas station attendants with hand-painted swastikas on their work gloves. And then, there'd been darkness. And miles and miles of crests and hollows. And fried egg sandwiches at the Riverside Motel. And speed, furious speed, as if the car were an icon of her own desperate needs. For freedom. For independence. For oblivion. Finally, at Rivière-du-Loup, she'd made that sharp dip downward into the fog.

"Dammit!"

She hadn't been able to leave work in May. They said an aunt wasn't a close relative. They said she'd have to wait until her holidays came up in July. And now she's sorry she left at all. Like most people, Rebecca has a hydra in her life. A multi-headed evil or sorrow she just can't kill. She doesn't exactly know what gave birth to this serpent, or where it lives or how it survives, but she does know that whenever she succeeds in emulating Hercules and cutting off one of its heads, it just hisses — and then replaces that severed head with at least two other writhing ones. Every miracle, it seems, is matched by two monsters. Her adult heart has always been a thick red muck that's pretty difficult to slither through. Brian's told her that often enough. But since there's no telling what it'll become back home in Aylesford, with the remains of her childhood, she isn't sure she wants to get there. After all, something might step on her hydra by mistake and make it grow more heads. But she's sure she wants to get there fast, without stopping, without thinking, without taking time to wonder whether she'll be able to be civil or not.

"Dammit all to hell!"

Never once, in the twenty-one years since she left Nova Scotia, has she ever been homesick. She knows she should feel guilty about it — and goodness knows her mother has tried to make her feel guilty about it — but she can't help it. She just doesn't care. She can't make herself care. She can't make herself miss them at all.

Her mother still keeps in touch but it's mostly just to gossip now. "Uncle Donald took a very bad turn." Or "Darrell's wife gave us all quite a scare." Or "I think we're all OK. Ha! Ha!" And sometimes to tell her who's died. Right after she left, it was her Dad and her Grammie. And then Irene Andrews, who had a heart attack, and whose husband Alvin took pictures of her in her coffin. And Herbert Armstrong, who had Lou Gehrig's disease and left nine thousand dollars to Nora and Wilfred Dean so they could build a big pen and take care of his cats. And Doris Pudsey, who survived lymphatic cancer but then got Alzheimer's disease and is now as good as dead in Roach's Nursing Home. And now Marion, who's crashed her car into a telephone pole on Old Post Road.

Rebecca peers through the windshield. The fog is as thick as ever. She presses down on the gas pedal.

Marion was her favourite aunt. Her mother's favourite sister. Everyone's favourite something.

"*Was*," she smirks.

As far as anyone can tell, there isn't a formal will; just a handwritten note, dated Sunday, November 7, 1965, and addressed to "My dear Dick Tracy."

It's early morning, barely light.

"What the hell's that?" murmurs Rebecca, as she coasts into the rest area at the border. She can make out the sign all right. WELCOME TO NOVA SCOTIA. But not the sound — a sort of deep and mournful drone.

She puts the car into neutral and rolls down the window. "Oh my God!" she laughs. "An agony bag! I wonder who...?" She peers through the mist.

Standing in the dew-soaked grass near the information booth is a young woman. She's dressed in a Nova Scotian tartan and working a set of Scottish Highland pipes.

"'Lament for the Children,'" groans Rebecca, as the young woman adds a line of shrieks to that annoyingly incessant drone. "Agony in the key of D." She leans out the window to listen.

The bagpipes are usually too harsh for her. Too harshly wild or harshly pathetic, depending on which of the two shrillnesses the situation requires. She's surprised, then, when these notes are so subtle, so intricate, so inescapably sad.

She watches the young woman's fingers fly over the chanter. It isn't just her ease with the long line of melody which makes her so good. Every competent player can learn that heart-wrenching succession of shrill and haunting cries. It's her ease with the grace notes and with those echoing beats in the ground. It takes good technique to play those. Good fingering. Good elbows. Good concentration. And more than a passing familiarity with the humour and horror of life's variations.

"Bloody bitch!" snorts the young woman, as she spits out the wind tube.

"What?" laughs Rebecca.

"Oh, sorry. Not you. This." She pumps at the bag. "It's hard enough to play without this damned fog."

"I would imagine it is."

"They're supposed to be better now. You know, not crack or shrink or anything. Because of all the plastic stuff. Imitation blackwood. Imitation ivory. But they're still so god-damned..."

"Yes," smiles Rebecca. "Anyway, you're up early."

"Summer job. I have to practice." She flips the wind tube back into her mouth and begins the pitiful introduction to "The Daughter's Lament."

"Whoa! Can't you play something cheerful?"

The young woman spits out the wind tube again. "Like what?"

"I don't know. A jig or a reel or something. Even a call to battle, for Christ's sake! Ha!" There's a twinkle in her eye now. "Or maybe something modern?"

"Bet you think I can't," laughs the young woman, as she flips the wind tube back into her mouth.

There's a rush of air and then a drone and then...
"Hey! Mr. Tambourine Man, play a song for me."
"Oh, my God!" Rebecca claps her hands with glee. "I don't believe it!"
"I'm not sleepy and there is no place I'm going to."
"Wait! Wait for me!"
"Hey! Mr...."
Life has to have a good chorus, decides Rebecca, as she bawls out a duet with those piercing pipes. A good, rousing chorus, no matter what the rest of it sounds like.
"In the jingle-jangle morning I'll come followin' you."
She claps her hands again. "Come on. Come on."
The young woman pauses for a moment...as if trying to decide whether the bloody bitch's nine-note range is wide enough for the verse...and then keeps going.
"And take me disappearin' through the..."
Rebecca stops singing.
But the rest of it is always there, she grieves. Always. You can't just disappear. You can't just go merrily down the foggy ruins of time pretending there are no frozen leaves, no haunted, frightened trees, no *you*.
"Sorry," she whispers. "I have to..." She rolls up the window.
Lost in the shrillness, beyond the reach of feeling and meaning and reason and Rebecca, the young woman keeps playing.
"I have to..."
As Rebecca pulls slowly away from the rest area, she's overwhelmed with yearning. For knowledge and oblivion. For punishment and comfort. For the company of the dead.
"Marion," she whispers. "Marion. Marion. Frankie."
Behind her, the pipes are still calling. But there's another sound now — a sound she'd hoped she'd forgotten.
Chink. Chink. Chink. Hissssssss.

She could take Highway 101 all the way to Aylesford. But she exits instead at Kentville, so she can drive the last few miles down Old Post Road, through what the tourist brochures describe as "the beautiful, bountiful Annapolis Valley."
As she glides past the stately elms and maples on the outskirts of

town, she turns on the radio. The disc jockey at FM Magic this morning
is Karen Bergin, the woman who supposedly broke up the relationship
between Julia Roberts and Kiefer Sutherland. Before she can share
any juicy tidbits, however, it's time for the news. First, there's a lengthy
account of the parole hearing for Sidney Paul Felch, who's been in a
psychiatric hospital for twenty-seven years — ever since he murdered
five people in Auburn. And then there are brief updates on the racial
clashes in Spryfield, the segregated bars in Halifax, the growing
resentment over the new road and terminal planned for the park
commemorating Africville.

Bloody liars, seethes Rebecca, as she remembers the mid- to
late-sixties, when the city fathers invoked the gods of integration and
urban renewal and forced the residents of Africville to leave. They
promised to replace the community with a thriving industrial complex.
Instead, they left a wasteland. And then, finally, a pretty, little, symbolic
park, which, in 1991, they're threatening to desecrate.

She switches off the radio and goes back to the world of the
brochures.

The most impressive sight now is the apple orchards. Some of the
gnarled trees in that sandy soil have been there for over a hundred
years, and yet to her they're still more natural than those new
experimental ones, with no branches, and leaves growing out of their
trunks. But most of the trees are young, tender, barely ready to grow
fruit. Beyond these, there are marshlands and meadows, farmlands
and forests. And a scruffy stretch, which means she's getting close to
home. Further north — she can almost smell it — there's a rugged,
treeless coastline which belies the "genial warmth" of the standard
guidebooks. But this is hidden from view right now.

"Oh, my God! I don't believe it!"

She was just gliding past the cranberry bogs at the east end of town
when she saw the sign. WELCOME TO AYLESFORD — NATURALLY
BEAUTIFUL.

"Yeah, right." She peers at the white clapboard houses on either
side of the road.

They give the impression of a pretty, quaint, old-fashioned town —
one of those quiet, sleepy towns, nestled in the hawthorns and
flowering black locusts, where nothing much happens and no one
much matters.

She glances in the rear-view mirror. The sun is a soft brown globe in the early morning sky.

Don't stay in Aylesford, whispers a quietly vehement voice inside her head.

And suddenly, she's sleeping on the front veranda at Marion's place. Her parents are drunk. Her pajama bottoms are soaked. The millers are beating against the tall, damp screens. And then she's sensing something and rubbing the sleep from her eyes and creeping down the hall toward the living room.

Marion is sitting on the chesterfield, in the dark, gazing at the glowing brown globe she bought at Birks the last time she was in Halifax.

"Auntie Marion?"

Marion doesn't answer. Rebecca sits down beside her and gazes at it, too.

Each year, from 1934 to 1965, the George F. Cram Company of Indianapolis made twenty-five hundred seven-inch globes. Rebecca can recite almost all of the statistics Marion's told her. But this isn't a measly seven-inch globe. This is a huge ten-and-a-half-inch floor model with light inside. And a metal base shaped like a fish. It also has a Natural Scale of one to forty-seven million, eight hundred thousand, and all kinds of facts printed on it — like the direction of the ocean currents and the location of Babylon. But to Rebecca, those aren't the neatest things about it. The neatest things are the colours. Not the usual pinks and greens and blues but a mixture of browns — for the water as well as the dirt.

"One inch equals seven hundred and fifty-five Statute Miles!" announces Rebecca proudly.

"Don't stay in Aylesford," answers Marion quietly, vehemently.

Rebecca blinks. Now that she's older, she can see a little of what Marion saw. That the soft brown glow was strange but also strangely inviting. That everything in the world was in it — not just the facts and figures but the dreams and adventures. And the hostilities, too. And the hunger and sorrow and imperial rule. But somehow the browns made those things seem older, warmer, a lot less terrifying than the things at home — whether those things were coloured in pastels or primaries. And she can feel Marion's longing. To swim in those golden seas, to trek across those caramel continents, to escape into that soft brown glow.

Rebecca glances in the rear-view mirror again. The sun is now a bright red ball of fire.

"Christ! I almost missed it."

On the corner of School Street and Old Post Road, there's a large, white clapboard house which needs a coat of paint. She pauses for a moment to watch its burnt-red metal shingles gleaming in the sunlight...and then yanks the car into the driveway.

There's a woman sitting on the concrete steps at the side of the house. Her sandy brown hair has patches of grey where the home colouring kit didn't quite take. Her rosebud pajamas are rolled up to the knees. Her pale and haggard face is turned toward the sun.

"I'll say one thing for her," murmurs Rebecca, as she coasts up the driveway. "She's tougher than a boiled owl."

The woman squints toward her.

"She's had asthma and survived it. She's been hit by a car and survived it. She's been a bloody drunk and survived it. Ha!" She yanks at the parking brake.

"Unlike Dad." She snatches the keys from the ignition. "Who just passed out on the chesterfield and never woke up."

There's a brief moment of expectation...as the car door creaks open, as the woman shades her eyes, as Rebecca stands alone on the gravel driveway.

"So," the woman finally wheezes. "You're here."

Rebecca smiles. "Yes, Mum. I'm here."

"Ha!" The woman struggles to her feet. "Then you might as well come inside."

"Jesus!" gasps Rebecca, when they reach the kitchen. "What happened? Did you win the lottery?" She waves at the shiny new washer and dryer.

"No," cackles Vivian. "But I won the jackpot."

"Again?"

"Yes, again. Last month down to Kingston, where they have that big, you know...What?"

Rebecca is staring at the rotting apple on the floor behind the garbage can. She thinks she recognizes it. Or was it a rotting tomato that was lying there the last time she looked?

"Nothing. I was just...Oh, hi, Peter."

A stocky man with huge forearms is standing in the doorway to the east living room. He doesn't answer her. He doesn't meet her eye. He just snuffles and grins as he brushes by her toward the table. "Ha!" Vivian ladles out a bowl of split-pea soup. "If you want something, you know, to eat, you'll have to hurry." She places it in front of him. "Otherwise your brother will..."

"Yes," smiles Rebecca.

It's all so familiar. They never ate in the dining room when they were kids either — except at Christmas time, when the white arborite table with the wobbly metal legs wasn't quite festive enough. It was always catch-as-catch-can in the kitchen. Only there was never anything as nourishing as split-pea soup, with huge pink chunks of ham.

"Anyway." Vivian tosses a box of saltines onto the table. "You'll have to, you know, keep each other company while I..." She pours him a glass of grape Kool-Aid. "While I go and get dressed."

Rebecca is sitting at the kitchen table, watching Peter lap up his third bowl of split-pea soup. No one would guess he's four years older than she is. He's just a big, strange, nervous kid, with two souvenir wrestling watches on his right wrist.

"Those are nice, Peter. Where did you...?"

"Corn Flakes," he snuffles.

"Oh."

He's never been much of a conversationalist. But he's usually better than this, especially when Vivian isn't around.

Rebecca peers at the watches. One of them has a photograph of Koko B. Ware on its face. The other has what looks like a cartoon drawing of Ricky Steamboat demonstrating the full nelson but she can't quite tell.

"There." Vivian scurries back into the room. "I'm all..."

"More crackers!" snorts Peter.

"Ha!" She pulls her pink sweater over the waist of her pale blue skirt. "And you say I haven't, you know, been a good mother all these years!" She tosses another box of saltines onto the table. "Well, I think..."

"Here she goes." Peter crushes a stale cracker into his soup.

"Damn right I do! I think, after all the cooking and cleaning and, you know, washing up I've done for all you kids...especially you, Peter, since you still live at..."

"More Kool-Aid!"

"... since you still live at home!"

Rebecca isn't listening anymore. Instead, she's testing that "amazing memory for detail" everyone at work says she has.

When her Mum was a girl, she went to Acadia University for a year and then to her Aunt Gertie's business college for a year. It didn't work out. Finally, in 1969, after a series of part-time jobs that didn't work out either, she went back to high school — Grade Twelve Commercial, they called it — to brush up on her typing and bookkeeping. The first thing she learned was how to apply for an official birth certificate. The second thing was that her real name was Lois. Nothing was a shock after that. She and Peter got their diplomas from West Kings District High School at the same time.

In fact, their pictures were side by side in the WKDHS yearbook, *The Torch*. Peter's was the same one they'd used the year before, when he was in 11F, when he listed his favourite place as outer bohemia and his pet peeve as girls with moustaches and his future plans as "morpheme," whatever *that* meant. They just changed the caption and now claimed that he was a car enthusiast who enjoyed working and reading and whose favourite saying was: "He who cannot remember the night before must repeat it."

Rebecca snorts. Just beneath it, as if to add an ironic emphasis to his warning, was the picture of her mother.

Jesus, she thinks, as she remembers the caption for the other half of the school's only mother-and-son combination. It made her sound so happy-go-lucky. There was nothing wrong with the activities listed in it. She couldn't argue with cooking, reading, watching TV, bingo and bridge — although drinking should have been in there somewhere. But it hadn't got her character quite right. *Ambitious, dependable all the while. Always ready with a cheerful smile.* And it had made a complete mess of its prediction for her future. *Her secretarial course may finally get her out of the kitchen.*

Rebecca can't help snickering.

"What?" cackles Vivian. "What's so funny?"

"Nothing." Rebecca stops testing her memory. "Nothing. Tell me the news. How's Sunny?"

"Ha! Like an old woman!" She scrapes the last of the soup into Peter's bowl.

"What do you mean?"

"Well, your sister Sonja's very efficient and seems to have everything, you know, under control. And she looks awful good for forty-two."

"So?"

"So she's not any fun! She works too hard!"

"Sounds familiar. Is she still nursing?"

"Yes, for the Coast Guard."

"Cherry Ames to the rescue!"

"Only this week, she's up to St. John's. To learn about stress. So she won't, you know, try that business with the pills again."

"And Randy? Last I heard he was smoking dope but cutting back on salt."

Vivian lights a cigarette. "Randy's over to Alberta...aagh...to work on the..."

"You shouldn't smoke."

"To work on the oil rigs. Aagh."

"And Pam? And the kids?"

"Jesus, she used him awful hard. Made that beautiful furniture and then said she couldn't, you know, stand the lifestyle."

"You mean they aren't together? They aren't still living in that cabin he built on the North Mountain?"

"Oh, no! Not for years! Aagh. It got so they didn't, you know, do anything but fight. There were always marks on his face whenever he came by to...Aagh. Jesus. I wish he'd, you know, gone into teaching instead of..."

"Drinking," snuffles Peter.

"You be quiet!" Vivian tosses her cigarette into the sink.

"Well, what about Donnie?"

"Ha! Donnie's still the same. Still ignorant. He got fired off his job, you know, at Hostess last month. After twenty years! But then he got work at the peat plant and now he's..."

"Drinking," snuffles Peter.

Rebecca elbows him.

"Well, Susan's promised, you know, to keep him in line but I bet it won't be...Oh! Before I forget! His daughter Donna was just crowned Miss Grafton! So I guess at least one of the kids has, you know, turned out all right."

"What do you mean? What's wrong with Billy?"

"Ha! Billy's as ignorant as his father. And eat! Jesus! You should see Billy and Peter when, you know, they're together. They can eat a whole casserole between them. And a whole loaf of bread, too."

Rebecca laughs.

"Oh, and speaking of food. You should've seen the beautiful Christmas dinner Darrell's wife Shirley made for us. There was a big turkey. And all the trimmings. And only a few months, you know, after her heart attack. Ha! Darrell said she had it because of...By the way, his leg's real bad now, but he's, you know, too scared to have anything done to it. Anyway, he said she had it because of excitement. You know, over winning the seventy-five dollar pot in that Booklet Bingo down at the Lion's Centre. But I think it was, you know, because Curtis Holt works her so hard at that christless store of his. Anyway, she gave us all quite a scare."

"Yes, you told me," murmurs Rebecca.

"Oh." Vivian tugs at her sweater. "Well, I guess that just leaves Peter. And you can see for yourself how *he* is."

"Yes."

"Your cousin Melanie tried to get him work with her at Michelin. Jesus! She even, you know, gave them a twenty-three page letter with all the odd jobs he's done. But they said he was, you know, too...Maybe they heard he's been hiding my wooden dolls. Those little painted *babkabooshes* that, you know, fit inside each other. Anyway. So now he's pruning trees for Barss's and taking long walks around town with that huge, maroon-covered Bible the Pentecostals gave him when they, you know, talked him into joining their church. Ha! I'm surprised he didn't bring it to the table with him. Like those Hardy Boys books he always, you know, carried around when he was little. Anyway, how long are you staying?"

"Just a few days. I have to get back to work."

"Ha! I don't mean that. I mean, you know, *here*, in *this* house. You're not sleeping here, are you?"

"I don't know. I thought maybe I'd..."

"Well, you always slept down at Marion's when you were a girl. You might as well, you know, sleep there now."

"Yes."

"Because George's away and Florence says she wants, you know, to come and sleep in the extra...Ha! She just bought the Marshall's old K-car. It's a real cheapo, according to George. But then my fat bitch of a sister'll never spend a dime more than she has to."

"When's the last time you saw her?"

"We all played bridge down to Alice Marshall's last night. Me, Wanda, the bitch. My brain's still, you know, foggy from all the...Oh, Jesus! Wanda! I almost forgot!" She rushes out of the kitchen.

"Where's she going?" sighs Rebecca.

"To the sun porch," mutters Peter. "To make sure the old whore hasn't gone without her."

"Ha!" laughs Rebecca. "So that's the kind of language you pick up from your huge, maroon-covered..."

"She says she's taking me to bingo for my birthday," pants Vivian, as she rushes back in. "All the way, you know, down to Halifax. To that big one they're having at the Metro Centre. But you can never, you know, trust her. She sometimes..."

"Jesus. It's July 8 today, isn't it? Happy Birthday, Mum."

"Ha! Don't remind me! Anyway, she sometimes sneaks out alone." She begins to clear the table. "And she only offers to drive me places if she, you know, hears I already have a ride. So I told her...Jesus, Peter!"

She's peering into the little shelf below the sink.

"How many times have I asked you to rinse these things before you...? Hoo!"

Rebecca bends down to take a look.

Her Dad made that shelf to hold the home-made beer he was always trying to brew. But it was never really tall enough for that and now it looks like Peter keeps his pop cans there. And his milk cartons and his pickle jars and anything else he can't bear to part with.

He's like Mum, really, thinks Rebecca as she straightens up again. She still has the boxes and wrapping paper from every single present she's ever received. Only *her* keepsakes don't smell — or attract the ants.

"And how is old Wanda Willoughby anyway?"

"Wait!" Vivian rushes out to the sun porch again.

"Do you see her very often?"

"Yes!" whoops Vivian, when she returns. "Too often! At bingo on Monday and seniors on Wednesday and...Ha! She's still the same old Wanda. Still bouncing her ass around the room; still getting into fights with the other women. Everyone wonders, you know, why I stay friends with her. Since she's so hard, so tight with her money. But I don't want her money! I only want her to drive me to bingo! Even though she's, you know, the worst driver in the town."

"Do you play a lot?"

"As much as I can. Whenever I..."

"Whenever I give her the money," mumbles Peter.

Vivian glares at him. Rebecca can see that her Mum wishes she had a jackpot in her hands right now. So she could fling it to the floor at Peter's feet — like she did that time with her husband Harold.

"But it's, you know, changed now. You have to get there real early for the big ones...you know, at six o'clock...or you won't get a chair at one of the tables. And they don't use chips anymore. They use, you know, dabbers or dubbers or...whatever they're called. Big, fat magic markers to colour the squares on your cards. Some of the women are real neat with theirs, but I have to, you know, bring my own paper towel. So I don't get pink and blue ink all over my hands and clothes."

"And how many cards do you play?"

"Well, I get bored if I don't play at least fifteen. Elsie Smeltzer says...Oh, Jesus. Elsie. She hasn't, you know, been the same since Bobby died. Had one of his, you know, real low moments and swallowed a whole bottle of Javex. Anyway, Elsie says she can't see how I keep that many straight. She says I've turned into one of those, you know, bingo bangers."

"What's a bingo banger?"

"Someone who bangs her dobber down on her cards."

"Oh."

"You know, real fast. So she can keep up with all of the...Anyway, you don't have much chance at the Lucky Seven or the Fifty-Fifty or the Bonanza if you don't, you know, play a lot of cards."

"How much does it usually cost?"

"Twenty-eight dollars," slurps Peter.

"OK!" Vivian rushes out of the room again. "But the money isn't wasted! Not now that there's, you know, a Commission and everything.

It goes to charity. Except for the private bingos which were, you know, already going before the...There she is! Ha! I swear those tits are hanging down to her knees!"

Rebecca and Peter can't help laughing.

"Oh, and before I, you know, forget," sighs Vivian, as she drifts back into the kitchen.

"There it is." She tosses a copy of the *Berwick Register* onto the table. "There was a full moon that night...Saturday, May 18, I think it was...so it's beyond me why she, you know..."

"Don't you have to go?" murmurs Rebecca as she loses herself in Marion's obituary.

"Well, it'll take her a little while to get down the steps. Ha! Not to mention down her driveway and then, you know, up around ours. We're none of us as young as we used to be."

The first paragraph is filled with the usual details about dates and times and places.

Vivian smooths out her skirt. "You never came home when your Dad died," she whines. "Or your Grammie. But then you always, you know, liked your Aunt Marion better than us."

"I liked you," murmurs Rebecca, without looking up. "I just got fed up with you."

The second paragraph recounts how kind, caring and committed Marion was. It's a jumble of her many hobbies and charities. Red Cross, bridge, School Board, bingo, Children's Aid, Eastern Star, the Liberal Party.

"She was a beautiful person," says Vivian softly. "She took care of everyone in the family, almost as if she was, you know, the oldest instead of the youngest."

The third paragraph marvels that she never married.

"Of course, she took care of strangers, too. Anyone who was, you know, hungry or in trouble. Ha! When she was still a girl, she started tearing the slips out of her chequebook so Mum couldn't, you know, tell who she'd given all her money to. Jesus! It's no wonder the church was packed."

Rebecca finally looks up from the page. "Who gave the eulogy?" she whispers.

"Well, it was supposed to be Reverend MacKay. You remember him. But he wasn't, you know, up to it. He took it awful hard. So it was that new one; that dark-skinned boy who transferred here from Jamaica. Jesus, things have changed! I remember the time when a coon wouldn't, you know, dare set foot in..."

"Yes." Rebecca closes her eyes.

"Jesus! They say he uses a microphone when he preaches! And the church! Wait till you see what they're doing to the church! You won't recognize it! Not with that white *aloo...aloo...*whatever you call it...siding going up over all that, you know, rotting wood! Which I suppose is about time. Anyway, the bitch and I didn't go to the grave. We couldn't face seeing her placed in the ground. George says the bitch just, you know, locked herself in the bathroom and cried. But I stayed home, keeping an eye on Peter, making sure he didn't, you know, eat all the food for the party."

Peter snuffles. Rebecca opens her eyes.

"Oh, and there's this, too, of course." Vivian lays a hand-written note on the table.

"My dear Dick Tracy," murmurs Rebecca.

"Yes. That's you, isn't it? I thought it was you. I sometimes, you know, have a fifth sense about these things. Anyway, I don't know what got into her. Jesus Murphy! Look at the date! Sunday, November 7, 1965! So many years ago! What was she thinking?"

Rebecca stares at the single sheet of white paper.

"Of course, there was lots of, you know, whispering at the party. There weren't any skid marks. And there was nothing wrong with the car. A beautiful, blue Ford Tempo. Although I can't see how they can tell after it's, you know, been all...Ugh! It makes me shiver. And the weather was perfect. No rain. No wind. So they started saying she must have, you know, fallen asleep at the wheel. Or swerved to miss a rabbit. Or something."

Rebecca can't bear to pick it up.

"Anyway, what they can't figure out is why she wasn't, you know, wearing her seat belt. She always wore her seat belt. Remember how she was always telling you to...? Jesus, I can't believe she's gone. We've all had a couple of months to recover, but I still can't, you know, believe she's...Jesus. I remember Peter asking me about dying after Grampy Newell passed away. 'You mean the world goes on and on without me?' he said. 'The sun comes up, the birds sing, and I'm not here?' Jesus, Jesus..."

Suddenly, a horn blares from the driveway.

"Oh! There's Wanda!" Vivian springs to the side door. "I've got to go!"

"Bye," murmurs Rebecca. "It was nice to see you."

Vivian turns to her. "The queer thing wasn't, you know, the seat belt. The queer thing was what she was wearing. A little, yellow plastic ring. Like a toy wedding ring. No one knows where she got it."

"What did you do with it?"

"Well, we didn't, you know, bury her in it, if that's what you mean. It wouldn't have been right. We put it..." The horn blares again. "I think it's, you know, with...Or did we throw it...?" And then again. "Coming, Wanda! Jesus, you'd think she'd been..."

"Go, Mum, go! Have a good time!"

"I will! I will!"

Peter snuffles.

Vivian pushes open the screen door. "Oh, and you can, you know, go over to the house anytime you want. The old coots are away with their women in Bermuda. Jesus! I don't see how she stood living with those two old men all those, you know...Anyway, the keys are where they always are. Bye!"

Rebecca takes a deep breath and then reads.

There are some things for you in the back chamber. You'll know which they are.

She closes her eyes.

It isn't much of a will. Just a few mysterious words, caught, someplace sane and secret perhaps, between life's howl and its whisper.

Suddenly, Peter taps the face of his Koko B. Ware watch.

"What?" smiles Rebecca.

"I'll sure need some nourishment," he snuffles.

She recognizes the line. It's from one of his old Hardy Boys books. *The Clue In the Embers*, she thinks.

"If I'm going to hassle with a lot of shrunken heads."

"Ha!" laughs Rebecca. "I agree!" She reaches for the box of stale crackers.

4

Rebecca is gliding down Old Post Road, on her way to Marion's house, when she spots the scaffolding. It's a tall, unsteady framework of poles and planks rising up the front of the church.

There's the church. The child's verse slowly comes back to her. *There's the steeple. Open the door...Where's all the people? Where's all the people? Where's all the...?*

Suddenly, there is no tangle of metal and wood. No plastic sheet flapping in the wind. No siding. There is only a simple ladder. And a man at the top, painting the steeple white. And three kids at the bottom, sprawled in the grass.

"How do you do that?" whines Alan, as he clasps and unclasps his fingers.

"What a dummy," sniffs Brenda.

"Well, there's two ways you can do it," says Rebecca earnestly. "You can either..."

"My Wild Irish Rose. The sweetest flower that grows."

The kids look up.

The short, sturdy man at the top of the ladder is dressed entirely in white. White cotton T-shirt, white cotton pants, white cloth shoes. He's also singing. He always sings when he paints. With that wonderful, deep, rich baritone that everyone admires.

"My Daddy's the best singer in the whole wide world!" boasts Rebecca.

"Is not."

"Is too, Brenda. Otherwise, why would he be in the glee club and the barbershop quartet?"

"You may search everywhere but none can compare..."

Rebecca watches the brush flash over the shingles. "And the best painter, too."

"No, he isn't."

"Well, he's way better than *your* Dad. I'd like to see *your* Dad do around windows as good as..."

"My Dad doesn't paint. He sells wieners."

"Yeah, well, you don't have to be brave to do that and my Daddy's brave."

"Yeah? Who says?"

"Everybody says. See that steeple." She points to the slim white spire rising up from the bell tower.

"So?"

"So that's way high up and nobody else will do it."

"Look!" shouts Alan. "I got it! I got it!" He thrusts out his hands. Rebecca examines them carefully. "OK, that's one way, Alan. Now do it *with* people."

"OK, but...What, Brenda?"

"That's a funny thing to be up there."

"What?"

"That!" Brenda points to the weather vane at the top of the steeple. It's a big, fat copper bullfrog. "I thought churches just had crosses on top."

"No," states Rebecca firmly. "My Dad says that some have roosters or even fish. So what's so funny about a frog?"

"Well...for one thing..." Brenda grimaces. "Frogs are yicky."

"No, they're not. They're neat. Randy and I catch them all the time, down at Sandy Beach."

"My Wild Irish Rose. The dearest flower that grows."

"Ugh. You mean you actually touch those ugly, slimy things?"

"Sure I do. And they're not just ugly and slimy, you know. They have real good eyes and ears. That can see and hear practically everything. So you have to be real careful when you..."

"Yuck."

"Oh, yeah! And their sex cells and their poop come out of the same hole! At least that's what Mrs. Armstrong told me when I..."

"Double yuck!"

"And some day for my sake, she may let me take..."

"And they sing good, too."

"Ha! No, they don't. They just croak."

"The bloom from My Wild Irish ROOOOSE!"

"Just like your Dad!"

"Hey!" Rebecca shoves her. "Don't you say that about my...!"

"There's all the people! There's all the people!" shouts Alan. *"See? I did it!"* He holds up his hands in triumph.

"Who cares, Alan?" mutters Rebecca. "Anybody can do that."

"Yeah," grins Brenda. "Just like anybody can paint."

"Can not."

"Can too."

"Can not." Rebecca looks up at her Dad again. He's up so high. So close to that big, fat copper bullfrog. And it's such an awkward reach. But his strokes are as quick and as sure as ever.

"Yeah, well, that's what I'm going to do when I grow up," she murmurs.

Brenda rolls her eyes. "You're mental."

"Too many ghosts," whispers Rebecca, as she stands on the back veranda at Marion's house. Pet squirrels. Christmas leftovers. Clothes that Doris Pudsey pushed along the line. She reaches up to the ledge above the door.

It's a clapboard house, of course. Rambling, predominantly white, with black trim and a red foundation. Marion bought it from Ben and Malcolm Kelly when she was just a girl, straight out of business college. But she didn't have the heart to evict those two old bachelors so the three of them lived there together, sharing the costs and the comforts and never giving much thought to legalities, like what actually belonged to whom, or to courtesies, like which of them was actually in charge. Everyone said she was crazy.

"OK!" whispers Rebecca, as she turns the key. "Come and get me!" She pushes open the door.

There are ghosts in the kitchen, too. Syrup on the French toast. Crackling from the dark brown plastic radio. Bright red splotches on the creamy white handkerchiefs.

"Ha!" She glances from the match-safe to the sleeve-board and back. Some things don't need ghosts. Some things still have themselves.

She wanders over to the fridge and peeks inside. "Jesus." She throws open the door. Steak, Stay-a-bed Stew, boxes of strawberries. It's almost as if Marion's expecting her.

"And wouldn't Brian love these!" she chortles, as she stares at the boxes of strawberries.

It was the first thing Brian ever bought her — not a box of chocolates, but a box of strawberries. He claimed he was going through his Ingmar Bergman phase, but Rebecca knew it was something else. She knew he meant it as a symbol of that wild righteousness, that cultivated succulence, which would someday take hold of their virginity. Brian was like that.

"But *I'm* not!" hoots Rebecca, as she looks inside the freezer. And orange-pineapple ice cream, too.

"It can't be," she laughs, as she flings the doors shut. The ice cream hasn't crystallized. The strawberries haven't grown fuzz. The steak still smells fresh. So. It isn't strange. It isn't crazy. It isn't Marion, making her childhood stand still for her. It's only Ben, being thoughtful, before he rushes off to Bermuda with his woman.

Chink. Chink.

"Jesus," she shudders. "Just get it over with." She pulls open the door to the back chamber and begins to climb the stairs. It's so dark she can barely make out the shelves where the oil lamps were kept; where the winter boots were stored in the summer. She reaches up and pulls the string.

"Not as bad as I thought," she murmurs, as she climbs up into the light.

The back chamber is pretty dingy — lots of dust and that old familiar musty smell — but it's not a mess. There's a gleaming barrel, an unmarked box, a prim little bag of Christmas decorations, a tidy pile of mattresses and a row of men's jackets and shirts, hanging neatly on the string which is stretched across the room. From the window to the door. The one to Marion's bedroom.

Rebecca's relieved. It doesn't look like anything of hers is here. But then she spots the doll house.

It's made of brightly painted metal, not wood — as if it really belongs to another town — and consists of two stories and an open deck, with a green and white striped awning over it. Marion gave it to her for her seventh birthday. And Rebecca decided to keep it here so it wouldn't get wrecked. Sunny played with it, too — not because she liked dolls but because its cartoon colours reminded her of Versailles. She'd seen a picture of that wondrous place in a magazine. And fallen in love with its gaudy splendour, its luscious gardens and gilt-edged drapes. It was so different than the filth at home. And exactly the sort of image Sunny needed to prepare her for fulfilling their mother's oft-repeated prophecy — that Sunny was going to marry Prince Charles someday.

"Home," whispers Rebecca.

She isn't really sure what that means. Mum's? Marion's? Grammie's? She grew up in so many of them — shuttled back and forth between extremes of indulgence and neglect. But those homes were usually painted white, like the church, where she felt so much anger and regret. She'd liked this brightly painted metal one better. No moral atmosphere. No bedrock of firmly held beliefs. She hadn't had to worry about some underlying evil lurking beneath its colourful claims of solidity and security. It was just a steady, supportive home base, where she could get all the approbation she needed — without the misery and the mystery.

"Ha! Perhaps that's because there weren't any people!"

It's true. There isn't a soul in sight. In fact, she threw out the little metal people the second day she had them. She kept the little metal furniture, however, so her little plastic animals would have somewhere to sit and sleep when she let them clank around in there.

"God!" She peers into the uninhabited doll house.

It's occurred to her that there was never really a place for her in there either. In fact, there was never really a place for her in *her*. It isn't a surprise. She's spent most of her life trying not to belong anywhere. Or have anything belong to her.

There are some things for you in the back chamber. Marion's note is still nagging at her. *Some things for you...some things for...*

"All right!" She stares at the unmarked box in the middle of the floor.

That must be it, she thinks. But she doesn't move toward it. The past may be possessive but it's not going anywhere. There's still lots of time to rip it open and spill it out on the floor.

"Jesus, I'm starved!" She tumbles back down the stairs to the kitchen.

There are initials gouged in the table behind the chesterfield. They appeared there in the spring of 1965, the day she graduated from elementary school. Of course, she swore she didn't do it and no one was actually able to prove she did it. But they were her initials, after all. It wasn't likely that anyone else carved them. She wishes she could sand them off.

There's also the ghost of a bluish green feather duster lying there, beside the ghost of a crystal bowl of licorice Allsorts. She stares at the duster for a few seconds, then takes a deep breath and turns toward the mantelpiece. Doris was nice and lots of fun — even when she hadn't had a sip of her beloved gin — but every once in a while she broke things. Rebecca made it a habit to check on the Old Balloon Seller whenever she got back from school.

"Jesus, I'm tired," she comments to the Royal Doulton figurine before wandering out of the living room and into the hall.

There are familiar things there, too. The mirror. The bookcases. The hall tree. The Bing Miller ball glove. The card table with Mont Sainte-Victoire painted on it. She trudges past them and up the steps.

"Ha!" she laughs, when she reaches the top. "Why am I not surprised?"

The little cot in the upstairs hall is all made up for her. There's a large, empty house with three large, empty bedrooms, but someone was sure she'd want to sleep where she always slept, beneath the open window at the front of the house.

Too tired to change, although she's sure there'd be a pair of her pajamas in the cedar chest at the foot of the bed, she crawls down under the covers and closes her eyes.

Chink. Chink.

Her eyes pop open.

"God, I must be crazy! That's the second time I..." She peers down the hall, to the room where Marion used to sleep. There's no one there now, of course, except perhaps some noisy, mean, impatient ghosts.

"Christ! I might as well see what they want!" She flings off the covers and stomps down the hall.

Chink. Chink.

"Coming! Coming! God, you'd think you were Wanda or..." She barges right through Marion's door. "...or something the way you're carrying..." And then through the door on the other side of the room.

"Jesus," she whispers. "Now it's worse than I thought."

Things are different in the back chamber now. Creepier. The wooden beams seem to be creaking in the wind. The giant cobwebs seem to be dripping from the window sill. That old familiar musty smell has been replaced by the stench of the past.

"Phew." Once again, she stares at the unmarked box in the middle of the floor. "It's you," she whispers.

Her memory becomes a murmur; its message a clammy hand.
"It's you who's stinking so much." She creeps up to the unmarked
box.

There's a moment of indecision...when she wonders if it's wise to
expose herself to all that reeking chaos...and then she rips open the
box and dumps its contents onto the floor.

"Ha!" She drops to her knees. "A shoehorn!"

It's not the only thing there, of course. There's actually a jumble of
things. A deck of cards. A pack of Matinées. A book of matches from
the Lord Nelson Hotel. A string of salmon-coloured plastic pop-it beads.
A hard, red leather key case with a flashlight in it. An assortment of
novels. An apple blossom handkerchief stained with blood. A set of
datebooks. But the shoehorn is the only thing which doesn't seem
eerie and threatening. Which isn't a sign. Which isn't a clue. Which
doesn't mean anything except that Marion was fond of shoes.

Once again, she's relieved.

The shoehorn is just what she needs right now. Her memory is
already aching. She's not yet ready to face the jumble of tricky clues;
not yet ready to do anything but sit there, trying to be impervious to
their stinking possessiveness. Unfortunately, she can't. She's already
spotted something she knows.

"God, I don't believe it!"

Sunny was always calling Marion and Rebecca detectives. "There
go Eliot Ness and Dick Tracy," she'd always say, whenever the two of
them went on their evening rounds to make sure the town was all
right. So Rebecca decided to buy *Nancy's Mysterious Letter* for Marion
as a joke, with money earned collecting pop bottles. She thought
Marion would get a kick out of it, even though Nancy was only an
amateur sleuth, not a professional one with a wrist radio and
everything. She never dreamed Marion would use it to torment her.

"How appropriate!" She reaches into the jumble and pulls out the
book.

It's missing its dust jacket now. There's only a grainy, pale blue
cover, with navy blue lettering and a navy blue silhouette of Nancy,
peering through a magnifying glass.

"As if she ever did that!" Rebecca laughs, as she folds back the cover.

The endpaper has blue and white drawings on it. Of Nancy peeking
through a curtained window, running from a burning house, kneeling

beside a dilapidated boat, rearing back on a creamy white horse, hiding behind a pillar, a statue, a chesterfield, a tree. They're silly and yet tantalizing pictures, filled with promises about what lies ahead…if only she turns the page. But she's afraid to do that. The years of dust and damp have made the book brittle — especially along the spine, where it's been glued rather than bound. If she turns the pages, she might pull them all out. At the very end, they might all be separated. She timidly peeks inside. "Ha!"

She can already see how it goes. Lots of dialogue. Plenty of run-on sentences to move the plot along. An abundance of active verbs. Hurled. Leaped. Swarmed. Gulped. Glowered. Gasped.

"God!" she laughs. "I can't believe we read this stuff!"

But then she remembers that at least there was always a "moment of truth," when the relationships became clear and the perpetrators of evil were exposed. She cracks open the book and begins to read.

"Now in my day young women didn't go flying around like…like wild turkeys."

It's that mean old Mr. Cutter. He was always spitting out some prejudice or another.

"Girls didn't go around inviting men below their station in life to come into their houses." Her heart beats faster. *"That's the reason we have so much lawlessness these days. The young people aren't brought up right. They have no discipline."*

She closes her eyes.

Marion didn't circle the passage but she might as well have, since she was always getting bawled out for something.

"Anyway." Rebecca's eyes pop open again. "I can't sit here all night reading silly old…" She turns back past the table of contents…*Prisoners in Darkness, Clues and Clouds, "You Are to Blame!," The Scent Grows Hotter*…and the registration of copyright…1932, by Grosset and Dunlap…and the handwritten inscription…*For Marion because it's her thirtieth birthday*…and the black-and-white drawing of Nancy having an excellent view of the perpetrator as he dashes down the stairs…to the page at the front, where the other exciting mysteries by Carolyn Keene are listed. She doesn't know what made her buy this one. She could easily have gotten *The Secret In the Old Attic* or *The Mystery of the Brass Bound Trunk* or *The Clue In the Diary*.

"Jesus." She flings the book on top of the jumble. "I have to get some sleep."

Rebecca is standing in the middle of the downstairs den.

"Something's missing," she whispers. "Something's definitely missing." She puts her hands on her hips and scans the room.

She's already checked the walk-in closet. It still contains her spinning top, her ball glove, her plastic pinball machine, her Chinese Checkers, her 101 Games In One, her golf clubs. And everything seems the same in the bookcases, too.

Her eyes rest on Marion's big, old oaken desk. It was never this tidy, she thinks. There were always pens and blotters and ledgers and datebooks and...

"Oh, my God!" she rasps. "*The Clue In the Diary!*" She rushes out of the den and up the stairs.

Lying on the floor of the back chamber are years and years of datebooks. Fancy ones, bound in leather, which Marion got from Fawcett's Fire and Auto to keep track of her meetings and appointments.

"Great." She slumps down beside them. "I can't possibly read all these."

But something tells her she has to try. One of them would contain an essential clue — a cryptic note or a secret code, some handwritten equivalent of a freshly made footprint.

"OK, but which one?"

And which mystery exactly would this "clue in the diary" help her to solve? There have always been so many of them — scary ones, sad ones, and scary ones that have tricked her into thinking they were sad ones — but only a few that she could bear to acknowledge, let alone investigate. Right now, everyone around her seems anxious to know things. Brian wants to know why she's so repressed. Her Mum wants to know why the beautiful, blue Ford Tempo smashed into the telephone pole. And she wants to know...why she doesn't want to know. She'll settle for finding out why Marion left her these things. And why she was so sure she'd come all this way for them; why she expected her to want them, recognize them, know what to do with them. As for the other mysteries...She doesn't really want to remember

why she's so angry. She doesn't really want to find an essential clue to
what happened to them all those years ago.

"Eenie, meenie, minie..." As she reaches for the datebooks, her
heart is thundering in her chest. Except for the colours — navy blue,
burgundy, black — they all look the same.

"Oh, hell!" She snatches the one for 1958, not because it stinks the
most, but because its navy blue cover reminds her of that silly
silhouette of Nancy with the magnifying glass.

"Wait! Didn't I see a...? Yes!" She strikes a match from the Lord
Nelson Hotel and lights a Matinée. "Ugh. Stale as hell. Anyway..." She
opens the datebook and begins to read.

The boxes for January are filled with endless notes and reminders.
Her disappointment is overwhelming. She wasn't expecting a page
right out of *The Domestic World*, something which vividly recalled
the happy-go-lucky fifties. That would be too easy. And she wasn't
expecting a *True Confession* either. Marion wasn't like that. But she
was hoping for something a little more exciting.

She blows a smoke ring.

Details about church suppers, Children's Aid benefits, Eastern Star
functions and insurance meetings aren't nearly juicy enough. They
don't begin to explain why the datebooks were left to *her*.

She watches the smoke ring begin to break apart.

Still, there's something alluring about these boring details. They're
just a starting point, after all — a point of overwhelming tedium from
which different worlds can rise.

She flips through the pages.

It won't be easy finding any revelations. For one thing, the detective in
her is both rusty and reluctant. For another, the essential clues to these
revelations are strung across three different worlds — the world Marion
knew and the world she knew and the world the world is keeping to itself.
But perhaps the truth will be a kind of partnership, with pictures formed
from Marion's notes and her own memory and the world's unspoken secrets.

Before it can break apart completely, she slips through the smoke
ring into the past.

It's spring, 1958. The blossoms are out. Harold has paid for his
insurance with a bag of last year's potatoes. Marion is making out the
receipt at her big, old oaken...

5

"I guess I won't be getting a new pair of shoes with that," laughs Marion, as she leans back in the swivel chair.

"With what?" Rebecca dumps her set of Chinese Checkers onto the floor.

Marion pats the ledger. "You'll have to come and see for yourself."

"OK." Rebecca scrambles over to the desk. "Show me."

Marion points to a line on the ledger.

Rebecca sounds it out. "One bag of po-ta-toes." And then she grins. She loves her Aunt Marion. In fact, she thinks her Aunt Marion's the best person in the whole wide world. And the best at selling insurance, too — even though she's only twenty-three years old. Of course, she herself is only four, so she doesn't know very much about insurance. *Life. Personal injury. Fire. Theft. Auto.* They're just words to practice her reading on. But insurance does seem to be a way to meet people. Everyone, from the President of Acadia University, who gave Marion her first ride on a motorcycle, to some bigwig politicians in Halifax, who always drop by when Marion takes that suite at the Lord Nelson Hotel at Christmas time, to farmers from the mountains, families from the air force base in Greenwood and relatives. And insurance does seem to be a way to be nice to people. For Marion anyway. Rebecca's not sure, but she doesn't think everyone would let people drop by at night, with their little two-dollar or five-dollar instalments; doesn't think everyone would sign bank notes and accept bags of potatoes as payment.

It was probably my Dad, thinks Rebecca. He probably dug them up from the tiny garden at the back of the house. She runs her hands over the smooth brown top of Marion's desk.

"Do you like it?" asks Marion.

"It's OK. Where did you get it?"

"From the Bank of Nova Scotia on Commercial Street."

"Didn't they want it anymore?"

"Well, they're going to be moving soon, to a brand-new red brick building on the corner, next to the pool hall, so they're getting new furniture."

"Oh."

Marion smiles. "Remember my first desk?"

"Sort of."

"The one that came from that hotel in Fredericton? From the very room, it was rumoured, where Edward VIII entertained Mrs. Simpson."

"What's *entertained* mean?"

"It had a matching bureau, too — where presumably His Highness kept his underwear — but I didn't bid on that. In any case, that first desk faded and splintered and attracted a strange assortment of..."

"Oh, yeah, I remember! It got filled with bugs and moths! Millions of them!"

Suddenly, Marion flinches. "What's that?"

"What?"

"I could swear I saw a tiny grey shadow on the carpet." She peers at the expanse of blue wool. "But it was probably just the hump."

"The what?"

"The hump. Haven't you noticed? Ever since we put that addition on the west side of the house, so Malcolm could have a larger bedroom, the floor of the den has had a slope to it. There!" Marion points to the closet.

But the only thing there is a pair of little yellow glimmers.

"No, Marion!" squeals Rebecca. "It's only my Chinese Checkers!"

"Oh." Marion opens her datebook and squints at the crowded pages. "Well, then, I must be crazy!"

Rebecca squints too. "What's next, Marion?"

"Children's Aid meeting. Although I'll have to squeeze it in between a meeting of the Apple Blossom Festival Float Committee and a meeting of the School Board."

Rebecca knits her brow. She likes doing things, lots of things, but her Aunt Marion seems to like doing the most things. If she doesn't have a bridge date, she has a bingo date or a church supper or an evening of collecting for the Red Cross or a bake sale sponsored by the Order of the Eastern Star. And then there's going on her evening rounds to make sure the town's all right. Her Aunt Marion could never leave that out. Rebecca once heard Grammie warn Marion to slow down; that she couldn't do everything for everyone; that self-sacrifice — a word Rebecca didn't understand — can sometimes lead to self-annihilation — another word Rebecca didn't understand. But Marion said she couldn't help it. She was always being asked for advice.

She was expected to pitch in. It just wasn't possible for her to spend any less time on the phone or on the road. And besides, she said Grammie wasn't right about that self-annihilation bit. She was never going to be so busy that she lost her way.

Rebecca reaches across the desk.

"What are you looking for?"

"That gold compass. The one Grampy Newell brought back from his second big war."

"About nine years before he surprised everyone and died of bone cancer instead of booze," murmurs Marion, as she hands the compass to Rebecca. "I didn't know you liked that."

"Better than his dumb old magnifying glass. I can't get it to set fire to anything!"

Marion's eyes cloud over.

Rebecca backs away a little. "Why are you sad, Marion?"

"It's a secret."

"I like secrets."

"Oh, you do, do you? Well, then, perhaps you should know that my Dad brought back a gold watch, too. Which Mum never let anyone touch. Which Mum kept to herself in a hand-carved jewellery box."

"Yeah? So?"

"And so the day I went swimming with some friends down at Kirk's Brook and lost it, I didn't say a single word about taking it. I didn't even make things up. I should have. I should have said that Cyril Neily swallowed it. That George Best stole it from my pile of clothes. That Jack Hall had been tossing it up and down when suddenly it fell..."

"I don't get it."

"But I just let Mum blame the woman who cleaned the house. Of course, the woman was fired and I've felt terrible about it ever since." Marion stares at her datebook. "And tried to make up for it ever since."

"Yeah, but I still don't see..."

"No, I don't suppose you do. But wait until you're older. Wait until you have...Iyee! I knew it!"

Within seconds, Marion's standing on top of the desk, waving her compass at the little grey mouse which is scurrying back and forth across the carpet.

"Get away! Get away!"

In late May, the Annapolis Valley is bursting with blossoms — pale pink and white flowers which, according to Rebecca, smell almost as good as the bubble gum she gets with her Topps baseball cards. She knows a bit about the terrible things to do with apples, too. Like codling moths and red-banded leaf rollers and black rot and rust and scab, but being just four years old, she doesn't spend much time worrying about them. To her, they're something to spell, not to understand.

"Where are you going?" hollers Marion, as the screen door slams shut.

Rebecca puts on the brakes by the Bishop Pippin apple tree at the side of the house.

It's an old, gnarled tree which no one takes care of any more. This year, there are only a few clusters of blossoms which may or may not provide enough sour, pale yellow apples for Marion to make her jelly.

"Over to Ruthie's!" Rebecca hollers back. "To watch them build the float!"

"What did you say?"

There's a formation of Vampires roaring overhead, practicing for that Armed Forces Day which CFB Greenwood holds every year at Apple Blossom Festival time.

Rebecca squints up at the sky. "I said..." There are huge gaps in her mouth where she's lost some of her baby teeth. "I'm going over to Ruthie's to..."

The planes perform a noisy sequence of aerobatic loops and rolls.

"Forget it." She races down the driveway.

The Apple Blossom Festival is held every year. Rebecca can recite the list of attractions. Plays. Games. Big fat cows with ribbons stuck on them. And she's heard the radio describe the Festival as a celebration of "wholesome country living"; a time of "fun, excitement and fond memories for all." But she doesn't care about that. All she cares about is the food and the floats.

Ruthie Sutherland's house is on the corner of Maple Avenue and Old Post Road, opposite the Baptist Church. As Rebecca slips past the big, black Chrysler Imperial parked in the driveway, a pair of white Samoyeds scramble to greet her.

"Hi, Caesar. What a good boy. Hi, Cleo. Have you two been...?"

"Jesus, Charlie!"

Rebecca flinches. And then peers toward the barn at the back of the house, where the volunteers are busy hammering and painting and gluing.

"What?"

"Do I have to tell you which end of the friggin' brush...?"

"I don't think you have to swear, Martin. I don't think..."

"Ha! That's right. You don't think."

Everyone snickers.

"What do you mean, Martin? I think. I think all the time!"

"Come on, everybody! Please!"

Ruthie is standing over them, wringing her hands. She's a delicate little woman with beige hair dyed the colour of a frightened fawn. She has nice clothes, and lots of rings and jewels, but she's one of Harold and Vivian's favourite drinking buddies and she always smells of booze — and perfume, to cover up the booze. Rebecca likes her better than her husband, however. Dr. Glendon Sutherland may have a cranberry bog, where the kids can go to get their sneakers soaked, but Rebecca's heard he's also the one who made her cheek all crooked when he pulled her out with the forceps.

"Jesus." Harold runs a hand through his thin, dark grey hair. "I don't see what *you've* got a stick up your ass about."

"Yes, well." Ruthie smooths her dress. "If all you're going to do is act up, we'll never get finished in time."

"Look, Ruthie. We're all volunteers here. And some of us don't even know which end of the friggin'...Sorry, Charlie."

There's more snickering.

"Anyway, I don't see why we shouldn't have some fun with..." He waves at the float. "...whatever that's supposed to be."

"Yes, well." Ruthie smooths her dress again. "We haven't won a prize since 1950, you know. And I just thought..."

"You, too, eh, Ruthie?"

"I just *know* that if we really...well, it might actually...Oh, it looks terrible!"

"No, it doesn't!" blurts Rebecca, as she hops up onto the flatbed trailer. "It looks neat!"

Her Dad told her that the theme for this year's floats is Nature's Abundance. She doesn't know how the other towns and villages from Digby to Windsor will portray it, but Aylesford's effort is going to be a mass of tissue-paper blossoms and a gigantic papier-mâché apple. Rebecca can't help imagining what it would be like to be riding it down Old Post Road, on her way to next Saturday's parade in Kentville. So many of her neighbours would come out to watch. And she'd be waving to each and every one of them — with her left hand, of course, since that's her *real* hand.

"Hello," says Rebecca serenely. "Hello. How are you?"

"Best friggin' princess we ever had," laughs Martin.

Everyone snickers.

"Yes, well. Say what you like," murmurs Ruthie, as she watches them resume their hammering and painting and gluing. "It won't win a prize. And we haven't won a prize since..."

"Oh-oh."

"What, Rebecca? What is it?"

She points to the punctured tire at the rear of the trailer.

"That's it!" wails Ruthie. "This is the last time! Next year you can all go over to Harvey Rawding's again!"

Suddenly, the pair of Samoyeds starts barking.

"Oh, gaaawd."

"What's *she* doing here?"

"Jesus, that's all we need."

Carol Ann Fancy, this year's Princess Aylesford, is trying to make her way to the barn. She's a plump young woman with short, dark brown hair. And a pretty face. And, as Harold says, the most artificial smile in the kingdom.

"I hope you don't...Quit it!" Carol Ann swats at the dogs. "I hope you don't expect me to ride on that."

Carol Ann comes from what Harold also says is a family of snobs in Millville. Every Christmas, they go all out, decking their neat little one-storey house in hundreds and hundreds of gaudy lights. People come from miles around to see the display. And to roll their eyes. And make faces. And laugh.

"Well, it's not finished," protests Ruthie. "You'll have to wait and see how it looks when we've..."

"Will you shut up!" Carol Ann screams at the dogs. "I can't hear myself...Oh, nuts!" She whirls away from them. "I'm going to get my hair done!"

"Gawd," drawls Charlie, as they watch her stomp down the driveway.

"Who chose *her*?"

"Yeah, Ruthie. Jesus." Harold slaps some red paint on the side of the apple. "You mustn't have had much to choose from."

"You can blame Connie Blackadar," sniffs Ruthie. "We had a half-dozen contestants. And all those dances and teas to help us decide. But every time the committee voted, it was always tied. So Connie just announced that the chairman would decide and since she was the chairman, well…"

"Hey, *I* know!"

"Yes, Rebecca," sighs Ruthie.

"We could always paint a worm!"

"What?"

"A worm. A big, fat, juicy worm. Right there." She points at the papier-mâché apple. "Right near where Carol'll be sitting when she…"

"What a good idea," grins Ruthie. "I'm sorry I didn't think of it myself."

Everyone roars with laughter.

Moments later, Rebecca is racing uptown to Marilyn Addy's beauty parlour. There are six days to go before the Grand Ball at Acadia University in Wolfville, where they'll choose this year's Queen Annapolisa, and Carol Ann is trying out another new hairdo. The first thing Rebecca passes when she turns down Commercial Street is Mack Tuttle's barbershop. It hasn't got a big, red and white pole out front — just a tiny metal bar with a thermometer on it. But it's got a pool hall out back, where the guys with greasy ducktails and steel combs jutting out of their back pockets can gather to smoke cigarettes and brag about things — like the size of their dicks or who's burnt down the most barns. Right next door is the building Marilyn shares with Stuart Hiltz. It's got a long porch, with a single step and two entrances — to the beauty parlour on the left and the barbershop on the right.

People sure make a fuss about their dumb old hair, thinks Rebecca, as she leans in Marilyn's doorway. Or else, why are there two barbershops and two hairdressers in town — counting Gladys Hodges, who does it out of her home?

Inside, there's a delirium of sights and sounds and smells. The smoke from the cigarettes. The fumes from the rinses. The hum of the dryers. And a half-dozen women, looking like either drowned rats or space people, as they flip through the pages of their juicy magazines. Rebecca hops up onto the only empty chair and listens.

"Gracious!"

"Whaaat, Ireeene?"

"Well, it says here...Oh, I can't say it out loud, Alice!"

"Whaaat!"

"Well...that there's a new...You say it, Edna."

"Hormonal contraceptive."

Everyone giggles.

"A new..."

"Just call it The Pill, Irene, and get on with it!"

"A new pill that will...oh, my gracious...be a great sexual liberator."

"Yeah, right."

"Ha!"

"Juuust whaaat I neeeeeeed!"

"Oh, gawd. Not me. Not in a million years. I get enough..."

"We know."

"Hey!"

"Yes, but don't you think...?"

"Ha! Vivian! Almost thirty and already the voice of authority!"

"No, but really. Don't you think it will just make people more, you know...*premuscuis*?"

"*Premuscuis*? What the hell's *premuscuis*?"

"Oh, you know Vivian. She has trouble pronouncing her own name."

"Can we please just get on with it?" sniffs Carol Ann. "I have another appointment this afternoon."

"Sorry. Sorry."

For a moment, there's no sound except the hum of the dryers and the clank of Carol Ann's rollers as Marilyn drops them into the sink.

"Anyway. Carol Ann. Have you picked out your dress yet?"

"Ages ago. Me and Connie and Marion went to Halifax, where there's this really expensive...Ow!"

"Sorry." Marilyn eases the roller out of her hair.

"What colour is it?"

"Pink, of course."

"And length?"

"You know they have to be long. Ow! I think you're doing that on purpose, Marilyn."

"No, I'm not. Really." She turns to one of the space people sitting under the dryers. "FIVE MORE MINUTES, MARION!"

"I just hope the banner doesn't spoil it," sulks Carol Ann.

"Oh, I'm sure you'll look very pretty."

"Yes, probably. If my hair turns out."

"It will. It...Oh! Just a sec!" Marilyn reaches over to check on Vivian, who's trying a new rinse today.

Vivian usually does her colour herself, with either Nestlé Colorinse or Colortint, depending on whether she wants "sparkling highlights" or a "thrilling new shade." But today, Marion's paid the five dollars for her to come to Marilyn's.

"And hooow was Haaalifaaax, Caaarol Aaann?"

"All right, Alice. Except for the negroes, of course. There's something about them that makes me..."

Marilyn starts combing out Carol Ann's hair.

"Are you sure it's not too curly this time? After all, I don't want to look like a..."

"*Volare. Wo, oh.*"

One of the space people has started to sing. It's obvious she can't hear herself.

"*Contare. Wo, oh, oh, oh.*"

Rebecca can't help giggling.

"Ha!" snorts Vivian. "How long have you been here?" She squints over at Rebecca.

"A while."

Marion lifts the silver helmet off her head. "Well, then, here." She waves a ten-dollar bill at Rebecca. "Go make yourself useful. Who wants coffee?"

Rebecca hops off her chair.

"God! I'm dying for one!"

"Me, too."

"And a pack of Player's."

"And another magazine. Jesus." Edna tosses *Liberty* into the wastebasket. "Like *McCall's* or *Good Housekeeping* or *Canadian Home Journal*. Preferably with words your mother can pronounce."

There's a tumult of laughter, as Rebecca memorizes the orders.

"And ask the men what *they* want!" Marion reminds her.

"Now, Carol Ann." Marilyn holds up a mirror. "How's that?"

"Well, it's certainly..." Carol Ann peers at herself. "No, I don't like it. You'll have to do it again."
Rebecca scrambles out the door.

"Thank you, Edna." Marilyn slips a five-dollar bill into the pocket of her white workdress. "We'll see you next week?"
"Yes. And you know, Marilyn..." Edna pauses in the doorway. "If you charged the stuck-up little so-and-so for every style she tried, you'd make a bloody..."
"Hey!" Rebecca barges past them. "I thought you were finished Carol Ann! I thought she...!"
"Shsh." Marilyn glances at Carol Ann, whose brand-new headful of rollers is lolling under a dryer. "Let's just let sleeping...bitches lie."
After she hands out the orders, Rebecca wanders over to watch her Mum's reddish brown highlights set. Vivian normally has sandy brown hair, quite a bit lighter than her sister Marion's. But lately she's been trying out different glimmers and streaks.
"Nancy Drew used to have yellow hair, you know." Rebecca reaches into the pocket of her pants and pulls out a Chickenbone. "But now she's got brown hair."
"Is that right?" cackles Vivian. "Who told you that?"
"Sunny." She sucks on the slender pink stick of candy, which, as she'll tell anyone who'll listen, is one of her favourite things in the whole wide world right now.
"Ha! What does *she* know about anything?"
"Lots! She even knows about that Pill you guys were..."
"Yuck!" Carol Ann heaves her silver helmet into the air. "I asked for double cream, not double sugar!"
"Sorry," grins Rebecca. The gaps in her teeth look bigger than ever. "I got mixed up."
"Yes, well...I suppose it's hereditary." Carol Ann yanks the silver helmet back down on her head.
"What's *hairytary*?" asks Rebecca.
She's sucking harder now so she can get past the cinnamon to the chocolate. She could just bite it but it's no fun to bite it until the very end.
"Never mind," laughs Marilyn. "Come on over here and we'll

make you look grown up."

"How?" Rebecca hops onto the chair.

"Well...your hair's pretty short, so we can't put much curl in it. Unless you want to try a perm like your Auntie Marion."

"No way!"

"OK. Then how about we just tease it back from the bangs? And then put some clips in it to make it wavy?"

"OK, but...just don't make me look like her, OK?" She points toward the dryers, where Carol Ann's latest headful of rollers is beginning to loll.

6

Early Saturday morning, under the gentle glimmer of steel blue and straw, Marion's 1953 Buick Skylark pulls slowly into Kentville.

"Look at that!" gasps Sunny.

Marion, Irene and Grammie all crane their necks.

"Wow!" Randy leans over Rebecca to get a better look.

Lining both sides of the road, as far as they can see, are hundreds of abandoned floats, all waiting for the parade to begin. There's an eerie potency to their stillness. Perhaps because there aren't any people around. Perhaps because all that suppressed energy and glamour is actually more thrilling than motion.

"So?" Rebecca folds her arms across her chest. "What's so great about that?"

She's still upset about the car. It's an old, standard-transmission estate car, with a two-toned body — creamy white at the bottom, emerald-green at the top — and four little portholes along the sides. And plastic covers over the greeny-grey cushions, since three of the Peterson kids still pee in their sleep. She was hoping Marion would buy the brand-new, pink and white Fairlane 500 Skyliner they'd seen at the new Ford dealership in Coldbrook — the one with the hardtop that retracted into the trunk — but she was told it wasn't practical. She'd have settled for the long, sleek, golden-brown Thunderbird, too — the one with the spare tire in a special case at the back — but she didn't even bother to ask about that. Marion wouldn't have thought the whitewalls or the splashy hubcaps were practical either. But then

Marion doesn't care about the latest innovations. Twin headlamps. Hood ornaments. Accentuated fins. Long bright strands of stainless steel trim. All Marion wants — Rebecca heard her tell the salesman over and over — is a big, serviceable, second-hand car that can hold six or seven people. Like today, when she's driving Grammie and Irene Andrews and three nieces and nephews to see the Apple Blossom Parade in Kentville.

At least it has a neat grill, muses Rebecca, as they glide to a stop. Like big, gleaming teeth. Of a big, ferocious… "Hey! Why are we stopping here?" She peers at the black-and-white sign over Lonergan's store.

"To look at shoes, of course. Come on, everyone."

The others pile out of the car.

"But what about the parade?" Rebecca doesn't budge.

"There's plenty of time for that."

"Yeah, well…" She doesn't see what's so great about shoes either. "I'm not getting a pair of those dumb old brown things. You said I didn't have to get those until I started school."

"Suit yourself," laughs Marion. "But then you only have two choices. You can either sit here and sulk or you can come inside and say hello to your mother."

Rebecca knits her brow. She's never understood why feet are so important to Marion. But then, it's probably not something to sulk over. She'll save her sulking for when Marion rounds them all up for the dentist.

"Hey! Wait for me!"

"Bad perm, Marion?" cackles Vivian as she watches them all troop into the store.

"Well, it was just for body. I'll still go…"

"My bangs fell out in one day!" blurts Rebecca.

"I'll still go every Saturday to have it set and…"

"Three dollars and fifty-seven cents!" gasps Irene. She's staring at the price tag on a pair of green stiletto heels. "That's an awful lot to pay for something that'll just poke holes in your linoleum."

"Ha! Don't blame me!" wheezes Vivian. "I only work here."

"Not for long," murmurs Grammie.

"What? What do you mean by that, Mum?"

"Your breath, Vivian. I can smell it on your breath."

"Yes, well..." Vivian looks away.

Grammie is a straight, strong, wiry woman with curly grey hair and soft, unwrinkled skin. She's shorter than all three of her daughters — Marion, Vivian and Florence — but she can still make them squirm.

"Well, some of us have to work, you know," splutters Vivian. "Some of us..."

"They do have an awfully thin heel, Irene." Grammie admires the pair of green spikes. "Whatever would you wear them with?"

Vivian persists. "Some of us don't get to go and have fun at the friggin'..."

"Well, they say that dress styles have changed from *chemise* to *empire*, Ivy. Although, personally..." Irene pats her hips. "I've never been able to fit into either of them."

Rebecca giggles.

"Yes, but do you think they're really the sort of thing to show off your...?"

"I know what you're doing!" snaps Vivian. "You're ignoring me! You're trying to make me...Sunny! Put those down! You can't afford those!"

Sunny has slipped her tiny feet into a pair of black, patent-leather shoes. Rebecca thinks they'd be perfect with Sunny's red, white and black plaid dress — the one with the pleats on the skirt. And her red cardigan. And her matching red barrettes. And her dark, Prince Valiant hair.

"I know, Mum," pleads Sunny. "But I just thought..."

"You'll have to get these instead." Vivian holds up a pair of blue plastic sandals.

"Yuck! They're worse than saddle shoes!"

"They're using a lot of straps this year, aren't they?" interjects Marion. She's been gazing at the shelves of ladies' shoes. Silky suede, patent leather, small-grained leather, cloth.

"Not on these!" shouts Randy, as he clumps around in a pair of men's square-toed oxfords.

"Little bugger," cackles Vivian.

"I tried those boys' ones." Randy points to the plain-toed bluchers, where the upper laps over the vamp, and the moccasins, both soft-soled and hard. "But they're not nearly as neat as…Hey! Rebecca!" He tries to clump after her. "Where are you going? Where are you?" But he topples out of his shoes to the floor.

Outside the shoe store, Rebecca makes sure she's not being followed, then slips two doors down into Neil Mackin's clothing store. She's not interested in anything from his fine line of ladies' apparel. She's pretty sure she'll never be interested. But she does want one of those tiny, silk, apple-blossom handkerchiefs she's seen in his display window. As a present for Marion. Even though she's still mad at her about the car.

Across from Memorial Park, where the parade always ends, there's a small white clapboard house which belongs to Irene's friend Julia Carey. A few hours later, as the parade begins to wind toward it, Marion and her gang are in the backyard, having their annual picnic.

"Did you hear…?" Rebecca gags on a mouthful of potato salad. "Did you hear something, Randy?"

"No." He gulps down his third glass of cherry Kool-Aid.

"Well, I did. It sounded like bagpipes. Like…It is!" She throws down her ham sandwich. "They're coming!"

They race around to the front of the house.

"They're always first," snorts Rebecca, as she clambers up the veranda steps. "And they don't even come from around here."

"Yeah, well, who cares?" Randy watches the pipe band from New Glasgow march by. "There's always tons more." He clambers up after her.

"They're expecting a hundred thousand spectators this year," remarks Marion, as she leads the adults up the steps.

"Ha!" Grammie glances at the crowd, which is lining both sides of the street. "Well, at least that's something."

"What do you mean, Ivy?" pants Irene.

"Well, the Festival's gone downhill since 1933, if you ask me. When it first started, it was a way of promoting the apple industry and encouraging local talent. But it's turned into a week-long orgy. Too much food, too much fun and too much religion."

"Oh. Well." Irene adjusts her glasses. "At least the apples are still going strong. I mean, I thought the pruning went well this spring. Didn't you? Not too many broken branches or branches with cankers or limbs that were crossing over one another."

"Look!" gasps Sunny. "The princesses are coming!"

The first one is Princess Middleton, who's riding on what looks like an overturned barrel of rotting apples, placed between the drum majorettes from Bridgetown and the brass band from Berwick. They'll be several more princesses, from towns in all three participating counties — Annapolis, Kings and Hants — but there's always something special about the first one. At least there is for Sunny, who thinks being one of those might be a good way of preparing to marry Prince Charles.

"She looks fat," snorts Randy.

After Princess Middleton, there's a succession of energetic bands. Some of them are professional but most are from high schools along the Evangeline Trail, like Horton District and Central Kings. The din is tremendous.

"Look at that one!" cries Rebecca. "It has *tangerines*!"

"Yes," laughs Marion. "Only they're called tam-bou-rines."

There's a tremendous clinking and hissing as the group from Windsor marches by, alternately hitting and waving its single-headed drums. And then, suddenly, a gigantic papier-mâché apple looms in the distance.

"Here she comes!" cries Rebecca.

"Gracious!" laughs Irene. "She's looking a bit flustered, don't you think?"

"I suppose," agrees Marion. "But you know Carol Ann. At least her hair hasn't fallen out."

"And such a sourpuss. You'd think she'd be able to..."

"Smile, Carol Ann!" shouts Randy. "Smile!"

Carol Ann gives them a perfunctory little wave.

"She can't," giggles Rebecca.

"Why not?"

"Well, for one thing, she's sitting on that big, fat, juicy worm we painted on the..."

"Hey! Maybe if we threw a water bomb at her! Maybe..."

"You needn't t'bother," interrupts Grammie.

"Yeah, well..." Randy snaps his gum. "I'm just glad she didn't win the Queen."

"Yes," sighs Julia, as the gigantic apple veers into the park. "That would have been quite the..."

Suddenly, there's a commotion on the sidewalk.

"Oh, my God!" gasps Grammie.

"What is it, Mum?"

"Look!" Grammie points to the rusty green pick-up which has somehow gotten wedged between the band from Greenwood and the float from Kingston.

"Hey! That's Uncle Filly's old truck!" squeals Rebecca.

"Jesus," laughs Marion. "I think it is. I wonder how on earth it got..."

"Oh no, Ivy!" Irene points, too. "Isn't that...?"

"Oh my God!"

Standing at the back of the rusty green pick-up is Vivian.

"I've been fired!" She shouts and waves to the crowd. "I've been friggin'...whoa-oa-oa..." She teeters from side to side. "Fired!" She plops down on her ass.

The crowd erupts in laughter.

"Let's go find Mum!" hollers Randy, as he and Rebecca scramble across the street.

"What for? There's too much else to...Come on, Marion! Hurry!"

"All right, all right!" Marion strolls after them. "It's not all going to disappear, you know."

Memorial Park is always busy, with its tennis courts, swimming pool, commons and ball diamond, but today, it's a mass of colour and chaos — a grand culmination of the week's festivities. Crafts booths, games booths, food booths. Streamers, balloons, gleaming instruments.

As Rebecca races through the commotion, she overhears some of the band members, arguing about whether or not they should change out of their uniforms before throwing balls at milk bottles. And then some of the princesses, wishing out loud they'd chosen different colours for their dresses, since sweat seems to show right through their pastel pinks and greens. And then she spots Princess Aylesford, who's simply trying to get down from her float.

"What's the matter, Carol Ann?" Rebecca grins up at her.

"You can see what's the matter, dummy. My dress has caught on that stupid nail, sticking out of that stupid...Will someone please...help...me...down!"

"Here." A tall young man leans his rake against the apple. "Let me..." He reaches up and takes her hand.

"Aaaaagh!" shrieks Carol Ann. "Get away from me! Get away!"

"Take your hands off her, nigger!" Someone shoves the young man.

"Yeah, nigger!" Someone else pins his arms behind his back. "Go back where you belong!"

Rebecca's never seen anything like it. She's so excited that all she can think of is a line from one of her brother's Hardy Boys books: "*Let go, you goons!*"

"Beat it, kid!" someone yells at Rebecca.

"No, *you* beat it!"

"Not before we teach this jungle bunny a lesson!" Someone punches him in the face.

"Yeah, a lesson he'll never..."

"Barry! Drew! Stop that!" Marion pushes herself into the fray. "You should be ashamed of yourselves."

"Yeah, well, he started it. He should know better than to..."

"*He* didn't start it!" splutters Rebecca. "*You* started it! You just came right up and...!"

"Never mind who started it." Marion brushes the hair out of her eyes. "Barry. Drew. I want you to leave...before you do something you'll..."

"Suits me."

"Yeah, something stinks around here anyway."

They swagger toward the crowd of pastel pinks and greens.

"*There's blood on his face!*" exclaims Rebecca. "*He's been slugged!*"

"Yes, I can see that," says Marion softly.

They peer at the gash near the young man's eye. Then Marion reaches into her purse and pulls out a tiny, silk, apple-blossom handkerchief.

"But maybe if we..." She dabs at the cut. "There. I think it's stopped." She slips the handkerchief into her purse. "But maybe you should see a..."

For the first time, their eyes meet.

"Just to make sure you don't need..."

"Thank you." His voice is as deep as the gash.

It's evening now. Marion and Rebecca are sitting together on the chesterfield.

"Did you have a good time?" whispers Marion.

Rebecca fiddles with the lid of her shoebox. "It wasn't as much fun as last year."

"No, I guess it wasn't."

"But at least..." Rebecca peeks into the shoebox. "At least I got..."

"What? Don't you like the colour? We could always take them back and get another pair."

"No." Rebecca closes the lid. "I like blue. I always wanted blue sneakers. It's just that...Marion?"

"Yes?"

"Was that man burnt in a fire?"

"No. Why do you say that?"

"No reason. I just thought..."

"You've seen men like him before, haven't you?"

"Yeah, but only on baseball cards and in the movies. Billy Bruton and Floyd Patterson and guys like that. And I always wondered if they'd been burnt in fires, too, 'cause their skin's all black and brown and...Marion?"

"Yes?"

"What's a nigger?"

"There's no such thing."

"But I heard Barry and Drew..."

"There's no such thing."

"Bullshit!" Rebecca slams shut the datebook. "I don't need this. I don't want this. I don't..."

But she's dragged inside the cloud of dust which has leapt up off the navy blue covers.

They found Frankie's body on a Sunday morning, when they were all arriving for church. It was a terrible mess. Gashes, bruises, compound fractures.

"We warned you about him, Marion."

"Yes."

"We told you time and time again that he was no good."

"Yes."

"We only hope that now we can all put this...unpleasant business...behind us and move on to..."

"God, I hate you, Marion! I hate you so...aaach." Rebecca chokes on the cloud of dust. "I wish I'd never come back!"

Uncle Filly loaded Frankie into the back of his rusty green pick-up and took him to Shunamon's Funeral Parlour in Berwick. But they wouldn't have him there so he drove him all the way to Halifax, where he was buried beside his mother. No one from Aylesford went with them.

"Bloody coward!" she cries, as she breaks out of the cloud of dust. "Bloody...bloody..."

She's not really sure whether she hates Marion or just doesn't understand her. The three of them had been such good friends. Why didn't Marion stick up for him? Why did she let the whole town think such terrible things about him?

Rebecca shudders.

She wants to know why. But she doesn't want to find out.

Suddenly, it's Marion's body she sees...lying amidst the jumble on the floor. It's a terrible mess, too. Gashes, bruises, compound fractures. But the face. The face is a tiny, silk, apple-blossom handkerchief, stained with her lips. Overwhelmed with grief and guilt and confusion, Rebecca breaks down and sobs.

A few minutes later, she slips quietly down the stairs and out to the yard.

When she was a little girl, there was nothing to remember, to admit, to understand. Life was simpler. Hearts were stronger. When she was a little girl, there were six wooden lawn chairs out there. A big, cream-coloured one for Marion. Three little, cream-coloured ones for her and Sunny and Sunny's friend Winifred. And two big, dark green ones for the men. A place for everyone. They'd been made by a retired apple-grower named Firth Harper, who once went fishing off Annapolis Royal with two of his friends and was the only one who didn't drown. But now there's only one chair. And it isn't cream-coloured anymore. It's white. And rotten. And peeling. It's still big, however. It still has that elegantly curved back. It's still Marion's.

Rebecca slides onto the chair.

She used to love being outside. It was so much better than reading; so much better than...

She takes a deep breath.

The smell of manure invades her nostrils; creeps up past her reluctance into her memory. She can't do anything about it. It's 1958 again.

7

It's only seven in the morning but already Rebecca is sitting at the arborite table, eating a bowlful of Fluffs. It's going to be one of the best days ever. The barn. Swimming. The warehouse. Grammie's. She can't wait to get started. But first, she has to get through this bowlful of Fluffs. She hates Fluffs. But that's all there is. That's all there ever is. She glances at the bag of cereal leaning in the doorway of the pantry. It's a huge bag. Like a bag of discount dog food, except it's as light as a feather. And it never seems to go down.

"Good." Sunny slips into the kitchen. "You're dressed."

"Yeah, but I think I'm going to need a new one pretty soon." Rebecca peers down at her bathing suit. It's made of beige stretchy material, with a big, green and white double V on the front. "This one's got holes in it."

"Yeah, so does Winifred's. That aqua one with the black and white diagonals on it. I told her she should have gotten one like mine." Sunny fondles the ruffles on her bright red romper suit.

"Yeah, well, I hope she isn't coming with us."

"No, she's going to sleep in."

"Figures." Rebecca gulps down her glass of Crino.

"Ugh." Sunny makes a face. "I don't know how you can drink that stuff. In fact, I think powdered milk is just about the yuckiest thing in the whole wide..."

"Ready!" Rebecca slams her glass down on the table.

"Great! Then I'll race ya to the barn!" Sunny springs toward the door.

"Hey! That's no fair!" Rebecca scrambles after her. "You've got a head start!"

Now that it's summertime, and Sunny's out of school, she and Rebecca go over to Carl Porter's barn almost every day. To get there, they have to cut through the pasture behind the Spinney house — a big, white sprawling house with a porch that goes all the way around to the back.

Rebecca stops running.

This morning, the pasture is lush and green and filled with cows. She slides her feet through the rich young grass.

But back at Christmas time, it was covered with a ratty blanket of ice. Everywhere else, there were huge drifts. Sheer cliffs on either side of the driveways. And sleds being pulled along the tire tracks. And red mittens. And silver buckles. And blue woollen hats with white balls on them. But in the pasture, there were tufts of grass poking through the ice.

She keeps sliding.

It was hard to skate there, with the thin ice and the stubble and the bumps. Once, she got going downhill so fast she couldn't stop and Holly Stoddard's skinny father Gerald had to pick her up when she fell.

Sunny was the one who kept trying to skate. After all, Vivian had named her after a famous figure skater. It was supposed to be Barbara Ann Scott, who won an Olympic gold medal for Canada at St. Moritz in 1948, but someone else in town had beaten her to it. So it ended up being Sonja Henie. Not that Sunny minded. When she saw a picture of that young Norwegian dressed in a short ermine-and-silk outfit, with *three* gold medals dangling around her neck, all Sunny could talk about was the adoring crowds and getting on TV and being showered with gifts, like royalty. If only she could skate.

"Ow!"

"What's the matter, Sunny?"

"Those stupid burdocks!"

In the winter, their feet were always so cold and so sore. Their skates were always too big or too small. If their mother had wanted Sunny to be an Olympic champion, she shouldn't have given her hand-me-downs.

"I like those ones the best," gushes Rebecca.

"What?" Sunny picks at the prickles in her leg.

"Those cows." Rebecca points to a big Brown Swiss, standing with a group of shiny, black and white Holsteins, chewing its cud. "They remind me of Siamese cats."

"Yeah, right."

"They do!"

"OK, then, tell me why a huge cow — Mrs. Porter says they weigh fourteen hundred pounds and give more than fifteen thousand pounds of milk a year — would remind you of a cat. Unless, of course, it's the colour. Which is stupid."

"Yeah, well, *Mr.* Porter says he's going to get more of them. 'Cause their milk doesn't have as much butterfat as the Jerseys and Guernseys he always..."

"Ha! How would you know? You're only four."

"Yeah, well, you're only eight."

"Anyway. Who cares how much butterfat it has? At least it isn't Crino!"

Rebecca examines the cows. They have such big, round, sad eyes. But they also have those funny sacs — those heavy, sagging, swaying udders. She can't help giggling.

"Wouldn't it be funny, Sunny? Wouldn't it be funny if the milk just came out of their tits as powder? Then they could squeeze it right into a box instead of a..."

"Oo-ah! Oo-ah!"

It's Calvin and Murray Loomer, the teenaged boys who work for Carl on the farm. They come from Dogpatch, the poor part of town up behind the slaughterhouse, but they're the best around at calling the cows in for milking.

There's a gentle tinkling of bells. And one or two moos of relief.

"There they go," marvels Rebecca, as she watches the cows move slowly and surely toward the barn. "They always seem to know when it's time."

"Yes," says Sunny softly. "Although...they don't look like they could jump over the moon, do they? I mean..."

"Even old Agnes," laughs Rebecca, as a big patch of buff and white bolts away from the herd.

Most of the cows have already been hooked up to the milkers. Rebecca thinks it's wonderful. The suction cups. The pails. The ten-gallon cans.

All that shiny silver. And that sweet-smelling steam. From the *real* milk. But she also thinks it's a little sad. They've been strapped into their stalls. There are stanchions fitted loosely around their necks.

"Carl! Carl!" squeals Rebecca.

"Over here, little one."

A tall man with reddish brown hair is setting up a stool next to Agnes, that scruffy old Guernsey who's never gotten used to modern technology.

"You should've seen her this morning, Carl!"

He begins to squeeze Agnes's teats.

"Was it ever neat! She ran all the way out to the back fence and Calvin had to go out and...!"

Some of the milk splashes into the gutter. Rebecca knits her brow.

Her mother once told her that, if she didn't behave herself, she was going to end up in the gutter.

She peers into the narrow trough.

It's an ugly place, filled with dirty water and milk and straw and shit. She certainly doesn't want to end up in there.

"Where's Sunny, Carl? Have you seen Sunny? I thought she was going to..."

"Shsh." Sunny's voice is mingled with a gentle lowing. "I'm over here."

Rebecca darts toward the stall at the back of the barn. "What is it, Sunny? What are you...? Wow!"

Sunny is standing with Carl's wife May and their son Turk, who was named after the famous Toronto Maple Leaf goaltender. They're all gazing down at a newborn calf.

"Isn't she sweet?" whispers Sunny.

"I guess." The mother cow licks the gooey discharge from one of the calf's little legs. "But a bit yucky, too. Did you give it a name yet?"

"Not yet," smiles May. "But I do know one thing. It's not going to be a hockey player this time."

Sunny reaches down to pat the little leg.

"Don't, Sunny! It's still all...!"

"Hey!" shouts Carl.

Rebecca spins around.

"What the hell are these?" He kicks at a pile of turds on the floor.

"How should *I* know?" giggles Rebecca, as she glances overhead.

"Have you kids been having your shitting contests again?"
"Not me!" hollers Rebecca. "I'm too little!"
"Or me," murmurs Sunny.
She wouldn't be caught dead sitting up there on that beam with her brothers, straining to see who could make the biggest turd. It just isn't something that royalty would do.

"See ya at four-thirty!" shouts Rebecca, as she and Sunny swish through the back pasture toward Sandy Beach.
"We'll be here," drawls Carl.
Closer to the banks of the little creek, where Sunny's teacher says the mighty Annapolis River actually begins, the ground gets spongier. And prettier, too. There are hundreds of cuckooflowers, poking their pale rose heads out of the luxuriously wet meadow. But that shouldn't fool anyone. Apart from a tiny stretch of yellow soil, Sandy Beach isn't a very glamorous place. The water isn't deep enough for swimming — just for splashing around — and it's on its way to being polluted.
"Looks pretty gunky today," muses Rebecca, as she gazes into the ripples.
"Never mind." Sunny slips out of her blue plastic sandals. "Just close your eyes and pretend it's Bermuda."
"OK, but…" Rebecca pulls off her soggy blue sneakers. "But what if…?"
"Come on." Sunny wades into the creek. "It's nice and…"
"Hey, wait for me!"
Seconds later, they're splashing around in the gunky water. At first, they're just themselves. Laughing, squealing, shouting. But then they turn into frogs. Beige frogs with green and white stripes. Red frogs with bands of ruffled camouflage.
"Ribbit!" shouts Rebecca, as she leaps from one pile of stones to another.
"I don't think they…" Sunny rests on her long, powerful hind legs. "I don't think they actually jump and croak at the same time, you know. I think they…"
"Who cares, Sunny? Ribbit, ribbit, ribbit, ribbit…"
"Hey, I've got an idea!" Sunny pulls in her forelegs.
A gentle breeze ruffles the tiny paired leaflets on the cuckooflowers.

"What?" Rebecca stops jumping.

"Let's take off our bathing suits."

"Are you crazy?"

"Come on. It'll be fun."

"No. I'm afraid."

"Of what?"

"Well..."

"Tell me!"

"OK, then. Snapping turtles."

"Oh, come on." Sunny tugs at her sister's bathing suit. "You're not going to let a little old..."

"Quit it, Sunny!" Rebecca tugs back. "Quit it or I'll...!"

"Weeeeeee!"

Suddenly, a green and white V flies into the air.

"Wee, yourself!"

Followed by a mass of bright red ruffles.

"Ha-haaa!" shouts Sunny, as she splashes naked in the gunky water. "I told you it'd be fun! I told you! I told you! I..."

"Sunny!" gasps Rebecca.

There's a break in the delirium.

"Now what? No, don't tell me. A snapping turtle, right?"

"No, Sunny, look!" She points to their bathing suits, which are sailing merrily down the creek.

"Oh my gawd!" squeals Sunny. "I thought they'd just float! I thought they'd just...Come on!"

They splash madly after them.

"Where're ya going?" shouts Sunny a little later, as she watches Rebecca veer down School Street.

"To the warehouse!" Rebecca keeps running. "To visit Ben!"

"Yeah, well, what about your bathing suit? Don't you want me to...? Forget it." Sunny pins her bright red ruffles to the long grey rope stretched across the yard.

In its heyday, Ben Kelly's always telling Rebecca, the K.S. Bowlby and Co. warehouse was an important depot for feed, flour, fertilizer, coal and apples — millions of apples. There isn't as much going on now — Acadia Insurance forms aren't nearly as exciting as huge mounds of Gravensteins — but Rebecca doesn't care. It's still one of her favourite places in the whole wide world.

Across the street, beside the lane where Jerry Veinotte keeps his big yellow caterpillar, there's a gigantic maple tree. It's emerald green now, so no one pays much attention to it, but in the fall, when it's turned burnt orange, people will come from miles around to take pictures of it. Even Ben, who gets to see it every day, will stand outside on the warehouse steps, beneath the wooden sign which proclaims MASSEY-HARRIS FERGUSON FARM EQUIPMENT, and take another snapshot. He must have at least fifty of them.

Rebecca glances once at the tree, and once at the red, yellow and blue sign hanging over her head, and then reaches for the doorknob.

Clang! Clang! Rattle! Clang!

"Marvin?" She lets go of the knob. "Is that you, Marvin?" She wanders around to the side. "Oh, hi, Marvin."

A slight, middle-aged man with thin grey hair and a weather-beaten face is tinkering with one of the battered green Lawnboys strewn on the gravel.

"Come on, now. Come on, my little beauty."

Rebecca can't help giggling. "You mean me, Marvin?"

Besides farm equipment, Ben sells household appliances and lawnmowers. And then gets Marvin Bennett to deliver them. And fix them, too, although Rebecca can't quite see how a man who says it rains "when the moon's crescent tips sideways and the water falls out" *can* fix things.

"OK, now." Marvin pushes his floppy brown hat to the back of his head. "Let's try 'er."

There's a series of splutters and groans.

"What's the matter, Marvin?" she finally asks, after she's watched him yank on the long, frayed cord for the seventh time. "Can't you get it to work?"

He tugs at his suspenders. "Nope."

"Well, then, what are you going to do?"

"Hmmm…I know what Ben would do." He loads the mower into the back of a dark blue pick-up which once belonged to Buster Nichols, the old Fish Man, before all that salt and water made the bed so rusty he couldn't use it anymore.

"What?"

"Drive 'er over to Morden and fire 'er into the Bay of Fundy."

"Really? He would? Ever neat! Is that what you're going to do, Marvin? Can I come with you?"

"Nope." He loads another mower. "I'm just going to drive 'er back to the owner and tell 'im she's died."

"Oh. Well, then…" Marvin's idea isn't nearly as exciting as Ben's. "I guess I'll just…" Even though it'd be fun to bounce down the road on the dark blue seats, with a rope strung across her lap from one broken door handle to the other. "See ya, Marvin."

"Yup."

The warehouse smells like it always smells — so good, so pure, like freshly cut wood. She takes a deep breath, then peeks into the office.

She sees the things first. The tall wooden cupboards. The long wooden bench. The calendars with K.S. Bowlby and Co. stamped on them. The tall wooden counter. The long wooden desk. The silver-grey safe with the door wide open. The silver-grey typewriter, too — a No. 5 Underwood. And the National cash register — mahogany, inlaid with ivory and finished with brass. And then she sees the people.

Ben Kelly has snow-white hair. It's been that way since he was twenty, he tells everyone. Since he saw those ghosts making love in the bell tower of the church, he always chuckles. Right now, he's leaning back in the wooden, wraparound chair by his desk, reading the *Chronicle Herald* he gets delivered from Halifax, and sucking on the straight black stem of his *pot* pipe. Rebecca loves the pipe words. He's got a *churchwarden*, too. And a *bulldog* and an *apple* and a *prince*, but he likes the little round bowl of the pot pipe the best. It holds just the right amount of his favourite *Amphora Brown*. And those other things, he scoffs, like *saddle-bit stems* and *diamond shanks*, are a little too fancy for him.

Rebecca stares at the back legs of the chair — Ben's tilted over on them for so many years that they're at least two inches shorter than the front ones — and then slips onto the long wooden bench by the wall. It's where Marvin always sits when Ben's run out of things for him to do. Or the customers, when they're waiting to buy a tractor or fire insurance or a plot in the cemetery.

Ben's wearing what he always wears — trousers, a long-sleeved shirt and a sweater vest; what he's worn since 1949, when he quit the bank to run K.S. Bowlby and Co. He said he was tired of moving around; that this would provide the stability he needed to settle down and get married. He hasn't done that yet. In fact, as far as Rebecca can tell, what he's mostly done is sit there, reading and smoking and wearing down the back legs of his chair. He's still way nicer than his dumb old brother, however. Malcolm Kelly may be a respected stockbroker, but he's also crabby and mean.

As for the two old women who work part-time for Ben, Rebecca likes Eldie Walker a little better than Millie Henshaw. Millie is tall and skinny, just like her husband Vaughan, and lives in a fancy grey house up on Park Street, across the yard from Grammie's. Grammie says she's a bit of a snob. Eldie is the short, slim woman with wavy white hair and wing-tipped glasses who's presently standing at the counter, filling out receipts in the big green book. Eldie isn't a snob, even though, as far as Rebecca's concerned, she's got something to be a snob about. Her house is on Park Street, too, beside the Fire Hall, and it's her husband Loring's job to run next door and activate the siren after Ruby Sanford has plugged an emergency call into their number on her big magneto keyboard.

Bling.

Eldie looks up from the big green book. "Gracious!" Her high voice crackles. "How long have you been here?"

"Hi, Eldie! Hi, Ben! I was wondering when you'd..."

Bling bling.

Ben stretches towards the wooden box on the wall. "Hello. Yes...Who?...Ha! Not worth the powder to blow him to hell, if you ask...Yes...Yes...Just a minute."

He leaves the receiver dangling from its long black cord while he crosses from the desk to the counter, where there's another big book. This one's really just two boards, with hinges, which open up to show a diagram of the plots in the Aylesford Memorial Cemetery.

"Heh, heh," he chuckles. "I guess I could squeeze him in beside old Bunty Bishop. I don't think old Bunty would mind." He moves to the phone again. "Yes, there's still plenty of...Right, Mona. With perpetual care that would come to...Yes. Marvin cuts the grass every...Yes, as long as you don't...Bye."

"Old man Spurr?" asks Eldie.

"God!" He snatches a ballpoint pen with K.S. Bowlby and Co. printed on it. "He hasn't been dead two hours and already she's asking about putting up those god-awful plastic flowers." He scribbles

Baldwin Spurr on the diagram, then flings down the pen and strides
to the door.

"Where're you going, Ben?" Rebecca slides to the front of the bench.

"To take a piss."

"Oh."

There isn't a bathroom in the warehouse. You either have to hold it
until dinner time or go outside. It's just as bad at Marion's house,
when Malcolm's taking his usual two hours over his toiletries, but
there the choices are the kitchen sink, the woodhouse, behind the
garage or next door at Alice Marshall's.

"And *I'm* going," smiles Eldie, "to do the inventory out back. Do
you want to come?"

"No, thanks." She cranes her neck, to watch Eldie drift back through
the clocks and the stoves and the fridges, and then slides to the back
of the bench again.

Rebecca hates waiting. But at least there's lots to look at. You can
usually look *out*, too, but Ben's still got cardboard over that huge hole
where the front window used to be. When she came by last week, he
was just standing there, with a glitter of glass at his feet. He said
someone broke in. And then he swiped at the jagged fragments. He
said it was probably Drew Saunders. And then he swept the pieces
into a dented dustpan that had rusty brown marigolds painted on it.
He said the little bugger wouldn't go to jail. That Marion would drive
him over to the county courthouse in Kentville, convince the judge
that he was really a good boy who'd learned his lesson, and then pay
his fine. Like she always did. And then he dumped the glass into the
wastebasket by the door.

The memory of this last tinkling fades into another tinkling. Softer.
Less threatening. She doesn't have to look. She knows Eldie's doing
something near the shelves on the far wall. Not in the little slots and
boxes for the different sizes of nuts and bolts and washers. But in the
big brown barrels filled with nails. *Masonry. Finishing. Brad.* She
chants the names to herself.

"You still here?" mutters Ben, when at last he returns. He blows his
nose, hard, into one of the white handkerchiefs she gave him for
Christmas. It turns bright red.

"Yes." She can't take her eyes off the handkerchief. She's pretty sure the
red's just from the Vicks nose drops, like it always is. But she's not positive.

"Now why would that be, I wonder." He stuffs the handkerchief into the pocket of his trousers.

"You *know* why."

"I suppose I do. Well, come on, then!" He flings open one of the doors on the tall wooden cupboards. "Before the mice get it all!"

She leaps off the bench.

The shelves are stocked with goods Ben's bought from wholesalers. Boxes of Morse's Orange Pekoe tea. Jars of Chase & Sanborn coffee. Cans of Campbell's soup and Allen's fruit cocktail. Sometimes, when he knows she's just having bread with margarine on it for dinner, he gives her a can of tomato soup, which doesn't taste great mixed with Crino but is still better than nothing. One of the shelves just has chocolate treats. Cadbury's Dairy Milk bars. Raisin Glossettes. Maltballs.

"Hmmmm. Let me see. How about...?" He reaches for a jar of coffee.

"I'm not old enough to drink that," she frowns.

"No, you're right. It should be something a little more nourishing; something that will...How about...?" He reaches for a can of chicken noodle soup.

"Be-en!"

"What?" He turns to face her. "You don't want that?"

"Not really," she sulks.

"Well, you didn't mind it last week." His eyes are twinkling.

"I know, but..."

"Oh, I see." He turns back to the shelves. "You want something that will rot your teeth. Hmmmm. Well, then...Catch!" He spins around and tosses her a Dairy Milk bar.

She grabs it with both hands. "Thanks, Ben!"

"You won't be thanking me when Dr. Doane yanks out all your teeth!"

"Who cares?" She tears at the wrapper. "It's my very favourite! Way better than Nielson's Jersey Milk!"

"One cow's as good as another, if you ask me."

"I know what *she's* doing," giggles Rebecca, as she tiptoes up the back steps at Grammie's place on North Park Street.

She licks the inside of the Dairy Milk wrapper, then peers through the screen door into the kitchen. "I was right," she whispers.

Grammie's standing next to the big black woodstove, squinting, with a round black lid in one hand and a smouldering cigarette in the other. She'd be more comfortable if she sat on the rocking chair, on the other side of the woodbox, but then she wouldn't be able to lean over and blow the smoke into the round black hole on top of the stove.

"Caught ya, Grammie!" shouts Rebecca, as she bursts inside.

Grammie flings the butt into the hole and clangs down the lid. "I don't know what you mean." She smooths her flowered housedress. "I was just..." She tugs at the elastic bands around the tops of her thick brown stockings. "I was just checking to see if it needed more wood."

"Yeah, sure," giggles Rebecca. "Then what are those?" She points to the pack of Player's on the arborite table, beside the tin of baking soda.

"Yes. Well." Grammie tucks it into the pocket of her housedress. "You're notta gonna tell anyone, I hope."

"No, Grammie."

"Good. Then you can go down and fetch some wood."

"Yes, Grammie." She hops toward the cellar door.

"And you needn't t'bother giggling all day either."

"Sorry, Grammie."

As Rebecca creeps down the wooden steps, she takes care not to squish the four loaves of bread lying on them. Grammie doesn't believe in fresh bread. She says it has to sit for a few days or it gums up your stomach.

The cellar is filled with wood for the stove. Piles of it. Everywhere you look. She's just bending down to gather a few of the stray logs when, suddenly, she hears mewing.

"Is that you, Zeke? Oh!"

There's a burlap bag spread under the steps. The short-haired cat on it — she's grey with splashes of gold — is nursing a litter of kittens.

"Hello, Zeke." She tiptoes towards them. "You're a mother again, are you?"

Grammie always has three or four cats, with strange, incongruous names, and they're always having kittens. Rebecca loves taking them saucers of Puss 'n Boots and then playing with them in the wood for hours.

"They're so cute, Zeke. They're so...one, two, three, four..."

Suddenly, she remembers. If Grammie can't find homes for them, she'll stuff them in a thick brown stocking that's got a run in it. And then take them down to Sandy Beach and drown them.

"Here, Zeke," she whispers, as she lays the Dairy Milk wrapper on the burlap bag. "Here's a little treat for you."

She gathers an armful of logs and trudges back up the steps.

Near the top, she sees the rockers, rolling gently back and forth. Grammie's had that chair for as long as anyone can remember. But it's looking worn now and she says she's going to get Stan Freeman to cover the seat and back in fake leather. And then she sees the hem of the flowered housedress. Grammie has plenty of hand-made housedresses. But she says this one's her favourite. Because it means something to her. Because it isn't just an off-white abstract with blue and green splotches on it. Even though she wouldn't be caught dead outside the house in it. And then she sees the thick brown stockings.

"Grammie?"

"Hmm?"

Rebecca dumps the logs into the woodbox. "I was just wondering..." She watches the stockings sway back and forth. "Have you got a run in any of them yet?"

"No," Grammie answers softly. "Not yet."

"Good. I'm glad."

The stockings sway one last time and then stop.

"Well, come on." Grammie pushes herself out of the chair. "Let's bake cookies."

"OK."

Grammie reaches up to the shelf above the sink and takes down her cookbook. "What kind do you want?"

"I don't care."

Rebecca doesn't care, really, as long as it's cookies and not cake. Grammie isn't good at cakes. She has several different recipes for them, but they always end up tasting the same — probably because she always puts jelly between the layers.

"Come on." Grammie flips through the pages. "I thought you liked baking cookies."

"I do, but..."

"Well, then, choose!"

"OK. How about those brown sugar ones? You know, the ones with the jam in the centre?"

They're not fancy cookies. But she likes how soft and chewy and

golden brown they are — especially near the centre, where the gooey
hole is; where they never cook as much.

"Right!" Grammie strides into the pantry.

Within seconds, she's furiously passing things through the hatch
above the sink. Milk, brown sugar, brown eggs, flour, bowls, spoons,
butter.

"Wait, Grammie! Wait!" Rebecca rushes back and forth from the
hatch to the arborite table. "You're going too fast!"

"Come on, come on!"

"OK! But don't blame me if I...!"

"There!" Grammie tosses her a measuring cup. "I think that's the
last of it."

"No, it isn't, Grammie," giggles Rebecca. "You forgot the most
important part. You forgot the jam."

"Gracious! Well, what kind would you like? There's orange
marmalade and..."

"Yu-uck!"

"Well, then how about ginger? They might taste good with a bit
of...I know. Let's try Velveeta!"

"Nooooo! Grammie! I want the kind we always have!"

"Ha! I figured as much." She hands Rebecca a gooey jar of
strawberry jam.

"Grammie?" asks Rebecca, as she stares at the little mounds of dough
on the tarnished sheets.

"Hmmm?"

She's standing by the small, white electric stove next to the sink —
the one she uses in the summertime, when it's too hot for the big,
black woodstove.

"What's a *sex kitten*?"

"Ha! I've never heard of such a thing." She checks to see if the oven
is hot.

"Is Zeke a sex kitten?"

"I'm sure I don't know."

"Well, I heard Barry Connors call Marion a sex kitten and I just
wondered...Do you think I'll be a sex kitten when I grow up?"

"Ha! You needn't t'bother."

"Why? What's so...?"

"Right." Grammie turns away from the stove. "Now we just have to..."

"Can I do it, Grammie? Can I?"

"Certainly."

"Neat!" Rebecca bends over the tarnished sheets. "It's the best part, you know."

She presses her thumb into each little mound of dough. And then spoons a bright red blob into each of the cream-coloured indentations.

"What the hell does she want from me?" cries Rebecca, as she stomps back into the house. "If she wants me to understand, I don't! I don't understand! Anything!"

She slumps to the floor of the back chamber.

"Ha! If only you were a cookbook!" She flips through the pages of 1958. "Maybe then I could find the right recipe. Maybe then I could...God! I should have known!"

July is just another series of meetings and appointments. She chooses one at random.

Bridge. Here. 2 pm.

She remembers the deck of cards in the unmarked box. And then that Blackwood Convention Marion was always talking about. The one which is based on aces and kings. She's never really understood conventions in cards, except that they're supposed to be like giving clues; like telling your partner secrets about your hand, without really saying anything.

"Well, it's a start."

8

Since Marion's freezer is too small to hold much, one of her daily rituals is to go uptown to shop for food. Rebecca usually tags along.

"Which one are we going to this time, Marion?"

Martin Selfridge's store is on Old Post Road, across from Hal Jackson's Fina Station. It has a large supply of clothing and paint as well as food. Fred Johnson's store, on Commercial Street beside the Post Office, is mostly stocked with food.

"Well, let's see. I need meat, cheese, a can of asparagus...How about Fred's?"

"Great! Fred's way nicer than that Mr. Selfridge."

Marion laughs. "What do you mean? Martin's nice. And so's his wife Lillian, for that matter. Although I must admit that whiny voice of hers does get on your nerves after a while."

"Yeah, well, they're both kind of snobby, if you ask me." Rebecca scuffs along the path. "And he's always picking on Uncle Charlie. And his store always smells like his dumb old pipe."

They turn left, down Commercial Street.

"Marion! Oh, Marion!"

Judith Jefferson is calling from the doorway of the Post Office.

"Oh, hi, Judith!" Marion waves to her. "How are you?"

"Good. Good. Listen, Marion. I wanted to tell you that your...Oh, wait a minute. Wanda wants some...Wait."

Judith and her husband Laurie are in charge of the Post Office. He's a short, roly-poly man who always wears a sweater vest and tie. She's a tall, hefty woman, with dark grey hair and glasses, who once brought Marion a lovely music box back from Switzerland.

"Goodness." Judith is back in the doorway again. "I've never in my life met anyone who haggles over prices as much as Wanda does. Laurie tried to tell her that the price of stamps is set by the government; that we aren't allowed to give discounts on prices set by the..."

Wanda brushes by her.

"Harrumph, yourself, you old...Anyway, Marion. Your purse is ready."

Judith also makes leather purses, wallets and bags. She's a pretty fair seamstress, too.

"Oh good, Judith. How much do I owe you?"

"Well, I thought I'd just pay for my insurance premium with it. If that's OK with you."

"That's fine, Judith. Fine. I'll come by for..."

Rebecca tugs at Marion's sleeve. "She'll come by for it later."

As they walk the last few steps to the store, Rebecca keeps her eyes fixed on the red and white metal sign suspended from the window frame. ICED COCA-COLA HERE. She's dying to go inside. Before they can, however, Fred's wife Cookie and their three young sons Eddie, Timmy and Clark come tumbling down the stairs at the side of the building. They all live up there, over the store.

"Oh, hi, Marion. Rebecca. Some hot, eh?" Cookie wipes her brow.

"Yes, it is."

"I guess." Rebecca looks down at the ground.

Cookie is a big woman, with a pudgy face and glasses and dark brown crimped hair. She seems nice enough to Rebecca. But Grammie says she's really "hard" — and all because of the time she went to bingo on the very night she found out her mother had cancer.

"Are you coming on Tuesday, Marion? We need a fourth." Cookie wipes her brow again.

"Yes, I think so. I think I can make it. Let me check." Marion pulls her datebook out of her purse.

While she confirms the time and place — eight o'clock, in Cookie's big, wide living room at the front of the house — Rebecca runs her fingers over the green and white metal bar across the screen door. FRESHEN UP — 7-UP. It's so smooth and cool.

"Want one?" whispers Eddie.

"No." She snatches her hand away. "I don't like 7-Up. It's boring."

"Yeah!" agrees Timmy. "Way more boring than root beer or Mountain Dew or...!"

"I like grape!" interrupts Clark.

"You would."

"And Nesbitt's Orange," adds Rebecca. "That's my..."

"Yeah, sure," snickers Eddie. "You probably just don't have the money."

It's true, thinks Rebecca, as they all go inside. She likes pop. But no matter how much you like it, you still have to have the six cents. And you only get a penny back for the bottle.

"OK, Marion. I'll talk to you later."

Cookie takes up her position at the cash register. Marion drifts toward the back. The boys run off to find their Dad. But Rebecca just stands there, staring down the aisles.

It's a wonderful place. Two aisles. Hardwood floors. The candy on the right. The potato chips straight ahead. The fruits and vegetables to the left. She never knows where to go first.

"Boys! Boys!" laughs Fred, as he tries to stack some cans of soup on the shelves near the back.

He's wearing what he always wears, too — a bow-tie, suspenders, glasses, a white shirt with the sleeves rolled up to the elbows and a soiled white apron.

"I didn't spend all morning...just to have you...Slow down!" He runs his fingers through his thin grey hair. "Let me know if there's anything I can help you with, Marion."

Rebecca makes a mental note of what she'd like. Two five-cent bags of Scotties potato chips. A big handful of Chickenbones. A bottle of Nesbitt's Orange, with lots of pulp in it. A cardboard container of ice cream, with a little wooden spoon. And a cherry popsicle. Or maybe lime. She can't decide.

"Here." Eddie hands her a Buried Treasure. "From Dad."

"Thanks!"

The kids wander toward the big square vent in the middle of the floor. In the wintertime, when the furnace is on, the huge grill can fit as many as six people. Nearly everyone who comes into the store spends some time standing on it, talking and laughing and trying to keep warm. In the summertime, there isn't as much use for it, but the kids go there anyway because it seems cooler and they've gotten into the habit.

For a while, they just stand there, licking the orange and white ice cream off the plastic sticks. But then Eddie gets impatient.

"What d'ya get, Rebecca? A clown?"

There's always a little plastic figure hiding under the orange and white swirls.

"I don't know yet. I haven't got there."

"Well, lick faster!"

"I'm trying!"

Suddenly, there's the piercing whine of a saw.

"I'm going to watch Walter!" cries Rebecca, as she races to the back.

Behind a large display case of chops, breasts, cutlets and steaks is a large walk-in cooler. That's where the whining is coming from. Loud whining. So loud, in fact, that Walter doesn't hear her creep inside.

There are sides of meat hanging all around them and a large, thick, wooden table, where Walter is sawing one of them in two. Right through the neck, where the patties and stews come from. And then down an invisible line between the steaks and roasts and chops and the parts that are only good for grinding and braising. To the cutlets at the other end.

It used to be a baby cow, she thinks, in wonder and disgust. And now it's just…She doesn't know what to call it. But at least it can't feel anything anymore.

She creeps closer to the table.

She's glad Walter can't hear her. She doesn't want to talk to him. She just wants to watch him. Everyone says he's the best butcher around. But she still can't see why anyone would actually want to do that for a living — unless, of course, like Walter Keddy, they'd come back from the Battle of Ortona with a glass eye and a wooden leg and couldn't think of anything better to do.

The whining stops abruptly.

"Oh, hello." Walter smiles at her. "When did you get here?" He heaves the bottom half onto his shoulder and limps over to an empty hook.

"Just a little…Yu-uck!"

The orange and white ice cream has dripped off the stick onto her hand. There's a ballerina underneath.

"You can wash that off in the sink," says Walter.

"It's OK."

Walter limps back to the table. It's a little concave now, because of all the chopping that's been done on it. And it comes right up to Rebecca's eyeballs.

"What are you going to do now, Mr. Keddy?" She peers over the edge.

"Well…" He thumps the top half onto its side. "I'm going to chop it first. And then trim it up a little so there won't be so much…"

"With those knives?"

There's a pair of gleaming silver blades lying on the table.

"Yes," he says solemnly. "With those knives."

"Hel-lo-o! Wal-ter!"

"Yes, Marion! Be right with you!" He wipes his hands on his apron and clumps out of the cooler.

"Ha!" laughs Marion, when she sees Rebecca come sidling out after him. "I should have known! I hope you weren't…"

"Oh, she's no bother," smiles Walter. "No bother at all."

"Well, that's a first!"

Marion chooses a big, juicy steak, which Walter grinds up for hamburgers. And then a few slabs of cheese, which he cuts from a huge orange block. And then it's time to go.

Rebecca's waiting by the cash register, with her two tiny bags of Scotties potato chips, when suddenly she remembers something. "Oh, I almost forgot!" She shouts toward the fruit and vegetables aisle. "Can I have the bottle caps, Fred?"

"If you like."

She races to the back again.

The pop machine is an old red, horizontal one filled with ice water and bottles hanging from rungs. Anyone who wants one just lifts up the cover, slides one of the bottles to the end of the rung, and pulls it up. The opener is on the side, with a metal container underneath to catch the caps.

"Ever neat!" she hollers, as she stuffs the dented caps into the pockets of her jeans. "There's millions of them!"

"Whatever will she do with them?" sighs Cookie, as she wipes her brow for the fiftieth time.

"I have no idea," laughs Marion. "But I'm sure she'll think of something." She turns toward the door.

"Hey! Wait for me!" Rebecca drops the plastic ballerina into the cap container. "Wait for meee!" She clinks and jingles after her.

Marion is standing near the sink, chopping up a bowlful of hard-boiled eggs. On the counter beside her is a loaf of white bread with the crusts cut off.

"How many of those are you going to make?" mutters Rebecca.

She's sitting on the black vinyl chair by the stove, sulking. She'd rather see the silver meat grinder on the counter. And a bowlful of cooked roast beef. And a jarful of mustard.

"Well, let's see." Marion drops a handful of shells into the garbage can behind the chair. "There'll be nine of us altogether."

"Eight," says Rebecca firmly. "I don't like egg salad sandwiches. Not even when they're in those coloured checkerboards you sometimes make with the bread."

"That's news to me," laughs Marion.

"So, then, what else are we going to have?"

"Guess."

"Ummm..." It's more of a wish than a guess. "Strawberry shortcake?"

"That's ri-ight."

"Neat!" Rebecca leaps to her feet. "Where are they?"

"Where do you think?"

Rebecca bounds across the room and throws open the door of the Kelvinator. It's filled with quart-sized boxes of strawberries.

"Wow! Where did you get them? At Small's?"

"No. Corkum's."

"Hey! Maybe they're the ones we picked. Remember? The time you took Randy and me up to...?"

"No," laughs Marion. "I don't think so. Vesta never grows this kind."

"Oh."

At first she's disappointed. She feels she got covered with daddy-longlegs for nothing. But then she brightens. These Bounty strawberries are the special ones; the sweet ones with the great big hole in the centre. Corkum's always keeps a few boxes of them out back, to give to their special customers.

"OK, now." Marion has finished with the sandwiches. The big bowl of yellow goop has been transformed into dainty little white and yellow triangles. "Hand me one of those boxes of strawberries, will you?"

Rebecca just stands there, gawking at them.

"Rebecca? Did you hear me? If I don't start hulling them..."

"Wait! I can't decide!"

"Any one will do!" laughs Marion.

She's still laughing, a few minutes later, when both of her hands are stained with red.

"What?" gasps Vivian. "Wasn't that right? What are you laughing at?"

When she tries to take back her card, the others all slap their hands down on hers.

"OK, OK," she sulks. "But what was I supposed to do? My cards aren't worth the salt they're printed on!"

There's another burst of laughter.

There are two tables for bridge this afternoon. At one of them — the one with the big square impression of Cezanne's Mont Sainte-Victoire which Marion keeps folded up in the front hall — Marion and

Irene Andrews are playing against Cookie Johnson and Thelma Peel, the big round woman who sings in the choir. At the other one — the plain brown one Alice Marshall always drags over from next door — Vivian and Frances Hazelwood, whose husband is that President of Acadia University who once gave Marion her first motorcycle ride — are going against Alice and Edna Ogletree, who has a nice house and nice furniture and a cocker spaniel named Teddy, but no chin.

Rebecca, meanwhile, is watching from the Eastern Star chair near the fireplace — the ornate chair with the high arms that Marion got from the Masonic Hall after its members voted to buy new furnishings.

The time comes, however, when she can't sit still any longer. "But I thought you were only supposed to take…"

"Shshsh!" everyone hisses.

"Sorry."

Rebecca stares down at the card case on her lap. It's an elegant one, made in Italy, with lovely varnished wood and a thin leather covering and slots for three decks of cards. Marion's put her signature on the bottom, in blue ink.

Rebecca tries again. "I was only…"

"Shshsh!"

Marion's explained a little about the hands to her. But she's still too young to understand; still too young to grasp the meaning of *vulnerability*, *void*, *dummy tricks*, *sacrifice*, *dummy reversal*, *squeeze*. She has a feeling that words like those are supposed to resonate with magic and mystery but they just seem stupid to her. She knows some of the rules, however. She knows you're not supposed to take forever over a bid or a play; that if you can't come up with something in fifteen seconds, you're supposed to…

"Come on, Thelma! We haven't got all day!"

"I told you," whispers Rebecca.

"Shsh, everyone. I'm thinking."

"That's a first!"

"OK, OK. *By me.*"

"What?" snaps Cookie.

"I mean *pass.*"

Everyone laughs except Rebecca, who's watching the smoke from Marion's cigarette twist and curl up the burgundy walls toward the creamy white ceiling. Marion doesn't smoke much — just the odd

Matinée or Cameo Menthol when she gets together with the ladies to play bridge. She doesn't curse much either, except, again, over bridge, when the odd "shit" or "damn" slips out. She does wear her glasses quite often, however — the ones with that popular wood-grain look to their dark brown plastic frames. Especially when she's playing the piano. Or peering down at her cards, with her chin up, and the smoke from her cigarette twisting and curling toward the ceiling.

"This is dumb!" cries Rebecca, as she springs out of her chair.

She's headed for the dark brown wooden table behind the burgundy chesterfield, where a large crystal bowl is filled with Bridge Mixture. On her way by the card tables, however, she can't resist taking a peek at the hands.

"Oh-oh," she giggles, as she dances from Alice to Vivian to Edna. "You're not going to get very far on..."

"Stop that!" snaps Marion.

"What?"

"*Kibitzers* are supposed to be seen and not heard. Just like children."

"Yeah, well, I'm bored. It's way more fun playing Crazy Eights. Or Fish! Can we play Fish after you're...?"

"Here." Marion hands her the silent butler. "Make yourself useful."

"OK, but..."

"Now!"

Rebecca stuffs a handful of Bridge Mixture into her mouth and then stomps around the room, dumping ashtrays into the silver dish.

"Alice, Alice, Alice," seethes Edna, when the hand's finally over.

"Whaaat?"

"Nothing."

"No, teeell me. Whaaat?"

"OK, then. What distribution did you have?"

"I dooon't knooow."

"Jesus. You only had a singleton. You shouldn't have..."

You're not supposed to pick on anyone, thinks Rebecca. She lets the cover clank down on the bowlful of stained white filters. You're supposed to just say "Bad luck" and then...

"You shouldn't have bid so many hearts when you only had a..."

"Oooh, my gaaawd! I diiidn't seee thaaat. I diiidn't..."

"Ladies. Ladies," laughs Marion. "It's only a game."

Rebecca places the silent butler on the oval coffee table, near the flowery chesterfield by the front window.

"Yes, of course, Marion. But we should still try to follow the...What are you doing, Cookie? You're not supposed to look at your cards until the dealer has..."

"Iyee! Now look what you made me...!"

"Misdeal!"

Irene flings the deck into the centre of the table.

"Jesus Christ, Irene! You should pay more attention to what you're doing!"

"Yes, well, if you didn't all talk so much, maybe I'd..."

Marion springs to her feet. "I think it's time to eat."

Rebecca is standing in the southwest corner of the dining room, staring up through the windows of the china cabinet.

Marion has nice things, she marvels. Lovely, shiny, silver things. A two-handled meat platter, a two-tiered cake basket, a sauce-boat, a biscuit box, a water pitcher and some really old knives and forks with what she thinks Marion called a "go thick design" on their tips. But the nicest things are the china cups. Not the flowery ones. And not the ones with the stripes and the flecks and the faces of the Queen. But the ones from that secret women's group Marion belongs to — where she's the secretary and gets to wear a badge with crossed pens on it.

The Order of the Eastern Star cups have a crest on one side, with the letters F-A-T-A-L arranged around it. Rebecca hasn't a clue what they mean or even what order you're supposed to say them in. On the other side is a five-pointed star with funny little pictures in its tips. A cup, a broken pole, a crown...

Rebecca frowns.

Marion's told her over and over what those pictures mean, but she doesn't remember. And she doesn't remember the names of those five Bible heroines the pictures are supposed to stand for. But she does wonder what will happen if she decides she doesn't want to grow up like any of those women. She's pretty sure the tips of that star should have a baseball bat, too. And a racing car, a butcher's knife, a deck of cards, a mystery novel.

"Are we supposed to drink our tea right out of the pot?" calls Marion from the living room.

Rebecca doesn't answer.

"Remiiinds me of Claaary," drawls Alice.

"What do you mean?" Edna fluffs at her hair.

"Weeell. He neeever aaanswers meee eeeither. Sooometimes he goooes for daaays withooout…"

"Rebecca! Bring those cups in here now!"

Within seconds, the ladies are all sipping their tea.

"These are pretty cups, Marion. Where did you get them?"

"Which?"

Mrs. Hazelwood holds up the one with apple blossoms on it.

"Oh, those. Uptown, at Harriet's. Remember, Edna? Remember how Opal accused Harriet of importing them from Japan?"

Mrs. Hazelwood runs her fingers over the lime-green branches, through the gaudy pink blooms.

"I'd liiike to gooo to Japaaan," whines Alice.

Rebecca watches Alice's lips curl down past the bunch of wheat to the broken pole.

"I neeever go aaanywheeere."

"Ha!" snorts Thelma. "You go to get the mail. And you visit your daughter. Jesus! Every day, I see you walking back and forth from Sheila's place with that brown paper bag of yours!"

"Yes, Alice," chuckles Irene. "What the hell do you keep in that damned bag anyway?"

"Her nightdress, probably." Cookie takes another sip. "In case she finally decides to leave the old coot."

"Weeell, maaaybe I wiiill."

"Oh, right!"

"If he doooesn't taaake me sooomewhere soooooon."

Rebecca watches Alice lick the drip off the sword with the cloth around it.

"Oh, it's probably just her purse," cackles Vivian.

Everyone snickers.

There are a few minutes of relative silence while they devour the heaping bowls of strawberry shortcake — made properly, Cookie comments, with biscuits, instead of that awful, yellow, spongy cake. And then they begin to deal out the hands again.

"*Honours, stoppers, finesse, false cards, the distributional echo,*" chants Rebecca, as she helps herself to a second mound of shortcake and then settles back into the ornate chair by the fireplace.

"What did you think of that business over to Yoho?" asks Cookie, as she arranges her suits.

"What business?"

"You know. That trouble with the coon and the white woman."

"Two hearts."

"Three diamonds."

"They can't be very bright, you know. To think they can get away with raping..."

"Well, it wasn't rape exactly. The two of them just..."

"Ha! That's what I call it. They've only got one thing on their minds, you know. To sleep with as many white..."

"Of course, it doesn't seem to make any difference the other way around. When the woman's a coon and the man's..."

"Can women be coons? I thought only men were..."

"Just another notch in his belt, you mean."

"Right. And kind of...well, exciting, if you..."

"Four no trump."

"Well, I think it's terrible! Either way. People should stick to their own kind...or we'll all look like zebras in a few generations!"

"Oh, I don't think they come out that way," muses Thelma. "Not with stripes. I think they just..."

"Vivian!" snaps Mrs. Hazelwood.

"What?"

"Stop that!"

"What!"

"Stop dancing around behind me!"

"Yes, Vivian. When you're the *dummy*..."

"Isn't she always?"

"When you're the dummy, you're not supposed to look at your opponent's hand or your partner's hand or..."

"Or dance around behind the *declarer*, which is me," seethes Mrs. Hazelwood.

Vivian slumps back into her chair. "I don't see what difference it makes. You're the best player here. Well, you and Marion, with your fancy duplicate bridge clubs over to Greenwood and everything. And with your Master's Card...ha!...there's not much chance you're going to..."

"Oh no!" cries Cookie, from the other table. "Sorry." She looks sheepishly at Thelma.

"Let me guess." Irene glares at her. "You should have doubled, right?"

"So?" Cookie glares back. "What do you care? You're not my partner."

"I know, but you didn't double last time either. At your place, when you were my..."

"That's it!" Mrs. Hazelwood throws her cards onto the plain brown table.

"Oh, please, Frances," urges Marion. "Just one more hand and then we can tally up the..."

"No, thank you, Marion. I have to be going."

"Well, OK, Frances. But I hope you'll come back next..."

The screen door bangs shut.

"We'll have different partners!" Marion calls after her. "I promise!"

"Yeees. Maaaybe Rebeeecca can plaaay with heeer."

"Or put up with her."

"Ha! The old..."

"No way!" Rebecca shoves the last, gooey red spoonful into her mouth.

Marion is pushing her old General Electric vacuum cleaner across the sculptured design on the living room carpet. It's a dark blue leafy pattern on a light blue background, with an occasional gob of eggy yellow or strawberry red near the impressions left by the legs beneath Mont Sainte-Victoire. Everyone's gone now except Rebecca, who's sitting at the Baldwin upright in the southeast corner of the room. She doesn't know how to play it yet. But when she does, she's going to play every single piece in those books piled on top of it.

She climbs up onto the stool to look at them.

"*The Mammoth Folio of Music for the Piano. 123 Christmas Songs. Tales from the Vienna Woods.*" Beneath the steady roar of the vacuum cleaner, she sounds out all of the names. "*Tennessee Ernie Ford's Book of Favourite Hymns.* 'The Desert Song'. 'Pomp and Circumstance.'" She's glad Marion's already taught her how to read. "'My Wild Irish Rose.' 'Without a Song.' 'I'm Forever...'"

The steady roar ends abruptly.

"What's this one, Marion?" Rebecca holds up a piece of sheet music.
"'I'm Forever Blowing Bubbles.'"

"I know, but..."

"It's my favourite. Now, come on. We have to..."

"But how does it go?"

"Never mind how it goes." Marion yanks the plug out of the wall.
"We have to get this place cleaned up before the men get home." She
starts to wind the long brown cord around the clamps on the stand-up
vacuum cleaner.

"Hey, wait!" Rebecca hops down off the stool. "That's *my* job!"

9

"I hate church," grumbles Rebecca, as she tosses her wet pajama
bottoms into the closet.

"Me, too," sighs Sunny. She does the same with her baby dolls.

"They never talk about any good stuff. Just God and junk like that."

"Well, we won't have to go there next month anyway." Sunny slips
into her red, white and black plaid dress.

"Why not?"

"Because it's closed. It's always closed in August."

"Oh yeah. I forgot." Rebecca does up the pearly white button at the
top of her cardigan.

"Of course, we're supposed to go down to the United Church instead.
But we never do. There." Sunny gazes into the tall mirror on the
closet door.

"You look nice," coos Rebecca, as she skips up beside her.

"I guess. Except that my dress smells like Javex."

"Yeah," sniffs Rebecca. "Mine, too."

"I don't know why she has to put it in *everything*. It's really only to
get the pee smell out and we never pee in our...Here. Let me do that."

"Thanks."

Sunny strings a white ribbon through Rebecca's hair and then ties
it into a bow. "OK. I guess that's it."

They gaze at themselves in the mirror again.

Everything on Rebecca is white — her dress, her cardigan, her
ribbon, her ankle socks — except her shoes, which are scuffed blue

sneakers. Sunny's feet don't match the rest of her either. The only things she could find that fit are her blue plastic sandals.

"I...hate...!" Rebecca jams a pair of sunglasses onto her face. They're white plastic ones, with a big yellow cut-out of Tweety Bird on the nosepiece. "Church!" She whirls away from the mirror.

When Rebecca sashays into the kitchen, everyone else is already there, waiting for Harold to finish the next batches of bacon and eggs and pancakes. It's his Sunday morning special — and a welcome break from Fluffs.

"Oh, you beautiful doll. You great big beautiful..."

"Maybe if you didn't sing so much," mutters Darrell.

"What?" Harold waves a grimy yellow spatula at him.

"Maybe they'd be ready sooner."

"Yeah, and maybe if you didn't eat like pigs, they'd be...Oh, hi, Rebecca." He moves slowly toward her, with the grimy yellow spatula in one hand and a rusty brown lifter in the other. *"Let me put my arms around you. I could..."*

"Daddy, don't!" She leaps away from him. "You'll get me all dirty!"

"OK, OK." He drops a spoonful of Domestic shortening into a big black pan. "Then how about some...? Yow!" The grease spits on his white cotton T-shirt and pants. "How about some grub?"

"No, thank you." She saunters toward the door.

"Ha! And where do you think you're going?" Vivian glares at her.

"To Marion's."

"If you ever leave me, how my heart will..."

"Shsh, Harold. And why, may I ask?"

"Because I don't like eggs like that. They're too runny. Either too runny or too cold."

"Well..." Harold places the pale brown egg back in the carton. "How about some pancakes, then? They'll be ready in..."

"In a million years!" the boys shout in unison.

"No." Rebecca pushes open the screen door. "I like French toast better."

"Well, don't be late!" Vivian calls after her. "We're all going up to Lake Paul this afternoon! And don't...!" She scrambles out of her chair to the door. "And don't you dare wear those sunglasses in church!"

"Oh! Oh! Oh! Oh! Oh, you beautiful doll!"

Marion's already left to teach Sunday school to the Big Kids. But there's still some breakfast waiting for Rebecca — two strips of crisp bacon on the warming rack and one slice of gooey yellow bread in a bowl on the counter. Heavy. Saturated. Just the way she likes it.

"It better not have *rooster sauce* in it this time, Ben!"

As soon as he hears her pounding up the back steps, Ben lifts the dripping slice of bread out of the bowl and into the hot black pan on top of the stove. "Or what?" he chuckles, as the bread begins to sizzle.

"Or..." She tumbles into the kitchen. "Or I'll..."

A big, white, enamel pot of water is boiling on the stove. Rebecca tries not to look at it. She doesn't want to see the gooey yellow handkerchiefs. The gummy red ones either. It might spoil her appetite. The men never use disposable handkerchiefs. They prefer those cloth ones they get for Christmas — white, with snazzy borders of burgundy or grey. Boiling them is a weekly ritual. But it doesn't usually happen on a Sunday.

"Or I'll make you go to church with me!"

"Gracious! Church! A fate worse than..." He checks the bottom of the bread. "Death. Is Vivian going this morning?"

"No."

"Probably half-tight," snorts Malcolm from the living room.

Rebecca leaps to the doorway. "She is not!"

"First time for everything, I guess."

"Yeah, well, what about you, Malcolm? Are *you* going?"

"No. I wouldn't be caught dead in that place."

"Well, then, why do I have to go?"

"Because you're an idiot, like the rest of them."

"I am not an idiot! *You're* an idiot!"

"Jesus H. Christ." He pushes himself up from the chesterfield and shuffles out to the front veranda.

Rebecca, meanwhile, just stands there, with her face turning purple. She and Malcolm don't like each other; can hardly stand being in the same room together. But he's especially mean this morning — maybe because she used his best shaving mug for her grasshopper collection. Still, she doesn't think that's what made his brush skitter into the basin, made his lather too watery, made him cut himself when he folded that long, unguarded blade back into its handle.

"OK, Rebecca." Ben places the slice of French toast on a plate. "Come and..."

"The biggest idiot in the whole wide world!"

"Don't let it get cold now." He settles into the rocking chair by the fridge and lights his bulldog pipe.

At ten-thirty, the church bell starts ringing.

"Gracious!"

"What's wrong with it, Ben?"

"I don't know. Sounds like nails inside a tin can. Probably cracked." He slips his pipe into the pocket of his shirt.

"Can they fix it?"

He can't help chuckling.

"Can they?"

"Well..." He's still chuckling. "Not today."

"Be-en! It's not funny! It's the worst thing I've ever heard!"

"Go on, now. Or you'll be late."

Rebecca doesn't know why exactly, but there's something about that awful clanking that makes her want to run.

The church is a tall white structure on Old Post Road, a few buildings up from Marion's place. When Rebecca reaches it, there's a throng of people standing out front, pointing and staring and shaking their heads. At first, she thinks it's because of the bell. But then she realizes they're not looking up; they're looking down — at the black and white sign on the manicured lawn.

She peers at it through their legs.

There's nothing wrong with the permanent letters. AYLESFORD UNITED BAPTIST CHURCH. They're the same big black letters that are always there. But there's something wrong with the temporary letters; with that weekly message the deacons always place underneath.

Rebecca sounds out the words.

I HAVE LOVED YOU WITH AN ELERLASTIN VOVEG.

"I don't get it," she murmurs. "What's that supposed to...?"

Suddenly, there's another awful clank. She squints up at the tower.

"Marvin!"

There's a shadowy figure in the little round window, straining to pull on the rope.

"Marvin! What do you think happened to the...?"

He can't hear her over the awful clanking.

"Marvin!" She bounces up and down on the pavement. "Marvin! Marvin!"

"Shshsh."

Monica Hill is tugging at the sleeve of Rebecca's cardigan.

"What?"

"Don't you know it's Sunday?"

"So?"

Monica pushes her toward the door. "So go inside."

Rebecca doesn't answer back this time. But she does stick her tongue out at Monica, all the way up the steps and into the vestry. She likes the French toast and the bell part of Sunday all right. But she doesn't think much of the people.

As the throng begins to push into the sanctuary, the Big Kids come tumbling down the stairs from their classrooms.

"Look what I got!" squeals Monica's daughter Winifred, as soon as she spots Rebecca. "Isn't it pretty?"

It's a brand-new Bible, with a bluey green picture of a forest on the front cover.

"It's OK, I guess. Who gave it to you?" She reaches out her hand to touch it.

"Mrs. Swinnimer." Winifred snatches it away from her. "For perfect attendance."

"Did you get anything, Sunny?"

"Yes. This." Sunny hands her a thin white book.

"But it looks like only half of one! How come you only got half of one?"

"I missed one Sunday," drawls Sunny.

As the throng continues to edge forward, the organ drones out the familiar introit.

All things bright and beautiful. All creatures great and small.

The ushers today are Sam Gates, Gordon Rogers, Alvin Andrews and Larry Swinnimer. But most of the worshippers don't have favourite spots. They just fill up the long wooden pews from the back to the front. All except Winifred, that is, who squeezes through to the very first row, to sit beside her mother.

All things wise and wonderful. The Lord God made them all.

Not yet ready to find a spot, Rebecca sidles up to the doorway to the sanctuary, where Reverend Andrew MacKay is greeting everyone.

Reverend MacKay is a short, round man with thin, blonde hair. He also has the calmest, gentlest smile, although Rebecca can't quite figure out why, since every Sunday he has to race around conducting services in Aylesford, Morristown, Millville and Lake Paul.

"Oh, Marion!" he calls, when he spots her near the stairs to the classrooms. "Marion! May I have a word with you?"

"Yes, Andrew!"

As she drifts toward them across the vestry, Rebecca can recognize the faint scent of her perfume. Marion once told her that she didn't go in much for "accessories". Just a little powder for her face or a touch of lipstick, whenever it's a special occasion. Never any "eye junk," as Rebecca calls it. And only rarely, a dab of perfume. Today's is from the aqua-coloured bottle of "Here's My Heart" which Nancy Bezanson brought by with an assortment of Avon products.

Each little flower that opens. Each little bird that sings.

"Here, Rebecca," whispers Reverend MacKay, as some of the kids jostle by. "You're a big girl now. How would you like to take my place for a minute while I talk to Marion?"

"Me?" she answers shyly. "But I don't know what to do."

"Well…" He smiles at her. "You just shake everyone's hand and ask them how they are and say that it's a lovely day for…Marion. Hello. I just wanted to…" He ushers Marion a few feet away.

He made their glowing colours. He made their tiny wings.

"Marion, I just wanted to…" He lowers his voice. "Well, the deacons, really. The deacons have asked me to speak to you about…"

"Good morning, Mrs. Woodbury," Rebecca says firmly. "It's a lovely day for…for fishing, don't you think?"

Everyone chuckles.

"Most of them don't even know who this Matthias is," continues Reverend MacKay. "And the gospels aren't very helpful. In fact, he's only mentioned…"

The purple-headed mountain. The river running by.

"And you, Mr. Franey. How are you this fine morning?" Rebecca strains to hear what's going on between Marion and Reverend MacKay.

"And the rest is speculation," whispers Reverend MacKay.

Rebecca wonders what "specks of patience" have to do with anything.

"I understand, Andrew. But, you know, I just wanted them to use their imaginations for a change and to realize that...any one of them...could someday be chosen to..."

"Hello, Mr. Cragg. Did you manage to get your lawnmower fixed? I hear it was making an awful racket."

Everyone chuckles again.

"I'm sorry, Marion. It's just a little too exotic for them. If it were up to me, of course..."

"And you, Mrs. Graveline. Is your vacuum cleaner still losing suction?"

The sunset, and the morning, that brightens up the sky.

"I understand, Andrew," smiles Marion. "Anything else? I have to hurry and get changed."

"Well, yes," he laughs. "Now that you mention it. They'd appreciate it if you'd stop giving Chiclets to the children."

"Ha!" Marion laughs, too. "Is that also just a little too exotic for them?"

He gave us eyes to see them. And lips that we might...

"I'm all done!" cries Rebecca. "They're all in!"

"Great," Reverend MacKay says softy. "And from what I was able to hear, you did a fine job. Now go and take your seat."

"OK, but...Aren't you going to sing today, Marion?"

"In a minute."

"OK, but...I hope they've saved you a spot!" She skips through the doorway into the sanctuary.

How great is God Almighty, who has made all things well.

Not so great if you ask me, thinks Rebecca, as she slides across the long wooden bench.

She's glad she missed the hymn — mostly because she's pretty sure it just isn't right. God didn't just make the ripe fruits and the meadows. He made the big, ugly, scary things, too. Like hornets and centipedes. And no one thought to include those in the verses.

She looks around her.

He made the people, too. And some of those aren't bright and beautiful at all. Some of those are meanies and retards and drunks. Some of those have only one eye or a wooden leg or too little money to pay for their food...

She closes her eyes and begins to chant softly. "It just isn't right. It just isn't right. It just isn't..."

Her eyes pop open again.

I HAVE LOVED YOU WITH AN ELERLASTIN VOVEG.

She starts to giggle.

It makes a lot more sense now — or at least as much sense as anything.

"Shshsh," hisses Edna Ogletree, who's sitting beside her. "We don't want to miss the readings."

"*I* do. They're boring."

"Yes, well, then close your eyes and think of something else."

"Like what?"

"How should *I* know? Something nice."

"OK."

The first thing that comes to mind is pretty nice. French toast. But not half as nice as the second thing. Lake Paul isn't nearly as big as Lake George, and there aren't nearly as many ritzy cottages on it. You just turn off the road at a farmer's lane, a little past the fire tower, and then go through the woods until you reach the sandy beach. But the swimming is great and the...

"*Clouds they are without water!*"

Her eyes pop open.

"*Carried about of winds!*"

It's the thundering voice of Herbert Armstrong, who's been asked to read the scripture this morning. Ben Kelly says Herbert learned to bellow like that when he attended a few classes at divinity college. But Rebecca's not interested in that. What she thinks is neat are his big, bushy, mutton-chop sideburns.

"*Without fruit, twice dead, plucked up by the roots!*"

I hate the Bible, she decides. Once in a while, it's pretty. But mostly, it's just scary and mean. For every Twenty-third Psalm, there are hundreds of Judes, verses twelve and thirteen.

"*Raging waves of the sea, foaming out their own shame!*" Herbert pauses to scowl at them. *"Wandering stars, to whom is reserved the blackness...of darkness...forever!"*

The Bible slams shut.

"Let us pray," murmurs Reverend MacKay.

Rebecca's afraid to close her eyes.

"Amen."

With that, there's a single chord from the Marshall organ and the choir rises to its feet.

"Take my life and let it be consecrated, Lord, to Thee."

Today's the first day that Rebecca notices that there are more women than men in the choir. And that they have a little touch on their flowing black gowns that the men don't have — a sparkling white collar.

"Take my moments and my days. Let them flow in ceaseless praise."

There are a few giggles from the congregation as the organist Hattie North struggles with the stops. Edna whispers that Hattie's probably been too busy giving fifty-cent piano lessons and helping her husband Arthur in the fields to brush up on the intricacies of the hymn. But Rebecca thinks she's still better than her Uncle Charlie, who sometimes fills in when Hattie's sick. And there are a few more giggles as the choirmaster Dr. David Dempsey flaps his arms and tries to get his sister Constance Harry, who Ben says sounds like a pin on a stovepipe at the best of times, to sing more quietly. Rebecca thinks it's probably a lost cause. In fact, she's heard people say that the whole choir is a lost cause.

Dr. Dempsey is a short, blonde bachelor — a bit of a Momma's boy, almost everyone whispers — who came to Aylesford late last year to help old Dr. Sutherland with his practice. So far, he's been pleasant, competent, and more successful as a doctor than a choirmaster.

"Take my voice and let me sing always, only, for my King."

The congregation feels sorry for him.

Every Thursday evening at seven o'clock, he leads the choir through a rigorous rehearsal. Some of the men are OK. There are his brothers John and Robert, for instance, who, along with Michael Ackroyd, sing in a barbershop quartet with him. And Sheila and Gloria, the two oldest Marshall girls, aren't bad either.

But the rest of the women are horrible. With those horribly high, grating voices. Even Marion and Irene only have, to put it charitably, good, wobbly, church voices. In any case, Rebecca's heard Herbert Armstrong bellow that there certainly aren't any Marian Andersons among them; only Thelma Peels. The real Thelma has the worst wobbly voice of them all. You can always hear her screeching above the rest when you wander by the church on your way to bingo at the Fire Hall. Thursday is a really neat day of the week, according to Rebecca, but it's not choir practice which makes it that way. It's bingo. And, much earlier in the day, Buster Nichols' son Dorn, the new Fish Man, who lives up near the railway tracks and every Thursday morning drives his greyish green half-ton truck filled with herring, mackerel and salmon right up your driveway to the side door.

"*Take my lips and let them be filled with messages from Thee.*"

As the choir proceeds, the inevitable whispering begins.

"Oooo. Look at Irene!"

"Jesus. *She's* put on a few pounds since Christmas."

"She sure couldn't get *that* ass through the eye of a needle."

Rebecca giggles.

"Shshsh." Edna elbows her.

"But I was only..."

"*Take my will and make it Thine. It shall be no longer mine.*"

"It's no fun if you can't..."

"*Take my heart, it is Thine own. It shall be Thy royal throne.*"

"Well, I think she's lovely," the whispering continues.

"A vision of loveliness."

"Ha! Three or four visions!"

The choir gives every last thing that it has to the Lord, and then abruptly sits down.

Reverend MacKay says there's only one announcement today. Rebecca hopes it's something really neat — like about yesterday, when Althea Gibson won both the singles and the doubles at Wimbledon — but it isn't.

"I have been asked by the deacons..." Reverend MacKay looks embarrassed, "...asked by the deacons to inform you that the American Baptist Association has recently passed a resolution reaffirming its..." He clears his throat. "...its opposition to enforced integration."

"Good."

"Here, here."

"They couldn't possibly have done anything else."

Amid that murmur of approval, Reverend MacKay nods glumly to the ushers, who are standing in pairs at the back of the sanctuary. While Hattie plays an instrumental reprise of "Take My Life and Let It Be," the four men walk slowly up the aisle to the foot of the pulpit, where the collection plates are lying. Then the four of them split up, two for each side, and begin to pass the plates along the rows — solemnly, with one hand held behind their backs.

The organ swells.

"Oh yeah!" Rebecca reaches into the pocket of her dress and pulls out a little white envelope. And then she smiles.

You have to put your name on it, she says to herself. You aren't allowed to give anything in secret. But that doesn't matter today. Today she has a whole quarter. Today she's printed her name in especially big black letters.

As she watches the ushers move slowly toward her, Rebecca wonders what each of them would do if they could actually keep all the money they collected. Sam Gates, who lives up near Grammie, would probably buy a new foot or maybe send his three mean kids away to boarding school. Gordon Rogers, who helps his father Harley dig graves in the cemetery, would probably move to Halifax and get a job driving a bulldozer or a garbage truck. Alvin Andrews, who's married to Marion's best friend Irene, would probably get another job, too, but closer to home, since he doesn't like travelling and has always wanted to be the manager of a hardware store in town. Larry Swinnimer, however, would probably just keep growing apples and being superintendent of the Sunday School and getting a little richer, that's all.

The organ swells again.

But the money doesn't go to the ushers, thinks Rebecca. The money goes to the office out back, where Alvin, who's been treasurer for as long as anyone can remember, counts it and records it and keeps it safe in the offering boxes. But why? What for? Who gets it after that?

She grips her envelope.

"Psst. Rebecca." Mr. Swinnimer is waiting at the end of her row. "Are you going to hold onto that?"

"What?"

He hands her the collection plate — a big, deep golden dish with a red felt bottom.

"Oh, sorry." She drops her crumpled envelope into it.

After they've finished the rows, the ushers meet for a moment at the rear of the sanctuary. Then, while Hattie resumes her struggle with the organ stops, they begin walking in pairs again, back up the aisle to the front.

That is, three of them walk.

As Sam Gates clumps by on his way to the blessing, Rebecca can't help staring at the thick black heel on his big black shoe.

This week's children's story is about Lazarus. Rebecca thinks it's dumb. If it weren't dumb, she reasons, then there wouldn't be any Sam Gates guys in the world, wearing big black shoes with thick black heels. But at least the story's the last thing she has to go through down here. While the choir makes a mess of "I Love to Tell the Story," the Little Kids all scramble out of their seats and up the stairs to their classrooms.

"I love to tell the story of unseen things above; of Jesus and His glory, of Jesus and His love."

As Rebecca stands at the door of her classroom, listening to the thumps and squeals coming from inside, she smiles. This is the last month she'll have to go in there. When she turns five, she'll get to go to real Sunday school, at ten o'clock, with the Big Kids like Sunny and Winifred.

She waits one more minute, so she can hear the faint and wobbly strains of Marion's solo…*"I love to tell the story because I know it's true. It satisfies my longings as nothing else would do"*…and then barges into the classroom.

"Settle down!" cries Elizabeth Ackroyd, in a high nasal voice. "Did you hear me? Settle down!"

Rebecca's heard that Mrs. Ackroyd has more trouble controlling the younger kids than her husband Michael has with the older ones. But then she doesn't have his mean and sneaky eyes.

"That's better. Now. Today we're going to draw our favourite Bible stories."

"Aw."

"Do we have to?"

"That's no fun!"

"That'll be enough! Rebecca! Pass these around, please!"

While Rebecca hands out the crayons and the construction paper, the others try to decide what to draw.

"A burning bush! Like my brother set fire to last...!"

"Daniel in the lions' den! Only I'm going to have them eat his head right...!"

"A pillar of salt!"

"A pillar of salt? What's so great about a pillar of salt? David and Goliath's way better than that!"

"No, it isn't," insists Rebecca. "It's dumb."

"Rebecca!" chides Elizabeth.

"Well, it is. I feel sorry for Goliath. Nobody liked him."

"Well, then, you can draw something else."

"Like what?"

"I'm sure you can think of..."

"I know! I know! The loaves and the fishes! Only I'm going to make it brown bread and...lobster! I love lobster! It's...!"

"Rebecca!"

"What?"

"I don't think that's very appropriate."

"What's *appropriate* mean?"

"It means you can sit down and be quiet. Now, let's see how the rest of you are..."

"How about crackers and sardines?"

Elizabeth points to the doorway. "Out!"

"But I don't see..."

"Out!"

Rebecca is standing alone in the hallway. She's not upset about it. It isn't the first time she's been kicked out of Sunday school. But she's not quite sure where to go.

"*Just as I am, without one plea, but that Thy blood was shed for me.*"

"Oh yeah!" she whispers when she hears the choir. "I forgot! Baptism!" She tiptoes up to the doorway down the hall and peeks inside. "Great!"

There's no one in the special classroom today — the one with the big plate-glass window looking down over the sanctuary.

"And that Thou bidd'st me come to Thee, O Lamb of God, I come."

She tiptoes up to the window to watch.

The dark brown doors of the dunking pool are open today. The tank is filled with water. But there's no one standing in it yet except Reverend MacKay, who's wearing his best black robes.

"Get on with it."

As the choir drones on about Jesus' blood — about how it can cleanse all conflict, doubt and fear — she knits her brow. It's news to her. The only blood she's ever seen didn't clean up anything. It only stained it.

"Just as I am, Thou wilt receive…"

Someone in a white robe creeps out from behind the dark brown doors.

"It's Louise Marshall," whispers Rebecca, when she recognizes the girl who lives next door to Marion.

"Wilt welcome, pardon, cleanse, relieve…"

Louise hesitates a little and then, with Reverend MacKay gently beckoning to her, steps gingerly down into the pool.

"Because Thy promise I believe…"

There's a single moment of suspended animation, when there's nothing moving except the concentric circles in the pool around their waists.

"O Lamb of God, I come."

And then Reverend MacKay cradles the back of Louise's head and pushes it under the water.

"Well, don't drown her," whispers Rebecca, before Louise's head finally emerges. "Gee."

While Louise splutters and then drags herself back up the steps, the choir begins the hymn all over again.

Rebecca's puzzled. It seems a lot to go through just to get to Jesus. She wonders if there's another way he'll take you.

As soon as the next white-robed person appears in the doorway, Rebecca has an idea.

"Do a cannonball!" she shouts through the big plate-glass window. "Do a cannonball!"

She's sure Jesus would like cannonballs.

"Do a cannonball!"

But no one hears her.

The choir keeps singing. Reverend MacKay keeps beckoning. The next white-robed person edges down the steps toward her total immersion.

"Chicken!" Rebecca jams her Tweety Bird sunglasses back on her face.

1 0

The kids are in the lake now, shouting and squealing and splashing one another.

"Don't!"

"Quit it!"

"Crybaby!"

"I'm telling!"

Peter and Randy are the best swimmers. But they don't spend much time actually swimming. They're too busy pushing everyone else's head under the water. Or stealing Rebecca's goggles. Or Sunny's Sea Queen bathing cap.

"Don't!"

"They're too big for you anyway!"

"Mu-um!"

"It makes you look like a hard-boiled egg!"

A little while later, while Harold's teaching the others how to propel themselves out of the water like Esther Williams, Rebecca is tramping alone through the sand on the beach. She's wearing red pants now, rolled up to her knees. And a grubby wet T-shirt. And her sunglasses, of course.

"What's the matter with you?" calls Vivian.

Rebecca squints toward her Mum. Vivian is sitting a little way down the shore, on a red and blue plaid blanket, with the bottoms of her jeans turned up, and her Viyella blouse freshly ironed, and her hair pulled back off her face. Rebecca thinks she looks young today.

"Nothing."

"Then why aren't you swimming?"

"I don't feel like it."

The evening sun glints off Tweety Bird's beak.

"Well, come over here and sit by me, then."

"No."

"Come on. I won't bite."

"I will if you peel me an orange."

"Oh, all right."

A few minutes later, the two of them are just sitting there, sucking on their oranges and gazing out across the lake. I HAVE LOVED YOU WITH AN ELERLASTIN VOVEG, Rebecca suddenly remembers.

"Are we nearly there?" asks Rebecca the very next day, as Marion's car races down a hill near Welton's Corner.

"Almost," laughs Marion. She peers up through the windshield at the seagulls soaring and swooping in the white-capped sky.

"That's what you said last time. How much farther?"

"About five miles."

"Still?"

The car speeds by an apple orchard, a field of corn, a herd of Holsteins. Rebecca rolls down her window and leans outside.

Lake Paul is OK, she thinks, as the wind whips through her auburn hair. But, after all, it's only a lake. She can hardly wait to get to Morden. Marion says it used to be known as French Cross, and that something really sad happened there. But Rebecca doesn't care about that. She also doesn't care that it sits just below the North Mountain, that huge chunk of volcanic rock which runs along the Bay of Fundy from Brier Island to Cape Blomidon — where Ben Kelly says men push their wives over the cliffs. She only cares that it's a wild and special place. Always windy. Always cold.

Rebecca closes her eyes.

All summer long, her aunts and uncles will make excursions there. They won't all rent cottages at the same time, but, with Howard coming from Sudbury and Clifford from Granby and Donald from Montreal and Gene from Kentville and Vivian and Marion and Florence all living nearby and all the wives and husbands and kids that most of them have and all the other kids belonging to all the other people who have cottages there, the place will be noisy and crowded.

Rebecca's trying to decide what she's going to do first — play on the rocks with Fred Johnson's kids or have a lupine fight with Hal Jackson's kids or maybe just watch Lester Greaves pull fish from the weir —

when, suddenly, the air changes.

She opens her eyes. "Why are we stopping?"

"I promised Florence we'd visit her at the trailer."

"But why?"

"Because George is away and she wants company."

"Well, I'm not going." Rebecca folds her arms across her chest.

"Oh, yes, you are." Marion gets out of the car. "And you're going to behave." She swats at the door. "Or I'm never taking you anywhere with me again." She strolls across the grass toward the trailer.

Florence is sitting in one of the wooden lawn chairs her husband made for her. She's a big-boned woman — typically Henderson, Marion says — with light brown hair pulled back into a ponytail.

The dumb old trailer isn't even *in* Morden, thinks Rebecca, as she squeezes her arms even tighter. It's up above everything. Nowhere near the wind and the cold and the fun.

"Hello, Florence."

Florence takes a weary little sip from her tumbler of white rum and coke. "Hello, yourself."

Marion smiles at her. "Where *is* George today anyway?"

"Over to Waterville.

"But it's Saturday."

"He promised to teach the kids how to make sleeve-boards." She takes another weary little sip.

George Best teaches industrial arts to mentally retarded kids at Kings County Hospital in Waterville, where Florence keeps the books. Even Vivian has to agree that his wooden floors are beautiful — the best example of what she calls *tongue-in-cheek* work she's ever seen.

"That was good of him," smiles Marion, as she slaps at the sand fleas nipping at her legs. "And I have the prototype, I believe. Sitting on top of my fridge."

"So what," mutters Rebecca, when she remembers that ugly little two-decker thing covered in white flannel.

"Yes, well, I'm hungry." Florence leaps to her feet. "Are you hungry? I've made baked beans and brown bread."

Rebecca unfolds her arms. She doesn't like the trailer. But she likes baked beans and brown bread. A lot. Almost as much as she likes "puke-on-toast." Which is that toast with mushy junk on it — cheese, asparagus, cream of mushroom soup — that Marion always makes.

"Great," smiles Marion. "Let me give you a hand."

When the two women disappear into the trailer, Rebecca slips out of the car. As she makes her way toward the lawn chairs, she catches little snippets of their conversation.

"She *says* she's going to leave him. She *says* if he keeps..."

"Oh, you know Alice. She hasn't been quite right since that business with the coat hanger. You know, when she..."

Rebecca stares at the big white globs of seagull poop on the slats of the lawn chairs.

"And as for Vivian...I'm not going to take it any...I'm not going to allow her to hurt me any..."

"Well, maybe if you paid her back the..."

"Ha! Do you see the way she treats Peter? Is it any wonder he's scared to...?"

"It's worse when she's drinking. I've tried to talk to her but..."

They come back outside.

"Oh, look, Marion," sighs Florence. "We'll have use for this third plate, after all." She winks at Rebecca. But it's not a happy wink, full of that joyful conspiracy that winks are supposed to have. It's a sad, withdrawn, depressed little wink.

"Ha!" laughs Marion. "You decided to join us, did you?"

"Yes."

It wasn't because of Florence that Rebecca didn't want to stop at the trailer. She and her aunt are great pals. And a lot alike, so everyone in the family says. Rebecca's heard their stories. About Florence borrowing a car she didn't know how to drive. About Florence stealing a party dress someone else was planning to wear. Since Rebecca's never done any neat junk like that herself, she doesn't know whether they're a lot alike or not. But she does know one thing they don't have in common — their attitude to pressed tongue. Florence starts gagging the moment she sees Marion boiling it, peeling it, curling it around a bowl and putting a saucer and flatiron on top. Florence never even makes it to the cutting it into slabs and serving it with a bit of potato salad part. But it's one of Rebecca's favourites.

"Well, sit down," orders Florence. "There's plenty for everyone."

"I know but..."

"What?"

Rebecca points to the big white globs.

"Oh, sorry. Sorry, your highness. I didn't know you were so..." She wipes the slats with the sleeve of her blouse.

"How come there's so many cars up here today?" asks Rebecca, a few minutes later.

"Tea meeting, I think. Jesus!" Florence slaps at another sand flea. "Over to the Anglican Church."

"What for?"

Rebecca and Marion both slap at their legs.

"I don't know for sure. Something to do with that ceiling of theirs. You know, the one that's modelled after the keel of a ship. I think it leaks."

"Oh."

"Of course, knowing the Anglicans, they'll use any excuse to raise a bit of money and stuff their mouths with strawberry shortcake. Which reminds me..." Florence stands up. "The biscuits aren't the best. The friggin' things just didn't rise this time. But if you want a little strawberry..."

"I do! I do!"

"Great. Then maybe you can do me a little favour in return."

"What?" Rebecca stuffs the last forkful of baked beans into her mouth.

"Maybe you can stay with me in the trailer tonight."

"No, thank you," sputters Rebecca.

"Why not?"

Rebecca swallows. "'Cause nothing ever happens up here."

"Well, you're right there," sighs Florence, as she gathers up the grimy plates.

The next morning, Rebecca's desperate. She just has to get out. Not just out of the back chamber, which is so hot and dusty she can barely breathe, but out of the house. She doesn't really have a destination. She doesn't really care if she ends up at the railway tracks or the ball park or Dogpatch even, which is sadder in the daylight but not nearly as scary. She just tosses a datebook onto the front seat of the car and starts to drive.

Within minutes, she's glad she didn't bother having a destination.

There are no tracks anymore. The rails have been ripped out of the ground and carted away. All that's left is a pile of ties.

She pulls the car right up to the gooey black beams and turns off the ignition.

It's hard to know how sad to feel. Ben once told her that Aylesford had been one of the liveliest towns in the Valley. He said they'd needed parallel tracks and all the sidings they could build in order to service the warehouses, the slaughterhouses, the two big fruit companies. But it hadn't been that way when she was a girl. In fact, by 1971, when she was seventeen, they'd sold the last ticket. And a few years later, when she was long gone and didn't care anymore, the station had been torn down and burned.

Still, there's something sad about that pile of ties. It's a little like that stone cross at Morden. A reminder of those who'd made it a regular stop. A memorial to those who'd made it a final stop. A belated sign of respect, of futility, of loneliness, of death.

Her memory gets stuck in the thick black goo.

11

"Hurry!" cries Rebecca, as she peers out Grammie's kitchen window. "Or we'll miss her!"

In 1958, steam-driven trains go through Aylesford three or four times a day. The Dayliners have a single car and an engine. The Midnight Run does too, but she's not allowed to stay up for that — not even when it's bringing her Uncle Donald from Montreal for the summer holidays. It's always a big event when a train goes through, but Sunday, August 10 is the biggest event of all.

Rebecca squints one last time at the distant stretch of glistening rails and then whirls away from the window. "I'm going!" she cries, as she races out the door.

The train station is on Station Street, on the south side of the tracks. It's a grey, unpainted wooden structure with an office, a ticket window, a waiting room, a freight area and a snack bar. Since there's never a dining car on the trains that pass through, passengers often get off here to stretch their legs and to buy little bags of chips or licorice Allsorts.

When she sees the crowd of spectators all dressed up in their Sunday best and carrying brightly coloured bouquets of flowers, she slows down a little. Her own frilly pink dress smells like Javex. She can't pick out a single person she knows. But when she spots Cam Shaw, the stationmaster, who's sweeping the same spot on the platform he was sweeping yesterday, she speeds up again.

"Mr. Shaw! Mr. Shaw! Caaaaaaam!"

Cam Shaw is huge and bald and lives with his wife Audrey in a big white house opposite Grammie's back door.

"Where's the fire?" he laughs, as he takes a final swipe at the wooden planks.

"Has she come yet?" pants Rebecca.

"Not yet."

"Are you sure?"

He laughs again. "Come on. I've saved you a spot." He leads her to a tiny opening in the big blob of garish colours, between Opal Rawding and Leafy Ruggles.

There's such a large group of Ruggles families living near the station that people call that area the Ruggles Block. They're a fairly ordinary bunch, except for their names. Rebecca feels sorry for kids called Spurgeon, Treasure, Burpee and Melon. She feels sorry for kids who have Opal Rawding as a mother, too, but that's just for the usual reason — because she's such an old bag.

The two women glare down at her, then continue their conversation over her head.

"I don't mind riding trains," sniffs Mrs. Rawding, "as long as I don't have to sit with the common people."

"I know what you mean," Mrs. Ruggles sniffs back.

Rebecca makes a face, but not a big one. She doesn't want to take a chance on losing her spot. She's a little worried about the others, however. The place has filled up so quickly that the spots right next to the tracks have all been taken. If the others don't hurry, they'll be stuck way back in the fourth or fifth row.

"Hey!"

"Watch it!"

"I was here first!"

Rebecca claps her hands with glee. Somehow Vivian and Sunny have managed to squeeze their way to the front.

"What took you so long?" she giggles.

"Never mind," wheezes Vivian. "We're here."

"Where's Grammie?"

"She's with Ardeth. Over there. See?"

They all lean forward and peer down the track.

Harold Peterson's older sister Ardeth is so frail that Grammie looks like her bodyguard.

"Lucky for her," remarks Sunny.

They all lean back again.

There's a lull while the throng shifts its feet and murmurs...and then, suddenly, Rebecca squeals. "Is that where Uncle Donald's head was?" She points a few yards down the track.

Everyone looks.

"Shsh." Vivian elbows her. "Keep your voice down."

"OK!" she whispers. "Is that where Uncle Donald's head was?"

Everyone laughs.

According to the story, Donald Henderson was so drunk one night that he fell asleep with his head on the railway tracks. When his wife Joyce found him, her first reaction was to leave him there. Her second and third reactions, too. It was Marion who finally persuaded her to drag him off to the side.

"Yes!" hisses Vivian.

There's another lull while the crowd inspects its bouquets of flowers, which don't seem to be holding up as well as the Jesus flannel growing wild by the tracks...and then the gossiping begins.

"I hear she went to the West Indies. You know, to open up that coon parliament of theirs."

"Yes, but not on this trip. She went to Niagara Falls on this trip."

"Oh, I've always wanted to go there!"

"And then had lunch in Ottawa with Diefenbaker."

"Son of a whore."

"Ha! At least he doesn't make drawers for a living. If you ask me it's Stanfield who's the..."

"And then...I think it was Montreal and Quebec City and..."

"Bloody Frogs."

"And Fredericton."

"Ha! What's there to do in Fredericton?"

"Nothing, I suppose. But then what's there to do in...?"

"Ha! What do you bet Edna tries to have her over for tea?"

"What do you mean?"

"Well, she's always strutting with doctors and politicians, always showing off how classy she thinks she is."

"Who cares? I just wish she'd get here!"

"Me, too. My feet are killing me."

Everyone titters except Sunny.

"You know, I'm not sure I approve of her. She's real...high-spirited."

"Yes, well...I like her better than that stuck-up sister of hers. She's so..."

Sunny tugs at Vivian's sleeve. "Will there be a cup and saucer, do you think?"

"I don't know. There'll be a spoon, I know that."

"*Hard*. That's the word I was looking for."

"Still, they say they're inseparable. And I suppose her sister's sense of duty will rub off on her. You know, be a steadying influence."

"Ha! I wouldn't bet on it. They say she's a playgirl; that she carries on with young boys until all hours of the..."

"Oh, not any more! Not since her father died!"

"Ha! That's not what did it. It was..."

"Well, I saw a picture of her standing with Danny Kaye and some other show business types. In a strapless evening gown. And she sure didn't look like she'd..."

Rebecca glances at Sunny, who's wearing her tawdry red, white and black plaid dress, with crisp white ankle socks and those blue plastic sandals. But her eyes seem to be slipping into a vision of that strapless evening gown the women were just talking about. It's what Sunny will have to be wearing, decides Rebecca, when she meets Prince Charles for the first time...although maybe not at Buckingham Palace, since Sunny's heard this is the last year any *debutantes*, whatever *those* are, will be presented there.

"Is he going to be with her?"

"I think so."

"Well, I think she should have married the other one."

"Oh, so do I!"

"He was some romantic, all right."

"They say they used to meet...you know, in secret...so that snotty sister of hers couldn't spy on them."

"Oh, but she couldn't have!"

"What? Spy on them?"

"No! She couldn't have married him!"

"Why not? What was wrong with him? He was handsome. He was brave..."

"He was divorced!"

"Big deal. *You've* been divorced."

"Yes, but I'm not..."

"What?"

"Royalty."

"Damn right!"

Once again, everyone laughs except Sunny.

"Well, I think she should have been able to do what she bloody well felt like doing."

"Yes, it's a friggin' shame."

"And *I* think..."

"It shouldn't matter which side of the tracks you..."

"And *I* think we have to obey the laws of the church."

"Oh, my gaaawd!"

"Can you believe it?

"She's an even bigger arsehole than her..."

"Look! Here she comes!"

A tiny black smudge is drifting towards the station.

"Where?"

"I don't see anything."

"There, you idiot."

There's a puff of white steam and then a long, shrill whistle.

"Yes! Oh, my God! I think I'm going to faint!"

It's a big black smudge now, edging closer and closer and...There's a hiss and a squeal and then a gentle roll of thunder, as the train glides by the platform.

"My God!"

"Jesus."

"She looks like..."

Princess Margaret is standing at the rear of the last car, smiling and waving at them. She's wearing a lovely satin dress — white and apple-blossom pink.

Just like Marion, thinks Rebecca, who isn't looking at Princess

Margaret's dress but her face. Large dark eyes, short dark hair, and a funny smile. Sort of small and crooked and sad.

The big black smudge drifts further away.

"Is that it?"

"She didn't even stop!"

"Typical."

"Well, at least I'll get a spoon out of the deal."

Suddenly, although she's well past the throng, Princess Margaret looks impishly over her shoulder and smiles.

"That's funny. I wonder…" Rebecca follows her smile.

There's a man standing off by himself, a little way down the track.

"Look!" she squeals. "There he is again! That man who looks like Billy Bruton! She's smiling at *him*!"

The crowd leans forward. And then erupts.

"Hey!"

"Who's that?"

"What the hell's *he* doing here?"

There's another puff of white steam.

"Bloody coon!"

"You'd think he'd know better than to…"

"Get him out of here!"

The man strolls across the track.

A few years later, Donald Duck would come all the way from Disneyland to visit the town. But that wouldn't be nearly as memorable as the day Princess Margaret smiled at Frankie Lewis.

12

Vivian is sitting on the concrete steps at the side of the house, waiting for the booze to arrive. There are lots of celebrations going on in the area tonight, for even skimpier reasons than Princess Margaret drifting through town, so Cyril Neily has more deliveries than he can handle. In the meantime, she's having a good time just watching over her kingdom. It isn't much. There isn't even really a lawn — just bare patches, with a few clumps of clover and grass. And a dirt and gravel driveway — circular, with a sandpit in the centre. But then, she isn't much of a Queen.

A little while ago, her "hairs," as she called them, were all there in the yard. Darrell and Donnie scrambling up and down the huge maple tree. Sunny swinging gently below them on an old black tire. Peter trying to get up enough nerve to boost himself onto the footrests of his stilts again. And Randy and Rebecca digging strange little tunnels and ramps in the sandpit. For a while, they were all quite content to suck on their Sweethearts. *Could Be. Smart Guy. Happy Days. OK, Baby.* But then Arch Ballou, the Meat Man, cruised by in his panel truck — dark red, with a dented white box on the back — and most of them went running after him. They couldn't wait to get their little free slices of bologna with the rinds still on.

The only one who didn't go was Rebecca, who's standing in the middle of the sandpit now, twirling her dirty yellow hula hoop.

"My little angel," wheezes Vivian, as she twists a stray strand of sandy brown hair around a pin curl and tucks it back under her multi-coloured kerchief.

The hula hoop is this summer's biggest fad. Rebecca got *her* two-dollar ring of plastic from Marion, on one of their many trips to Michie's five-and-dime in Kingston. She could have had a red one, like everyone else's, but she thought the yellow one looked "a little more special". In fact, she liked it so much that she gave her blue, plastic skipping rope to Holly Stoddard, the tiny girl with strawberry-blonde hair whose Aunt Muriel is one of the telephone operators.

"Jesus," marvels Vivian. "Look at her go now!" She claps her hands with pride.

Spurred on by the clapping, Rebecca eases the dirty yellow hoop from her legs to her hips to her neck and back to her hips again. Then she swivels and swivels and swivels until she's got it twirling faster than ever. It's at that point, when the dirty yellow hoop is nothing but a colourless blur, that something possesses her. At first, she just squishes up her face — a defiant little squish, a disdainful little squish, as if nothing in the world could make that hoop clatter to the ground — but then she sticks out her tongue and starts jabbing her forefingers into the air. It's not just clowning anymore. It's not just jiving. It's a dance of feverish joy, of feverish guilt, of feverish faith and impudence and alarm. And of ultimate obliteration.

"Jesus."

Vivian doesn't know whether to laugh or to cry. It's funny, really.
But it's also terrible. At that exact moment, she has no idea what's
going to become of her youngest child.

The spell of that furious twirling lasts a long time. But only until
Vivian spots the brand-new Chevy Impala with the electric TAXI sign
on top.

"About time, Cyril!" She struggles to her feet. "About bloody…!"

As Vivian goes to meet the taxi, she catches a glimpse of a round,
red face with its wild, exuberant eyes, its unmistakably demonic grin.

She quickly looks away. The bottles clink into her arms. Rebecca
keeps twirling.

"OK, OK. How about…? *Thirteen years of marital bliss, makes me
want to*…Wait, wait…Ha! *Makes me want to take a piss!*"

There's a chorus of laughter coming from the sun porch. But Vivian
and Rebecca are still in the west living room, gazing fondly into Vivian's
china cabinet.

Mum hasn't got as many nice things as Marion, thinks Rebecca, but
they're still pretty neat. A browny photograph of her Dad as a young
man, when he looked so sturdy and defiant. Like Peter, really, but
with some brains and self-confidence to back it up. And a fuzzy
photograph of Sunny as a newborn, right after the nurse had shown
her Mum how to oil the baby's jet-black hair up to a greasy little point.
And her Mum's Royal Souvenirs.

Every time one of the Royal Family makes a visit or has a wedding
or a baby, her Mum buys something to commemorate the occasion.
Not those silly pin trays and dolls, neckties and socks, buttons and
coasters and egg cups and bars of soap that some people buy. But
something "real nice," as she often says. Like a plate or a cup and
saucer or a spoon.

"Oh, why not," whispers Vivian, as she admires the gleaming
intricacy on the handle of her brand-new Princess Margaret spoon.
"It *is* a special occasion, after all."

"It is?"

"That'll be enough out of you, young lady."

The spoons were ready earlier than the plates. In fact, her Mum
told her that Harriet Bill had them in the back room of her store even

before the big black smudge drifted through town. Harriet just didn't tell anyone. She wanted the decoration to be a surprise. It wasn't just engraving this time. It was real design. And that made it so much more collectible, even if it were only on the handle and not on the bowl.

After arranging three dainty little commemorative cups and saucers on a large platter honouring the memory of King George the Sixth, Vivian unscrews the top of the Seagram's bottle and pours Five Star whiskey into them. Then she stirs them vigorously, with the unadorned bowl of the Princess Margaret spoon, and heads for the laughter.

"Hey! Wait for me!"

Because Harold and Uncle Filly are both there, the sun porch is even noisier than usual tonight. In a family fond of stories, these two tell the funniest stories of all.

"Uncle Filly!" pleads Randy. "Tell us about getting fired!"

"Well..." Uncle Filly has a high, whiny, asthmatic voice. "There's not much to tell, really." He stops to take a swig from his Coronation cup. "Some good, Vivian. Some friggin' good."

Rebecca giggles. Randy snaps his gum.

"I was cooking for the lumber camp," continues Uncle Filly. "You know, the one over to Dalhousie. And..."

Charles Filson Parker is Grammie's younger brother. His grey hair is always greasy. And the baggy suit he wears is always rumpled. Everyone agrees he's a good cook, but they're always arguing about his character. Ben Kelly claims he's a drunken liar — "the most useless man I ever met" — and Vivian insists he's got a great, kind heart. Randy and Rebecca don't care either way. All *they* know is he's funny.

"And I woke up in the middle of the night with a powerful thirst," he wheezes.

"What did you do, Uncle Filly?"

"Well..." He stops to light a cigarette. "There wasn't a single, god-damned drop of booze in the place so I... Ha! So I drank up all the vanilla!"

Vivian begins to cackle.

"And then I shit in the dish-pan!"

Everyone whoops.

"I think it was shitting in the…" He farts loudly, "…dish-pan that did it."

Everyone whoops again.

"Jesus, Filly," laughs Harold. "Remember the time Charlie and I had a contest to see who could fart out the old oil lamp?"

Uncle Filly chuckles. "I sure do. You were both so god-damned…"

"What happened, Dad?" interrupts Rebecca. "Did you win?"

"Well, no. Nobody won. We had to call it off."

"How come?"

"Ha! Because your Uncle Charlie burnt his ass!"

The room erupts in laughter.

"Jesus," cackles Vivian. "Old Charlie always was a bit funny in the…"

With that, Harold takes a swig from his Royal Wedding cup and leaps to his feet. Everyone knows what's coming.

"Yay!" shouts Rebecca.

Her Dad may be old — almost twenty years older than her Mum — and a bit rough. But he's also what she's heard Ruthie Sutherland call a "fun drunk" and he gives the longest, funniest, filthiest recitations in town.

They begin clapping, rhythmically, to urge him on. He clears his throat and begins.

"*I'll tell you a story, that's certain to please, of a grand farting contest on Synamontese.*"

"I knew it!" roars Uncle Filly. "I knew it was going to be that one!"

"*This fine Easter morning had drawn a large crowd and betting was even on Mrs. MacLeod.*"

"Because of all the cabbage and peas she ate," wheezes Vivian.

Randy sneaks a sip from her Royal Christening cup.

"*'Twas said in the paper, the sporting edition, that this woman's ass was in perfect condition.*"

"Ha! I've known a few of those in my time!"

"Shsh, Filly!"

"*And Old Mrs. Brown had a perfect backside, with a bunch of red hairs and a wart on each side.*"

Rebecca claps her hands with glee.

Her Dad is real smart, just like everyone says he is. With the best memory in the whole wide world. Well, tied for first, she admits, when she remembers *she* knows the poem by heart, too. In fact, as he continues through the opening verses, getting old Mrs. Brown and Mrs. MacLeod ready to show their stuff against Mrs. Potluck, who's fond of gassing the Vicar, and Old Marmeduck Morgan, who makes more noise than the organ, she almost mouths the words. But she likes it best when just her Dad says them.

"Eeeeeee!" wheezes Vivian, as the Vicar ascends the stage and explains the rules against injections and pills. "I can't stand it! I can't...!"

Mrs. Brown wins the toss and prepares to go first.

"Eeeee...eeeee!"

"On your mark," interrupts Filly, as Mrs. Brown pulls down her drawers. "Get set..."

Everyone blows a raspberry.

"The crowd was astonished, in silence and wonder. This beefy old girl gave them plenty of thunder."

"Yeah!" hollers Randy. "Way to go!" He reaches for the Royal Christening cup again, while Mrs. Potluck parts her cheeks and clenches her hands and blows the roof off the twenty-cent stand.

"But Mrs. MacLeod simply snickered at this. She copped up some beer and was all wind and piss."

Vivian snatches the cup away from him.

"With her hands on her hips and her legs stretched out wide, she suddenly..."

Harold pauses for effect. Everyone's eyes widen.

"She suddenly shit and was disqualified!"

The room erupts in laughter. But not for long. There's still a dark horse waiting to take her turn. There's still Mrs. Bugle, who's got a fairly small ass, albeit a pretty one.

"More! More! More! More!" they shout and clap in unison.

"OK, OK!" laughs Harold. "Just wait till I...Hey!" He turns his Royal Wedding cup upside down. "Who drank all my...?"

"Never mind that!" pleads Uncle Filly. "Keep going! Keep going!"

The others cheer as Mrs. Bugle steps forward and, with a sound that rings as clear and as true as a saxophone, out-farts them all.

They blow another raspberry. Harold grins.

"She walked to the next room, with maidenly gait, to receive from the Vicar a set of gold plates."

"Ha!" Uncle Filly tosses his butt into his Coronation cup. "That's probably not all he gave..."

"Shsh, Filly. Or we'll miss..."

"*And as that great throng stood up to sing...*"

The others join in.

"SHE FARTED THE FIRST VERSE OF GOD SAVE THE KING!"

"Yeaaaaah!"

There's another tumult of laughter and clapping. Harold takes a bow.

"OK, you two," he announces on the way up. "Time for bed."

"Aw, Dad."

"Just one more. Ple-ease!"

"Go on now, or I'll..."

"What?" giggles Rebecca.

"Ha!" Harold peers into his empty Royal Wedding cup. "That's a good question."

A little later, Randy and Rebecca are huddled on the bottom step, still listening.

"I suppose you met him at the last camp?" asks Vivian, as she screws the cap off the second bottle of Five Star.

"Yes," wheezes Uncle Filly. "He was...Jesus! What's the occasion anyway?"

Vivian pours another round.

"I was expecting a can or two of beer."

"Ha!" snorts Vivian. "I only get bottles. I can't work the tabs on those god-damned *aloominee*..."

"Anyway. From what *I* know, he's a good fellow. He..."

"But why did you bring him here?"

"I didn't *bring* him. I only told him about the place."

"Yes, well, we've never had any coons living here that I can remember." She flops into the armchair. "They usually live in Waterville or Yoho."

They drink in silence for a moment.

"Where did he come from anyway?"

"How should *I* know? Look. He's a good fellow. He works hard. He...You're not going to have to lock up the offering boxes or anything."

"And where's he going to live?"

"On Pierce Road."

"Jesus."

"By the railway tracks. Next to Stronach's, I think." Uncle Filly lights another cigarette. "Down the road from McClare's, at any rate."

"Jesus."

"Don't worry, Vivian." He tosses the match to the floor. "He won't bother anybody."

"Does he work?"

"Yes, he works."

"Where?"

"Over to Millville, on Newton Webster's lot."

"Well, at least that's something."

"Look. I'll say it again. He's a good fellow. A right good fellow. He'd give you the shirt off his back. Ha! Which is more than I can say for..."

"Oh, God," sighs Harold. "Here we go."

Once Uncle Filly gets drunk, he starts orating. Tonight's subject is one of his favourites — people who are tight with their money.

"Oh, you're a great preacher, Filly," remarks Vivian.

"I'm serious! She accused me of stealing her bed!"

"Who did?"

"That lady friend of mine into Berwick."

"Well, did you?"

"No, I did not! Her god-damned son had it put in storage!"

They all chuckle.

"And last week...Ha! Last week she..."

"Well, nobody can be as mean with her money as Florence."

"Why? What'd she do?"

"What she always does. Ha! Never spends a dime of her own money if she can help it. Says she forgot her pocketbook. Says she forgot to go to the bank. And then asks *me* to loan her five dollars."

"So?" Uncle Filly's eyes are twinkling.

"So that's the last I ever see of it! The bitch never pays me back! Aaach, aaach. And she's probably got more money in her purse than the Queen of...aaaaaaach!"

"But she's got a good heart, at least. I hear she's nursing old Mrs. Palmer."

"Oh, that's only so she can get into the will."

With that, there's a flash of light from across the road. Wanda Willoughby is pulling into her driveway.

"And as for *that* old whore..."

"I thought she was your friend!"

"She is but she's still tight with her money. You know what she brought to the last potluck supper? A can of Spam! And then she bounced her ass around the room and ate everybody else's food! Jesus. And she's worn the same god-damned dress for twenty years! She must think she can take it all with her or something!"

"Now look who's preaching," drawls Harold.

The kids can't help giggling.

"If you're not in bed by the time I count to ten," warns Vivian, "I'll..."

They scramble up the stairs.

A few hours later, Rebecca creeps back down again.

Harold and Uncle Filly are passed out on the sun porch, with their mouths open. There are bits of vomit caught in their teeth. Vivian is standing in the east living room, holding her wooden seagull in her cupped and trembling hands.

Vivian claims she never drank a drop before she was married. She claims it was her sister Florence who was the wild one when they were girls. Now she goes on six or seven binges a year, mostly on weekends, but she never passes out. Not like Harold and Filly, who always pass out laughing and puking.

"Are you all right?" she whispers to the seagull.

Rebecca rolls her eyes.

"You'll be fine." she strokes the seagull's painted plumage. "As long as Peter doesn't get to you."

Rebecca puts her hand over her mouth, so her Mum can't hear her giggling. Peter knows how much Vivian likes her seagull to perch on the window sill in the east living room. Maybe that's why he keeps moving it around.

"Sssh. Go to sleep, now." Vivian places the seagull back on the window sill, then turns and drifts outside.

Rebecca rolls her eyes again, then tiptoes after her.

The yard is bathed in moonlight. The clothes are twisted on the line. Rebecca's yellow hula hoop is lying in the sandpit.

Rebecca hides in the shadows near the door, as Vivian climbs into the two-dollar ring of plastic, raises it slowly to her waist and then twirls it.

"Whoa-oa-oa..."

The first few spins are pretty wobbly. But gradually, as she finds the rhythm, they get tighter and faster and more and more furious until finally...

"Ha-haaaaa!"

...There's just laughter. And a big blur. And Vivian, who doesn't seem to know where she is any more.

Soon, however, the spell is broken.

Standing in the glassed-in sun porch across the street is a shadow with its hands on its hips.

"Well! Now I've seen everything!" the shadow hollers.

"Monica? Is that you, Monica?" Vivian tries to wave, but she quickly loses the rhythm and the dirty yellow hoop twirls up from her waist to her breasts to her neck...and then whirls off over her head.

"Weeeee!"

For a moment, it just hangs there, suspended — like a gigantic halo.

"Wow!" whispers Rebecca.

13

The Golden Hawk glides down Pierce Road, past McClare's place and Stronach's place, until it reaches the railway crossing. Then it bumps unceremoniously over the tracks and pulls sharply into a dirt driveway on the right-hand side of the road.

"This better be the last place," grumbles Rebecca, from the back seat. "You said we only had two more places to go and that was five places ago."

"I think this is it," says Reverend MacKay, as he pushes open his door.

"Yes." Marion stares through the windshield.

The house is a shambles. The log part at the back looks sturdy enough, but the plywood part at the front is cobbled together with strips of tar paper and dented sheets of scrap metal. The patchwork roof looks like a quilt of rotting boards and shingles.

"Awfully noisy, I would imagine." Reverend MacKay waves at the glistening tracks. "What with the trains going through day and night."

"Yes." Marion is still staring.

"Who cares?" whines Rebecca. "Let's just get going!"

"Well, come on, Marion," says Reverend MacKay, as he leans inside the car. It smells faintly of "Magi," that Spanish perfume in a red and black box, that Marion gets from Harriet's. "Let's do our Welcoming Committee bit."

Marion reaches into the back seat for the cardboard box of books and clothes and food which is sitting beside Rebecca.

"Anybody home?" calls the Reverend, as he strolls toward the house.

The front door creaks open.

"Frankie? Frankie Lewis?"

"Yes?"

"Wow!" whispers Rebecca, as she peers through the window. "It's that man again."

"Oh, hello. We weren't sure if you'd be at work or…"

"Well, I was," says Frankie gently, as he tucks his pale green shirt into his dark green pants. "But I…" He stops when he spots Marion.

"Well, anyway. We've come to…" Reverend MacKay looks from Frankie to Marion and back. "Do you two know each other by any chance?"

Frankie smiles at him.

"Silly of me," splutters Reverend MacKay. "Anyway, Mr. Lewis, we've come to welcome you to Aylesford!" he announces cheerfully.

"Thank you."

"Wow!"

Behind Frankie, there's another shambles. From the car, Rebecca can see the water stains, the cracked gyprock, the rotting linoleum, the tattered furniture. And no woodwork, no cupboards, no sink.

"And we thought," continues Reverend MacKay, "that you might find some use for these. Marion?"

She hands Frankie the box.

"Thank you." He smiles at her.

"And if there's anything else you need, just…"

"Would you like to come in, Reverend?"

"No, sorry. We can't. Not today. We've got a Red Cross meeting down at the…Well, actually, we promised little Rebecca we'd take her…"

"Some other time, then." Frankie says this to Marion.

"Yes."

Once again, Reverend MacKay looks from one to the other.

Thwap. Thwap. Thwap. Thwap.

Rebecca is scuffing along Park Street, trying to pound a pocket in her brand-new glove with her brand-new ball. They're both presents from Darrell, who got a job loading bags of Bluenose Peat Moss at the plant up Old Post Road. The glove is the first one she's ever had. And it isn't one of those plastic baby gloves either. It's real leather and fits on her proper hand.

Thwap. Thwap. Thwap. Thwap.

The ball isn't real. It's one of those rubber-coated ones with simulated stitching. But she doesn't care. At least it won't get soaked in the rain. And it's way better than those tennis balls Winifred Hill sometimes gives her after she and her father have bashed all the fuzz off them.

Thwap. Thwap…

She stops for a moment by Cyril Neily's place. Cyril was born the very same day Marion was. He has a real gas pump in his side yard, and he just got married to the woman who runs Caroline's restaurant, but Rebecca still doesn't like him. He's the one her parents always call to fetch them booze after hours. She knows his number by heart. Twenty-seven. The same as Frank Mahovlich. And when it's not Cyril driving the taxi over to Bootlegger's Lane, it's his younger brother Waldo, who has a wooden left leg and is so fat that he can barely squeeze behind the steering wheel.

She pauses a moment longer, to examine the pale green smudges on the face of the ball…and then starts running down Park Street.

She loves baseball. She loves the sound of the words which describe it. Monstrous, scary, religious words like *double-header* and *twin killing* and *spikes*. She doesn't really understand what they mean, but she's mesmerized by them. They seem to make promises to her; to call out to her that life will be dangerous, glamorous, romantic…and, if she's lucky, will get played out on a glittering diamond. To her, baseball is somehow a much bigger game than dodgeball, which is played in a circle, and hopscotch, which only uses squares.

Near the Fire Hall, she stops running. The ball park is right behind it, next to the woods. But the infield is just gravel, with bits of broken glass in it, and the outfield is just patchy brown grass, with devil's paintbrushes poking through. There's no need to run any more. Behind home plate, there are creaky wooden bleachers. Painted dark green. Empty. In fact, there isn't anybody here except Frankie, who's volunteered to prepare the field. She hooks her fingers through the backstop and watches.

It's hot today — a typical Saturday afternoon in August — but Frankie is wearing his pale green cotton dress shirt and his dark green cotton slacks. He's finished the rolling and raking now and is busy pouring a bag of chalky white powder into a silver container. When it's full, he begins to push it along the base paths.

As the chalky white lines appear on the gravel, Rebecca's fingers clench the big, bent screen. It's Frankie who's making the diamond for her. Frankie who's making sure the game will have guidelines, standards, rules...

There's a sudden burst of laughter from the third-base side.

"Not bad, not bad," chuckles Marion, as she ducks out of the tool shed.

Frankie smiles at her.

"Yeah!" blurts Rebecca. "Not nearly as wiggly as when Marvin Bennett makes them!"

"Oh! Rebecca!" Marion glances at Frankie. "You scared me half to death! Where did you come from? Have you been here long? Why didn't you...?"

"Come on, little one," calls Frankie.

"What?" Rebecca peers through the rusty lozenges of the screen.

"You can do from third to home."

"I can? Me?" She scrambles across the gravel toward the silver container.

At last, the volunteer firemen, who've been polishing the ball-shaped pressure dome over the engine in their Ahrens-Fox Piston Pumper, push open the hatch at the back of the hall and begin to set up their canteen. The man in charge is Hal Jackson, who's secretary of the

Fire Commission this year.

"What *I'd* like to know..."

Rebecca can hear him hollering from inside the hall.

"... is what we're going to use to wrap around the bloody wieners if we can't find the bloody bags of buns!"

Before long, however, Rebecca and the other kids are lining up for their usual hot dogs and the fans from both sides are taking up their favourite positions around the park — near the trees along the third-base line, past the misshapen chain link fence surrounding the outfield, in the creaky green bleachers behind home plate — and the players are milling about in front of their dugouts. These are painted the same dark green as the bleachers but they also have bright white facings with HOME and AWAY in big, bold green letters.

The Aylesford players wear blue jerseys, with MOHAWKS in a white diagonal across the chest. Their caps are blue, too, with a white arrowhead on the front. Some of the players are from out of town, like Marty Grainger, who Uncle Filly says is kind of fruity but covers a lot of ground at shortstop and is some good as a hitter. But most of them are from Aylesford. There's Arnie Oyler, who lives next to Grammie with his wife Iris. And Reggie Matheson, who helps his father run the pharmacy. And the two Genes. Gene Patterson, who lives next to Marion, and Gene Henderson, who has the best outfield arm in the league. And then there's Wayne Sanford, the telephone operator's son, who's the envy of all the kids because he's the batboy and gets to wear a blue and white uniform.

Chink. Chink. Chink. Chink.

As Rebecca drags the Allen's Apple Juice crate along the curve of the fence, she's nearly overcome by the greasy glamour of the grill, the sweet seduction of the floss. But she keeps her eyes fixed on the scoreboard beyond centre-field. It's an old wooden one, green and white with an ad for 7-Up at the top. Soon, she and Frankie will be kneeling at the foot of it, sorting through the crateful of metal placards.

Suddenly, there's a commotion in the bleachers.

"Look, Frankie! They're fighting already!"

There's a tremendous clatter and clang as she drops the crate and rushes to the fence. But it's just some shoving and shouting...and it ends when the Mohawks run onto the field.

"Yaaaaay!" She's too excited to notice that the white lines are already smudged. "Here comes my Uncle Gene!"

While Gene Henderson jogs toward his position in centre field, Frankie carries the apple juice crate to the foot of the scoreboard.

"He's the best player on the whole team, you know." She swivels to face him. "Only he won't be here much longer."

"Why's that?" He stares at the dented white placards.

"'Cause he's getting married," she snorts. "And then moving away to be a Newfie." She spins back to the field. "Hi, Uncle Gene! You're going to cream them!"

Frankie and Rebecca are perched on the wooden bench attached to the scoreboard. It's a different game when watched from here, almost a dream — with all those indistinct faces and the backs of things instead of the fronts. Except for the numbers.

"Rats!" She hands him a dented white placard with a big black zero painted on it.

"What's the matter, little one?" He hangs it on the rusty nail at the bottom of the fourth inning.

"Nothing." She props her face in her hands.

"Oh, come on. It must be something."

Rebecca senses that there's a certain magic to keeping score this way. But it's not really fun. It's not perfect. You have to do exactly what you're told.

"Well, they're never going to get any runs!"

"Who says?"

"And it's no fun hanging dumb old zeroes all day!"

"Never mind," he laughs. "Come on. I'll quiz you."

"On what?"

"Baseball, of course. Now, tell me. Who's leading the National League in…hitting?"

"Ummm…Richie Ashburn!"

"Right! And who's leading the American League in…home runs?"

"Minnie Mackerel!"

He laughs again. "Right! And…"

"I like Minnie Mackerel OK, but my favourite player is Billy Bruton."

"Why's that?"

"'Cause he's little, like me. And fast. And 'cause he plays centre field, like Uncle Gene. I bet if Uncle Gene didn't have to get married, he could try out for the Milwaukee Braves and..."

"Oh-oh."

"What, Frankie?"

"You'd better hand me a two. Those dreaded Berwick Bruins have just got a..."

"Nooooo! They don't deserve it! We're way better than they are! Put it on crooked, Frankie!"

During the seventh-inning stretch, the ladies always pass around the sand pail. Today, it's Marion who's climbing up and down the bleachers, collecting dimes and quarters to pay for the balls and bats and extra uniforms.

"Frankie?"

He doesn't answer.

"Frankie!" Rebecca tugs at him.

"What is it?" His gaze is fixed on the bleachers.

"Do you think I'll ever be big enough?"

"For what?"

"To get chosen."

"I don't know what you mean."

"Well, when the kids choose sides for baseball, they never choose me. They choose all the bums and the creeps. And Charlene and Jimmy Gould, who cry if they can't be on the same team as each other. And Chuck Chisolm, who always holds the bat by the wrong end. And Mary Mapplebeck, who has the worst B.O. I ever smelled — even though she's real smart and takes a bath every day. And Sherry Lynn Goddard, who sits off by herself so she *won't* get picked. But they never choose me. They say I'm too little. Do you think I'll ever be big enough?"

"Yes." His gaze is still fixed on the bleachers. "We all get chosen for something."

"Good." She hops down off the scoreboard.

"Hey! Where are you going?"

"To get some pop and chips!"

She checks the apple juice crate, to make sure her brand-new ball and glove are still inside, and then races toward the canteen. By the time she reaches the hatch at the back of the Fire Hall, however, it's too late. Donnie Taylor has just bought the last bag of Scotties.

"Too bad! Too bad!" He stuffs his mouth full of chips and dances around her.

"Yeah?" She glares at him for a moment, then pushes him down on the gravel and runs all the way back to the scoreboard.

"What was *that* all about?" laughs Frankie, as she climbs back onto the bench.

"He deserved it," she pants.

"Oh?" He peers at Donnie, who's still sitting on the gravel, rubbing his eyes. "And why's that?"

"'Cause he's always bothering me."

"Always? I thought he just moved here?"

"Yeah, well…he's always trying to use the swings Marion bought me and…"

Just then, a huge black crow flies overhead.

"Wow! Look at that!"

She and Frankie watch it land on the peak of a pine tree at the edge of the woods.

"And he's a tattletale, too."

"What?" Frankie turns to her.

"Donnie. He's a tattletale. Last week, when Randy and I were…"

Suddenly, there's a great roar from the crowd. And a ball, winging toward them.

"Frankie!"

When it gets so close they can pick out the neat red stitching on its shiny white face, he puts up his hands to catch it.

"No! Let it go!" screams Rebecca. "Or it won't be a home…!"

Frankie drops his hands. They both duck. The ball goes crashing into the scoreboard, knocking off all the bent and dented numbers.

At first, they just look at one another, their eyes wide with fright and astonishment. And then they start laughing. They laugh as long as the crowd cheers the three-run homer hit by Gene Patterson. In fact, they're still laughing as they leap down off the bench and start rummaging around in the tall grass.

"Boys, oh, boys!" squeals Rebecca, as she collects an armful of metal placards. "It's the neatest thing that ever happened!"

They climb back up and start hanging the numbers again. First, the three. And then the zeroes. And then…

There's a howl of protest from the crowd.

"Oops," she giggles. "Wrong place."

She starts to move Berwick's big black two up to the top of the fifth, where it belongs, but Frankie reaches out and stops her.

"What?"

"Leave it there," he chortles.

"But, Frankie, it isn't supposed to…"

"Leave it."

There's another howl of protest from the crowd.

Rebecca glances up at the huge black crow, as it continues to sit on the peak of a pine tree at the edge of the woods.

It's dark now. The white lines have been obliterated. Frankie, Marion and Rebecca are the only ones left at the park.

"Here! Catch!" He tosses a mushy hot dog bun into the cardboard box Rebecca's carrying.

"Thanks a lot!"

They're all friends now. They enjoy each other's company. But Rebecca draws the line at mushy hot dog buns.

"Hey, look at this!"

Frankie's kneeling on the ground, with his hand in a half-eaten box of Cracker Jack.

"What?" Rebecca wanders over to him.

He holds up a little, yellow plastic ring. "Someone forgot the prize. Here." He offers it to Rebecca.

"No, thanks. I already have one."

"You do?"

"Yeah. A great big one. A hula hoop!" She laughs at her own joke.

"Oh. Well, then, how about you?" Frankie offers the ring to Marion.

"Don't be silly, Frankie. Whatever would I do with…?"

"Please?"

He's still kneeling.

"Yeah, Marion," urges Rebecca. "Put it on!"

"Oh, all right," she laughs. "If it'll make you both…" She slips the ring onto the fourth finger of her left hand. And then holds out her hand to admire it.

"God, Frankie. Wouldn't it be funny...?"

Frankie hasn't got up yet.

"Yes," he says softly. "It would certainly cause a stink."

For one more moment, Marion gazes down at him.

"Well!" She yanks the ring off her finger and stuffs it into the pocket of her slacks. "Come on, you two! We've got work to do!"

There's plenty of garbage left around the diamond.

"God, it must be the heat."

Rebecca coasts up the driveway, past the back veranda and the double garage, to the shade beneath the poplar trees. Then she leans her forehead on the steering wheel and disappears — not into the past, exactly, but into something she's now making of the past.

It's early morning, barely light. There's a forest of balsam fir, quivering in the mist. Some of them are going to be novels. Some of them are going to be plywood. Some of them are going to be hung with lights. DOWN HOME CHRISTMAS TREES, the signs in the parking lots in Ontario will say. NOVA SCOTIA FIR.

And there's also a man. A young, strong, sensual man, with his pale yellow sleeves rolled up to his elbows and an axe stuck in the waist of his black cotton dress pants.

Oh, dearest Mary. Do not break my heart. There's nothing but slavery for you and I to part. Oh, dearest Mary, with arms on shore outstretched...

And then there are men in plaid shirts and blue jeans, hopping off the backs of trucks, searching the skies for signs of rain.

Most of them work in pairs; one of them cutting, the other piling the sweet-smelling wood into cords. They share the cost of their saw. They share their pay at the end of the day. And they only fell trees marked with their own initials. But one of them works alone. All day. Through the flies, the splinters, the heat, the grinding of saws. And the trucks leaving for the sawmill in town.

It's early evening, barely light. There's nothing left of the quivering forest. But there's still a man, deep in the mist, carving two sets of tiny initials on the drooping limb of a sugar maple bush that no one will ever touch.

Do not break my heart. Do not break my heart. Do not break my...

It's dark now. And still. Except for the heavy breathing of the sea. Except for the gentle moaning of the breeze. Except for the ghost of desire, which is hiding in the bed of lupines in front of Lizzie Peterson's place.

It's a two-storey cottage, made of wood, painted ivory, starting to lean, with a sun porch at the front and another around the side. Downstairs, there's some ratty wicker furniture and a grubby linoleum floor, with a threadbare Persian rug thrown over it. Upstairs, there's a large room with nine mismatched beds.

Suddenly, there's a rustle and then a creak. And then something besides the breeze is brushing past the bed of lupines.

The ghost of desire tries not to follow it. It likes the big bold bed of lupines. The pinks, the whites, the mostly purples. They look like multi-coloured steeples. But the breeze's tender touch of genius has turned ravenous and the ghost is pushed to the edge of the cliff.

Down below, the sea is pounding against the dark rocks. It's a very old duet, sung by the bully and the stoic. But tonight the bully seems sad, lonely, as if it wishes it could stop. A little back from this struggle, there's a woman, walking alone on the beach. As she picks her way through the field of stones, the waves crash, the wind whips her hair, the cold mist sprays over her face. She clutches the grey woollen blanket which is wrapped around her. But she also smiles.

It's not a pleasant place. But it's a beautiful one.

The ghost of desire smiles, too.

"Jesus." Rebecca lifts her head from the steering wheel.

She's embarrassed by the soft, sensual secrecy of her hallucinations. She doesn't know why they came to her. She doesn't know what they mean. She doesn't even know who the people are wandering through them.

"Ha! Except they're not me. I know that." She wipes the sweat from her face.

She's never been what anyone would call a wild and passionate woman. She's not prim, exactly. Just a little too calm and concise for her own good. Or Brian's, for that matter. In other words, she's never had trouble getting the facts straight, just the poetry.

"Which is why…" She snatches the datebook from the front seat of the car. "I'd better stick to this." She wanders across the grass to the wooden lawn chairs.

As soon as Rebecca opens the dark blue cover, she realizes she's been driving around with the wrong one. It's the same colour as 1958, but it's 1965 instead.

At first, she just flips aimlessly through the pages, not really paying attention to the notations; not really caring which obligations they signify now. But then she spots something strange. From a distance, it looks like a tiny black squiggle, something Marion would make if she dropped her pen on the page. Only when Rebecca lifts the book and squints at it, can she make out the tiny little letters.

Black paint.

It doesn't mean anything to her.

She flips through the pages again.

There are other black squiggles, too; mysterious bits of memory like *His eyes are my sky.*

"Ha!" she laughs. "So Marion wrote poetry!"

The black squiggles are funny things to find among the legions of appointments, but they're also a relief. Until now, the books were filled with oppressive details about the endless things to do, to make, to see; the endless people to call, to visit, to cheer up. Now, at least, there are one or two squiggly moments of joy or sorrow, ecstasy or desolation.

"I wonder why she was so shy about it."

She closes the datebook. And then turns her face to the sun and whispers "Black paint, black paint, black paint," as if the mere repetition will jog her memory.

But it's no use.

She stares across the patchy brown grass. The only things still thriving are the devil's paintbrushes.

14

"Stubborn little buggers," laughs Florence, as she stares at the clusters of orangey red heads which have taken over the lawn.

Rebecca can't help giggling.

"Yeees," drawls Alice. Her eyes are fixed on the naked green stalks. "You haaave to caaatch them iiin the spriiing, or they juuust keep…"

"Where the hell's Marion with the food?" interrupts Vivian.

Reverend MacKay clears his throat.

"Frankly," muses Kay Armstrong. "I prefer dandelions. They may have a lot more petals, but at least you can dig them up."

"If you must have anything, of course," sniffs Evelyn Pierce.

"Yes, of course," splutters Florence.

It's August 1958 and they've all gathered at Marion's place to make plans for Evelyn's marriage to Gene Henderson. The circular driveway is big enough to fit the extra cars. Ben's and Malcolm's Bel Airs are where they always are, pushed right up against the double garage. And Marion's Skylark is parked in its usual place, too — around the back, with the keys still jammed in the ignition. So there's still plenty of room at each end for the Silver Streak and the Golden Hawk belonging to Florence and Reverend MacKay, who live too far away to walk. There aren't enough big wooden lawn chairs, however. The Reverend came late, so he missed out on the dark green ones, and on Marion's big cream-coloured one with the rounded back. When he tried to squish himself into Rebecca's little cream-coloured replica, everyone snickered, and he settled for one of the fold-up chairs Alice dragged over.

"If she doesn't get here soon," wheezes Vivian, "we're all going to die of hunger."

"Yeah," agrees Rebecca. "We're all going to…"

"Weeeee!"

From inside the house comes a tumult of squealing and shouting.

"Hey, you guys!" Rebecca leaps out of her chair. "You were supposed to wait for me!"

As soon as she gets inside, she joins Sunny and Winifred as they take turns sliding across the newly waxed kitchen floor in their stocking feet.

"Weeeee!"

Meanwhile, Doris Pudsey is leaning in the doorway to the dining room, watching them. Doris is a short, wide woman with short, crimped hair who comes from Millville one day a week to do housework for Marion. She also works one day a week for the Armstrongs, for Edna Ogletree, for Grammie and for Dr. Dempsey. But she likes it best here. The pay is only five dollars a day, the same as everywhere else, but she says she's fond of the kids, squealing and shouting and polishing her newly waxed kitchen floor. And she says she's fond of Marion, who, for some strange reason, is especially good to her — treats her like a sister; doesn't even get mad when she uses flour with mealworms in it or takes sips of gin between swipes with the feather duster or breaks things.

"Weeeeeee!"

"My soul!" Doris smooths her orange and yellow print dress — the one with the buttons all the way down the front. "My soul and..."

"Watch this, Doris! Watch! I'm going to...Iyee!" Rebecca crashes into the fridge.

"OK, you kids."

Marion has been standing at the counter near the sink, obliviously pouring tea into six of her best china cups.

"Watch out now."

When she turns towards the room, she's balancing six cups of tea and two plates of sweets on a large, silver tray. One of the plates just has Peek Freans creams on it. The other has squares — big, gooey, home-made squares, with layers of fruit and coconut and chocolate on their butter-and-crumb bottoms.

"And don't give Doris any trouble."

Rebecca watches Marion pick her way down the stairs and across the yard, toward the lawn chairs. She's wearing a pink sundress with huge white roses and thin black straps. Her ample breasts are white, too — like a pair of roses spilling out of the material.

"OK, Alice! Christ!" Florence slams her cup into her saucer. "I'm sick and tired of hearing you whine about how much Clary ignores you."

"Weeell, I was ooonly..."

"So." Marion scribbles something in her datebook. "Now that we've decided about the flower arrangements..."

"Wait!" Vivian wipes the crumbs from her lips. "Who did you say the best man was?"

"Gene Patterson!" they all chime together.

"OK!" laughs Vivian. "I just asked." She reaches for another gooey square. "There are so many Genes."

"Yes," sighs Evelyn. "Well, I'm sure even you can get that straight, Vivian."

"Yeah, Mum!" Rebecca makes a face at her. Even she knows that there are two main Genes.

Gene Henderson is one of what Grammie calls her "sober, sensible kids." As opposed to the "drunken liars," she always sighs. Right now, he's a chartered accountant with D.L. Young & Company in Kentville, but after he marries snobby old Evelyn Pierce, he's moving to Grand Falls, Newfoundland to work for Goodfellow's Construction. Gene Patterson, on the other hand, is a fat man with duck lips and a crew cut. He lives in the little house next to Marion's and hits three-run homers for the Mohawks. Rebecca thinks his wife Monta looks like a farm horse, but she admires two of his three kids. Darlene and Rosemary are so supple they can pull their legs right over their backs onto their shoulders. His son Craig can't do much of anything.

"So." Marion's writing again. "The wedding is set for the second Saturday in October. With the ceremony to be held in the Aylesford United Baptist Church. And the reception to follow in the vestry. There." She closes her datebook.

"Goodness, Marion!" marvels Kay. "Don't you go anywhere without that thing?"

"Oh, she couldn't do that," Rebecca says earnestly. "She wouldn't be able to keep everything straight."

"No rest for the wicked, eh, Marion?"

They all laugh.

"Yes, well, before we get *too* carried away." Evelyn's the first to stop laughing. "I want to ask Vivian…"

"What? What did I do now?"

"I want to ask you if Filly's going to be there."

"Yes, why?"

"Well, I don't want a repeat of what happened at Florence's wedding."

"What do you mean?"

"I mean…"

"Oh, *I* remember!" blurts Florence. "Ha! We were all standing there, saying the Lord's Prayer, when Filly...when Filly..." She's laughing too hard to continue.

Vivian picks up the story. "When Filly, who was in the row behind me, suddenly hollers...eeee...eeee...suddenly hollers out: 'Jesus! I forgot the words!'"

Everyone hoots except Evelyn.

"Gaaawd!" Florence wipes her eyes. "George and I nearly pissed ourselves!"

"I did piss myself!" squeals Vivian.

Once again, Rebecca can't help giggling.

"Well," sniffs Evelyn. "See that he keeps his mouth shut this time."

Marion glances at Reverend MacKay.

"I don't think you can shut up Uncle Filly," he says gently.

Once again, everyone hoots except Evelyn. "OK, OK! Let's move on! What about the dresses?"

Marion opens her datebook again.

As they begin to discuss colours and corsages, Ben strides past the lawn chairs and into the tall grass.

"Wheeere're you geeetting the mateeerial, Eeev?" Alice watches him shift his way toward the woods. "At Haaarriet's?"

"Oh, no! We're going to Halifax for that!"

"And who's going to make them?" asks Kay.

"Who cares?" mutters Rebecca, as she pushes herself up from her chair.

"Well, I thought Janet Pine. She made lovely dresses for..."

Rebecca was going to follow Ben into the tall grass, but she changes her mind and wanders over to watch Sunny and Winifred on the swing set instead.

It's a shiny new swing set at the edge of the short grass and the tall grass, halfway between Marion's house and the Marshall's house, which they made her Dad paint dark brown this year. The really special thing about this set is that it's got three swings, not two. But that doesn't help Rebecca right now. Winifred's gone and propped her great big doll on the third swing. That fancy new doll with the curly red hair and frilly white dress.

Moments later, however, it's Sunny who's watching from a seat in the sandbox, and Rebecca who's playing with Winifred. She wishes she weren't. They've moved on to the teeter-totter now and Winifred's dangling her high in the air.

"Put me down, Winifred! Put me down, you big bum, or I'll...!"

"Hmmm. Now let me see." Winifred flicks at some fluff on her yellow and white striped shirt. "Whatever shall I...?" She stares up into Rebecca's face. "Eenie, meenie, minie, mo. Catch a nigger by the..."

"Stop that!"

The kids all flinch. Marion's never yelled like that before.

"But we're not doing anything," sniffs Winifred. "We're only..."

"You can catch a tiger by the toe instead."

"Yes, well, my Mum taught me the verse and she says it goes...Eenie, meenie, minie..." Winifred begins to bump the teeter-totter on the ground.

"Winifred!...ugh." A jolt goes right up Rebecca's spine. "For the last time...ugh. Put...ugh...me...ugh!"

"Whatever you say, Rebecca." Winifred suddenly hops off her seat.

Rebecca goes crashing to the ground.

"I'm going to get you for that!" she screams, as she chases Winifred around the yard. "I'm going to rip your stupid blonde ropes right out of your...!"

"No, you're not. No, you're not. No, you're not."

When she finally decides Winifred's right, Rebecca marches over to the swing and starts pulling at the great big doll's hair instead. Soon there are curly red balls flying everywhere.

"You little brat!" wails Winifred. "You little..."

"Rebecca!" snaps Marion. "That's enough!"

"But she started it!"

"Never mind who started it. Now come over here and sit by me."

"Oh, all right." She shoves the doll off the swing and stomps over to the lawn chairs.

"I don't know what I'm going to do with you," hisses Vivian. "You're always getting into fights."

"So?"

Winifred scoops her doll out of the dirt, gapes for a moment at its filthy white frills, and then runs off towards home.

"Crybaby!" Rebecca hollers after her.

"Rebecca!" Vivian pulls her down into a little cream-coloured chair.

"Right," laughs Florence. "Now where were we?"

Rebecca folds her arms across her chest.

"Oh, yes." Florence winks at her. "The men. Is Gene going to rent a tux or...?"

"Uncle Gene's my favourite of all my uncles!" blurts Rebecca.

"Why is that?" asks Reverend MacKay.

"'Cause he promised to send me cans of lobsters for Christmas! After he moves away to be a Newfie!"

"Well, good." Marion makes another notation in her datebook. "Then you'll be glad to know you're going to be a flower girl at his wedding."

"Oh. Do I have to wear a dress?"

"Yes, you do."

Rebecca grimaces.

"You and Sunny will have the prettiest dresses there."

With that, Sunny gets up from her seat on the sandbox and wanders over to join them. "What colours will they be?" she asks quietly.

"Well, there'll be two layers. The bottom layer will be yellow, with a matching yellow headpiece."

Sunny's eyes light up.

"And the top layer will be white; a white, filmy material with little white flowers embroidered on it."

"Neat!"

"Yuck!"

The grown-ups all laugh.

"Whaaat's the maaatter, Rebeeeecca?" drawls Alice.

"I don't want to wear a pretty dress."

"Well, then, we'll get you an ugly one," sighs Marion.

"I don't want to wear *any* dress."

There's another round of laughter.

Rebecca suddenly sits up. "Will there be food?"

"Yes, there'll be food."

"Pop and chips?"

"Typical Henderson," snorts Evelyn. "Always thinking about her stomach. You'd think..."

"OK, then, maybe I'll come," interrupts Rebecca.

"Good." Marion shuts her datebook again. "Then I guess that's everything." She pushes herself out of her chair. "Now who wants more tea?" She begins to gather up the cups and saucers.

"Ha!" chuckles Florence. "Now that we've taken care of Gene,

Marion, when are we going to marry *you* off?"

"Yes, Marion," adds Kay. "Weren't you seeing the youngest Beveridge boy?"

"Oooh, my gaaawd!" drawls Alice. "Iiisn't heee the ooone who…?" Marion turns with her tray toward the driveway.

"Seriously, Marion," snickers Evelyn. "Don't you think it's time you…?"

As soon as she disappears around the side of the house, they all lean forward.

"Hasn't she ever been in love?" whispers Kay.

"Well," muses Florence. "I don't know whether you'd call it love or not, but there *was* Wes Hepburn. He stole her shoe at graduation or something."

"Yes, but that was ages ago."

"Whaaat does looove have to dooo with iiit?"

"Well, in your case, Alice," cackles Vivian. "Not much."

"I still don't see why she never married," insists Kay.

"She says she never met anyone *worth* marrying," murmurs Reverend MacKay.

They all look at him.

Bored again, this time with what she calls "the mushy stuff," Rebecca leaps up and swishes through the tall grass toward Ben. Along the way, she swats furiously at the gnats. They're the only thing she hates about the summer. Because of them, she usually spends it feeling like one huge, swollen lump.

When she reaches Ben, he's staring down into the pit. It's a big, deep hole he digs every spring — a new one, since luscious, dark green grass always grows back over the old ones. There's goopy garbage from the kitchen and the garden in there, with some chicken wire over it to keep the animals away. The paper stuff, he burns in the fireplace. The bottles and cans, he keeps in boxes in the woodhouse — to take to the dump on Millville Road.

"What's the matter?" he asks hoarsely.

"Bugs." She swats at another cloud of them.

"What bugs?"

It's what he always says.

The last time they were standing by the pit together, she asked him if he'd ever been bad. And he told her about the time he dared Rodney

Bent to eat a whole basket of bananas and the time he and Malcolm set fire to an abandoned barn back of the Masonic Hall — and then ran away. And she told him that she'd rather be the sort of person who burned down empty barns than the sort of person who made a retard eat three dozen bananas. And Ben agreed with her that sticking up for people was the most important thing in the whole wide world.

"Are you going to burn off any grass today, Ben?"

It's really the only way to keep the bugs away.

"Nope." He sucks on his empty billiard pipe. "Not until spring."

"Well, then, I'm going!" She marches back toward the lawn chairs.

"It's a shame about old Leander Blue," murmurs Kay, as she takes a sip of her tea.

"Yes," sighs Reverend MacKay. "He was a nice man."

"Real nice," agrees Rebecca, as she flops down again. She's going to miss that tiny old man with the thin white hair. He reminded her of a miniature Santa Claus.

"What'd he do for a living anyway?"

"Well..." Reverend MacKay wipes a drip from the lip of his cup. "He hadn't worked in years, of course, but they say he used to be a fireman on the boiler down at Scotian Gold."

"He put new handles on some knives for me once," adds Marion.

"Did he haaave any faaamily?"

"Oh, yes, Alice. A sister, I think. Or was that a daughter who used to come down from Armdale to visit?"

"Anyway, Marion." Florence gestures beyond the garage. "What are you going to do with the cabin now that Leander's passed away?"

It's a small white building, about ten feet by twelve, with a flat black roof and a white wooden brace to hold up the chimney. At the front, over the white wooden door, and the disproportionately large horizontal window, there's a façade, like those over the saloons and livery stables in the Old West movies.

"Well, what *can* she do with it?" Evelyn waves her hand dismissively. "Not many people would want to live in a place that doesn't have any...facilities."

"I could put my racoons in there!" blurts Rebecca.

"You haven't got any racoons," wheezes Vivian.

"Yes, but I *will* have. Randy says Darrell shot a mother racoon down at the dump yesterday and now there's two little babies that..."

"You aren't going to keep any racoons and that's that!"

"But Mu-um! They don't have anyone to take care of them!"

"I'm going to let Frankie Lewis live there," says Marion softly.

There's a moment of stunned silence. And then a burst of indignation.

"Marion!"

"Yooou're nooot!"

"What will people say?"

Reverend MacKay quietly sips his tea.

"I know what they'll say," huffs Evelyn. "They'll say she shouldn't be carrying on with…"

"Who says they're carrying on?"

"Carrying on with someone who's…"

"What's the matter with Frankie?" asks Rebecca.

"Well, nothing," splutters Evelyn. "Not really. In fact, I have nothing against…well…*them* in general. Although they're a little too…*niggerish*, for my tastes. It's just that…well, it's pretty uppity of him to never wear a T-shirt or jeans, don't you think? And living here…well…it's just not right, that's all. People should stick to their own…"

Marion gets up abruptly. "I'm going to drive Doris home."

"Can I come?" Rebecca jumps up, too.

"And me?" says Evelyn stiffly. "Remember, Marion. You promised to give me a ride."

Millville is only a ten-minute drive from Aylesford. To Rebecca, it's usually an exotic drive, through orchards and woodlots and farms. She usually finds the smell of blossoms or manure or freshly cut wood intoxicating. Today, however, she's too busy watching the adults to notice.

"Thank you, Marion," says Evelyn curtly, as the Buick glides to a stop.

Marion doesn't answer.

Rebecca looks from the back of one head to the back of the other head and then peers out of the window.

The nice, clean house on the corner belongs to Evelyn's parents Edson and Lydia. It's a two-storey house with a large, open veranda and a brand-new coat of gleaming white paint. Across the road is the log cabin that Doris rents. It's a small place — just a kitchen and a bedroom, really — but Doris says it's big enough for her and her son Andy, who lives there with her.

"Well," huffs Evelyn. "If that's the way you want to..." As soon as she heaves herself out of the car, it starts moving again.

She reaches out and slams the door. "But don't say I didn't warn you!"

By the time they roll up Doris's lane, the yellow Lab tied to a post outside the door is squealing.

"Shsh, girl. Shshsh. I told you it was her."

It isn't Andy who's leaning in the doorway. It's Milfred Parkes, the rural route mailman. He's a tall, fat, balding man with thick, grey-rimmed glasses and Rebecca's heard from Sunny that he and Doris are an "item" now.

"Thanks, Marion. You're an angel. Do you want to come in?"

"Not today, Doris. I think I'll just go right home."

"OK." Doris eases out the door. "Same day next week, then? I'll make my famous apple thing."

"Yaaaaaaay!" shouts Rebecca.

It's the best dessert in the whole wide world. Apples wrapped in pastry and soaked in syrup, with a huge white drift of whipping cream on top. She doesn't know whether she'll be able to wait.

"Yes. I'll pick you up," replies Marion, as she starts down the lane.

Once they slip back past the gristmill, the sawmill and the tannery, Rebecca begins to fidget.

"What's the matter with you?" sighs Marion.

"Well...nothing. Except I was wondering...are we really going right home?"

"Why?"

"Nothing. I just thought you might need gas."

"Ha! Come to think of it, I could use..." Marion suddenly applies the brakes.

"No! Not here!"

Up ahead, on the right, is Alex Hudgins's Car Repair. He does have a gas pump, and Rebecca likes how he's always covered from head to toe in black grease, but it's not the place she means.

"Just teasing." Marion releases the brake. "Just teasing."

A little further on, she does turn off the road, into the red, white and blue Irving station run by Kathleen and Tommy Kern.

"Yaaay!" shouts Rebecca, as she yanks on the door handle. "Yaaaaaaay!"

"Hi, Marion," calls Tommy. He shuffles toward the car. "What'll it be this nice, fine...? Whoa!"

Rebecca races by him.

"Slow down! Slow down! Or you'll break your neck!" He leans in the window. "Break *my* neck, at any rate."

"Fill it up, Tommy," laughs Marion.

"Be glad to." His eyes are twinkling.

A little later, when Marion and Tommy go inside to settle the bill, Rebecca is leaning on the counter, staring at Kathleen's assortment of home-made sandwiches and baked goods and pickles.

"I can't decide what to get, Marion! I can't decide between...!"

"Shsh. In a minute. How are you doing, Kathleen?"

"Good, Marion. Real good. I'm thinking of opening a shop in town, you know. Now that Lulu's old enough to help. I hear there's a place on Commercial Street that's gone vacant."

"Really? Well, that would be a nice change for..."

"Would you like to try one of those?" whispers Tommy.

Rebecca is peering into a large glass jar filled with browny white ovals.

"What are they?" she whispers back.

"Pickled eggs."

She keeps peering.

"No, thank you," she answers at last.

She wouldn't try a pickled egg if he paid her. But she has to admit they're the neatest things there.

15

Rebecca is clambering over the big, black, moulded rocks along the shore at Morden. It's even trickier than usual, since she's clutching a straggly bunch of buttercups and daisies and dangling Sunny's brand-new Brownie Starmite around her neck. She wanted to swim today. She even put on her stretchy, beige bathing suit. But it's way too cold. It's almost always too cold. So she just kneels for a moment, on one of the darkest, slipperiest rocks, and peers out into the bay.

"Brrrrr." It's not long before she's scrambling back over the field of stones which forms the beach. "Brrr. Brrr. Brrr."

When she reaches the gently sloping rocks near the cliff, she finds a dry spot for the wildflowers and the box camera and then plops down in the little brook which is trickling through the crevices. It's a lot warmer, gentler, safer than the sea.

"Weeeee! Yeaaaaah!" She splashes around in it.

Looming overhead is a cross made out of beach stones. Rebecca glances up at it. Marion's told her the story about that cross. About how it's a monument to some expelled Acadians who spent the winter there, on the shores of that cold and windy bay, waiting for passage. And then about how it's also a monument to what Marion called "separated lovers," like Evangeline and Gabriel, who didn't find each other until he lay dying.

Suddenly, there's a peal of laughter. Rebecca looks up.

Marion and Frankie are standing by the stone cross, talking and giggling and jostling one another.

Rebecca's surprised. She thought no one else would be here. Marion said it was probably too cold for anyone else to be here.

"Stay there!" shouts Rebecca.

"What?"

"I said...!"

The wind whips up. Marion puts her hand to her ear.

"Oh, brother." Rebecca grabs the camera and scrambles up the hill.

"What did you say?" laughs Marion, when at last she reaches them. "We couldn't hear..."

Rebecca squints into the viewfinder.

"Oh, no, you don't!" Marion turns her face away. "Don't you dare take our picture!"

"Why not?"

Frankie wanders away.

"Because...because my hair's a mess!"

Frankie bends down and picks up an empty purple shell.

"No, it isn't! It's the same as it always..."

The wind whips up again. Frankie gazes out to sea.

At dusk, the beach is deserted. And the sun is hanging, red and proud, like the last ripe apple that no one can pick. And then, suddenly, there's a great commotion and the six Peterson kids are stampeding down the hill. Behind them, walking more slowly and calmly, is Marion. She's carrying a bunch of pointed sticks in one hand and an enormous black pot in the other. The rest of the grown-ups are up above, in Lizzie Peterson's cottage, trying, as Vivian always says, to out-drink and out-lie one another.

As soon as they find a fairly flat spot, the kids rip open their paper bags and dump the supplies onto the stones. There are wieners and buns and marshmallows and ears of corn and little yellow plastic pokers shaped like cobs, for sticking in the ends of the real cobs so no fingers will get burnt.

"OK," pants Marion. "Who's going to gather the wood?"

"I will, I will!" bellows Peter.

"And the rocks?"

Nobody answers.

"We have to have rocks."

"Get Darrell to do it," snickers Donnie. "He's the biggest."

"Yeah," sneers Darrell. "And you're the dumbest."

The boys start shoving one another. Sunny wanders over to help Peter.

"What can *we* do, Marion?" asks Rebecca, who's been left behind with Randy.

"Well...you can take the husks off the corn."

"That's no fun."

Marion laughs. "Then you can open up the buns and the wieners."

"OK."

The buns are from the Berwick Bakery. They look like slices of bread that have been folded over and then pinched at the corners. The wieners are from Larsen's. Each one is wrapped in its very own little plastic jacket.

"I love hot dogs," whispers Rebecca.

"Me, too," Randy whispers back.

"I wish we got them at home."

"Yes, well, you won't get them here either, if you don't hurry up and..."

They tear open the bags with their teeth.

As soon as they peel off the first little plastic jacket, they start giggling and elbowing one another.

"What's so funny?" asks Marion.

"Nothing," giggles Randy.

"Do you always laugh about nothing?"

"Yes!" Rebecca takes a bite off the end of her wiener.

The flames are leaping around the big black pot of boiling water.

"Don't get too close, Rebecca," pleads Marion.

They're all sitting in a circle around the crackling fire.

"Why?"

"Because you'll burn yourself."

"No, I won't." She drops a plastic wrapper into the flames. It immediately shrivels and turns black.

"Look!" marvels Darrell. "Just like lava!"

"Yeah!"

"Neat!"

"Let *me* try!"

They all drop wrappers into the flames.

Suddenly, from up above in Lizzie's cottage, comes a torrent of laughing and screaming and coughing.

"Sounds like *they're* having a good time," murmurs Sunny.

There's a moment of sad and sullen silence, except for the spitting of the flames. And then Marion claps her hands.

"Well, come on, everybody! It's time for marshmallows!"

Soon they're all jabbing creamy white puffs onto sticks.

"I like mine burnt," announces Rebecca, as she thrusts it into the flames.

"So do I," snuffles Peter.

"Well, not burnt exactly, but all crispy and black on the outside and all gooey and white on the inside."

"Not me." Sunny is turning hers slowly, carefully, just above the flames. "I like mine a light brown."

"But that takes too long!" cries Rebecca. "By the time you've eaten *one*, everybody else has eaten …!"

"Never mind that!" interrupts Donnie. "Who's got the pop?"

"Here it is!" shouts Randy.

Moments later, they're passing a gigantic bottle of Nesbitt's Orange around the fire. It's a silent communion. Each of them takes a sip and then, wordlessly, passes it on.

"Oooo! It's gone up my nose!"

The spell is broken.

"You're not supposed to put your whole mouth around it, dummy. You're supposed to..."

Suddenly, there's a crackle and then a crack, as a cinder leaps out of the fire.

"Ow!" Marion puts her hand to her mouth.

"Are you all right, Marion?"

"Where did it get you?"

"Let me see!"

She points to her upper lip.

"Here." The voice is as deep as the shadows surrounding it. "Let me kiss it better."

"Is that who I think it is?"

"Where did *he* come from?"

"He's not *really* going to, is he?"

There's a great deal of gasping and giggling as Frankie actually starts moving out of the shadows toward Marion. "Shame, shame."

"Oooooo!"

But then Marion springs to her feet. "Oh, no, you don't! It's not *that* bad!" And flees toward the water.

Marion and Frankie are standing together near the water. Most of the kids are dozing by the fire. All except Rebecca, that is, who's listening to the squabbling coming from up above.

"Hey! It's *my* turn!"

"Let go of my leg!"

"Jesus, it's cold!"

The rest of the kids sit up.

It seems the grown-ups have stumbled out of Lizzie's cottage and are now climbing on the stone cross.

"Oh, God, Frankie." Marion touches his sleeve. "Maybe you better..." He slips back into the shadows.

"Get down!" Wanda tries to pull Harold off the cross. "Give somebody else a...!"

"Oh, look. How sweet. A little bunch of buttercups and daisies." Clary slumps to the ground.

"Sentimental old bastard," chuckles Filly.

"Ha!" snorts Florence. "He's just too pickled to stand."

"Hey, everybody! Look at me!" Harold has escaped Wanda's grasp and is now towering above the cross, with a foot on each stone bar. "I'm John...John...! What the hell was that fellow's name? Florence? Vivian? Jesus, Wanda, your tits look even bigger from up...whoa-oa!"

"He's going to fall!" gasps Sunny, as he sways a little.

"No, he isn't," snorts Darrell. "He never falls."

Rebecca's eyes are shining. "He's been up millions of ladders at millions of houses and he's never fallen yet," she boasts.

Sunny crosses her fingers.

"I'm the Strong Man of Morden!" roars Harold. "The Samson of Nova Scotia! I can carry two-hundred-pound bags of flour under each arm! I can lift an anchor with...! Oh, hi, kids!" He's spotted them down below. "How the hell are ya doing? Are ya behaving yourselves?"

"Yes, Daddy!" they cry in unison.

"Well, good! Don't do anything I wouldn't dooooooo!" Harold throws back his head and howls.

Marion gazes out to sea.

Rebecca stares at the patch of brown grass where the swing set used to be.

It lost its parts gradually. First, the paint cracked. And then the metal rusted away. And then the screws fell out. And then whole parts went missing...a seat, a crossbar, a handle, a long silver chain...until she was left with nothing but that old rubber tire hanging from the maple tree at home. And the devil's paintbrushes, of course.

"Black paint. Black paint. God! I have to get the right book!" She pushes herself up from the lawn chair and goes inside.

When she gets to the back chamber again, it's not quite as stuffy as when she left. There's a little breeze sifting through the screen on the back window.

Chink. Chink.

"Oh, shut up."

She knows what's making that sound. She just doesn't want to look at it.

16

"It's just for one more night," her Mum keeps telling her. "Just until your Dad puts on the second coat of..."

The first few days of school, Harold pretends he's painting the inside of their house, but he and Vivian are really on their end-of-summer binge. Rebecca doesn't mind. She gets to stay overnight at Marion's, on the cot in the upstairs hall. And in the morning, she gets to set the black arborite table with Lotte dishes — thick white bowls with cheerful blue Norwegians painted on them. And start the Dripolator going on the stove. And make sure Ben's can of evaporated milk is waiting for him by his place near the door. And she gets to drink real chocolate milk, delivered in the dark by an Acadia Dairy truck, and choose between Shreddies and Special K — and maybe even porridge with brown sugar and whipping cream on it. And she gets to feed the birds.

She used to just throw the hunks of stale bread on the ground. But then Marvin Bennett made a large wooden tray, with a wire, so it could hang from the Bishop Pippin apple tree. Now she slips across the driveway, overturns the bagful of ripped bits onto the tray and then slips across the driveway again.

On this particular morning, she's standing alone in the kitchen, watching the birds eat. Her favourites are the sparrows. Everybody says they're common and drab — just about the homeliest birds there are — but she thinks they're cute. And she *knows* they have the best voices. Not like those mean, ugly, noisy...

"Oh-oh."

She can see through the window that the starlings are being mean again, chasing the sparrows away from the feeder.

"Shoo! Shoo!" She leans over and bangs on the glass.

But it doesn't work the way she wants it to and *all* of the birds, not just the starlings, dart away.

"It's not fair," she mutters.

Because their house is right there, on the corner of School Street and Old Post Road, Sunny and Rebecca don't have far to walk to school. They don't always cover the distance quickly, however, especially on the mornings they've promised to wait for Winifred.

"Where *is* she?" grumbles Rebecca, as she wiggles the post for the wooden street sign.

"I don't know." Sunny squints across the road. "She's probably got her nose buried in a book or something. You know Winifred."

"But we're going to be late!"

"You go ahead, then. I'll catch up."

"No!" Rebecca throttles the post. "I want to walk to school with you!"

"Look! Here she comes! At least, I think that's Winifred."

A girl with yellow pigtails is wheeling a shiny new bicycle across the road.

"Gee," murmurs Rebecca. "Look how pretty it is! Like the sky!"

Winifred wheels right up to them. "It's a Norman," she announces proudly. "From England."

"When did you get it?" marvels Sunny, as she peers at herself in the silver bell attached to the handlebars.

"For my birthday, silly." Winifred hesitates for a moment, then begins to wheel it down the dusty side road.

"I'm going to get a bike for *my* birthday!" exclaims Rebecca, before very long.

"No, you're not," smirks Winifred. "You're too little."

"Am not."

"Are, too."

"Am not."

"And sooo childish." Winifred wheels a little faster.

Sunny scurries to keep up.

"Yeah, well, I bet I can ride better than you can!" Rebecca hollers after them.

She's standing all alone, in the middle of the dusty side road, scowling. She doesn't think Winifred *deserves* a bike. Not when she already has a tow truck — a yellow Bedford tow truck, with tiny black wipers and a bright red winch, that she never lets anyone ride. And not when *she's* still stuck with a tricycle. It's a pretty good one — big, dark blue, with hubcaps on the wheels and a pouch hanging from the seat and a silver bell, which she rings over and over as she pedals around the sandpit — but it's still just a tricycle. You can't really get anywhere on it. Not far, not fast.

"Ha! Don't be silly!" Winifred turns a little red, but she keeps on wheeling.

"Well, if you're so hot, let's *see* you!" yells Rebecca.

"No. That wouldn't be polite."

"C'mon! I dare you! Let's see you ride it!"

"No!" Winifred hooks her free arm through Sunny's. "I want to walk to school with my friend."

"Ha!" shouts Rebecca. "I told you! You can't even ride the stupid thing! And it's only got twenty-four inch wheels! Mine's going to have twenty-six!" She races to catch up to them.

Sunny and Winifred are best friends this year. For the time being anyway. Until the novelty of the swings at Marion's place wears off. In the meantime, they certainly don't have much in common. Sunny, who has a rough-and-tumble side as well as a royal side, would much rather play outside than read a book. Skipping, free the bunch, baseball, hide and seek, dreaming about Prince Charles while swinging on an old black tire...anything that's fun; that leaves her sweaty and out of breath. Winifred, on the other hand, is always reading a book. She's also a little standoffish about games, as if all the squealing and laughing might be mistaken for vulgarity. And she hates vulgarity, she tells anyone who'll listen. Almost as much as she hates mess. Her teachers are always commenting on how neat her scribblers are.

"Would you look at that!" smirks Winifred, as they approach the schoolyard.

"What?"

"Look who's ringing the handbell today."

"So?"

"So she smells!"

Catherine McClare is standing in the middle of the schoolyard, looking like she's done something wrong. Rebecca's puzzled. The principal usually picks kids from the upper grades to ring the bell. Or maybe kids who have the nerve to ask or kids who get in the nineties on their reading tests. But Catherine has a hard time getting thirty-seven. She even has a hard time with her colours. Just like the other thirteen kids in her family.

"Why don't you take a bath?" sniffs Winifred, as she and Sunny draw a little nearer.

"Winifred!" Sunny unhooks her arm. "They don't have a bathtub!"

"So?"

"So you're a meanie!" cries Rebecca.

Catherine lives in a draughty, overcrowded shack on Pierce Road, just down from Stronach's place. It's really just a plywood box with sagging floors, a rotting stovepipe and cement blocks to hold the roof down. There's no insulation, no electricity and no bathtub.

"Oh, sorry." Winifred carefully folds down her kickstand. "I forgot. It isn't nice to tease a retard."

Sunny takes a deep breath. "She's not a retard, Winifred. She's just slow."

"Oh, really? What's the difference? Hey, retard! Are you just going to stand there or are you going to...?"

As soon as she sees those yellow pigtails moving toward her, Catherine starts lifting and lowering her arm, over and over, like a robot.

"Way to go, Catherine!" shouts Rebecca, as the bell resounds throughout the schoolyard.

Catherine grins at her. Rebecca grins back. And then swipes at Winifred's kickstand. The sky-blue Norman clatters to the ground.

Their mood of celebration lasts until some of the older boys start circling around Catherine.

"Your father makes babies with his daughters," taunts Ricky MacNair.

"You're next. You're next," hisses Stevie Cleveland, as he brushes past her.

Catherine almost drops the bell.

And then, as if that isn't enough, Dwayne Melanson comes pedalling into the yard.

"Oh-oh, here comes Bubba."

Dwayne is only five, but fairly big for his age. He says he's going to race Harley-Davidsons when he grows up, but he hasn't even got the hang of his bicycle yet.

"I don't think he can find the..."

As he hurtles toward them, it's obvious he's fumbling for the brakes. When it's equally obvious he isn't going to be able to stop in time, he just leaps off the bike and lets it skid and scrape across the ground.

There's a cloud of dust and stones. The circle of kids scatters.

"Swift, Bubba. Real swift."

"Yeah, you tub of lard!" Ricky grabs him by the shirt. "Watch it!"

"No, you watch it!" Dwayne slaps at Ricky's hand.

Before a fight can break out, however, there's a loud wail.

"My new pants!" Ian Baltzer is in tears. "Look what you've done to my new pants!"

Ricky takes a few playful swipes at Ian's dusty trousers. "My new pants!" He imitates Ian's high, nasal voice. "Look what you've done to my new pants!"

Everyone laughs.

"Sissy."

"Fruit."

"Quit it or I'm telling!"

Catherine, meanwhile, keeps ringing the handbell. It's the longest it's ever been rung.

There was a time, Rebecca's been told, when Aylesford School was a one-room wooden schoolhouse for all the grades. But then the town added a white wooden part onto the north side and a red artificial-brick part onto the south side and sent the high school kids off to West Kings in Auburn. The large wooden part is now the Big Kids end. It's divided into three classrooms — one for Kay Armstrong's fours and fives; one for Herbert Armstrong's sixes; and one which is empty. The artificial-brick part, which the Little Kids get, only has two classrooms — one for Peggy Blackburn's beginners and ones; the other for Myrna Hamilton's twos and threes. There are washrooms in the middle.

Rebecca looks up at the sign. AYLESFORD SCHOOL SECTION NO. 108, and then follows Sunny and Winifred into the red artificial-brick part. As soon as she gets inside, into the long, narrow hallway where the coat rack is, she makes a face. School smells like it always smells — like Dustbane.

"It must be ground right down into the floorboards," she murmurs, as she drapes her fuzzy, dark green jacket over a wooden hanger.

It's her favourite jacket — mostly because of the camel-coloured lining — but she likes her underneath clothes, too. Her dark brown corduroy pants. And her flashy new jersey, which Marion brought back from Halifax last month. It has blue and red fish on it. And men wearing big yellow hats and playing bongos and tambourines. She doesn't think she'll ever see real fish with colours that crazy — let alone play one of those wild, exotic instruments — but she sure likes the shirt. And no one else in her class has anything like it.

She adds her jacket to the ones already dangling from the long wooden pole and then takes a deep breath. There isn't anything special about the hall today, but Sunny says that, in the wintertime, when the coats stay soaked for days, it'll smell like wet wool — and Dustbane, of course.

"See you at dinnertime!" she calls to Sunny and Winifred.

They're heading toward Miss Hamilton's class, where they're in grade three together.

"If you're lucky," drawls Winifred, as they duck inside.

Beginners, Rebecca tells anyone who'll listen, isn't like kindergarten at other places. They don't just play with toys, take naps, eat Arrowroot cookies and then go home after half a day. It's real school, with reading and writing and everything. Mr. Armstrong, who's also the principal, calls it "primer" because, he says, it prepares them for life. Only the way he pronounces it, it rhymes with "swimmer."

Mrs. Blackburn's classroom is a light and airy place. This is partly due to the four gigantic windows, which look out onto the scruffy play area at the back of the school, and partly due to the walls, which are pale green on the wooden part, from the floor to half-way up, and then white on the plaster part, which extends to the ceiling. In fact, the walls wouldn't look like they belonged to a classroom at all if it weren't for the two big blackboards — one for beginners and the other for grade one — which today are missing that distinctive white film they always have before Mrs. Armstrong uses kerosene on them.

When everyone is present, there are thirty-one kids in the classroom — sixteen in beginners and fifteen in grade one. Rebecca's counted them all, including her brother Randy. She likes having him in the same room with her, even if he is on the other side and has trouble getting his letters in the right order.

"OK, everyone."

Mrs. Blackburn is standing in the doorway, surveying the swarm of kids. The only neat thing about her, Rebecca's already decided, is her wandering eye.

"It's time to settle…Children!" She claps her hands. "That's better. Now take your seats, please."

The kids don't have separate desks. They won't have those until Grade Three. Instead, they sit on dark brown wooden chairs at dark brown wooden tables — with drawers, Rebecca always mentions, whenever anyone says it sounds boring to them. There are six tiny chairs at each long, low table, but at least two of them are always empty.

"Now." Mrs. Blackburn scans the tables.

"Yes, teacher?" asks Catherine McClare nervously.

Sometimes, with that wandering eye, the kids can't tell if Mrs. Blackburn's looking at anyone in particular.

Mrs. Blackburn smiles. "The Lord's Prayer, Catherine."

"Oh."

Thirty-one tiny chairs scrape across the wooden floor.

The morning subjects are always the same — arithmetic and silent reading, with spelling and reading out loud saved for the afternoon. Rebecca does well in all of them. She smiles to herself as she remembers that her first progress report indicated both "excellent work" *and* "perfect adjustment." At least that's what Mrs. Blackburn told Marion at the Home and School meeting which Vivian was too drunk to attend. Rebecca could be bored, since Marion's already taught her to read and the numbers come so much easier to her than to the other kids. But she's not. It's fun to be with the kids. In the same room with them, at the same table with them, grumbling and giggling about the very same things. She looks at the kids who share her table — Kenny Jackson, Dwayne Melanson and Brenda Taylor, the new girl no one knows too well. She isn't looking forward to growing up and having a separate desk.

"Mrs. Blackburn?"

Bubba has his hand up.

"What is it, Dwayne?"

He clambers to his feet. "Rebecca's using a pen!" he announces.

There's a mixture of gasping and giggling.

"Rebecca, is that true?"

"Yes."

Mrs. Blackburn strolls over to the table. "Rebecca..." She stares down at the page of additions and subtractions, all of which have been done in red ink. "I thought I told you to use a pencil."

"I know, but why?"

"So you can rub out your mistakes."

"But I don't make mistakes."

"Rebecca." Mrs. Blackburn takes the pen away. "Sooner or later, everybody makes mistakes. Now use a pencil."

There's a brief pause.

"Pardon?"

"Yes, Mrs. Blackburn." Rebecca reaches into the drawer of her table. The teacher strides to the front of the room.

"Serves you right, you little..." Dwayne can't resist peeking over Rebecca's shoulder. "Mrs. Blackburn!" His eyes are as big as dessert plates.

"I don't want to hear it, Dwayne."

"But Mrs. Blackburn! Rebecca's..."

"Get back to work!"

He slumps into his chair.

"Tattletale," hisses Rebecca.

"Cheater," he hisses back.

The sums on Rebecca's new page are a bright and saucy green.

"Oh, no! My bicycle! Someone's knocked over my bicycle!" Winifred starts wailing the minute she gets outside at recess.

Rebecca squats down in the sandy soil near the driveway. "That's too bad, Winifred."

Morning recess is from 10:15 to 10:30. It's only September but already the kids have routines. Some of them wander to the scrubby area out back to play baseball, with the balls and bats they've brought from home. Others race past the Big Kids end to the hill on the north side of the building, where it's fun to slide on flattened cardboard boxes. Others skip rope on the bald area out front or mill about on the gravel driveway, smoking and sometimes ducking behind the teachers' cars.

"My bicycle! My bicycle!"

Rebecca starts tracing a circle in the sandy soil.

"My brand-new...!"

"Wanna play?"

Randy and his best friend Roddy Warner are lugging the crokinole board across the yard. It's the only thing the school provides in the way of games or toys. There aren't any balls and bats and beanbags, let alone any musical instruments — like those blocks and triangles Rebecca hears they have in the Halifax schools. Or like those bongos and tambourines she has on her favourite shirt.

"No, thanks." Rebecca keeps tracing.

"Why not, creep?" yells Roddy.

Rebecca squints up at him. Roddy's supposed to have a crush on her. At least that's what Sunny keeps telling her. She doesn't exactly know what a crush is, but she wonders whether it means he has to yell at her all the time.

"Because you always fight," she finally answers.

"What's wrong with that?" He gives Randy a little shove.

"Hey!" Randy shoves him back.

Before long, they're jostling each other across the yard.

Rebecca watches them for a moment, wondering whether Roddy's really going to grow up to be that big-shot politician he says he is, and then reaches into the pocket of her pants and pulls out a handful of marbles.

Most of them are *glassies*, with twists or speckles of colour. But there's also a large, opaque, yellow *boulder* she uses as a shooter and a few white peewees that are good for targets. She has an *orange custard*, a *purple shag* and a *green vaseline*, too, but she keeps those at home. There's always a chance she'll be really smelly one day and lose them all.

"Right there, Mr. Armstrong! See?"

"Yes, yes, Winifred. But are you sure it didn't just...?"

Rebecca places a peewee at the far end of the circle, balances the boulder between her thumb and her forefinger and then...flick, click. The peewee skitters off to the side.

"Hey, you're pretty good!" gushes Brenda Taylor. She and Alan Rawding have wandered over to watch.

"Thanks."

"So maybe you could..." Brenda sits down beside her. "Well, me and Alan thought that maybe you could teach us..."

"Breeen-daaa! Don't you get your dress dirty!"

Brenda and Rebecca roll their eyes. It's Brenda's older brother Donnie. The kids have already sized him up as a sissy — the goody-goody boy scout, bookworm type, who plays on your swings when you don't want him to and cries his eyes out when you push him down in the dirt at baseball games and isn't at all like Rebecca's brother Donnie.

"Brenda! Did you hear what I said?"

"Yes, Donnie!" She lowers her voice. "You big poop."

Rebecca smiles with approval. And then gives each of them a handful of glassies. Within seconds, there's a flurry of loud, sharp clicks.

"My Daddy sells Chevies in Middleton," says Alan proudly, as he sets up the targets again. "What's your Daddy do?"

Brenda leans over the dusty circle. "My Daddy sells wieners."

Rebecca giggles.

"In a store?" asks Alan.

"No, he drives a big red Fairlane with two black doors and SWIFT painted on the side."

"Neat! Wait till I tell Winifred! Her Daddy sells groceries from Windsor to Bridgetown, for R.B. Seton or something, but he doesn't get a car out of it!"

"What about your Daddy, Rebecca?"

"Well, my Daddy..." She's concentrating on a peewee at the far end of the circle.

"Your Daddy's a drunk."

Rebecca squints upward. Howie Shelton, whose parents are bootleggers, is standing over them.

"Is not."

"Is, too. He's always over at my place picking up..."

"I don't know if I have a Daddy or not." It's the high, nasal voice of Ian Baltzer.

"Ha!" Howie begins to mimic him. "I don't know if I have a..."

But the mocking is drowned by the roar of a big grey plane. They all look up. Big grey planes fly overhead, day and night, and the kids always look up. Usually it's just another Argus, on its way to CFB

Greenwood, but even that's a little scary. Ben Kelly once told them that an Argus has a hundred eyes. And that it uses them to spy on little children when they're bad.

Suddenly, there's a commotion at the far side of the yard.

"It's *my* turn, you little wiener!" Stevie Cleveland shoves Gavin Sturk in the chest.

"Hey!" Rebecca's brother Darrell leaps between them. "Pick on someone your own size."

Stevie eyeballs Gavin. He's smart and he's quiet, but he's not a pipsqueak.

"He *is* my own size, dummy."

"Oh-oh." Rebecca knows what's coming.

"What did you call me?" Darrell shoves Stevie in the chest.

"Nothing."

There's usually fighting when the Petersons are around. But this time, since it's Darrell who organized the game — and he's the biggest one there — things calm down quickly.

"OK." Darrell draws a line in the dirt with his foot. "Whose turn is it? Gavin?"

"No. It's OK."

"Aw, c'mon."

Gavin steps reluctantly up to the line.

"Now, remember..." Darrell claps him on the back. "The closest to that stone marker wins."

He always runs two contests — one for distance, the other for accuracy.

"Ready?"

There's a long pause.

"Ready, Gavin?"

A crowd gathers.

"Gavin! What the hell are you waiting for?"

"I don't know how!" he whispers.

"Oh, for...Jesus Murphy!" Darrell throws his hands into the air. "That'll teach me to let Juniors into the contest. What do you mean you don't know how?"

Just as Rebecca's about to leap to her feet, Linda Durling, a tiny grade-one girl with fuzzy brown hair, rushes up to the line. "I know! I know!" she squeals.

"Hey!"

"What's the big idea?"

"I thought you said no girls!"

Darrell gazes down at Linda.

"Well, I changed my mind. Any objections? Go ahead, Linda."

With that, Linda rolls her saliva into a tight, little frothy ball and then spits. The gob lands right on the marker.

"Yeaaaaah!" shouts Rebecca.

"I don't believe it!"

"She won!"

"God." Darrell shakes his head. "Beaten by a girl."

"Too bad, sucker," sneers Stevie Cleveland, as the handbell begins to ring.

"Yeah, well, wait until tomorrow." Darrell kicks at the line in the dirt. "She'll never get it as *far* as me."

After recess, it's silent reading time. Rebecca's already gone through the readers with Marion — the red one, the green one and the blue one — but she doesn't mind doing them again. She enjoys the adventures of Tom, Betty and Susan. They have nice parents and a neat little dog named Flip.

"Psst." It's Danny Stronach from the next table. "Psst!"

"What!" She glares up at him.

"I'm going to get you!"

"No, you're not." She looks back down at the page.

"Yes, I am!"

Danny lives on Pierce Road, in a little house that's part trailer and part freight car. He's one of twelve tiny kids and has an even bigger crush on her than Roddy Warner. Lately, he's been chasing her around the schoolyard, trying to kiss her.

"Right on the..."

"OK, everyone," Mrs. Blackburn suddenly announces. "I have to leave the room for a few minutes. Just continue what you're doing."

Rebecca makes sure Mrs. Blackburn's really gone, then turns to Danny and smirks. "No, you're not, squirt."

"Wanna bet?"

"Fat chance! You can't even run as fast as your Mum!"

As soon as she says it, she's sorry. Danny's mother Hilda is in a wheelchair. She can't even make it uptown by herself. She has to get her husband Ralph, who's scrawny and has a patch over one eye, to push her there.

"Yeah, well..." Danny's feelings are hurt. "At least she's not a drunk."

"Yes!" Mrs. Blackburn's voice cracks from the door.

The kids jump in their seats.

"And that's what you'll *all* grow up to be..." Mrs. Blackburn marches back into the room,"...if you don't finish your reading! Hanna?"

"What did I do?" squeals Hanna Clem. "*I'm* not a drunk!"

Alan, Catherine and Howie all giggle.

"Nothing, girl. Now sit up straight. You've been chosen to press the buzzers after school."

"Oh."

Hanna doesn't sound impressed with this honour.

"Well..."

Rebecca gawks over at the next table, where Hanna is sitting. She's a tall, dark-haired girl who lives up School Street, next to Sammie Gates. Her father Merrill is what Ben calls "fairly ordinary." Medium build. Wavy-brown hair. A nine-to-five job at the air base in Greenwood. But her mother Gerda is as wild and crazy as Elsie Smeltzer, one of Vivian's favourite drinking buddies — even if her kinky brown hair and pudgy round face do make her look like Shirley Temple. One of Gerda's wildest stunts was naming her seventh child Thumper, after the rabbit in the Disney movie.

No wonder pressing the buzzers isn't a dream come true for Hanna, thinks Rebecca, as they all wait for Hanna's answer. After all, Hanna's grown up with Thumper.

"No, thank you," says Hanna politely.

They're all stunned. All, that is, except Rebecca, who immediately thrusts her hand into the air. "I'll do it! Can I do it?"

"I don't see why not," sighs Mrs. Blackburn.

Rebecca beams.

Danny leans over and whispers. "Right...on...the...lips."

17

"*Northern Spy. Crimson Beauty. Golden Delicious. Gravenstein,*" chants Rebecca, as the Buick barrels along the Back Road.

It's after school in mid-September, and Marion is taking Randy, Rebecca, Frankie, Peter and Marsha Luddington, the grade-four girl who has a crush on Peter, up to Swinnimer's apple orchards. They actually have peaches, pears and plums there, too, but Rebecca likes the apples best — especially the crisp and juicy, sour-sweet Gravensteins.

As she drives, Marion tells them again why she especially likes going to the Swinnimer's. The regular pickers, she reminds everyone, come from places like Dogpatch or Yoho, where people live in tar-paper shacks without plumbing or electricity. Unlike most farmers, however, the Swinnimers don't take advantage of them; don't expect them to work twelve hours a day, seven days a week, for peanuts. The Swinnimers even try to find them jobs at the peat plant or at Larsen's packers when the picking season is over.

"OK, OK."

Rebecca doesn't care about all this. She just wants to get there. For her, this is a chance to earn a little pocket money. She isn't old enough to do the actual picking, but she can manage the picking up. She won't get paid as much for gathering the apples that have fallen to the ground as the grown-ups will for removing the ones still hanging from the branches. But she'll still make enough for a bag of Scotties or a handful of Chickenbones.

The only problem is the bees.

"Get away!" cries Randy, as Peter and Marsha drag a tall wooden barrel toward the next tree. "Shoo! Get away!" He swats at the air.

"What's the matter, Randy?" laughs Rebecca. "Aren't you having any fun?"

"No!" He keeps swatting.

"Well, it's better than picking strawberries."

"No, it isn't."

"Yes, it is."

"Aaaaaaagh!"

In early July, Randy and Rebecca went strawberry picking at Vesta Perry's place on Commercial Street, a mile or so north of town. Vesta is a wiry woman with short-cropped hair who puts her hands on her hips a lot. In fact, she did that as soon as they got there — put her hands on her hips and roared that they were too young to pick; that they had to be at least seven. But then Marion came and lied about their ages and Vesta gave in. Rebecca wishes she hadn't. She and Randy didn't think picking strawberries was any fun at all. First, there were too many daddy longlegs crawling all over them. And then the inching up and down the hill rows hurt their knees. And then Vesta put her hands on her hips again and shouted that she didn't want any crybabies working for her. So she and Randy had to stay.

"Aaaaagh!" cries Randy. "I'm getting out of here!"

"Scab!" hollers Peter, as he overturns the tall wooden barrel.

Marsha brushes his hand with hers. "And maggot, too. Right, Peter?"

Randy's still swatting as he disappears into the car.

Rebecca looks to the left and to the right, to make sure nobody's watching her, and then up through the branches, to make sure nothing's hiding overhead, and then slowly climbs the ladder. Once at the top, she tries to keep herself very luscious and still, like an apple. But she feels more like a tiny bird perched in the branches, nervous about sparrow hawks, about BB guns, about...

"What's that?" She holds her breath and listens.

There's bristling in the branches of the next tree.

She waits for a second, to give herself the chance to chicken out and climb back down again...and then leans forward and peeks through the leaves.

"It's Frankie and Marion," she whispers.

She watches Frankie reach up to the branch near his face and pull down a big red apple with yellow streaks. She watches him polish it on his sleeve and offer it to Marion. She watches Marion hesitate and then take a bite and then offer it back to him. She watches Frankie take a turn and then Marion again and then Frankie and then Marion until the juice is running down their chins and there's nothing left of the apple but the core.

"Pretty dumb game, if you ask...Aaaaagh! Get away!"

"Rebecca?" Marion calls out nervously. "Is that you? Rebecca? Frankie, I think you better..."

"Aaaaagh! Help!" Rebecca scrambles down the ladder. "Help!"

As she spins around and around, swatting at bees, Frankie drops gracefully to the ground. He's already moved four trees over by the time Mr. Swinnimer shows up.

"Rebecca!"

She stops spinning. "What?"

"Come over here a minute!"

She runs to him. "What?"

He points to a tall wooden barrel. "What are these?" he tries to ask sternly.

"Apples."

"But what kind of apples?"

"I don't know. You told me to pick up the apples and I did."

"Yes, but not the wormy, rotten ones."

"Oh. Well, no one told us. No one...Do I still get paid?"

Mr. Swinnimer bursts into laughter.

"It's not *all* my fault, you know. Randy picked them up, too."

"I bet he did."

"Before the bees came and he went to sit in the car."

"Yes, well. Help me sort through these." Mr. Swinnimer picks a bad apple out of the barrel.

"Are you going to fire me?" Rebecca picks one out, too.

"No."

"You're way nicer than Mrs. Perry, then." She drops her apple to the ground. "*She* fired me."

"And why did she do that?"

"She said I filled the boxes too full."

Mr. Swinnimer bursts into laughter again.

They've just begun to replenish the barrel with good apples when Rebecca feels a pang of loss. "Where do they all go anyway?"

"These are going to Berwick, to the Graves plant. Of course, in the old days, we just shipped them down the road to the United Fruit Company."

"Hey! That's the place my Grampy Newell used to run!"

"That's right. And it was going great guns, too, especially during the war, when it made all kinds of jams and preserves — and apple juice for the troops overseas. But then your grandfather...well, let's just say he got his notice and another fellow reorganized it into a Scotian Gold cooperative and it failed up."

"Yeah! And now it's all burnt down! Right to the cinder blocks! My brother Donnie told me that mean old Barry and Drew go over there all the time to smoke and drink and...Oh, yeah! Once he...once Drew...!"

"Slow down! Slow down!" Mr. Swinnimer tops up the barrel.

"Once Drew fell right through a hole into the old basement!"

"Is that a fact!" he chuckles.

"Yeah, but..." She sounds disappointed. "He didn't break anything, though."

Marion, who's gone back to picking now, starts chuckling too.

"Hey! What's so funny?" Rebecca looks from Mr. Swinnimer to the tree where Marion is and back. "What's so...? Forget it." She picks up a fallen apple, checks it carefully for worms, then drops it into the barrel.

Moments later, she's chanting again. "*Cortland. McIntosh. Red Delicious. King.*"

18

Most days after school, there's a succession of creaks and slams as the six Peterson kids, and sometimes the two Marshall girls, file through the screen door at Marion's place. They are there to do their homework. Marion makes them do it. But there are always compensations. There are always snacks. Sandwiches, home-made cookies, real milk. Randy and Rebecca are still too young to have any homework, but they always go to Marion's anyway — because they don't want to miss the food.

The first things Rebecca always does after the final buzzers, however, is say hello to her Dad. Harold has an after-school job as their janitor now. Just for a few hours. Just long enough to scour the washrooms and sweep the floors with Dustbane. "Which he'll probably be doing for a million years," Rebecca once snorted, after she discovered huge cardboard cylinders of the smelly green powder lying on the concrete floor by the school's furnace. And then after that, as she and Randy race away from the schoolyard, she usually plays a little game with herself. She usually pretends that mean old Myrna Hamilton is chasing her in her big black Champion. "Stop!" Miss Hamilton's voice is husky and clipped. "Stop, this instant!" She has the worst bad breath of any teacher in the school. "Stop, or I'll...!" Rebecca can almost make herself believe that if she doesn't hurry, Miss Hamilton's going to catch up to her. And pinch her on the arm. And pick her up by the skin. And stand her up on the hood of the car. And invite the whole town to come and gawk at her. Just like she stood her up on her table last week, when Mrs. Blackburn was sick, for getting everyone to put their cod liver oil capsules under the legs of their chairs. Rebecca's afraid that maybe someday Miss Hamilton'll strap her with a blueberry bush, like she did Ben Kelly, years and years ago, when he kicked a hole in the door to the girls' cloakroom after a bunch of the boys had locked him in. But for now, there's just the big black Champion. And Rebecca, running as fast as she can.

Today, when Randy and Rebecca come tumbling down the driveway, their clothes are soaking wet. Their arms and legs are streaked with mud. Rebecca is jingling a bag of bottle caps she got from the pop machine at Fred Johnson's place. As they climb the steps to the back veranda, they hear voices. And then they see the others, already huddled around the kitchen table.

"Here, let me," snuffles Peter.

"You did it yesterday."

"Watch it!"

There's a bit of jostling and one or two bumps. And then Darrell, who's the oldest and biggest, manages to switch on the dark brown plastic radio sitting on the table.

"There was another terrorist bombing in Nicosia today."

It's the CBC news from Halifax.

Rebecca takes a few swipes at her wet and grimy clothes. She doesn't understand the news. It's always about things so far away; things which have nothing to do with her — about Sputniks and Fifth Republics and Great Leaps Forward and Elvis being drafted into the army. But there's something mesmerizing about it, too. She and Randy just stand there on the veranda, watching and listening.

"Reports coming out of Cyprus are sketchy but it appears that…"

"Is anybody hungry?" interrupts Marion.

"Yeah!"

"I'm starving!"

"Whatta ya got?"

"And this just in from Montgomery, Alabama…Civil rights groups continue to petition Governor James E. Folsom to commute the death

*sentence passed on a negro man for robbing an elderly white woman
of one dollar and ninety-five cents."*
"Never mind that junk," snorts Donnie.
"Yes, Darrell," agrees Sunny. "Change the station!"
"Despite their best efforts, however, it appears that…"
There's a soft crackling and then a loud, irritating whine.
"Wait!"
"You missed it!"
"Back a little…"
"There!"
*"Just tell your hoodlum friends outside. You ain't got time to take
a ride."*
"Yeah!"
"That's more like it."
"Turn it up!"
They all join in on the chorus. *"Yakety-Yak. Yakety-Yak."*
Now Randy and Rebecca are mesmerized by something else — the
exuberant rhythms and chords of the Coasters. They don't hear much
rock 'n' roll at home. Vivian says it's "ignorant" music. She says the
singers can't sing; the words don't make sense; the tunes are too jumpy
and loud. She says listening to it will turn them all into crazed animals,
into rabid racoons, into coons, even. Rebecca can't help jingling her
bag of bottle caps in time to the music.
As soon as the song ends, Marion leaps over to the table and turns
down the volume. "Yakety-yak is right!" she laughs.
"Aw, Marion."
"We were only…"
Peter leans over and tries to turn it up again.
"No!" She grabs his hand. "It's time for homework."
There's a tremendous scraping of chairs as they arrange themselves
around the table.
"I thought you liked this music, Marion." Sunny is already bent
over a page of fractions.
"Well, I like some of it."
"Like what?" snorts Donnie, as he runs his hands through his long,
straight, sandy hair. "Elvis, I suppose."
"No. Well, yes. I like 'Don't Be Cruel' and 'Peace in the Valley.'
But…like 'Volare,' for instance. *We could sing in the glow of a star*

that I know of where lovers enjoy peace of..."

"Are you kidding?"

"'Volare?'"

"That's the dumbest song I ever..."

"OK. Well, what about 'Who's Sorry Now?'"

"Oh, brother."

"And 'You Send Me.'"

They all groan.

"What?" Marion's still laughing. "What's the matter with those?"

The kids pucker up their lips and make smooching sounds.

"You thrill me..."

"Drill me."

"Kill me."

"Honest you do. Honest you do. Honest you..."

"OK, OK. So what are your favourites? Something by The Impalas, no doubt." She smiles at Darrell, who's as obsessed with cars as Rebecca is.

"I like 'Witch Doctor,'" blurts Peter.

"Yeah!"

"You should hear him!"

"He sings it all the time!"

"OK, then." Marion tries to look serious. "Then maybe I should learn the words to that one. Who sings it?"

"Sheb Wooley," says Peter.

Marion laughs. "And how does it go?"

"My friend, the witch doctor, he told me what to say." Sunny beats Peter to it.

"No, Sunny!"

"That's not what comes first!"

"Yes, it is."

"No, it isn't. First, you have to tell the witch doctor that you're in love with him. Not the witch doctor, but the person you're in love with."

"Oh, yeah."

"And then he has to tell you what to say."

"Right. Now, I remember."

"OK, OK." Marion is laughing again. "Just tell me. What does the witch doctor tell you to say?"

"Ha!"

"That's easy!"

"One, two, three, four..."

They all join in on his momentous advice.

"*Oo, ee, oo ah-ah. TING, TANG, wallah-wallah, bing, bang. Oo, ee, oo ah-ah. Ting TANG, wallah-wallah, bing, BANG.*"

At the end of the tune, there's a tumult of howling and squealing.

Unable to stay quiet a second longer, Rebecca throws open the screen door. "Yeaaah!" she shouts as she bursts into the kitchen. "But it's not nearly as good as that Woolsey guy's 'Purple People-Eater!'"

"As his what?" splutters Marion.

"God, you scared me, you little creep," says Donnie.

"As his 'People Purple-Eater.' I mean his..."

"Yeah, well, *you* look a lot like a one-eyed, one-horned, flying purple people-eater yourself," retorts Darrell.

"Yes," laughs Marion, as she strolls to the refrigerator. "And you, too, Randy. You're filthy. What happened to you?"

"Nothing."

"We were just playing."

They hang their jackets on the nails in the corner, between the doors to the back chamber and the woodhouse.

"Yes, well, you better wash your hands." Marion places a plate of sandwiches on the table. "Quick. Or there won't be..."

"Yay!"

"Lobster!"

"I knew we were getting lobster!"

Randy and Rebecca race over to the sink, quickly splash water on their arms and face, and then reach for the towel on the roller overhead. For a split second, while their hands are buried in the thick, white, cotton nubs, time stands still for Rebecca. She loves that towel. How soft it is. How it's sewn together. How she can pull it and pull it and it'll never come off. Never end. Never run out. Malcolm says it's the most unsanitary thing he's ever seen.

"Hey!"

"No fair!"

"You got the biggest one last time!"

Randy and Rebecca spin away from the towel. "Save some for us!" they cry in unison.

Rebecca is sitting at the dining room table, examining her bottle caps. She can't figure out why she took them this time either. They're no good to play with. She can't make anything out of them. They're just a bunch of squished and dented circles.

"Randy, don't!"

He's just driven his Ford Zodiac into the pile of bottle caps.

"And put that away or someone will see!"

"OK, but..." He shoves the little pink convertible back into his pocket. "What's the use of stealing something if you can't show anyone?"

Rebecca doesn't answer. She buried the little yellow Vauxhall Victor — the one *she* stole — in the sandpit a long time ago.

"I'm bored," sulks Randy. "Let's play something."

"OK, what?" Rebecca scrapes the bottle caps back into the bag.

"Well...what about Chinese Checkers?"

"I don't really know how."

"I don't either but..."

"I know! Pinball!"

"Yeah!"

They race into the walk-in closet in the den.

The Big Score is the miniature pinball machine Marion gave them last Christmas. It's only three feet by one and a half feet, and made of plastic, but it's still lots of fun. Donnie used to play it with them all the time, after he finished his arithmetic, but that was before he turned eleven and got too busy trying to train his long, straight, sandy hair to stay slicked back.

"Where should we put it?" asks Randy, when they get back to the dining room.

"On the floor. No, wait! On the table." Rebecca props Marion's datebook under it, to give it a slight incline.

"Now what?" Randy stares down at it.

"Now we shoot the...Oh, I forgot!" Rebecca tilts The Big Score forward and to the side. There's a great clatter as the little white balls careen through the plastic loops, against the plastic walls, and end up in a neat little row in the bottom, right-hand corner. "OK. Ready." She places it on the datebook again. "You can go first."

Randy pulls the little white knob at the bottom of the machine. A little white ball springs upward, bumps into the plastic barrier protecting the bull's-eye, and lands in a loop marked 1000.

"Pretty good," nods Rebecca.

Randy steps aside.

"Well, keep going. It's still your turn. Your turn's not over until all the balls are gone. Then we add up the score."

"OK." He prepares to pull the little white knob again.

"And remember. Black balls...See that black ball?" She points to the lone black ball in the long line of white ones. "Black balls count double."

Within moments, they're so busy squealing and cheering they don't hear the car pull into the driveway. They do, however, hear Marion, as she moves to the screen door. "I wonder what Opal wants."

"Oh-oh."

They exchange a glance.

"We've had the biscuit."

"Keep playing. Keep playing."

The balls begin to clatter through the loops again.

"Probably came to show off Phyllis's new car," sneers Darrell, as he leans across the table and peeks through the curtains. "An Envoy, by the looks of it. Dinky, little English thing. Big rear window. Goofy-looking hub caps. Ugly, grey paint job."

"Opal or the car?" giggles Sunny.

"Shsh, you two," cautions Marion.

Opal Rawding lives with her husband Harvey and their two children Betsy and Alan in a big white house on Old Post Road, opposite School Street. Since she doesn't know how to drive, she's gotten Phyllis Horsnell, the elderly woman from the apartment upstairs, to take her and Alan down to Marion's.

As soon as the car doors swing open, Marion slips out to the veranda. "Hello, Opal. Alan. And you, Phyllis. How are you?"

Phyllis is still stooped over the steering wheel, with the sunlight gleaming on the wings of her glasses, on the strands of her wavy grey hair. She doesn't budge.

"This isn't a social call, Marion." Opal fires her door shut.

"Oh?" Marion saunters down to the driveway.

The kids all leap to their feet and peer through the curtains.

"What are they saying?" mumbles Peter.

"I don't know," whispers Sunny. "But look at Alan. He's soaking wet!"

"Serves him right, the little snot." Donnie runs his hands through his hair again.

"And Opal," snorts Darrell. "She looks like she's got a stick up her ass about something."

They all giggle.

Marion spins around. "Randy! Rebecca! Come out here, please!"

The balls stop clattering.

"Oh-oh."

"I told you we've had the biscuit."

They wander into the kitchen.

"What d'ya do?"

"I knew you'd done something."

"You're going to get it."

"Come on, you two." Marion's arms are folded across her chest. "We haven't got all night."

Randy and Rebecca edge through the screen door and onto the veranda.

"All the way. Come on."

They creep down the steps to the driveway.

"Now." Marion tries to sound stern. "Mrs. Rawding says you threw water on Alan and made him cry. Is that right?"

"We were just playing."

"Just playing!" sputters Opal. "Look at him! He's freezing!"

"Now, Opal," laughs Marion. "Really."

Rebecca thinks she and Randy might be safe. She knows Marion and Opal don't get along very well. She's even heard Marion say that Opal's a snob, that she treats her kids like babies, that she has the annoying habit of buying something, wearing it once, and then taking it back for a refund.

"I think he probably had a good time getting soaked," continues Marion. "Didn't you, Alan?"

Yeah, thinks Rebecca. He probably wasn't even crying until his Mum got to him.

"A good time!" roars Opal. "How can you say that?"

"Well, look at *them*." Marion gestures toward Randy and Rebecca.

"*They're* wet and *they* don't mind."

"Yes, well, that's different. They're…"

"What?"

"They're Petersons."

"Oh, I see."

The kids inside giggle and punch each other.

"Well!" sniffs Opal. "I can see I'm not going to get any satisfaction here!" She bundles Alan into the back seat of the car.

Rebecca can't help smiling. She once heard her Mum say that Opal Rawding was the only person she knew who was never satisfied. It wasn't possible for her to be satisfied. Otherwise, why had there never been a single Christmas gift that Opal hadn't exchanged?

"All I wanted was a simple apology," huffs Opal, as she climbs into the front seat and slams the door.

"Opal, Opal." Marion leans down and looks past Phyllis. "There's no need to get upset. The kids are going to apologize. Aren't you, kids?" Behind her back, she waves for them to approach the car.

"Sorry, Alan," mutters Randy.

"Yeah." Rebecca secretly crosses her fingers. "Sorry."

"That's OK," gushes Alan.

Opal stares straight ahead. Rebecca wonders if she's still mad at Marion for beating her to that Hummel at Harriet's. Coquette, it was called. Two little porcelain girls in kerchiefs, sitting on the top rail of a fence. With blue and green birds. And poppies. Opal said she especially liked the poppies.

"All right, Phyllis. We can go now."

The old woman coaxes the Envoy into reverse. And then backs slowly down the driveway.

"Hey!" Alan suddenly leans out the window. "Come over after supper, you two! We can mess around in the barn!"

"Alan!" Opal reaches back and yanks him into his seat.

"Ha!" scoffs Randy. "Old Mrs. Horsnell's driving so slow I could probably beat her there."

"No, you couldn't."

"Bets?"

Before Rebecca can answer, he's flying down the driveway.

"Aren't they finished *yet*?" grumbles Rebecca, as she wanders back into the kitchen.

"No, they aren't," laughs Marion. She's helping Donnie draw the outline of a Silver Dart on a piece of white Bristol board. "Now sit down. And see if you can keep out of trouble for five minutes."

"I bet I can!" Rebecca flops down in the rocking chair near the refrigerator.

Within seconds, however, she's jingling her bag of bottle caps.

"Shshsh."

She stuffs the bag into her waistband, folds her arms across her chest, and then looks around the room.

The kitchen is a place of wonder, merriment, abundance, confusion. And of mindless repetition. It has six doorways — two to the dining room and one each to the cellar, the back chamber, the woodhouse and the veranda. But even those with cream-coloured doors on them don't actually lead anywhere. Nowhere romantic and exciting, that is — unless you count pissing in the woodhouse or going down to the cellar for stoker pea coal. And then there are the calendars. There are never fewer than four of them hanging on the doors, cupboards and walls. Everyone gets them from businesses in the area — from the milk company, the insurance company, the oil company, the car company — but Ben's the only one who puts them all up, regardless of whether they show cars or cats or picturesque views of Peggy's Cove. In the daylight. Under the stars. Shrouded in fog. The result is that, everywhere you look, you're reminded what day it is. And then there are the five pairs of scissors hanging from a nail by the spice rack. They're all shapes and sizes, including a junior pair with blunt ends, and they're all legitimately useful. Different pairs are needed for different things — for cutting cloth, paper, carrot tops, nails.

Rebecca's arms are still folded. Marion, meanwhile, has moved to the sink, where she's filling a bucket with water.

"Arrrgh!" roars Darrell.

"What?"

"I can't get it."

"What?"

"This stupid problem!"

Marion stares at herself in the mirror on the back of the medicine cabinet.

"Ha! Are you sure it's the problem that's stupid?" teases Randy.

"Watch it, you little creep!"

"Or what?"

"Or you might end up with a black eye!"

When the bucket is full, Marion turns and starts for the screen door. Halfway there, however, she suddenly stops. "Who wants to take this out to Frankie?"

"I will!" Rebecca leaps out of the rocking chair. "Oops." She sits back down again. "Are my five minutes up yet?"

"Never mind," laughs Marion. "Are you sure you can carry it?"

"I bet she can't."

"She's way too little."

"No, I'm not! Watch!" Rebecca grabs the handle with both hands and lurches out the door.

As she stumbles down the steps, the others scramble to get a better look.

"You're spilling it!"

"Am not!"

They laugh as she staggers across the driveway. But as she swishes and sways through the devil's paintbrushes, they can't help admiring her.

"Tough little bugger, isn't she?"

"That's for sure."

She disappears around the corner of the garage.

The small white cabin has no running water. Leander Blue used to come up to the house to get a bucketful for shaving and drinking. But Frankie doesn't. Frankie always waits until they bring it out to him.

"Frankie!" she gasps.

She's standing in the shade, in the tall grass between Frankie's front door and Leander's old van. It's a navy blue Ford, with lots of dents and scratches, and it doesn't run any more.

"Frankie, can you...? I'm going to drop it!"

The door swings open.

"Come in." He takes the bucket from her. "Come in."

"Thanks."

He leaves the door open behind her.

There's not much in the cabin — just a narrow cot, a couple of straight-backed wooden chairs and a pot-bellied stove, near the tiny window at the back.

"Boys, oh, boys, that was heavy!" She plops down on one of the chairs.

Chink.

"What's that?" he asks softly.

"Nothing." She pulls the bag out of her waistband. "Just some old bottle caps I got at Fred's."

Chink, chink, chink.

She tosses them gently up and down.

"What are you going to do with them?"

"I dunno. Nothing, I guess." She drops the bag on the floor.

Chink.

"How's school?" he asks, as he pours some water from the bucket into a basin.

"OK."

"You don't sound very excited about it."

"Well, there's not lots to do. I know all the stuff."

"And what stuff is that?"

"You know. Reading. Junk like that."

"Oh, I see," he laughs. "And what about music?"

"We don't have music."

"No music? No instruments?"

"Nope."

"Not even cymbals or triangles? How about tambourines?"

"Nope."

She wants to ask what tambourines are made of, but she's getting restless. Frankie always keeps a paper bag full of chocolates in his cabin — to give to the kids when they bring him water or come for a visit. She can taste them. The saliva is spurting in her mouth. But she can't see the bag and she's beginning to think he's run out.

"I gotta go home for supper now." She doesn't get up.

"Sure." He pats his face with a towel. "Thanks for the water."

"That's OK, Frankie." She drags herself to the doorway.

"Oh, by the way, Rebecca…"

She spins around. "Yes, Frankie?"

"You forgot this." He dangles a brown paper bag in front of her face.

"Oh, yeah," she says forlornly. "My bottle caps." She takes the bag from him. "Hey! Those aren't bottle caps! Those are…" She tears open the bag. "Chocolates! Millions of them! Are they all for me?"

"Well," laughs Frankie. "Anyone who carries a heavy bucket all this way deserves to have millions, don't you think?"

"Thanks, Frankie! Thanks! Wait till I show…!" She races out the door toward the house.

Half-way through the devil's paintbrushes, however, she whirls around and hollers. "See ya at the game tomorrow, Frankie?"

"You bet." He steps back in and closes the door.

Chink, chink, chink.

Rebecca shuffles through the pile of datebooks, looking for 1958 again. When she finds it, she quickly flips the pages until she reaches Wednesday, September 10.

"But I always had a party," she murmurs, when she sees there's nothing written on the thin green lines. "Marion always gave me a party."

Chink, chink, chink.

And then she remembers. The party was on Saturday, September 13 that year.

She gazes at the box at the end of the week.

It's filled with notations about who was invited; how many card tables they needed to borrow; which person was making the Kool-Aid, bringing the serviettes, organizing the games.

She closes her eyes and dives into the box.

But her memory is jerky, restless, out of focus. Sometimes there's too much sky. And sometimes the heads are cut off. It's as if an amateur is holding the Super-8 camera that day.

She squeezes her eyelids.

The yard is quiet and still. No one has arrived yet. The only movement is the flickering of images in the garage windows…the breezes blowing through the poplar trees, the balloons hanging on strings from the mulberry bushes, the zinnias in vases on the card tables. But then the lens shifts away from the reflections to the things themselves. There's a neat line of tables, end to end. But there's also an odd assortment of tablecloths. Striped, flowered, bleached white. And a jumble of mismatched chairs. Canvas ones from the front veranda, vinyl ones from the kitchen, upholstered ones from the living room. Ones with black metal sticks for legs.

She relaxes her eyelids.

There are more adjectives now. Impudent breezes. Defenceless balloons. Superfluous flowers. And more animation. Opal Rawding rushing toward the armchair with the bluish grey leafy pattern. Alice Marshall sinking onto the straight-backed vinyl one with the yellow and black crosses.

"Isn't Frankie coming?"

"No. Why would he?"

"Well, I just thought since he was living..."

"Well, he certainly isn't invited, if that's what you mean."

Rebecca's eyelids flicker. The projector jams.

Suddenly, it's all "still life" again...carriages and strollers and tricycles askew on the lawn, under the poplars, against the garage. And dozens of dollies, with their eyes flipped open. And Eunice Dunn sitting in the miniature blue armchair with the matching blue footstool. And Audrey Shaw sitting in the light-green marbled one that Marion wiped the egg off. And Kay Armstrong stuck with the red, green and yellow canvas one that Ben burnt with his pipe. And the Peterson kids and the Marshall kids and the Dunn, Shaw and Rawding kids all frozen in chairs at the card tables. Scowling, pouting, bored. Most of them are wearing tissue-paper hats. Like pirates, clowns, dunces and kings. But Winifred has grabbed the foil one — the bright red fez with the long black tassels. And Darrell is in the middle of trying to decide how he'd look if he put on the cardboard one — the tall white one which looks like a wizard's. They should have been blowing off, of course. Like the poplar trees should have been shimmering and the zinnias should have been tipping over and the dresses should have been billowing up past their thighs. But it's just "still life." Nothing is moving.

Once more, she squeezes her eyelids. And then, like magic, the images are flickering again.

Grammie and Marion are bringing out the food. There's a tumult of energetic images. Of hands reaching for the plates. Of little peanut butter and egg wedges with the crusts cut off. Of Grammie standing over them, swatting at flies with the lid of a shoebox. Of ladies drinking tea out of the good cups. Of kids fighting over who gets the orange Kool-Aid and who gets the grape.

"Is he in there?"

"I guess so."

"He's probably watching everything we do."

"Now, why would he do that?"

"I don't know. He gives me the creeps."

"Yes. Me, too."

Marion is placing another jug of milk on the table. And the birthday girl is staring at her for a second, wondering what she meant by "Me, too," and then stuffing another wedge into her mouth and squinting at the camera.

Rebecca tries to squint back.

She's the only one not wearing a party hat. She hates hats. And she hates dresses. Hates the big, white drapey bits. Hates the big flowery patches which form the pockets. Hates the big pink bow which sticks out at the back. You can't sit down very well with one of *those* on.

She's thrusting out her jaw.

Winifred is looking pretty good in *her* dress. But then Peter is reminding everyone how she used to run around with her shirt off. And Winifred is turning as red as the roses on her puffy white sleeves and starting to cry and running off into the tent which is pitched in the tall grass behind the swings.

Suddenly, little Rebecca is throwing a peanut butter wedge at the camera. The picture is wobbling. Big Rebecca ducks.

And then the cake is coming. Marion's speciality. She's made a train this year, with an engine and box cars and a caboose. And then the bowls of ice cream. And the presents. Tons of presents. Panties, pajamas, a "Little Brave Sambo" record. A plastic snow shovel, a plastic skeleton, a paint-by-numbers set. An autograph book, a book about animals, a ball. A red, white and blue ball. Exactly what she wanted. A ball she could swing her leg over and play "one, two, three a-lara" with. A ball she would have to bring inside in the winter or else the paint would come off and it would get soaked right through and be no good.

And then the camera is tilting and everyone is laughing. And Peter is standing in the middle of the lawn, snuffling and snorting, with his arms at his side. And Winifred is stomping off into the tent again, with her yellow pigtails flapping. And Vivian is shaking him by the arms. And Peter is still snuffling and snorting. And Winifred is wailing.

And everything goes black.

Rebecca has dived so far into the box that she's hit bottom. It's actually Saturday, September 13 again.

19

That evening, Rebecca drags the long, green rubber hose out back behind the garage. Ben's already there. As she watches him poke around in the sandy, well-grained soil of the garden, inspecting a soggy tomato here, a spongy pepper there, she can't help noticing how sad he looks. Sadder than he looked in the spring, at least, when he was stirring up the soil with the rototiller and his shirt was drenched with sweat. Now that it's fall, and everything's dying, there doesn't seem much else for him to do but putter. And puttering doesn't seem to make him very happy.

"It's smaaaller than laaast year," drawls Alice, who's wandered over to watch him, too.

It's true, thinks Rebecca, as she twists the nozzle on the hose. Even *she* remembers when the garden was huge. When the rhubarb, for one thing, was in the southeast corner, instead of off by itself in the tall grass.

Ben lights his pipe, then wanders back toward the zucchini.

There are so many of them, thinks Rebecca, as she watches him prod at one of the long green fruits with his foot. And so many of them are so huge — too huge to be of any use.

"I tooold you nooot to plaaant so maaany." Alice is still watching him, too. "You ooonly eeend up feeding the crooows. Like you diiid when you leeet the peeeas go wiiild, whaaat, Rebeeecca?"

Rebecca doesn't answer. She's too busy trying to make a rainbow.

She knows she has to get the angle of the long, green rubber hose just right, so the sunlight glints through the gentle spray of water. But when she shoots down at the garden, she only gets dinky little flashes of colour. And when she shoots up at the sky, she only gets a few thin pale bands.

Maybe it's too late in the day, she thinks, as she adjusts the angle of the hose again. Or maybe I'm doing it wrong.

She knows it can be done. She's seen Ben do it. Maybe his wasn't a great, big, beautiful rainbow, like the one in the sky. But it was pretty.

"Oh, well." She turns the hose away from the sunlight, onto the last of the dirty brown onions.

It isn't long, however, before she hears a strange tinkling sound.

Chink, chink, chink.

She looks toward Frankie's cabin.

"Rebecca!" he calls to her from the doorway. "I have something for you!"

"I bet I know what it is!" she calls back. "The last time I was there I forgot my bag of bottle caps!"

"I bet you don't!"

"Oh. Well, then, maybe...Ben!"

There's a puff of smoke from the garden.

"Can I stop now?" she hollers at it.

Ben nods to her.

"OK, Frankie! I'll be right...!" She tries to turn off the nozzle, but it's on too tight. "As soon as I...Nuts!" She drops the hose and races toward the cabin.

The water starts forming a pool next to the rotting green peppers.

At the entrance to Frankie's cabin, there's a cluster of gooseberry bushes. If it were late July, she'd pop one of the crisp green berries into her mouth and then make a face. But the berries are gone now. Marion has turned them into jam. Rebecca brushes past the bushes through the open doorway.

"Hoo!" She takes a puzzled little sniff.

She's used to smoke — from Ben's pipe, from the canning factory, from the incense burning in the miniature wooden fireplace Marion puts out at Christmas time — but this smells like cigarette smoke. Frankie never smokes. She knows that. And Marion...well, Marion smokes, but mostly during bridge games, and she never comes out here to the...

Chink, chink.

The mystery isn't nearly enough to distract Rebecca from the excitement.

"What is it, Frankie?"

He has his hands behind his back.

"What are you hiding?"

Chink, chink.

"It's your birthday present."

"It is?"

"Yes. Listen."

Chink, chink, chink, hisssss.

"Oh, I know what it is! I know! I know! It's a tambourine!"

"Good guess," he laughs. But he keeps his hands behind his back.

"Oh, Frankie, Frankie!" She's jumping up and down now. "How many jingles does it have?"

"How many would you like?"

"Millions of them!"

Hisssssss.

"Well, then, your wish is my command." He finally holds it out to her.

"Oh, Frankie!" she whispers, as she draws back her hands.

The tambourine has a single, round calfskin head. Imbedded in its shallow wooden hoop are seven pairs of flattened bottle caps.

"It's so pretty!"

The shallow wooden hoop is painted as blue as the sea on a bright and sunny day. The calfskin head has a little white dog on it — just like the one that was hanging around the church supper last year. Only this one is burying a little red ball on a soft and sandy beach. A yellow beach.

"Is it mine?" she whispers. "To keep?"

"Yes, Rebecca. To keep."

At last, she reaches out her hands. He places the tambourine in them.

"When did you make it?" she whispers.

She can almost see the sand flying into the air, as the little white dog digs deeper and deeper.

"The last few days. After you told me you didn't have any instruments at school."

She gently taps a pair of jingles. Chink. And then another pair. Chink.

"How do you play it?" she asks timidly.

Frankie laughs. "Any way you like."

"You show me." She hands it back to him.

"OK." He holds the tambourine in his left hand and then, using two fingers of his right, taps it gently in the centre. Dum, chink. Then he does the same thing, nearer the rim. Tak, chink.

"Neat!"

Then he gently flicks the jingles and strikes the calfskin head against his palm, his knee, Rebecca's rear end.

She giggles with glee.

Then he holds it up near his shoulder and, with a steady rolling of his wrist, starts an ominous hissing.

Her eyes widen.

She can hear the sounds of summer. The shrill demands of the cicada. The contemptuous warnings of the rattlesnake.

Suddenly, he presses the inside of the vellum with the fingers of his left hand. The tone changes, creeps higher, suggest a new player...or a different kind of danger. Without stopping this new hissing, he quickly strikes the rim, the head, the rim, the head until the cabin itself seems to be hissing and jingling and vibrating.

"Oh, Frankie!"

Rebecca is hopping around the room now. She loves it but she can hardly stand it.

"Frankie! Frankie!"

He gives it a final shake and then stops.

"It's the neatest present I ever got!"

He hands it back to her. "Is it?"

"Well, I got some good junk for my birthday. Louise Marshall gave me an autograph book and..."

"What about Christmas?"

"We only get socks."

"Oh?"

"Well, we only get socks from home, but Marion gives me neat stuff, like candy and toys, and her friend Edna Ogletree...Do you know Edna Ogletree? The short, fat, rich lady with the pink Chrysler?...Well, she gives me mint coin sets. In plastic. So they won't get all brown or anything."

"That's nice."

"I guess. But they're not good for anything."

"Why not?"

"'Cause I'm not allowed to spend them."

He can't help laughing. "Things don't always have to be good for something. Sometimes they just *are*."

She knits her brow.

"Well...take your tambourine. Is it good for something?"

"Yeaaah! I can...well, maybe I can play it in a parade! Or a circus! Or build a fort and scare off all the...!"

He's still laughing.

"Well, it's better than those dumb old coin sets. Or anything else I've got."

"What else *have* you got?"

"Well, I've got some other coins. I press them into holes in those little blue books Marion gets me from Michie's five-and-dime. And I've got some stupid spoons that people gave me when I was born or when they came back from visiting places. You can't eat anything with them, though. Unless you want to take puny little sips of things. And...What's so funny? And I got a couple of little statues of horses. And some pencils with my name on them from Alison Chown, a friend of Marion's from..."

Frankie can't stop laughing. Rebecca shakes her tambourine at him. Hisssssss.

"Well." He wipes the tears from his eyes. "You better go now. People might be wondering what happened to you."

"OK, Frankie. But first, I want to ask you something."

"What's that?"

"This is a really neat present and everything." She taps the little white dog on the head. "But...well..." She looks up at him. "Are you one of my friends?"

"I sure am."

"Then how come...?"

"What?"

"How come you didn't come to my party?"

"Oh, you know me. I don't like crowds very much."

"Yeah, but..."

"Besides, I wouldn't have fit in."

"Yeah, but..."

"Oh, *yeah but, yeah but*. Is that all you can say?" He laughs and pushes her through the doorway.

As Rebecca wades back through the tall grass, she remembers something. She meant to ask Frankie to write in her autograph book. Not just his name but a little saying or poem or something. She's about to turn back when she notices the garden.

"Oh-oh."

The entire south end is flooded with water.

Rebecca's eyes snap up from the page.

Frankie *did* write something in her autograph book. A few days later, he wrote: *Never trouble till trouble troubles you.*

Her eyes snap down to the page again.

20

In October 1958, a few weeks after Vivian hears Van Cliburn's recording of Tchaikovsky's Concerto No. 1 in B Flat Minor, Rebecca starts taking piano lessons. It could have been a disaster, but the early verdict is that she's pretty good at it. "Has outstanding skill" is the first thing scrawled at the top of her *Teaching Little Fingers to Play* book. But she doesn't like it very much. The pieces are OK, and there's nothing wrong with her teacher Clara Whitman, the United Church minister's wife. The problem is her lesson's on Saturday, which means she either has to interrupt all the neat things she's doing outside or forget to come home in time for Marion to drive her there. She wishes her Mum had never heard that Van Cliburn guy. She wishes she'd swooned over Billy Bruton instead. Or even Luis Aparicio.

"How much longer?"

Rebecca and Sunny are sitting in the parlour of the United Church manse, waiting for Winifred to finish her arpeggios.

"How should *I* know?" Sunny unfolds the dollar bill Marion gave her to pay for her lesson.

Rebecca looks down at the tambourine lying on her lap.

She can't decide if it's the best present in the whole wide world yet, since she still likes her miniature pinball machine, but ever since Frankie surprised her with it, she's taken it everywhere.

"Tam-bou-rine. Tam-bou-rine," she recites softly, as she taps on one of the jingles.

Chink, chink, chink. Chink, chink, chink. Chink, chink...

"Sunny? Why does Winifred always take so long?"

"Because she isn't very musical."

"She isn't?"

"No. I heard Mrs. Whitman telling Marion."

"Oh."

Chink, chink, chink.

"Then I guess it's a good thing she doesn't take singing lessons, too!"

CHINK!

She slams her hand on the head of the little white dog.

"Shshsh!" begs Sunny.

"Why should I?"

CHINK! CHINK! CHINK!

"You're going to get it."

"So?" Rebecca stops banging. "I don't see why we have to take these stupid lessons anyway. We don't even have a piano."

"No, but we can always play at Grammie's or Marion's."

"But I don't want to!"

Hissssssss!

With that, Rebecca leaps out of her Queen Anne chair and starts dancing around the room. There are a few whoops and squeals, but mostly she just bangs and shakes her tambourine.

Chink, chink, hissssssss. Chink, chink, hissssssss.

Suddenly, the door flies open.

"Thanks a lot!" cries Winifred, as she bursts into the parlour. She has that same blotchy red face she always has after her lesson.

"What did *I* do?" Rebecca hops out of reach.

"You interrupted me!"

"So?"

"Just when I was getting it!"

"Oh, come on, Winifred," drawls Sunny. "You were not."

"I was, too! You ask Mrs...!"

"Rebecca?"

A slender young woman is leaning in the doorway.

"Yes, Mrs. Whitman?" Rebecca answers sweetly.

"Your turn."

"Finally." She reaches into the pocket of her jeans and pulls out a crumpled dollar bill.

"God!" sighs Rebecca, as she lifts her eyes from the page. "I don't know how they put up with us!"

She squints through the window.

There's not much left of the garden now. It used to be a place of hope and havoc. There was something both melancholy and thrilling about its vast potential — for abundant growth or for the messiest tomato fight in years. But then, there's not much left of the sky either.

Up in what's left of the sky, far away from harm and hilarity, there's a cloud with its mouth around the moon. It looks like an old grey dog chewing on a bingo ball.

She stares back down at the page.

21

Later that night, scores of women and children are crowding through the side door of St. Monica's Catholic Church on School Street. On the walls of the staircase leading down to the basement are drawings and posters commemorating the one hundredth anniversary of the Vision of Bernadette.

"Whatever became of Scott Herbert?" asks Beverley Stoddard, as they shuffle past a charcoal sketch of *A Woman at the Entrance to a Cave*.

"Elsie says he's surveying some land up to his Daddy's house," answers Wanda Willoughby. "She says he's going to...Hey!"

Chink, chink, chink.

Rebecca pushes past them.

"Where's the fire?"

"Sorry."

Rebecca's too excited to shuffle. Saturday night bingo at St. Monica's is always balls of fun. Not only does she get to stay up really late — sometimes three hours past her bedtime — but the basement is smaller than the Fire Hall, where they play on Thursday nights, so she can actually see things. And then, of course, there's the food, which is way better here than it is over there.

"Excuse me. Excuse me."

When she reaches the bottom of the stairs, she glances over to make sure the ladies' auxiliary has set up its little counter. Then she stands by the wall, beneath a finger painting of *Sick People Drinking Water From a Spring*, and waits for her Mum and Marion. The room is noisy, and already filled with smoke, by the time she spots them.

"What took you so long? I've been waiting and waiting."

Those in the vicinity chuckle. For a five-year-old, she has a loud and demanding voice.

"Well, we're here now," sighs Marion, "so what's the trouble?"

"I'm hungry."

"But you just ate!" exclaims Vivian.

"Yeah, but not very..."

"OK, OK! What do you want?"

"I want pop and chips and a hot dog and..."

The area explodes in laughter.

"Rebecca, you can have one thing! One! Now what'll it be?"

She thinks for a moment, then frowns.

"Come on. We haven't got all night."

"Nothing!" She stomps off toward the rows of tables.

Chink, chink, chink, chink, chink, chink, chink, chink.

When she finds a table she likes, she slams down her tambourine and begins to set up her cards.

"If you keep acting like this," hisses Vivian, as she slips up beside her, "I'm never taking you anywhere with me again."

"Big hairy deal."

"What did you say?"

"*You* never take me anywhere anyway. Marion does."

"OK, then, I'll see that *she* doesn't."

"But I'm hungry!"

"Well, you'll just have to wait." Vivian, too, begins setting up her cards. "And don't you dare let me catch you making a racket with that...whatever that is." She waves at the tambourine. "I heard what happened at Mrs. Whitman's this afternoon."

There are two kinds of cards to play — regular cards and jackpot cards. The regular ones are thick green sheets of cardboard with black letters and numbers on them. They cost three for a quarter and you can win five- or ten-dollar prizes by making diagonals or crosses or squares around the free one in the centre. The jackpot ones are thick white sheets of cardboard. They cost a dollar each but the prize is bigger, too. At St. Monica's, it starts at one hundred dollars. To win, a player must fill an entire card in a certain number of calls. The card can be played during any game and if nobody's won by the end of the night, the money is carried over until the next week. Rebecca always plays a jackpot card and three regular ones. Vivian plays four times that many.

Chink, chink.

"Where are you going?"

Rebecca's chair scrapes across the floor. "I need some chips."

"Rebecca, I thought I told you..."

"I can't play without chips!" She points to the little mound of red and green circles near Vivian's cards.

"Oh, ee, *those* chips," wheezes Vivian. "Ee, hee, hee, heeee."

As far as chips go, people either bring their own — usually those translucent plastic ones, so they can easily check the numbers underneath — or they use the metal slugs that the hall supplies. Tonight, Rebecca's come with a pocketful of bottle caps that Frankie didn't need for the tambourine. At the last minute, however, she's decided they're too big to fit the squares.

"OK, but hurry, or you'll miss the start."

Moments later, there's a tremendous hush. And then a great whoosh of air, as the caller flips a switch and the white balls start bouncing around in the wire basket. It isn't long before one of them slides down the chute.

"Under the B...10!"

The caller places the ball, gently, as if it's a swan's egg, in an indentation on the numbered board. The evening has begun.

As play continues, there's plenty of laughing and groaning, squealing and cursing. They're never completely quiet after that first hush. But they don't just react to the luck they're having. They talk about important village matters, like so-and-so, who's moving over to Baxter Harbour, and so-and-so, who's still living off the welfare, and so-and-so, who's...

"Under the O...69!"

After that, there's the usual outburst — raucous laughter, then snickering. Bobby Smeltzer leans toward Marion.

"Oh, by the way..." he drawls. "How's your coon working out?"

"Fine, thank you." Marion's voice is steady, calm, detached.

"Under the G...52!"

"I'm set." Marion places another chip on her card.

"I bet you are," chortles Bobby. "Anyway." He scans the nearby tables. "I hear their dicks get as big as..."

"Watermelons?" someone interrupts.

Everyone laughs except Rebecca, who's trying hard to concentrate.

"Well, I don't know about that." Bobby rubs the stubble on his chin. "Maybe a..."

"Under the I...28!"

"I'm set."

"Maybe a large zucchini."

There's another torrent of laughter.

"Ha! Ha! But I do know..."

"Shshsh!" complains Rebecca. "You're making me miss the numbers!"

Bobby lowers his voice. "I do know there's something magic about their dicks." He leans toward Marion again.

"No, there isn't!" protests Vivian.

"OK, then." Bobby straightens up. "Why do you gals all want to get laid by them?"

"We do not!"

"Who says we do?"

"I've never heard anything so..."

Bobby raises his hands. "That's what I heard. You sneak out of the house in the middle of the night and...".

"Well, you heard wrong!" huff Wanda and Beverley together.

"Under the B...9!"

"Hey!"

"What's the big idea?"

"We've had that number!"

The caller stares at the dirty white ball. "Sorry. Sorry. Under the B...6!"

"Look, I'm not blaming you gals," continues Bobby, as the others check their cards. "I wish *my* dick got as big as a zucchini. Maybe you'd all come to *my* house in the middle of the night, too. But if you ever get caught..." He leans one last time toward Marion.

"Under the O...72!"

"Well, someone's liable to get hurt."

Marion squirms away from him.

"Maybe even killed."

Rebecca gasps. She doesn't understand much of what Bobby was saying — not even why he was using that word "dick" so much. But she knows what "killed" means.

"BINGO!"

"Shit."

"Isn't that always the way?"

"Just when you think you're going to..."

"Jesus, Jesus, Jesus."

As the night wears on, Rebecca gets bored. She hasn't even come close to making a straight line, never mind a Z pattern. She leans back in her chair and begins to dream of Zorro, carving Z with his sword on bad men's chests. In this trance of danger and delight, she starts to jingle her tambourine.

"Rebecca?"

She keeps on jingling.

"Rebecca!" Vivian elbows her.

"What!"

"I can't concentrate!"

"So?"

With a great whoop of defiance, she lifts the tambourine over her head and starts banging and shaking it. There's a murmur of surprise and annoyance throughout the room.

"Rebecca!" hisses Vivian. "People are looking! Rebecca! Stop that racket this instant or I'll...!"

"NEVER TAKE YOU ANYWHERE WITH ME AGAIN!" Everyone at their table chimes in.

The room erupts in laughter. Vivian's face is as red as a burning coal.

"Come on, Rebecca," says Marion quickly. "Let's go see what there is to eat. I'm starved."

"Me, too! I've been starved for ages!"

By the end of the evening, Rebecca feels sick.

"Serves you right," smirks Vivian, as they coast up the driveway.

"It wasn't the food." Rebecca rubs her tummy. "It was the smoke."

"Ha!"

"Anyway, can I sleep at Marion's tonight?"

"No, you cannot."

"Why not?"

"Because you're always over there. She must get sick of seeing you."

"Pleeeeease."

"It's all right with me, Vivian."

Marion is gazing up at the moon.

I have to find out about the smoke, decides Rebecca, as she slips out of bed and down the stairs. It's dawned on her that if she sneaks out to Frankie's cabin, she might find out who's...

"Brrr."

She wishes she had her sneakers on. The linoleum floor in the hallway is cold enough, but the grass'll be even colder. Colder. Slipperier. Wetter.

"Nuts."

There's a light on in the kitchen. She peeks around the doorway. And someone in the rocking chair by the fridge. She rolls her eyes. She'll have to wait another night to find out about the...

Marion is just sitting there. Crying and rocking. Crying and rocking.

Rebecca creeps back down the cold and slippery hall.

22

Rebecca loves the late fall, when the churches in the area hold their suppers. These aren't snobby affairs, limited to members of a particular congregation. In fact, everyone goes to all of them. Around this time, people start kidding Marion again, saying the only reason she goes to church at all is for the socializing. It may be another outlet for her good works, they chuckle, but what she really likes is the fellowship and the food. As for Rebecca, she's already following in Marion's footsteps. Rebecca isn't particularly religious either. But she likes to feel good and to eat.

To most people, these suppers are big events — bigger even than

Thanksgiving, which is celebrated a few weeks earlier. To Rebecca, they come close to being Christmas. Her second favourite is the one at the Anglican Parish Hall on School Street, across from the warehouse — mostly because the hall used to be an apple evaporator. Her first favourite is the one in her own church. The ladies in the kitchen always give her a special plate, with white meat and mashed potatoes and tons of gravy. At the other churches, where they don't know her as well, she has to take what she gets, like big piles of carrots and turnips, maybe even a hunk of dark meat. She likes those OK, but it means she can't fit as much of the really good stuff on her plate.

It's early Thursday evening. In the kitchen, where the ladies are preparing to serve the multitudes, there's a gleeful clinking and clattering. But in the vestry, where Rebecca's waiting for the long, lonely rows of tables and chairs to fill up, there's only an odd, impetuous chink from her tambourine.

Right now, the tables and chairs look fairly forlorn — a few plates of sliced tomatoes and cucumbers sitting on the freshly ironed tablecloths; a few sweaters or scarves draped over the backs of chairs to mark them as "saved" — but soon they'll all be filled. And everyone will be together. And Rebecca will be thinking it's tied for first with Christmas again.

"I wish they'd hurry!"

Chink. Chink.

At Christmas, people are wrapped up in their own special customs, which means Rebecca doesn't get to eat with Florence and Grammie and Marion. If she's lucky, she sees them later in the day. If her parents get drunk, she sneaks over to Marion's for leftovers — including the best dressing and gravy in the whole wide world off Spode's Tower plates from the dining room cabinet.

Chink. Chink.

"Rebecca?" Marion leans across the counter into the vestry. Her face and arms are glistening. There are dark wet patches on her brand-new party dress — dazzlingly white, with big black polka dots.

"Gee. You look pretty."

"Thank you." Her smile is radiant. "Now why don't you go see if they need help at the fishpond."

"OK."

Irene and Thelma are standing at the foot of the staircase which leads to the upper rooms, cursing and laughing and trying to hang up a big blue curtain.

"Can I help?" Rebecca chinks over to them.

"Yes, you can," mumbles Irene. She has a nail in her mouth. "You can hold...No, wait!" She removes the nail. "You're too little. You won't be able to reach the..."

"Never mind, Irene." Thelma takes the hammer from her. "*We* can do *this*. And Rebecca can make sure there's a safety pin at the end of each line. OK?"

"Good idea," nods Irene. "Only don't prick yourself. Just tell us if there's a pin missing and we'll put one on. OK?"

"OK."

Rebecca feels more grown-up than ever. She's being let in on a great mystery — the Mystery of the Fishpond — and it isn't even spoiling things for her. Only now she knows that when little kids poke their rods through the curtain, it isn't a fish which gives the line a little tug. It's a person, pretending to be a fish. She can't wait until she's even older. She thinks it might be just as much fun being the person behind the curtain, putting little plastic bags on the ends of pins, as it is being the little kid who squeals with joy when she pulls out her rod and discovers a little plastic soldier or dinosaur on the end of the line.

"The pins are all here!"

It's so noisy now that no one can hear the gentle clunk, clunk at the front door, as the latest arrivals drop their donations onto the collection plates. But they can still hear Rebecca's relentless chinking, as she dances around the table off to the side where the ladies have set up their baked goods and quilts.

"Rebecca!" barks Vivian. "Come and sit down!"

"But Mum." She squeezes into the spot between Vivian and Grammie, directly across from Reverend MacKay. "I was only..."

"And give that to me!" Vivian grabs the tambourine.

"Please, Mum." She holds it very tight. "I promise not to play it."

"OK." Vivian lets go. "But if you do play it, even once, I'm taking it away from you."

"Ladies and..." Reverend MacKay pushes his chair away from the table.

"For good," hisses Vivian.

"Ladies and gentlemen, I just want to..."

"It's too late for grace, Reverend!" shouts Wade Kinsman, who already has a splop of gravy on his chin.

Reverend MacKay smiles. There's never a proper time to ask for the Lord's blessing at these affairs — not with people coming and going all evening; not with the incessant din.

"Don't worry, everyone. You're off the hook. I just want to..." He leans over and clinks his glass. "I just want to publicly thank Marvin Bennett...Marvin, where are you?...There he is." He points to the back door. "To publicly thank Marvin for donating these beautiful new lights you see hanging in the vestry."

For a moment, there's a curious hush as everyone looks up at the ceiling. And then the din returns.

"Way to go, Marvin!"

"Hip, hip, hooray!"

"Who wants seconds?"

When Reverend MacKay resumes his seat, the only one still staring up at Marvin's lights is Rebecca. And she doesn't think they're beautiful at all. In fact, they're the one thing about church suppers that isn't nearly as good as Christmas. At Christmas, there are thousands of red and green and yellow and blue lights strung around trees or under eavestroughs or through trellises. The Rawdings always have a lot of them and so do the Mathesons, and Carol Ann Fancy's family in Millville, of course. And then there are the other lights...The crooked rows of candles flickering on the sills. The strange little sculptures of snowmen and Santas glowing through the branches. The stars.

Rebecca can't help singing. "*O Holy Night*." Chink. "*The stars are brightly...*"

"A-ha!" Vivian snatches the tambourine away from her.

"But Mum!"

"You heard what I said." She slides it under her rear end.

"Well, don't squish it! It won't work if you...!"

A splutter of laughter comes from the kitchen.

"And don't you encourage her, Marion!"

Everyone hoots except Rebecca.

"Are you taking a break?" asks Grammie.

"No." Marion unties her apron. "I've been fired."

"What on earth for?"

Marion laughs. "For putting too much on the plates."

"Just like me!" cries Rebecca. "Remember, Marion? Remember when Vesta fired me for filling the boxes too full of strawberries?"

"Here." Grammie pushes herself up from the table. "You sit here and have some supper. I'll go see about cleaning up."

No sooner has Marion taken a mouthful of turkey than Rebecca is pulling at the sleeve of her polka-dot dress.

"For heaven's sake!" wheezes Vivian. "Let her eat in peace!"

"But I was only..."

"I know what you were *only* going to do." Vivian watches Marion mix her turnips and potatoes together. "You were *only* going to ask her to get your drum thing back."

"Was not."

"Oh, yes, you were. You can't fool..."

"What is it, Rebecca?" Marion pops an orange and white glob into her mouth.

"Well..." She has to think of something else quickly. "I just wanted to ask you...well...you had Leander Blue over for Christmas dinner last year, right?"

"Right."

"Well, are you going to have Frankie over this year?"

Reverend MacKay quickly intervenes. "Did I ever tell you what happened to me in California, when I went to visit my cousin Vorrie?"

"No, you didn't, Reverend."

"Well, there was a terrible rainstorm one night. And the next morning, when I was standing in Vorrie's back yard, at the foot of this lovely green hill, an avalanche of mud brought..."

"Gracious!"

"Brought a dozen coffins right down on top of me. It was quite a mess, I can..."

"I know what else is a mess!" blurts Rebecca.

"What's that?"

"When you catch a grasshopper and you have it in your hand and it poops on you!"

"Please," groans Vivian. "Not while we're eating."

"You know. That clear bubbly stuff."

"Rebecca, that's enough!"

Rebecca folds her arms across her chest. "Why can he tell his story and I can't tell my story?"

"You're excused, young lady."

"But..."

"Come on." Vivian lifts her out of her chair.

"But I'm not finished!"

"Yes, you are. Now go play the fishpond."

"I've done that already."

"Well, then, go play outside."

"There's nothing to do out there."

"Rebecca!"

"OK, I'll go! But can I have my tambourine?"

"No."

"Why not?"

"Because it makes too much noise."

"Mu-um!"

"Don't you *Mu-um* me!" Vivian raises her hand. "Or I'll...!"

Rebecca whirls away from her. "Missed me!" And then stomps straight through the kitchen and out the door.

There isn't much at the back of the church — just a little graveyard, all filled up, and a brand-new parking lot, overflowing with Fords and Chevies, and the woods. As she tramps across the sparkling black pavement, she frowns. If Marvin hadn't donated all that goopy black stuff, too — if he'd only had enough money to pay for the lights in the vestry — there'd be more grass; more places for her to play.

When she reaches the graveyard, she instinctively looks around...through the tall grass, behind the headstones, among the scary shadows on the ground...But it's no use. The little white dog hasn't come back this year. She thought it might. Even though a bunch of kids said they saw her brother Darrell shoot it with his twenty-two, she thought it might...just to chase the squirrels across the parking lot and poop on the grass between the gravesites and pick the cucumbers out of the garbage bins behind the kitchen. Like it did last year.

The wind slides through the branches of the trees. She shades her eyes. But the shadows are just scary branches. No matter how much she wants them to be whiskers...On the little white dog. Which she wanted to keep. Which her Mum said would cost too much to feed. Which hasn't come back this year.

She lies down on the grass between Catterick and Wade and shuts her eyes. She wishes it were Christmas, after all. So she could stay up really late and watch *Miracle on 34th Street*. And then ask Santa for the little white dog back.

She squeezes her eyelids tighter and tighter until, miraculously, the scene changes. It's colder, wetter, noisier...She's wearing red mittens and white snowpants and a navy blue woollen coat with snow stuck to it. Soon she's flying off the swings into the banks, building tunnels through the drifts, catching snowflakes on the tip of her tongue. And then she's doing nothing. The others have gone home to thaw their feet. She lies down on her back in the snow and begins to move her arms and legs, slowly, gently, in small angelic arcs.

"Rebecca?"

It's only grass swishing over her skin. She blinks open her eyes.

"Are you OK?"

Marion is standing over her.

"Oh, hi." She sits up. There's a gentle indentation in the grass.

"Now." Marion kneels beside her. "About the tambourine."

"Is she going to throw it out?"

"No, but you're going to have to keep it at my place. Or at Frankie's place. Yes. That's a good idea. Then you can go and play it any time you want. And not bother anybody. OK?"

"OK."

23

"Here's Howe, moving quickly down the right wing. He leaves it for Gadsby. Back to Howe. Oooooh! A cannonading drive!"

"God damn it!" Marion leaps out of the Eastern Star chair placed over the register. "Maybe they'd score if I left the room!" She stands for a moment between the doorways to the den and the hall, with her hands on her hips, glaring at the TV, then turns and stomps into the kitchen.

"Don't count on it!" Ben calls after her. He's a Canadiens fan.

"Ha! Just for that," she calls back, "I won't bring you a glass of Beep!"

"*Oooooh! A scintillating save!*"

"I'll live," laughs Ben.

"Well, *I* won't," mutters Rebecca.

Ever since the game began, she's been sitting in the Eastern Star chair near the fireplace, squirming. It's usually fun staying with Marion whenever her Mum and Dad get drunk, but tonight she's bored.

She waits a little longer, while Danny Gallivan rhapsodizes over the tremendous pad save made by Plante, and then swivels to face Ben, who's sprawled on the chesterfield, smoking. "Do we have to watch this?"

"Yes."

She folds her arms across her chest and sulks.

Ben Kelly was one of the first people in Aylesford to get a TV. The day it arrived, Rebecca was so excited that she raced right over to watch him unwrap it. It was a huge, stand-up General Electric model, with an enormous black screen and all kinds of buttons and knobs. But she was more impressed by the box. She played in it all day. After that, members of her family began dropping over to watch their favourite shows. Right now, Sunny likes *I've Got a Secret* and *Alfred Hitchcock Presents* and *The Miss America Pageant*, although Rebecca can't see what she gets out of something that's only on once a year. The boys like the *Merrie Melodies* cartoons — an hour of silent little animals running around, beating each other up. Vivian likes the "stories," as she calls them, especially *Guiding Light* and *Search for Tomorrow*, and the quiz shows — she insists her precious *Truth or Consequences* isn't among those they've rigged — and *Country Hoedown*. She also likes the Everly Brothers and Michael Landon, but they don't have shows of their own.

Rebecca scowls at the little black and white men skittering across the screen. "How much longer?"

"Until the game's over."

"When will that be?"

"Rebecca!"

Marion is walking briskly from room to room, with an afghan draped around her shoulders. It's what she always does when she wants to lose a few pounds.

"What?"

"Do you want some…some juice?" she puffs.

"No."

"Then what…what do you want?"

Rebecca's eyes light up. "I want my own TV!"

"Scorrres! Moore scores! It looked like an innocent enough shot when he let it go, but at the last second it was redirected into the net off…"

"Ha!" Ben lays his pipe on the end table. "I told you, Marion. Those Red Wings of yours don't stand a chance against the likes of Moore and Harvey and Richard and…"

"OK! I get the point!" Marion keeps walking.

Rebecca folds her arms across her chest again.

She knows lots of hockey players. She even knows Frank Mahovlich, who won the Calder Trophy last season for being the best rookie. But she likes them best when they're on bubble-gum cards. She'd rather look at other things on TV, like *Captain Kangaroo* and *I Love Lucy* and *Frontier Justice*. All the cowboy shows, in fact — even if they are on way past her bedtime.

As the play-by-play resumes, she starts rhyming them off in her mind…*Gunsmoke, Wells Fargo, Wyatt Earp, Cheyenne, Have Gun Will Travel*…but the rhyming doesn't make the wanting go away. It makes it worse.

"So I don't have to watch *this* boring stuff!" She springs out of her chair.

Seconds later, she's flinging open one of the cupboards near the refrigerator. As she does, she can't help noticing the calendar on the door. Wednesday, October 22, 1958. Five more months of hockey, she sighs. And then she frowns. She's looking for cookies. But all she can find is kippers.

"Ha!" Marion walks briskly into the kitchen. "If you're looking…looking for something…to do…why don't you…go down…and fill up the coal hopper?"

"Can I? Really? All by myself?"

Marion clutches the afghan to her throat and strides into the dining room.

The stairs to the cellar are cluttered. Starting at the top, there's a glass jug of Scotian Gold apple cider, then a sack of her Dad's potatoes, then a box of cooking onions. Rebecca takes care to step around them as she inches her way downward. When she gets to the bottom, she reaches over her head and feels for the string. It isn't long before the room is bathed in a dull, yellow glow.

There isn't much there — just some old stoneware jugs, which once contained pickles and molasses, and a narrow swing-bed, which can be moved upstairs if more than one kid is staying overnight, and some dusty shelves, which hold jars of strawberry jam and green tomato relish.

She runs her finger over the little blue racoon slip-trailed onto the side of one of the jugs.

By far the most impressive thing is the enormous black shadow rising up behind the furnace. Yesterday, a man with a big brown truck came and dumped it there — through the window and down the chute. Some day, it would be a puny little pile of stoker pea coal but, right now, it's a mysterious mound of energy which almost touches the ceiling.

She climbs a little way up the shadow and retrieves the shovel. Then she slides back the cover on the large green hopper, makes sure the screw on the inside is really tight and begins to scoop in the shiny black nuggets.

Suddenly, there's a terrible yowl.

"Iyeeeee!" She's so startled that she loses her footing, and the pile of coal comes tumbling down on her, burying her up to her waist.

"Stupid cat!" she laughs, as she flings a piece of coal at the crack in the wall. "Wait till I get *you*!"

The old black stray scurries back to the rock ledge under the veranda, where it's always liked to sleep. Rebecca, meanwhile, begins to struggle out of the minor cave-in.

At quarter after eleven, while Ben and Marion are watching their favourite singer "Our Pet Juliette" begin her opening number, Rebecca tries to sneak upstairs. As she inches by the staircase, she touches everything she sees...the hall tree, the feather duster, the card table, the Bing Miller ball glove Ben used when he was a boy. When she turns to the cabinet, however, she stops.

Behind the glass doors, there are rows and rows of books. Most are from the Book-of-the-Month Club, which Ben's belonged to for years. But some have come from Ben's sister Colleen, who once went up to the North Pole to...Well, Ben says it was the elves she was teaching English to, but Rebecca thinks it must have been the Eskimos.

Colleen Kelly drives down from Ottawa to see her brothers Ben and Malcolm every summer. Her hair is snow-white, too — probably from being up in the Arctic so much, reasons Rebecca — and she gives the biggest, boniest hugs in the whole wide world. She also takes everyone out to eat at fancy seafood restaurants in Wolfville and uses tooth powder from a red and white can and sits outside on the wooden lawn chairs, helping Marion with the darning and mending that's piled up — which everyone agrees is a good thing, since it's always touch-and-go whether a hem is coming up or down when Marion's involved.

Rebecca stretches way up onto her tippy-toes, and then taps at the huge black Bible lying on top of the cabinet. It's Ben's special Bible; the one he got some sort of deal on, so his name got embossed in gold on the leather cover for nothing. Even if he didn't believe in God. She always reaches up and touches it on her way by the cabinet — partly for luck and partly to see if she's getting any taller.

"Don't forget to have a bath!"

Rebecca jumps.

"Rebecca? Did you hear what I said?"

"But I only have baths on Sundays!"

"Yes, well, you're not going to wait until then to get that coal dust off, are you?"

Rebecca frowns. She can never figure out how Marion knows things.

"Are you?"

"I guess not." She scrapes her toe against the rubber flap on the bottom step; lifts it extra high, in fact, so its slap is extra loud.

"I'll be there in a minute," laughs Marion. "To tuck you in."

Rebecca slaps up the stairs.

"I can't find any bottoms!" hollers Rebecca, as she leaps under the covers.

"Try the cedar chest!" Marion hollers back.

"Brrrrrrr."

Rebecca peers at the big wooden box at the foot of the cot. But she doesn't get up. It's too cold to get up. She wishes she could use an electric blanket, like Ben does, but she can't — not until she stops wetting her bed.

"Hey! What's that?" She leans forward. The plastic sheet on the mattress rustles.

"What's what?"

Marion is tiptoeing up the stairs.

"That." Rebecca points to a big, black, jagged thing on top of the chest, beside the pile of clean and folded clothes.

"*That*," laughs Marion, "is a rock."

"Where did it come from?"

"Well, it's my guess that Buddy Matheson threw it through the window; probably when Doris opened it to air out the hall. He's been doing that lately."

"But why? Is he nuts?"

"Nobody knows." Marion starts sifting through the pile of clothes. "Least of all poor June. He just turns mean. For no reason. Anyway, here." She tosses Rebecca a pair of blue and white striped bottoms. "Put these on. They'll go really well with the buttercups."

Rebecca giggles. And then quickly squirms into the bottoms and snuggles under the covers. "Brrrrr. I'm still cold."

"I can fix that," says Marion mysteriously.

"You can?" She watches her lift the lid of the chest. "How?"

"With this." Marion holds up a light green, quilted bed covering.

"A new puff! Where did you get it?"

"At the church supper." Marion flings it on top of her. "While you were busy being…"

Rebecca brushes it off her face.

"… being a pain."

"No, I wasn't! I was only…!"

"Yes. Well…" Marion tucks it around her. "Time to go to sleep now." She turns toward the stairs. "Or you'll never get up in time to beat Malcolm to the…"

"Marion? Will you be my Mum?"

She stops at the landing. "You have a Mum."

"Yeah, but she's no good."

Marion pauses for moment, then turns back towards the cot. "What makes you say that?" she asks quietly.

"Well...she's always yelling at me."

Marion laughs. "Sometimes you deserve it."

"Oh."

"Anything else?"

"Ummm...Do I deserve her to be drunk all the time?"

"No, but..." Marion sits on the edge of the cot.

"Donnie says she threw me down the stairs when I was a baby."

"No." Marion strokes Rebecca's damp hair. "I think that was an accident."

"Did I do something to make her mad? Didn't she love me?"

"Oh, yes, Rebecca! She loved you very much! Ha! I remember how worried she was when you were born. Dr. Sutherland had to pull you out with the forceps, you know."

"I know."

"So you were all bruised and..."

"Was I?" Rebecca props herself up on her elbows. "Where?"

Marion laughs. "Mostly on your face. Your cheek, your eye..."

"Neat!"

"And I remember how proud she looked when she wheeled you up and down Old Post Road in that dark blue, leather baby carriage. Ha!" Marion's face is contorted in laughter. "Even when you had eczema so bad that all your hair had fallen out!"

"Was I ugly?" giggles Rebecca.

"Well, you wouldn't have won any beauty contests. But Vivian didn't mind. She took you everywhere with her. Wheeled you, carried you, showed you off to all her..."

"Did she feed me?"

"Of course, she fed you."

"What?" Rebecca flops back down again. "Fluffs?"

"No, not Fluffs. Formula, at first, then Pablum, carrots, bananas. I wrote...She wrote down all the dates and amounts in the Baby Book she got from Wanda Willoughby when you were born. Said she was going to make sure she did it right this time."

"OK, but how come I don't get any of that good junk to eat now?"

The crickets have stopped rubbing their wings together. There's no more traffic. The only sound is a tiny tinkling coming from the kitchen.

Rebecca's eyes pop open.

But it's only Marion, getting the milk money out of the little metal match-safe on the wall by the back door. Ben says the little box used to contain wooden matches to light the stove and the lamps, but now it mostly holds junk — old buttons, safety pins, loose change.

Rebecca's eyes flutter shut again.

As she drifts back to sleep, she listens for the creak and tap of the screen door...and the jingle and clink of the Farmer's Milk bottles...and the...

Her eyes pop back open.

She hasn't heard the second creak and tap. Marion hasn't come back in yet.

"I wonder what she's *doing*?"

Rebecca slides out of bed and creeps down the hall...past Ben's room and Malcolm's room and...She trips a little on the step by the bathroom. But when no one stirs, she keeps on creeping until, at the end of the hall, she quickly slips through the open door, across the Arabian carpet and through the door at the back of the room.

As soon as it clicks behind her, she gets scared. She's been in the back chamber hundreds of times. But never at night. When it's creepy. When the old suits hanging from the line seem to drip blood; when the old books stacked in the corner seem to whisper threats; when the cobwebs seem as big as dragnets.

Suddenly, her eyes grow wide, not just with terror but with determination. She's going to look out that dusty back window whether those scary things like it or not. She takes a deep breath and marches right through the creepiness. And then she frowns. The window pane is pretty grimy, but she can still see the lawn and the garden and the paths to the woods. What she can't see is Marion. Disappointed, she presses her face against the glass.

No sooner does her nose touch the pane than the dust goes up her nostrils and she sneezes. Scared the men are going to wake up, she scrambles back down the hall.

Just before she drops off, she hears a familiar sound.

Chink, chink, chink.

It's the wind, slipping through her bottle caps.

24

Every fall, Carl Porter moves his animals across the street, from his old barn to his new one. This is a two-storey structure set back from the road, just west of Marshall's house. It has a real wooden part at the front and a modern concrete-block extension at the back. The kids think it's neat, because it's painted white and has rows and rows of windows along its sides, but they don't go there very often. Just on weekends, when they don't have school.

"Ow!" shouts Randy. He and Rebecca are taking the shortcut through Alice's rosebushes. "Let's go the long way next time!"

Rebecca doesn't answer. She's pretending to stalk big game through a pretty pink and yellow jungle.

"Oh, no! She sees us! Run!"

Rebecca doesn't have to look. She knows he means Sissy. And if they don't hurry, she'll catch up to them. And then knock them over and slobber on them and make them throw the ball for her.

"Quick! Quick!" she squeals, as they scramble through the prickly shrubs.

The last few yards to safety are within sight of the Field of Bones. This is a large patch of scruffy grass behind the barn where Calvin and Murray Loomer dump the bones after the pigs have sucked the meat off them. Where the bones come from in the first place — Randy says the store; Rebecca says the slaughterhouse — is a mystery. But that's where they always end up — dried out, bleached, absolutely useless.

"Made it!" she shouts, as they dance through the door of the barn.

"Hey, you two!"

They spin around.

"Where are you, Carl?" cries Randy.

"Over here, changing the salt licks."

On the west side of the barn, there are two rows of stalls for the cows. They're a lot fancier than the stalls at the old barn — mostly because of the shiny metal troughs. Rebecca likes the ones for drinking. She thinks it's fun to watch the cows stick their noses into the gleaming bowls and then press those pedals with the holes in them. But she doesn't like the ones for shitting. Carl's always asking for volunteers to scrape the mess out of them — scrape it into that big smelly hole near the back of the barn — and she thinks that should be Calvin and Murray's job.

"Right." Carl rubs his hands together. "Now who wants to help me fill the mangers?"

"Me! Me!"

While Randy helps Carl pitch hay into the boxes, Rebecca wanders up and down the rows of stalls, patting the cows on their noses.

"It's OK. Shsh. It won't be long. It'll be warm soon. Just a few months. Shsh."

She feels so sorry for them. They don't have nearly as much fun over here as they do across the street. Over here, they never get any exercise. They just stand in one spot, like despondent statues, with their necks in those shiny metal braces.

"OK, what should we play with first? The chickens or the pigs? Hey!" Randy gives her a shove. "Did you hear me?"

"Ummmmm...pigs!"

Soon there are squeals coming from the east side of the barn.

"Come here, you little bugger!" screeches Randy, as he chases a tiny black pig around the perimeter of the pen.

Rebecca giggles. "Don't let Mum catch you saying that!"

"Why not?" He dives after the Berkshire. And misses.

"Oh, yuck, Randy!"

He rolls over on his back and spits out a mouthful of manure. "*She* says it."

They burst into laughter.

Pigs are luckier than cows, decides Rebecca, as she tries to remember what Carl once told her. Cows have to marry cows which look exactly like they do. But pigs get to fall in love with pigs that are different. So if Carl lets a...

Suddenly, one of the larger pigs — a cherry-red Hereford hog with white splashes on its face and tail — turns on them.

"There!" shrieks Rebecca. "Behind you! Get it!"

Randy leaps to his feet. "Are you crazy? That one's too big!"

"Is not!"

"Is too, you little twerp! Look at those bristles!"

"You're just a scaredy-cat."

"*Me!*" I don't see *you* trying to get it."

"OK, I will."

After a few deft dodges and feints, Rebecca has the Hereford trapped in a corner of the pen. She's just beginning to creep toward it...with her hands poised, ready to clutch at its filthy red neck...when the conveyer belt starts up.

"The new bales!"

"Yeah!"

"I forgot about those!"

They scramble out of the pen.

The bales are more fun than anything. Sometimes, after he's loaded them onto the wagon, Carl lets the kids sit on top while he drives them across to the barn. Once, the bales were piled so high that the kids had to duck under the street wires — either that or get their heads cut off.

"Jesus H. Christ."

Carl is waiting by the mound of bales he's dumped outside.

"What?" Randy and Rebecca skid to a stop.

"What's your mother going to say when she sees you?"

They peer down at their clothes, which are completely covered with muck.

"I don't know."

"What do you mean, Carl?"

"Never mind," he laughs. "Sorry I asked." He begins to load the bales onto the conveyer belt.

For the next few minutes, Randy and Rebecca watch the bales inch slowly upward, toward the open window in the loft of the barn. Then, as if it's all part of their ritual, Rebecca steps forward and clears her throat.

"Carl?"

"Hmmm?" He keeps loading.

"Can we...can we ride the escalator?"

"Sure," he chuckles. "Sure you can." He hoists one, and then the other, onto a bale.

"Yippee!"

"Ride 'em cowboy!"

"Here we come, you two!"

As he watches them crawl toward the top, Carl keeps chuckling. The ride may be magic, but it's very slow magic.

"Where's Calvin?" asks Rebecca, as she dips through the window and thumps to the floor.

Murray throws a handful of salt onto a layer of bales. "I don't know. I thought he was…"

The brothers are rarely apart. It's always Calvin-and-Murray this and Calvin-and-Murray that.

"No, wait. Come to think of it, he said he was going to drive a cow over to…"

Just then, the half-ton truck starts up. Rebecca rushes to the window. But Randy stays behind with Murray.

"Can I help?" he asks sheepishly.

"Sure. Be my guest."

"Gee, thanks." He takes a handful of big white crystals from the bucket and flings it at the bales.

"Hey! Take it easy! Not so much!"

"Sorry." He waits until Murray has piled a second layer of bales on top of the first one, then takes a smaller handful of salt and sprinkles it over them.

Rebecca, meanwhile, presses her face against the glass. She has a perfect view.

The half-ton truck rocks a little as Calvin tries to coax a Holstein into the box. When at last he does, he quickly kicks away the wooden ramp, slams the tailgate shut and hops into the cab.

As the truck pulls slowly down the lane, Rebecca takes a deep breath and then exhales. It's through a cloud of condensation, then, that she thinks she sees the truck idling at the end of the lane; thinks she sees the truck angling sharply into the road; thinks she sees a big black and white thing lying…Frantic now, she wipes the glass with her sleeve. It's true.

"Murray! Murray!" she screams.

"Now what?" He tosses another bale onto the pile.

"The cow fell off the truck!"

"What!" He rushes to the window. "Oh my gaaaaawd." He scrambles to the ladder. "Oh, my…"

"Neat!" Randy scrambles after him.

"What are you going to do, Murray?" wails Rebecca. "What are you going to dooooooo?"

"Stop your bawling and come on!" Randy pauses at the top of the ladder. "Or you'll miss everything!"

But Rebecca doesn't move. She already has a perfect view.

"Wait for meeeee!" hollers Randy as he scrambles down the ladder.

After a minute, Rebecca presses her face against the glass again. Even through the smudges, she can see the men standing with their hands on their hips. She can see them shaking their heads and backing away a little. She can see the cow thrashing around on the pavement. She can see Carl walking slowly up to it, then aiming his rifle right at the spot where she patted it.

"A perfect view," murmurs Rebecca, as she strolls to the window of the back chamber.

The world looks damp now and streaky brown — like a nest with a hole in the bottom. It's the same way Marion's face looked that evening when she was writing in her datebook; when she formed a mysterious word in those long, elegant loops of hers and then jerked her pen away from the page. Rebecca couldn't figure out what that word was then, while Marion was furiously erasing it, and she can't figure it out now. Most good people have transparent souls. There's no mystery to their relentless giving. No secrets. No ulterior motives. Nothing going on except "goodness." Marion's soul was translucent.

"A perfect view."

Rebecca knows there must be a reason why Marion looked so sad that night, but she can't get past the diffusion, the distortion of Marion's soul. It wasn't the gold watch and the cleaning lady business, however. Rebecca had asked her about that. And it couldn't have been just choir practice on Thursday, Red Cross on Friday, bingo on Saturday that made Marion whisper hoarsely, "No, I can't, I can't." And then, sickened, enthralled, bury her face in her hands. After all, she was used to being busy.

Rebecca can't help wondering what images exploded in the deepest recess of Marion's reluctance; can't help wondering what Marion saw on the back of her sheltering hands that made her dig her fingers into her eyelids. It was as if there were a ghost hiding in the margins of her hectic schedule. Something Marion couldn't quite see that was unbuttoning her reluctance, flinging it in the face of her objections, showing her the depths of her moist and miraculous pain.

"No, I can't, I can't, I can't, I can't!" Marion had practically shouted at her. "It would never work! I can't!" And then she'd squiggled something — in tiny, little letters this time — and slammed the datebook shut.

"OK!" Marion had said to her. "Where do you want to go tomorrow?"

Once again, Rebecca watches as Marion's soul clouds over and the desire behind it becomes indistinguishable — just another shadowy object behind the terrible translucency.

Rebecca slumps to the floor of the back chamber. She's cold, tired, barely tinged with hope. She wants to go home. Or at least somewhere that isn't filled with darkness and dust. Suddenly, she sees a band of colour; hears an exuberant cry. There's a red-winged blackbird dipping through her mind. A gaudy memory, a noisy promise, a brilliant reminder that sorrow is crazier than joy.

"Whatever that means," she murmurs.

25

As soon as the Buick creeps into Vivian's driveway, Randy and Rebecca come tumbling out of the house.

"We're ready!"

They're dressed in their good clothes — Randy in his grey shorts, starched white shirt and teeny-weeny, plaid bow tie; Rebecca in her short, white cotton dress, dark blue cardigan, white ankle socks and scuffed brown oxfords.

"Where's your Mum?" Marion asks wearily.

"Up to Elsie Smeltzer's place." Rebecca hops from foot to foot. "She's mad about not coming with us."

"Where *are* we going anyway?" Randy tugs at the crotch of his shorts.

"It's a secret."

"I bet *I* know!" blurts Rebecca. "Shubenacadie!"

Every year, Marion takes the kids to the Wildlife Preserve in Shubenacadie, where they pat the llamas, feed apples to the fawns and laugh at the big black bears rolling gently on their backs in the grass.

"I like the skunks!" shouts Rebecca, as she twirls around on the driveway.

"No, you don't," scoffs Randy. "You like the red foxes."

"That was last year. This year I like..."

"Yeah, well, I *don't* like the peacocks."

Rebecca stops twirling. "Why not? They're so pretty when their tails are spread out."

"Not from the back they're not. From the back they're ugly. Just big brown sticks." Randy snaps his gum.

"Yeah, but from the front..."

"Too many eyes."

Marion can't help smiling.

"Well, I was wrong anyway," drawls Rebecca. "We're not going there."

"How do you know?"

"Well, for one thing, it's not Sunday. We always go on a Sunday. And for another, we're all dressed up."

"Oh. Well, then, how about...Stewiake?"

Marion shakes her head.

Stewiake is where Aubrey and Mildred Roop live — on a big farm, with a big white house, and *three*, big burgundy barns. It's a magnificent place, compared to Carl Porter's, but it's not a place for good clothes either.

"I know! I know!" squeals Rebecca. "Gabriel Motors!"

"Yeah!"

"We could help Ben pump the gas! Or wash the cars!"

"Or maybe even sell them!"

"Yeah!"

Marion's still laughing.

Gabriel Motors is the Ford dealership in Coldbrook which Ben and Malcolm have invested in. The first time she took the kids there barely ten minutes went by before she was screaming at them to climb down from the big latticework tower beside the service bays. The last time they got so bored listening to Butch Beals tell stories about his prostate operation that they just went outside and sat by the big, yellow White Rose pump marked Premium and picked their noses.

"OK, OK." She puts them out of their misery. "We're going to Bridgetown."

"Oh." They're tremendously disappointed. Bridgetown's just where

Grammie grew up. There aren't any neat animals there.
"To see Gertie and Nanny Henderson. And Ernest Buckler, if he's home."
"Oh." They hate just visiting.
"And if there's time, we can stop at the bakery and get…"
"Egg tarts!"
"Molasses cookies!"
"YAY!"

As they turn into Grammie's driveway, "Honeycomb" is playing on the car radio.
"She's not ready," murmurs Marion.
"How do you know?"
"She's not peeking out the living room curtains."
The kids giggle.

There's a green corduroy couch beneath the east window in Grammie's kitchen. The kids think it's neat because it has ribs that go up and down as well as across and because it can be turned into a double-decker bed. When the upstairs gets so full that two of them have to stay down here overnight, they just pull out the bottom drawer, place two cushions from the top part into it, and then go to sleep — one up above and the other down below. But it's also a great place just to sit and watch, whether Grammie's applying Woodbury Dry Skin Cream to the five danger zones — frown lines, expression lines, crow's feet, flaky patches and crepey throat — or putting on her famous finishing touch, like she's doing right now.
"I swear that girl's on the phone…" Grammie leans toward the mirror to the right of the sink.
The kids lean forward, too, fascinated by the ritual of the droopy left eyelid.
"… more than anyone I…" She takes a bit of translucent beige tape and, with a deft little flick, grabs the top of her lid with one end and sticks it to her brow with the other. "There."
"You did it first time, Grammie!"
She whirls away from the mirror. "Now. Where's my coat? I thought I put it…"

"Is this it, Grammie?" Randy pulls a mound of rough grey wool from beneath him.

It's the tweed coat Marion bought her at Harriet's. She slips her arms into its finely twilled sleeves.

"OK, Marion! You can get off the phone now! We're ready!"

"How come *you* don't drive, Grammie?"

"I don't need to drive." She pulls open the back door of the Buick. "I have friends to drive me wherever I need to go."

"Oh." Rebecca thinks for a moment. "Well, *I'm* sure going to drive!" She slides into the back seat. "I'm going to drive the fastest, shiniest car in the whole wide world!"

"Yeah?" Randy bounces in beside her. "Who says?"

Marion and Grammie gaze at each other across the roof.

"Well, Mum. What do you think? I bet there isn't another five-year-old anywhere who knows as much about cars as Rebecca does. Now watch your fingers, everyone." She ducks inside.

They all shut their doors.

"Psst! Rebecca!" Randy elbows her.

"What?"

"You'll probably just have an old crate."

"No, I won't! I'll have one with...with *auto-pilot*!"

"Ha!" laughs Marion, in disbelief. "It's Chrysler's newest innovation," she says to Grammie, "and the little bugger knows all about it."

"*No wonder my happy heart sings. Your love has given me...*"

As they pull out onto Old Post Road, Marion tunes out "Volare." Then she laughs and turns to Grammie again. "She can tell the difference between them, not just by looking at their bodies, Mum, but their grills, their taillights even! It's amazing."

"Big hairy deal," mutters Randy.

Grammie glances over her shoulder. "Have you picked out what colour this shiny, fast car is going to be?"

"Yellow!" blurts Rebecca. "No! Red!"

"Yeah, right," Randy mutters again. "You'll probably just steal it, like you stole that...Ow!"

She's pinched him hard on the arm.

Grammie glances over her shoulder again. "You needn't t'bother fighting."

As they drive through Auburn, the new Johnny Mathis song is playing on the radio.

"Chances are...'cause I wear a silly grin the moment you come into view."

"Hey, look!" Rebecca springs forward. "Isn't that...?"

Just ahead, by Flewelling's Shell Station, there's a lone hitchhiker. The car zooms by.

"Hey!" She swivels around. "That *was* Frankie!"

"Was it?" murmurs Marion. She stares through the green-tinted glass at the top of the windshield.

"Yeah! Why didn't you stop?"

"We don't have any room."

"Yeah, well." Rebecca flops back down in her seat. "We could have squished together. This isn't a Triumph or anything."

The Buick is pretty rusty around the rear wheel wells. In fact, on the left-hand side, where Rebecca's sitting, there's an enormous hole in the floor where she can watch the road fly by. After thirty-five miles, however, it suddenly begins to drift and wander and creep until, finally, it stops moving altogether.

"Time to start visiting," sighs Randy.

Rebecca blinks.

Grammie's always strangely quiet whenever they visit Bridgetown. Probably because she's remembering her childhood, Rebecca guesses. Grammie's told her lots of stories about how her mother gave her away to a wealthy family in Annapolis Royal. About how she had to march all the way back home and convince her mother to keep her. About how she became the best of any of them at shearing, never mind tramping back and forth from Bridgetown to Annapolis selling the wool. About how her two younger sisters still live here, quite near each other on Route 201, just south of Highway 1 and the river. Gertie Phillips is generally regarded as the *nice* one. She once ran Phillips Business College in Kentville and is always making fudge and sneaking quarters into the kids' pockets. Edith Illsley, on the other hand, is the *hard* one. Rebecca once thought that maybe Edith was too busy running the orchards to be nice, but then she remembered the Swinnimers — who are really nice — so it must be something else.

When the Aylesford gang arrives at the Illsley place, Gertie is sitting in the spacious kitchen, making apple butter. Edith and her boys are out in the orchards. No one minds missing Cousin Edmund. He's as mean and tricky as his mother. But they're sorry they can't see Cousin Herman. He may sweat a lot when he gets nervous. And his eyes may twitch a lot when there's something in *TIME* magazine he doesn't understand. But he's as nice as his Aunt Gertie.

"Sorry we can't stay. We're on our way to..."

There's a lot less room in the back seat with Gertie there, but Rebecca doesn't care. She's too busy watching the road whiz by and taking big slurpy bites of her apple — which she barely has time to finish before the road suddenly leaps and swirls and...

"Hey! What's going on?" She drops her core through the hole in the floor.

"Nothing." Marion pulls into Nanny Henderson's lane. "I almost missed the turn, that's all."

"That would've been fine with me," grumbles Randy.

Grammie's mother-in-law is snipping at a cluster of Blossom Time roses on one of the many tall trellises surrounding her farmhouse. The kids hang around long enough to get their picture taken with her and then run off — but not so far away that they can't hear the grown-ups chatting about the differences between tea roses and everblooming climbers. Or gossiping about the latest troubles the cops are having with the negroes down near Brickyard Road.

"No, sorry. We promised we'd drop in on..."

For the next few minutes, Rebecca's attention is divided between the hole in the floor and the thorn in her finger. And then, suddenly, Marion jams the gear-shift into park.

"OK, everyone. We're here."

"I'm hungry," mutters Rebecca.

"Well, you'll just have to wait."

"Who *is* this Mr. Buckler anyway?" asks Randy.

Marion laughs. "Well, let's see. He's my second cousin, twice...or is it three times removed? Anyway, I knew him when I was a girl. I grew up in Bridgetown, you know."

"Yeah, well, I just hope he has food," mutters Rebecca.

As soon as they push open the car doors, they're besieged by strange, piercing cries.

"What's that?" Randy whispers to Rebecca.

"How should *I* know?" she whispers back.

Their eyes widen.

"It's opera," laughs Marion. "Now, come on. It won't bite." She strolls toward the small, white wooden farmhouse.

"Let *me* knock!" Randy rushes up the steps to the porch.

Before he can bang on the door, however, it flies open.

"Yow!" He leaps back.

"Oh, it's you." A man with slick grey hair waves a martini at them. "Well, come in. Come in."

As they follow him into the living room, where the music is even weirder and louder, Rebecca stares at his feet. She's never seen an old man with black, high-top sneakers before.

"I'm glad it's you." He jabs at the bridge of his dark-rimmed glasses. "Sit. Sit. Do you want a drink?"

"No, thanks. We only dropped by to..."

"I'll have a beer!" blurts Randy.

"No, you will not!" hisses Grammie. "Now behave! Sorry, Ernie. You know how kids can..."

"Such daring chromatics," he murmurs to himself. "And such fluid duality. Yes. All of life's pain and poison in a single..."

"Ernie?" Grammie tries again.

"Sorry? Oh, yes. I'm glad it's you." He takes a sip of his martini. "I thought it was the friggin' minister."

The kids giggle.

"Go ahead, laugh!" There's a stern twinkle in his eye. "But when you're older, you won't think it's so funny. When you're older, you'll find out what I already know."

"What's that, Mr. Buckler?"

"Ha!" The twinkle vanishes. "That ministers and rats are the lowest form of life!"

The kids don't dare giggle.

After the tirade, there's a long pause, during which nobody says a word. Randy wiggles his feet a little. And Rebecca watches Mr. Buckler's eyes, waiting for them to start twinkling again. But nobody talks. And Mr. Buckler just sits there, staring at his martini. He and Rebecca are the only ones with their eyes still open. Gertie, Grammie and Marion have all shut out the ordinary details of the outside world. They think that's the way you're supposed to listen to sad music. Maybe they need to listen to it that way, thinks Rebecca, as she watches their eyelids flutter. Of course, Randy's just bored. He's squeezed his eyelids so tightly together that he's probably seeing stars.

Tired of waiting for the twinkle to return, Rebecca shifts her gaze from Mr. Buckler's eyes to the room. Besides the furniture, it's really just a jumble of papers and books, some of which have his name on the cover. Marion's told her about the famous one — a sad tale about the place where they live — but she can't remember the name of it. And she can't understand why people write about dumb things like that anyway, when there's all sorts of really neat things, like baseball or cars.

Suddenly, her eyes fix on the one thing that isn't part of the decor or the jumble. The stereo. She's never seen a record player like it — with different parts, not just one big piece — and she's never heard one like it either. It makes the music seem so large. And so tricky, like it's coming from more than one place at the same time.

"*Nurse me, kill me. Nurse me, kill me*," murmurs Mr. Buckler.

"I have to pee," whispers Randy.

"No, you don't," she whispers back. "Now, shshsh."

Once again, Randy squishes his eyes shut. Only now he's mad as well as bored.

Rebecca, meanwhile, is actually smiling at the heart-breaking notes. And then shivering. And then smiling and shivering again. It's all so exciting. She feels like she's being gobbled up by those wavering voices. Which sometimes sound sad. Which sometimes sound nuts. She looks back and forth, from speaker to speaker. It's all so frustrating, too. The sound is beautiful, but she doesn't think much of the song.

Snap! Randy's gum pops loudly.

"Oops."

"Maybe I should get you that beer," mumbles Mr. Buckler. "Or would you rather have a magic potion that turns hatred and indifference into love?"

"Pardon?" Randy swallows his gum.

Now that Randy's gum has broken the spell, Rebecca doesn't see why she shouldn't say something.

"Mr. Buckler?"

"Hmmm?"

A terrible scream of pain and joy blares from the speakers.

"What is that song anyway?"

"The love duet from *Tristan and Isolde*," he answers quietly.

"Oh. What's it about?"

He takes a sip of his martini. "It's a simple story, really, about treachery, honour, betrayal and death."

The kids look at each other and giggle.

"Stop that!" hisses Grammie.

"What?"

"We were just laughing."

"Well, you needn't t'bother."

"OK, but…" Rebecca turns to Mr. Buckler again. "What's the *story*?"

"Well, let's see." He takes another sip. "There was once a beautiful Irish Princess named…"

"We saw the Princesses last spring!" she squeals. "The ones from the Apple Blossom Festival!"

"Ha! Nothing but a bunch of friggin' lunatics!"

"No, they weren't! They were pretty! And they were wearing their…!"

"Not them, child! The fellows who run the show! Those arseholes!"

"Oh."

"They can't do a thing without bringing religion into it. So they've pretty near ruined everything! Anyway, the Irish Princess is named Isolde."

The long pause after this tirade is punctuated by sniffling. Rebecca can tell that the music is filled with sadness — and that it's making Gertie, Grammie and Marion all need Kleenex — but she wishes she knew exactly what there is to cry about.

"Mr. Buckler?"

"Wait, child. Yes. Hear that? Those upper notes of longing? Those lower notes of suffering? That's what the whole friggin' world is all…"

"Mr. Buckler?" Her curiosity about the actual story is greater than her fear of having her head bitten off.

"Yes, child?"

"*Now* what's happening?"

He leans toward her, as he would toward another grown-up, and tells her about the two lovers. About how they've been caught; about how the knight Tristan has been wounded in a duel and is now dying in Isolde's arms.

"Oh."

"And pretty soon *she's* going to die, too." He sets his empty glass on the table. "Of a broken heart."

"Oh."

As they pile into the car again, a light rain is falling — gently, so gently it hurts. Not like hail hurts, perhaps, but just as much.

"OK, then," whispers Marion, as she watches the tiny rivers of raindrops flow like tears down the green-tinted slope at the top of the windshield. "We're all set."

She pulls a knob on the dashboard. The wipers pass over the tiny tears. Again and again, from the outside in. But it's no use. The rain just keeps lapping back again.

Once again, it's Randy who breaks the mood. "Look out, egg tarts! Here we come!"

Gertie rolls down her window. "Thank you, Ernie," she murmurs.

He nods, then taps lightly on the back window. Rebecca cranks it down.

"Did you like the music?" he asks gently.

"Yes." She knits her brow. "But I liked your sneakers better."

As they pull slowly away, Mr. Buckler is still standing in his driveway, laughing and laughing. And getting his sneakers soaked.

"Oh, God," rasps Rebecca. "Tristan and Isolde…"

But her memory is flooded with her own two-voiced prelude of terror and disgust. And the voices of the doomed lovers are drowned out completely.

"What was it I saw the night we got back from Mr. Buckler's? Let's see…it was the very next time I went to look."

It's occurred to her that the next time she slipped out of bed and down the stairs, it wasn't to find out about the smoke in Frankie's cabin. It was to find out about her tambourine.

Night after night, the door had edged open, the wind had slipped through, the bottle caps had jingled. Night after night, the pairs of jingles had brushed one another, lightly, beseechingly, as if there really could be magic in the rhythms of darkness. And then, suddenly, the jingling had stopped. And the night had lost its voice and its spirit and its gratification. She wanted to know why. She thought perhaps her Mum had come and stolen her tambourine.

As usual, it was a little tricky getting down to the kitchen and out the door. First, there was Marion, standing in her dimly lit bedroom, slipping her nightdress over her head — its field of buttercups rippling gently past her shoulders and hips — and then reaching for her brush. That sturdy plastic brush Rebecca had given her last Christmas. With the long black handle and the soft red pad, where the stiff black bristles were stuck. And then there was the knocking at the back door.

As Rebecca recalls now, Marion had said, "Jesus. Now what?" and then jammed her feet into her brown leather slippers — the ones with the big brown puffs of fur — and scurried downstairs.

She herself had said, "Nuts!" and plastered herself against the wall in the hall. And then tiptoed down to the dining room to watch.

"I'm coming!" Marion flings open the door. And then gasps.

Frankie is standing on the back veranda. His face is covered in white paint.

Rebecca's eyes widen.

"Is this better?" he asks calmly.

"What are you doing?"

"Is this what you want?"

"Go away."

He doesn't move.

"Go away!"

He backs down the stairs.

Rebecca cranes her neck.

It looks like Marion wants to close the door, but can't. It's as if he's pulling her toward him. And for a while, Marion just watches him…watches him turn, watches him push open the door, hears the jingling of those seven pairs of dented bottle caps…but then she follows him.

As Marion drifts toward the cabin, she looks like a flying carpet of yellow. The air is swimming through her. But then, suddenly, it's as if she's frightened by the shadows — and the spell is broken.

Rebecca creeps out to the veranda.

Marion is standing just inside the door of Frankie's cabin, watching him wash the paint off his face.

"I wish I could hear," grumbles Rebecca. But she's afraid to get any closer. "If I could hear, I could...Yay!" She's spotted her tambourine, hanging from a nail next to Frankie's towel.

Marion must have found what she was looking for, too, because as soon as Frankie buries his face in the towel, she moves to the door.

There's a plaintive chink, chink as she slips back outside.

"Oh-oh!" Rebecca ducks into the house. She doesn't go right upstairs, however. She stays in the kitchen, watching Marion drift away from the cabin.

At first, she sees nothing but a field of buttercups waving in the moonlight. But then she sees the other flowers, too — the devil's paintbrushes, with their naked stalks and their flaming orange heads.

26

"Marion, quick!" Rebecca bursts into the kitchen. "I've ripped my sheet!" She drops her brown paper shopping bag to the floor.

Marion laughs.

"Nooo! It's not funny! You have to fix it!" She drags the sheet off over her head.

"Well, I'll try."

"Quick!"

Marion's still laughing as she reaches for the greasy pin cushion stuck to the wall above the sink. "But, remember, I'm not very good at this." She pulls out a fuzzy needle. "You should really go over to your Grammie's if you want an expert."

"I can't!" Rebecca holds the sheet out to her. "She's too busy cooking!"

"Well, in that case..." Marion snatches the sheet. "I'll do the best I can." She plops down in the rocking chair.

Grammie often says that her sewing skills weren't inherited by her daughters. Marion, Florence and Vivian are all lucky if they can get a button sewn on properly. If they have any real mending to do, they pass it along to Grammie. Or to Janet Pine, who also knits those big bulky winter sweaters with hockey players and soldiers on them.

"How come you can iron, but you can't sew?" asks Rebecca.

Marion glances at the irons, hanging on the wall by the door to the woodhouse. A dry one. One for steam. "I really don't know," she laughs. "Maybe it has something to do with..."

"Hurry up, Rebecca!" comes a desperate cry from the back veranda. "Or there won't be nothing left!"

"Marion?" Rebecca leans toward the rocking chair. "How much longer will it...?"

"Done!" Marion breaks the thread with her teeth. "And it's the best I can do." She holds up the sheet. "So don't you complain if..."

"Neat! A scar! A big, long scar!" Rebecca grabs the sheet and pulls it back over her head. When she's got the eye holes adjusted properly, she makes an announcement. "I'm going as a ghost!"

"Yes." Marion sticks the needle back into the cushion. "I can see that."

"We're *all* going as ghosts. Big ones. Little ones. The most ghosts in the whole wide world!" She screws up her face. "Or white witches and wizards. I can't decide. I saw this picture in a magazine at Marilyn Addy's place." Her eyes are big black holes.

"Well, have fun," says Marion softly, as she drops a chocolate bar and a handful of candy kisses into the shopping bag.

"Thanks! And I'll come back later..." She flies out the door. "For the leftovers! Hey, Randy! Wait for meeeee!"

It isn't long before there's a cluster of little ghosts drifting from house to house, sometimes hollering "Trick or treat!" but mostly just knocking on doors. They aren't really interested in playing tricks. They just think you have to say that sometimes to scare the grown-ups into giving you candy.

"Yoo-hoo!"

"Hey!"

There's a clown and a tramp coming from Thelma Peel's place.

"What's she got this year?"

"Candy apples!"

"Yay!"

All but one of the little ghosts race up Thelma's drive.

Rebecca doesn't like candy apples very much. The red ones are pretty, but they're also pretty messy. You can't eat them without getting all gooey. The brown ones are better, but even they're all mushy inside. She once heard Grammie call them "Apples of Sodom."

Grammie never goes to church with us, she suddenly remembers. But she sure knows lots of neat junk from the Bible. Things other people don't know, like about apples that are pretty to look at, but just have ashes inside.

She keeps walking.

"Hey! Where are you going?"

"To the Hills's!"

"What?"

"Are you crazy?"

"They won't open the door!"

"I know. I'm just going to peek in the window."

"Why?"

"Because I feel like it." She tugs at her big, long scar.

"OK, but we're not going to wait."

"So? I'll catch up."

Rebecca's already seen witches — a whole bunch of them — walking down the street in Kentville. Marion told her they were really something called "nuns," but she knew they were witches. And she wasn't scared one bit! At any rate, she's made up her mind that there are two spooky places she's going to visit tonight. They're both pretty spooky on ordinary days of the year, so they must be really spooky on Halloween.

As she creeps toward the Hills's glassed-in sun porch, she sees they haven't left the light on. But then they never do. They just don't want visitors. Florence says it's because they have a deep, dark secret, but Rebecca doesn't know anything about that. She only knows that Winifred is a pain and that her parents are mean and keep to themselves.

Maybe they eat little children, she thinks, as she boosts herself up. Or maybe they drink blood instead of milk. After all, Emerson *is* in charge of collecting for the Red Cross. She cups her hands around her eyes and peers through the window. Her disappointment is instantaneous.

There isn't anything scary in the living room. Just a tall, skinny old man sitting at a piano, playing what sounds like "All Through the Night." And that stuck-up Winifred rolling around on the carpet with her Scottie dog Sue. But then, suddenly, a shiver goes up Rebecca's spine. She can see Mr. Hill and Winifred all right, but she can't see

Mrs. Hill. She must be in another room. Either that or...

"Boo!"

Rebecca falls to the ground.

"Ha! Got you!"

Mrs. Hill's voice is coming from the darkness of the glassed-in sun porch. It's a bit muffled, but it's still scary.

"Do you know what we do with little ghosts who trespass?"

"Yow!"

Rebecca doesn't wait to find out. She leaps to her feet and races to join the others.

The brown paper shopping bags get heavier and heavier as the evening wears on. By the time the ghosts get to Grammie's house, some of the handles have broken. It doesn't matter, though. Grammie always has an extra supply of bags; just as she always has an extra supply of presents, like candy and colouring books and pajamas, in case anyone needy drops by. Tonight, she's had hundreds of visitors, even repeats. Some came because they'd heard how much candy she gives out. Others were drawn by the smell of roasting chicken. That's an unusual smell for Halloween, but then Grammie is unusual. Ordinarily, she never lets strangers into the house. She never even answers the door. But she'll always feed any poor soul who comes to the back porch needing a meal. And there are lots of those on Halloween. People like the McClares, for instance, who this year are disguised as cowboys and clowns.

While the ghosts dump their goodies into brand-new bags, Grammie sits down at the kitchen table with a hobo and a harem girl and proceeds to find out how they are, where they're from, what they really need. When they finally leave, they're carrying a loaf of bread, a box of Shredded Wheat and a chicken.

A few minutes later, at the corner of Station and Commercial Streets, Rebecca breaks from the group again.

"Hey! Where're you going now?"

"There aren't any houses down there!"

She keeps walking.

"Well, it's your own fault if you can't find us!"

She looks up through the holes in her sheet.

The stars are twinkling, like diamonds on a black velvet cloth. They look so tiny — way tinier than she is. But Ben Kelly once told her that

that isn't true; that they're really bigger than the sun, which is pretty big, even though you can block it out with your thumb. Of course, you can't block out the stars. You don't have enough fingers.

She turns slowly around and around. The diamonds sparkle and whirl. She frowns.

She doesn't have a clue which one is the Eastern Star — the one she's been told hangs over Bethlehem. They all look the same to her. And then, suddenly, she can't help giggling. "The hardest hem to mend is a Bethlehem," she's heard her Day say more than once.

Moments later, she arrives at the second spooky place she promised to visit — the Masonic Hall on Commercial Street. Located between Kyle Bishop's feed storage building, where Wanda Willoughby works, and Olive Longley's grocery store, which is famous for its dark brown wooden cabinets and enormous rounds of cheese, it isn't very scary from the outside — just a two-storey building with pillars, and that ugly, cream-coloured metal siding with bumps all over it. But she's heard that the men who go there at night wear funny hats and call each other funny names. And that the women who go there do crazy things, too.

Unfortunately, they don't seem to be there tonight. The place is dark. The front door is locked.

Still determined to be frightened, she presses her face against the window. She can't see much, just the outline of an altar and a few ornate chairs, facing east. They look just like the ones in Marion's living room — with arms so high they hurt her shoulders when she tries to rest on them.

"Nuts!" She turns away from the window.

She's about to drift back to the Ruggles Block, where the other ghosts must be by now, when she spots the staircase. It has twelve lacy black metal steps rising up the side of the building. And then, at the top, a little metal landing and a big black door.

"Hey! Maybe that one's not locked!" She gazes up the staircase. "Maybe I can get in through there and steal some banners! Or that ugly purple scarf they're always snickering about — with the yellow tassels on it. The one that the Worthy Matron has to wear."

She tugs at her big, long scar and begins to clank up the stairs. The closer she gets to the door, the faster her heart beats. What if someone's there? she worries. What if someone captures her? And makes her swear that she believes in a Supreme Being and has a good moral character? What if...? And then she whoops with relief.

Marion once told her that when someone wants to join the Order of the Eastern Star, the members hold a secret vote, where they use balls instead of ballots. All white balls and you're in. Even a single black ball and you're out. Rebecca can't imagine getting all white balls, so she's probably safe. She wonders whether Marion is.

Clank. Clank. Clank.

Rebecca's reached the landing. There's nothing left for her to do but try the door. She was going to knock first, just in case there was actually someone there, practicing the secret signs and grips, but instead she just stretches out her hand and turns the knob.

"Nuts!" This door's locked, too. "After all that!"

Fed up with spooky places that aren't all that spooky, she clanks quickly down the stairs and races to join the others.

Rebecca finds a few of her fellow ghosts at McCarthy's and a few more of them at Rawding's. By the time the biggest ones come drifting down the road from way up near Duncanson's, there's a huge mob of them — the biggest they've had all night. As they stop for a moment to plan their next move, their white sheets billow in the wind.

There aren't many houses left to visit; just the ones in Dogpatch, where no one likes to go at night.

"Well, what about *your* place, Rebecca?" One of the older ghosts is towering over her. "We haven't gone there yet."

"Yeah!" Another tall ghost sidles up to them. "Your Mum makes great fudge."

"When she's not drunk, that is." Barry Connors spits through a hole in his sheet.

"Quit it, you two!"

"Or what?" Drew Saunders yanks at his hood, so the holes match up with his eyes.

"Hey! I almost forgot!" squeals one of the tinier ghosts. "Let's go back to Marion's!"

"Yeah! For seconds!"

"Yeah! She always has lots of good junk left!"

By the time they reach Marion's back veranda, however, Drew has a better idea. "Hey, you guys! We haven't gone *there* yet." He waves toward the cabin.

"Why bother?" Barry reaches beneath his sheet and takes out his lighter. "He won't have no candy."

"Will, too!" blurts Rebecca.

"Bets?"

"C'mon. Let's go find out."

As the mob of white sheets drifts toward the cabin, a few more of the bigger ones take out their lighters. That's one thing they like about Halloween, thinks Rebecca. They can do bad things, like smoke, without being recognized.

"An-y-thing for Hal-low-eeeeeeen!"

The ghosts flick their lighters. Tiny flames leap up into the darkness.

"I must be stupid," seethes Rebecca, as she closes the datebook for 1958. "Either that or there's nothing in these god-damned books to see." She tosses it onto the pile. "And Marion's just playing a god-damned trick on me."

She knows better. She knows there *is* something she's supposed to see — maybe even something she's supposed to do about it — if only she weren't so stupid.

"Well, I can't stay here forever," she sighs, as she leans over the pile of datebooks.

She wants to take one back to Ontario with her — as a souvenir of her failing powers of detection, if nothing else.

"OK. Eenie, meenie, minie..." She lifts the one for 1965 out of the pile. "Just as good as any, I guess."

A few minutes later, she's sorry she didn't follow her first instinct and just leave. Her Mum isn't home. No one's home. And now she's stuck upstairs, in the room which used to be hers — before her Mum moved in and got rid of the bunks.

"I can't even remember whether I *liked* being eleven." She peels open the datebook. "Ha! I can't even remember whether I liked being anything."

At first, she just flips indifferently through the pages. But then she has an idea.

"Maybe you can be the third base coach!" she cries, as she bends back the pages. "Or the catcher! Yeah!" She lets the pages slip past her thumb.

She was hoping the words would just flicker into pictures, like those Finger-Tip Movies put out by Gillette in the late fifties; like the one she had called *Signals...The Secret Language of Baseball.*

"Well, that was a bust," she sighs, as December 31 slides by. "I must be out of practice."

There was a real trick to flipping those booklets. You had to do it calmly, smoothly, so the signals looked real; so they weren't too jumpy and there weren't any important bits left out.

"Or else this book's too..." As she bends back the pages again, she senses that it is too big; that there's too much secret language being flashed at her. But she lets the pages go anyway.

This time, she doesn't try to get it all. She just looks for the most important *indicators*. By the time she reaches June, she's not having any trouble with the *flash signs*. It's just the *combinations* which she can't quite figure out...skin and skin, colour and colour, motion and motion...

27

It's ten o'clock on a warm June night. Harold and Vivian are with Ruthie Sutherland in the east living room, watching a Sonja Henie movie. Randy and Peter are over at Josephine Schwartz's house, playing croquet by the light of the back veranda. Sunny and Rebecca are slumped at the kitchen table, waiting for the potatoes to boil.

"What should I write on them?" asks Rebecca, as she sifts through a pile of dark blue folders.

"How should I know?" mutters Sunny.

She's too engrossed in *Harper's Bazaar* to bother with Rebecca's dumb old coin collection. Yesterday, on the radio, they'd heard a so-called expert claim that *"many of the young people who enjoyed improved educational opportunities are now seeking alternatives to what they consider a shallow, materialistic lifestyle."* But not Sunny. She'd love to have one of those lifestyles. Love to be tall, gorgeous, well-dressed, rich.

"Oh, *I* know!" Rebecca hunches over one of the dark blue folders and prints PROPERTY OF REBECCA PETERSON on it. Then she sits up and surveys the rest of her collection.

The most valuable things are the mint sets that Edna Ogletree always gives her for Christmas. But they aren't her favourites. It's great to have uncirculated coins in sealed plastic packages, if all you want to do is look at them. But if you want to hold them or play with them — and couldn't care less whether they get tarnished or discoloured — it's crummy. Her favourites are the dark blue folders. It's fun to press coins into holes — and then pop them back out again; fun to find exotic coins, when everyone else just has regular ones; fun to look them all up in the catalogues they have down at Michie's five-and-dime in Kingston.

"They're ready," drawls Sunny.

"What are?" Rebecca peers at the little, silver five-cent piece that Grammie found in the bottom drawer of her bureau. 1913. The date is smudgy and smooth.

"The potatoes, dummy."

"So?"

"So you can put them on the plates."

"No! You do it! I'm busy!"

"Yeah, well, how come you're never busy until…?"

There's a tremendous clatter, as Rebecca dumps an envelope of big brown Canadian Large Cents onto the table.

"Forget it." Sunny spins out of her chair.

A few minutes later, they're mashing little mounds of boiled potatoes with their forks.

"Just like sawdust," snorts Rebecca, as she flings a lump of margarine on top.

Sunny pushes the bangs of her short dark hair to the side. "That's what Darrell used to say, before he and Donnie moved out."

"Yeah, well, it wouldn't be so bad if we didn't have to eat them every day. Well, almost every day. I wish Mum and Dad didn't get drunk so much now. Then maybe we could afford to get steak and stuff, like regular people." Rebecca glances at the Glamour Puss on the cover of Sunny's magazine. She isn't sure whether the model's a regular person or not. But she bets the agency feeds her something besides boiled potatoes and Fluffs.

"Oh, by the way." Sunny scrapes her fork across her plate. "Did you hear?"

"What?"

"The Beatles got the O.B.E. today."

"So?"

"From the Queen!"

CHINK!

"What was that?" whispers Sunny.

"I don't know. It sounded like a bottle breaking."

"Shshsh."

The girls get up to peek into the sunporch.

"It was Howard," wheezes Vivian.

"What the hell are you talking about?" laughs Harold. "It was you. I saw you. You put your elbow right…"

"Excuse me," interrupts Ruthie. "But Howard isn't even here." She looks around the sun porch. "Is he?"

"No," protests Vivian. "Not that." She kicks at the bits of broken glass. "Howard. Howard and Donald who dared me to pee in the bottle."

"Oh." Ruthie looks around again. "So what happened?"

"What happened when?"

"Jesus, Vivian! What happened when you and Howard…?"

"Ha! I just got my panties down around my knees. You know, like…" She squats over to demonstrate.

"What kind of bottle was it?" chuckles Harold.

"Jesus! What difference does it make?"

"Let her finish!" pleads Ruthie.

"And was hunching over the bottle when…uuuuuh…when… uuuuuh…when…huck, huck, huck, huck…"

Vivian's asthma is bad tonight. Harold finishes the story.

"When Marion came in and caught her."

"What did she do to her?"

"Not much. But Vivian was some scared she was going to."

"Oh. Well, is that it? Is that the funny story she's been trying to remember all night?"

"Huck, huck." Vivian flops onto the chesterfield.

"Yup," laughs Harold. "That's it."

Rebecca and Sunny look at one another.

"Come on." Sunny pulls Rebecca back to the kitchen. "Even boiled potatoes is better than that."

A minute later, Sunny lays down her fork. "I won't be here after tonight," she says softly. "I'm going to go live with Grammie. And, well...maybe you should spend more time at Marion's, OK?"

Rebecca lays down her fork, too. "OK, but just for two or three weeks this time. To give Mum and Dad a chance to..."

"Sure. Now, come on." Sunny reaches for *Harper's Bazaar*. "You can help me decide what to take."

"OK." Rebecca gathers up her dark blue folders.

When they reach the bottom of the staircase, they stop for a moment and listen.

"Ha!" snorts Rebecca. "Probably passed out."

"Everyone but Mum." Sunny starts climbing.

"Wait!"

"What?"

"Is this where they found me?" whispers Rebecca.

"When?"

"When I was a baby."

"Oh, God. Not this again."

"When Mum threw me down the stairs."

"How should *I* know? Now, come on."

"But she did, didn't she? She did throw me. It wasn't just an accident."

"Look. All I know is...if she threw you, she threw herself, too, 'cause Marion found both of you at the bottom. Now, for the last time, come on!" Sunny turns and stomps up the stairs.

"OK, Sunny, but I only wanted..."

"Jesus Christ!" Sunny keeps stomping. "I don't see why you have to make such a big deal out of it! It's not like you got mangled or anything!"

At the top landing, there's a blank white wall. And two sets of stairs — one to the left and one to the right. Sunny stops stomping.

"Hurry up, Sunny! I can't squish by you!"

Tonight, the wall looks even blanker than usual.

"Move!" Rebecca buries her head in Sunny's back and pushes her up the stairs to the right.

"Hey! Watch it!"

As they tumble into the bedroom, Sunny turns on the lamp. Every inch of the ceiling and walls is papered with pictures of John, Paul, George and Ringo. Most of them were cut out of magazines she found in the lunch room at school and they almost succeed in making the room a shrine…except instead of smelling like incense, it smells like piss.

"Ready…aim…fire!" They throw their shoes across the room.

Thump, thump. Thump. Thump.

Sunny's land on the pile of books and toys and dirty clothes on the floor of the closet. Rebecca's go in separate directions. One of them hits the closet door; the other lands on the little shelf about halfway up the back.

"Brrrrr."

The bunk-bed is opposite the big bay window overlooking the driveway. Rebecca changes quickly into some mismatched pajamas, then dashes madly across the room and boosts herself up to the top.

"Brrrrr."

The plastic sheet on the mattress rustles a little.

"Brrr, yourself."

Sunny is sitting cross-legged on the floor, sorting through a pile of black and yellow records. Most of them are old and dusty. Some have scratches and cracks. One looks like a cookie with a bite out of it. But the newest ones, like the Swan issues of "She Loves You" and "Anyway You Want It," which cost sixty-nine cents down at Michie's five-and-dime, are still in their paper sleeves. Rebecca can see that to Sunny, their snow-white labels are almost as alluring as the lip gloss she's hidden in the bottom drawer of her bureau. She slips one of them out of its sleeve…and then frowns. "Red Roses for a Blue Lady." Her mother gave it to her on her last birthday. But it's "sooo square," she's grumbled to Rebecca. In the same boat as Andy Williams and Petula Clarke.

"*Downtown, downtown, downtown,*" she mocks.

Rebecca giggles. Sunny sifts through the pile again.

"Hey, look! 'Rock Around the Clock'! The first real record I ever got!"

"My first real one was 'Little Brave Sambo.'"

"What do you mean? That's just a kid's record."

"Yeah, but it was my first *black* one. Before that, they were all yellow."

Sunny laughs, then starts to sing. "*I'm poor little Sambo…*How does it go?"

Rebecca joins in. "*I'm sad as can be. The tigers have taken my*

*clothes from me. What shall I do? What shall I do? I'm poor little
Sambo and sad as can be."*

"Ha!"

Rebecca watches Sunny grab an armful of yellow records. "Dennis
The Menace." "The Poky Little Puppy." "Bumble Bee Bumble By."
"My Bunny." As Sunny throws them, one by one, back on the pile,
Rebecca notices they all have little holes in the middle. Most of the
black ones have little holes, too. "When I Grow Up." "Home Sweet
Home." "Please Mr. Sun." "Who in the World Are You?" But the
grown-up ones — by The Animals, The Temptations, The Grateful
Dead, The Doors — all have great big holes. You need a special plastic
centre to play those.

Sunny arranges the records into piles, according to the size of their
holes, then slips into her nightdress and ducks into the bottom bunk.

"Now don't play anything stupid." Rebecca watches her turn on the
record player. "And don't play anything by that guy with the funny
voice. I can't remember his name."

"Bob Dylan?"

"No, not Bob Dylan. But close. I think it begins with a D."

"Oh, I know, I know!" Sunny imitates Donovan's shivery voice. *"In
the chilly hours and minutes of uncertainty, I want to be…"*

"Yeah! That's the one. Don't play anything by him, OK?"

Sunny laughs. "OK."

The record player is the dark brown, plastic portable one Marion
gave Sunny for Christmas. She keeps it on the floor, close to the bed,
so she can easily reach over and change the records — which she has
to do every two minutes and thirty seconds or so since all she has are
singles. Tonight it's The Byrds's version of "Mr. Tambourine Man" which
is sitting on top of the big-holes pile. It's Number One on the charts
this month — even though the Byrds left out most of Dylan's good
words — and Sunny can usually stand its chiming twelve-string guitar
a lot longer than Rebecca. For five or six plays, not just one. But right
now, Sunny seems to want something else. She brushes "Mr.
Tambourine Man" to the floor.

Rebecca watches Sunny sift through the big-holes pile.

"Catch Us if You Can" by the Dave Clark Five. "It Hurts So Bad" by
Little Anthony and the Imperials. "Mrs. Brown You've Got a Lovely
Daughter" by Herman's Hermits. "As Tears Go By" by Marianne

Faithfull. And then there's a brand-new one, with a special plastic centre stuck in its hole. Sunny eases it out of its sleeve and onto the turntable.

Round and around and around it goes...black, gleaming, silent, threatening. The girls are mesmerized.

At last, Sunny places the needle on the edge of the blackness. There's a great rushing sound and then...

"One pill makes you larger and one pill makes you small. And the ones that mother gives you don't do anything at..."

It's the first psychedelic record Rebecca's ever heard.

"Go ask Alice, when she was just small."

She thinks she hates it...but then she loves it. That must be the way Sunny feels, too, decides Rebecca. Or else why would she say she was mad she wasted her babysitting money on it and then say she was glad she wasted her babysitting money on it?

"And if you go chasing rabbits and you know you're going to fall."

Rebecca watches the record spin round and around and around. But she won't let her mind go with it. Sunny has, by the look of her. Sunny's let her mind spin out of the present into nothingness.

"Feed your head. Feed your head."

Sunny's let her mind go to mush.

"Sunny?" Rebecca has to yell to get her sister's attention. "Sunny! It's over!"

"Oh. Sorry."

Sunny blinks, then peers through the darkness at the walls. It's as though she's expecting to see brightly coloured globs and swirls. But there are only Beatles, hiding the cracks and the rot and the peeling paint.

"What should I play now?" She lifts the needle from the record.

"I don't care. Just don't play *that* again."

"Why not?"

"Because it stunk!" The plastic sheet rustles. "What is that junk about white rabbits anyway? I don't get it."

"Well, they...Never mind. I'll play the Beatles next. As soon as you..."

"Well, I like 'My Bunny' way better than that. I don't care if it is a yellow record."

"Great. Now go have a pee."

"OK. But it never does any good."

The bathroom has two doors — one to the hall and one to the girls' bedroom. There are dark blue tiles on its walls, with crud between them, and an old white bathtub, with a big fat lip hanging over its casing, and a large glass jug to refill the toilet tank after the water's seeped out.

When Rebecca returns, Sunny's sitting up in bed, sorting through her Beatles cards.

"Have you got all of them yet?" Rebecca hikes up her mismatched bottoms.

"Almost. I still need No. 80 in the Second Series."

"Which one's that?"

"The one where John is making a snowball. Winifred has it — has two of them, in fact — but she won't trade me."

"Well, then, we won't let her come to Middleton with us when we go see *HELP!*" Rebecca scrambles up to the top bunk. "That'll teach her."

"I guess."

As Sunny gathers up the cards, Rebecca's eyes flit up the walls and across the ceiling, from one cherubic face to another. "Sunny?"

"Hmm?"

"Which one's your favourite again? I forget."

"Wait a second, while I put on another…"

"Well, I like Paul…because he's left-handed like me and Grammie. Hey! I just remembered something!" She hangs her head over the edge. "Have you got any of the gum left?"

"Ha! I was wondering when you'd get around to that." Sunny hands her a jagged piece of dusty pink bubble gum.

"Thanks!"

"And I like George." Sunny jams the yellow plastic centre into a different hole. "Because he's the dreamiest."

"No, he isn't."

"Well, then, he's the tallest." She eases the record onto the turntable.

"Tied with John."

"Well, then, the best guitar player!" She drops the needle. It skitters off the edge of the record.

"Swift," giggles Rebecca. "Real swift."

"Quit it, you little creep!" She places the needle more gently this time.

First, there's a crackling sound and then...

"Yesterday, all my troubles seemed so far away. Now it looks as though they're..."

"Sunny?"

"Hmm?"

"How come Peter doesn't wet his bed?"

"How should *I* know?"

"And Randy. And Donnie. They don't either."

"Maybe it's a rule. You know, every other kid or half the kids or..."

"Yeah, well, I don't like it."

"I know but...Hey! Maybe if you stayed awake all night!"

"I already tried that. It doesn't work."

"Oh. Well, look. Someday it'll just stop, OK? Like it did for me."

"I know, but when? I'm almost in high school! Everybody's going to laugh at me!"

"Why should they? Are you going to tell them?"

"No."

"Well, then, who's going to know?"

The plastic sheet rustles.

"No one, I guess. But..."

"Look! It stopped for me and it'll stop for you, OK? Now go to sleep!"

"Yesterday, love was such an easy game to play. Now I need a place to..."

"Sunny?"

"Now what?"

Rebecca is peering up at the freshly scrubbed faces on the ceiling again.

"Do you still think you're going to marry Prince Charles?"

Sunny breathes in deeply...and then smiles. "No." She slowly exhales. "I think I'll marry George instead."

"Ha! You're cracked."

"Takes one to know one!" She kicks at the sagging mattress over her head.

The next day, when Rebecca goes uptown for Vivian's aspirin, she rides her bike. It's a royal blue CCM with white fenders, a brown seat and twenty-six inch wheels. She's had it since she was six, when it was *way* too big for her, and she rides it absolutely everywhere.

The drugstore is on Old Post Road, between Harriet Bill's store and Violet McCarthy's store. Hanging over its entrance is a big, blue and orange sign. MATHESON'S REXALL PHARMACY. Rebecca leans her bike a little left of the mortar and pestle, so it won't block the door, and then goes to peek through the window at McCarthy's.

She used to peek into Harriet's, too. At the elegant clothing, the fancy linens, the fine china and other dainty gifts. Occasionally, there was a treat for kids, but mostly it was a store for sissies and she never went in unless she absolutely had to — unless it was Mother's Day or something. Not even for the plate of home-made doughnuts Harriet sometimes had on the counter. Now she doesn't even peek. She and Randy once stole two dinky toys from there. Slipped them right out of their boxes in that special cardboard display case by the cash register, when Harriet was out back helping Marion try on a dacron shirt-dress with vivid blue splotches and swirls. Even now, she can't help shaking. It's been seven years since they took those little Matchbox beauties, but there's still a chance that they'll get caught — that someone's on the verge of solving The Mystery of the Empty Boxes.

McCarthy's isn't actually owned by Violet. It's owned by Ron Hepburn, whose son Wes is drinking himself to death. But Violet's the only one anyone ever sees working there. When Rebecca cups her hands, she can just make out the rows of boots and the rows of overalls and the tall, hefty, grey-haired woman with glasses who's telling Clary Marshall that, if he buys that particular work shirt, it'll last him for twenty years.

McCarthy's is a magical place. It's where Fred Johnson gets his aprons, Lester Greaves gets his waders, her Dad gets his T-shirts and pants. And the strange thing is there's more magic when you peek. Inside, you have to behave. Outside, you can giggle all you want when Clary tugs at his collar and acts like "to buy or not to buy" is the biggest question of his life.

"Rats!" She suddenly remembers her Mum's headache. It's a real doozy this time. She better get going.

As she turns away, she spots a row of short-sleeved shirts she's never seen before. They have high, button-down collars, like a lot of the newer ones. And so many colours and shapes! Red, with dainty, little yellow flowers. Black, with big round puffs of white. Green, with golden swirls and fronds. She can't wait to tell Randy about them.

When at last she enters the drugstore, Gus Matheson is busy restocking the shelves.

"Don't we have any more tampons?" he hollers to his wife June who's standing at the cash register. "I thought I told you to order more tampons!"

Rebecca giggles.

"Oh, hi. We were just..." He grins at her. "I bet you don't even know what tampons are."

"Yes, I do! They're...they're for..." Her cheeks turn red.

"Anyway." Gus is embarrassed, too. "Are you going to the wrestling in to Berwick next Saturday?"

"No."

"Why not?"

Her eyes begin to sparkle. "Because it's silly and..." She pauses for effect. "Fake."

"Fake? Who told you that? It's not fake! I know for a fact that...!"

"Gus, that's enough," cautions June.

"OK, but..."

"Augustus!"

"All right! Jesus."

Everyone in Aylesford knows that the easiest way to get Gus Matheson all hopped up is to tell him that his beloved wrestling isn't real. Even eleven-year-olds can do it.

"So." He wipes his glasses to compose himself. "What can I do for you today?"

"Well, I'm supposed to get a big bottle of aspirin...but first, I'm going to get a float."

"Ha! I should have known." He waves at the soda fountain by the opposite wall. "One of the boys will get it for you."

"Oh. OK."

As she saunters toward the stools — round, chrome, with black plastic coverings on their seats — she crosses her fingers. She hopes it's going to be Reggie. Reggie is older and nicer and used to play for the Mohawks when they were here. His brother Buddy just used to throw rocks through Marion's windows. The doctors in Halifax have decided that he couldn't help it; that it's his schizophrenia which makes him mean and crazy all the time. As far as Rebecca's concerned, that may explain why he pokes pinholes in the condoms — she's seen him do it — but it doesn't make him any nicer to talk to.

"So?" The footsteps come from out back. "What do you want?"

It's Buddy.

"I want a float, please." She hops onto a stool.

"Yeah, well, I could've guessed that. What kind?"

"Chocolate and orange, please."

"What do you mean chocolate and orange? What kind of stupid float is that?"

"It's *not* stupid! It's..." She calms herself down. "You take two scoops of chocolate ice cream and then pour orange pop over them."

"Jesus Christ Almighty! I know how to make floats!"

"Buddy!" June loves her younger son more than anything, but she doesn't know what to do with him.

"Yes, Mommie?"

"When you're finished over there, I'd like you to help me with these boxes of rubber gloves."

"Yes, Mommie." He slams a tall glass down on the counter.

Rebecca tries hard to be pleasant. "What are you going to do when you get older, Buddy? Are you going to take over the store?"

"No, I am not!" He drops in a scoop of chocolate ice cream. "Didn't you read my obit in the yearbook?"

Hang Sorrow, it had said. *Care will kill a cat. Let's live for today.*

"Yeah, but...I don't see what that has to do with..."

He glares at her.

"What are you going to do, then, Buddy?"

"I'm going to be a banker." He drops in another scoop. "Either that or a hockey player, I haven't decided."

"What made you pick those?"

"Because you don't need physics, dummy." He snaps the cap off a bottle of Nesbitt's Orange. "It's twelve cents apiece now, you know. Two cents refund when you bring the bottle back."

She watches it fizz up. "Yes, I know. It's my favourite. Especially the little bits of pulp in the..."

"You know. You know. You think you know everything. Well, I bet you don't know how to play poker." He pours the pop over the ice cream. "I bet I could win you every..."

"Buddy, I'm waiting!" June calls out wearily.

"Coming, Mommie!" He holds the float in front of Rebecca's face. She watches it splutter and foam.

"I'll serve *you*," he hisses. "But I won't serve that coon friend of yours. You tell him that." He places the float on the counter, then turns away.

"Yeah, well, at least he doesn't throw rocks through windows," she mutters.

"What did you say?" He swivels to face her.

"Nothing." She slurps the foam through her straw.

As soon as Rebecca gets outside, she reaches into the pocket of her pants and pulls out a Chickenbone. They're the same slender pink sticks of candy, with cinnamon on the outside and chocolate on the inside, she's sucked on all her life. But now that Fred Johnson's sold his store to Curtis Holt and moved to Kentville, she can only get them at the drugstore. She takes a tiny pink end in either hand and closes her eyes.

"May I never be as crazy as Buddy Matheson," she whispers.

There's a brief pause...and then she snaps the slender pink stick in two.

28

According to Rebecca, 1962 was one of the greatest years ever, mostly because that's when Clay Corbett and Mortie Sands founded the Diamondview Golf and Country Club in Kingston. For the first few years, people seemed to go for the fun of it. To get their ankles bitten by sand fleas in the pasture on Number Six, lose their balls in the scummy pond at the dogleg on Number Twelve, pick wormy apples from the gnarled trees near the blind approach on Number Two. And laugh and curse and threaten to fire their clubs into the Bay of Fundy. And then, when it was all over, go into the greyish green clubhouse and eat. Chickenburgers, french fries, banana cream pie, lemonade. But now, Rebecca's noticed, their scores have become important to them and they've started inflating their handicaps so they have a better chance of winning their division at the club championships.

Rebecca is serious about her golf now, too, but she doesn't cheat. Cheaters won't be invited to play against Sam Snead on *Shell's Wonderful World of Golf*. And that's what she's planning to do. Beat Sam Snead, on TV, at five o'clock on a Sunday afternoon.

Late one Wednesday afternoon, there's a cluster of carts outside the clubhouse. Some of the women have finished their round and are busy getting ready for the potluck supper. It's all part of the ritual of "Ladies Day." The lesson, the eighteen hilarious holes, the food. Rebecca has just come from school, and is sitting on a bench near the section which acts as a pro shop, putting on her shoes.

"Ugh! I hate these things!"

They're the second straight pair of ugly golf shoes she's owned. The first ones were dark brown, with prissy little milky-white flaps. These are a pukey orangey colour. She can't wait to grow out of them — and then give them away to Brenda's grandmother Fern Ripley, who has really small feet and *likes* prissy things. In the meantime, she has an idea.

"Come on." She tugs at the leather flaps. "Come on. Oh!"

They tear off more easily than she expected.

"Great." She clumps in a circle on the pavement. "But I don't see why I can't just play in my bare feet."

As she strides toward her bag, which is leaning against the ball washer by the first tee, she can't help frowning. It's a beige tweedy material with chocolate brown plastic strips. The clubs are a Junior Set — authentic, well-made, but quite a bit shorter than grown-up ones and not complete. They're also right-handed. Mortie Sands told Marion he couldn't find a left-handed set, but Rebecca thinks he just didn't know how to teach things backwards. At any rate, she got the clubs when she was eight, from Marion. Along with an annual membership, so she can play whenever she wants.

"At least no one can make me wear a glove," she murmurs, as she takes out her driver and waggles it.

She likes the feel of the black rubber grip in her bare hands.

"And no one can…"

She gazes down the gleaming shaft to the sturdy wooden head.

Sam Snead is old now. So he doesn't win the big tournaments anymore. Not like Arnold Palmer and Carol Mann. But he still has a sweet swing and a great porkpie hat. And he's still won thirteen times in a row on *Shell's Wonderful World of Golf*.

The shaft gleams even brighter.

Maybe she can, too. After all, Mortie says her swing's a beauty — no yips, good weight shift, lovely follow-through; that her form's exceptional for her age.

Whoosh. Whoosh. Whoosh.

She slices the heads off some blades of grass.

"Except that my stupid clubs are…"

She decapitates a few more blades.

"Uuuuuuugh!"

Golf is full of tragedies. Babe Zaharias died of cancer. Mickey Wright has a bum wrist. And Rebecca's outgrown her Junior Set of clubs.

"Hurry up, Brenda! It's getting dark!" She fires the driver into the bag. It thumps against the bottom.

Brenda Taylor is obsessed with golf, too. She's just not quite as good at any facet of the game — and she's *really* terrible at putting. Right now she's on the practice green near the clubhouse, surrounded by dozens of little white dots.

"Brenda? Brenda!"

Brenda strokes another ball toward the hole. Rebecca puts her fingers to her mouth and whistles. She's no good at tunes — not like her Dad — but she's really good at shrieks.

"Whaaat?" Brenda lifts her head.

"If you don't hurry up, I'm going to start without you!"

"Big hairy deal." She lowers her head again.

Rebecca slings her bag over her shoulder and stomps toward the practice green. She doesn't always want to play golf with Brenda — who's a little too dense for her; who's had to wear brown oxfords longer than anyone else in class — but she has no choice. Sunny isn't interested. She prefers running and basketball. Betsy Rawding's interested, but she's too snobby to be much fun. And Winifred's given up — which is probably best, since she never played an entire round without crying. But that only leaves Alan, who doesn't play much, and Janice Tidman and Steven Huet, who live right in Kingston but aren't allowed to play on a schoolday. They may play more next year, when they all go for grade seven to West Kings, which has a golf team. But, for now, she's stuck with Brenda. Who did stick up for her with Myrna Hamilton, after all. Way back in grade two, when mean old Myrna stood Rebecca up on her table for saying there was nothing wrong with Kenny Jackson pumping gas for the rest of his life. Brenda called Myrna an old witch, twice, right to her face! And then got stood up on *her* table, too.

When Rebecca reaches the practice green, she lets her bag clatter to the ground.

"Hey! Watch it! I'm trying to concentrate!"

"Sorry." She slumps down beside her bag.

"What's wrong with you today anyway?"

There's a pause while Brenda misses another putt.

"My clubs are too short."

"Oh."

Rebecca rests her chin in the palm of her hand. "Too bad your puny little grandmother doesn't need new clubs."

"Yeah, well...Hey! Maybe Mortie's son could use them!"

"Yeah! And then I could...!"

"FORE!"

A ball thuds down a few yards away.

"It must be Edna Ogletree," giggles Brenda. "Nobody's as wild as Edna."

They peer over at the eighteenth fairway, where four women are trudging toward the final green.

"It's Edna, all right. And..." Rebecca spots a knitted yellow cap, with a knitted white ball on top. "Your Mum and..."

One of them takes a long, sweeping, elastic swing. The ball bounces onward.

"Ha! That's gotta be Marion. She says it's because she's using men's clubs — Clay's old set, I think — but I bet she'd swing that way anyway."

"Well, then, the other one's gotta be Nan. She always plays with them."

"I know, but I don't see her."

Suddenly, there's a withered arm poking up from the rough.

"It's OK, everyone," a voice calls snootily. "I found it."

The girls look at one another.

"It's sooo embarrassing," moans Brenda.

"Yeah, well, there may be some snots in your family." She's thinking about Brenda's brother Donnie, who's a sissy and always busy with Scouts. And Brenda's grandmother Fern, who sniffs on and on about the party line she has to share with the Petersons now that everyone has that new step-by-step dial system with the seven-digit numbers. "But, well, at least they play together. Ha! Can you imagine my Mum out there?"

"No. Not really," muses Brenda.

Amid gales of laughter, the four women putt out and then head for the clubhouse.

"Next time I'm going to pay somebody!" announces Fern, as she strides ahead.

"To do what?" pants Marion.

"To hit my ball over the water on Number Eleven."

There's more laughter.

"Well, don't ask *me*!" splutters Edna.

She's chomping on the hard green apple she picked along the seventeenth fairway.

"Don't worry, Edna. I won't."

The laughter continues.

"Oh. Good. But I thought my swing was better today, didn't you?"

The laughter erupts again.

"Oh, come on, Edna," teases Helen. "You swing like my father-in-law."

"I do not!"

"Yes, you do. You take the club up like this and then…whump…just drop it on the ball. The only difference is that Floyd knows where his ball's going. Yours squirts all over the place."

"OK, OK! I get the point! How *is* old Floyd anyway?"

"Well, he's a feisty old duffer, I'll say that for him. All those cold sores. And that metal plate in his head. And now he's getting his gallbladder out so he can eat baked beans again."

"And his crop? How's his crop doing?"

"Good. He says the cranberries are coming up good this year."

"Where's his bog again? I forget."

"Near the river, across from the peat plant."

"Mona Spurr has one there, too, hasn't she? Or is that Ruthie

Sutherland? I never remember which...Well, hello girls. Have you played already?"

"No. We were going to, but..."

"Then why don't you come and have something to eat?"

"Sure."

They leave their carts and bags with the others.

"Brenda," coos Helen, as they pile through the door. "Mortie tells me you're turning into quite the little golfer."

"Mu-um!"

"Well, you are. He told me this morning at the lesson. And you, too, of course, Rebecca."

"Thank you, Mrs. Taylor. But I'd..."

"Christ, there's a good turnout today. I'll say that much."

The room is alive with women, setting tables, pouring milk into jugs, ripping the cellophane off trays of pickles, and laughing.

Rebecca perseveres. "But I'd be a lot better — *a lot* — if I had new clubs."

"Ha!" Marion gives her a thump in the rear end. "I bet you would."

Rebecca laughs. "What did *you* bring today, Marion?"

"Tuna casserole. The one with the cashews and mandarin oranges on top."

"Great! But where is it?" She looks around the room. "We have to get to it before Edna does."

29

It isn't a long run from school to Marion's, but already Rebecca's legs feel moist beneath her burgundy brushed-denim jeans. And her arms are almost pasted to her brand-new short-sleeved blouse — off-white, with racy red buttons and stripes.

"Hurry or we'll miss it!"

"All right, Randy! I'm coming!"

They have lots of homework to do. Science, social studies, history...She wonders how Marsha Luddington will manage it. Marsha only got thirty-four on her arithmetic test today — and yesterday in science class, she told everybody that her Mum died of a "tuber" — but that's not why Rebecca feels sorry for her. Marsha's always been thick. But ever since she moved into the old Murphy house, she's been a bundle of nerves, too. They may have cleaned up the blood and plastered over the bullet holes, but Marsha still can't forget that the Felch boy went there last February and murdered his wife and his baby and his wife's parents and his wife's sister. "Four...I mean, five!" Rebecca's heard Marsha counting aloud. And she agrees with Marsha that it was a horrible thing. But it also put Aylesford on the map. *Star Weekly* featured it as having the highest violent crime rate per capita in Canada.

"Hey, look!" shouts Rebecca, as she and Randy shove each other up Marion's driveway. "He's almost finished the white!"

"Yeah! Pretty fast, eh?"

Harold has lost his after-school job as janitor — for being half-tight all the time — but he's still the best painter around.

"Yeah." Rebecca stops to study his handiwork. "But I think I liked the cream colour better."

"Aw, who cares?" Randy shoves her forward again. "Come on or we'll miss the show."

They're not as early as they are when Kenny Jackson sneaks up on Mr. Armstrong's desk and moves the big hand of the clock forward five minutes.

When they reach the back veranda, they hear whistling. Their Dad's the best around at that, too.

"Where is he? I can't see him."

"Probably on the other side."

They stop to listen.

It's a melancholy tune, but it's not a puny one. It seems to fill the sky. Rebecca's not sure, but she doesn't think he'd be able to do that if he were just an old drunk. He must be other things, too, like funny and brave. After all, wasn't he the one who volunteered to go to the old Murphy house to move the bodies and clean up the mess? And then wasn't he the one who plastered over the bullet holes and painted a nice cool blue where the big red splats had been? And then wasn't he the one who made everybody laugh by saying he hadn't seen so much blood since his wife had her last period?

Randy and Rebecca listen for a moment longer, while the tune leads them deeper into the crazy sorrow at the heart of the universe. And then they take a great big gulp of air and try to join in.

There's an eerie silence and then a thud, thud, thud, thud.

"Is that you, kids?" calls Harold, as he scrambles over the roof.

"Yeah, Dad!" they cry in unison. "How are you?"

"How the hell do you think?"

He's standing at the peak now — flushed, amused, dressed completely in white. There's another eerie silence.

"Hey, Randy!" he suddenly chortles. "What the hell's *that* you're wearing?"

"What do you mean?"

"That!"

Randy peers down at his paisley chest. "It's a shirt."

"A shirt! Jesus. I thought it was a friggin' sheet of wallpaper."

The program Randy and Rebecca don't want to miss is the *After School Show*. Radio stations in the Valley usually play old-fashioned music, like Perry Como and Rosemary Clooney, but from four to five in the afternoon, they do songs from the Hit Parade. When the kids get inside, they race right into the living room, where there's a huge, brown shortwave radio made by General Electric. The day Ben brought it home from the warehouse, they spent hours twirling the dial, trying to get exotic places. All they want today, however, is a clear signal from either Kentville or Middleton.

As soon as Rebecca turns the radio on, there's a pop and then a hush. She peers at the circular bands. But then there's a crackle and a roar and she hops back again.

"*The number of U.S. troops deployed in Vietnam now stands at seventy-five thousand,*" a man says serenely. "*Domestic criticism of the impending build-up has begun to escalate, particulary in academic circles. President Johnson, meanwhile, continues to defend his earlier decision to change the U.S. military role from advisory to direct, insisting that retaliatory strikes were proving ineffectual.*"

"Hey!" protests Randy. "Let's have some music!"

Her hand hovers over the dial.

"C'mon! What are you waiting for?"

She hasn't got a clue what that man with the serene voice is talking about; what he's been talking about every single day for a year. It makes her mad. She feels left out.

"Here. Let *me* do it." Randy pushes her aside. "Thanks to you, we've probably already missed the beginning."

He spins the dial. A long thin hand sweeps through the circles.

"What is it again?"

"1680."

A large green dot expands and then contracts.

"God damn it! Are you sure that's it?"

"Yes, I'm sure. You just have to be gentle, that's all. Here."

She rolls the dial. The long thin hand edges onto the station.

"Help! Not just anybody."

"Great! My favourite!" exclaims Randy.

"Help! You know I need someone."

"Mine, too, I guess."

"HE-E-ELP!" They both join in on the desperate plea.

"When I was younger, so much younger than…"

"The movie's on in Middleton, you know."

"I thought the one with the drunk horse was on."

"Cat Ballou? That was last week."

"Oh. Well, are you going?"

"And now these days are gone, I'm not so self-assured."

"I guess."

"Who with?"

"Probably Alan and Brenda."

"Oh. The Club."

"Help me if you can I'm feeling down."

"Maybe you can come, too. I'll ask at our next meeting, OK?"

"Don't bother."

"Why not?"

"'Cause I said so, that's…"

They both join in on the desperate plea again. *"WON'T YOU PLEASE, PLEASE HELP…"*

"Well, *I* think…" Marion is looming in the doorway.

"OH!" They leap back from the radio.

"… that it's better if you help yourself, don't you?"

"Marion!"

"You scared us!"

"Good. Now, come on, you two. It's time to study." She turns toward the kitchen.

"Tough titty," whispers Randy.

"What did you say?" Marion keeps walking.

"Nothing."

They turn up the radio and tramp after her.

The philodendron on top of the fridge has turned yellow. The silver sugar bowl by the radio needs polishing. There's a naked light bulb hanging over their heads.

"I don't get it."

"What?"

Randy points to Rebecca's page of fractions. "How you get *that* from *that*."

"OK, look." She leans toward him.

There are just two of them at Marion's in the afternoons these days. The others have either dropped out of school or found better things to do.

"But I *did* that!"

"No, you didn't. Look!"

Ever since Sunny moved in with Grammie, Randy and Rebecca do everything together — except golf, which he thinks is for sissies.

"OK, now *you* do one."

Randy bends over his scribbler and then, slowly, painfully scratches out the numerator and the denominator.

"Good. Now what comes next?"

He lifts his head. "I don't know."

"Yes, you do. Think! What comes next?"

He lowers his face a few inches from the numbers. There's a brief, unproductive pause and then...his stomach gurgles.

Rebecca giggles. They elbow one another.

"Hard at work, I see!" announces Marion, as she strides into the room.

Instinctively, they snap their heads back to their books.

"Yes, well, we *would* be, only..."

"Only we're too hungry to think straight."

Marion laughs. "Is that a hint?"

"YES!" they shout in unison.

"Well, in that case..." She strolls toward the cupboard. "Are lobster sandwiches OK? Your Uncle Gene sent another case from…"

"Yay!"

"Got what I wanted!"

Marion takes three Lotte plates down from the shelf.

Rebecca leaps up from her chair. "Can I help?"

"Yes. You can get the mayonnaise for me."

"OK."

"And the butter."

"Rats!"

"What?"

"I forgot to take it out when I got here."

"Ha!" laughs Marion. "Too busy oo-ing and ee-ing and asking for HE-E-ELP!"

Rebecca scowls.

Marion starts dancing in circles by the counter. "*When I was younger, so much younger than to-da-a-ay.*"

"Quit it!"

"*I never needed anybody's help in any…*"

"Why don't you just leave it out?" shouts Randy.

Marion stops dancing.

"Then it wouldn't get so hard," he adds quietly.

Marion and Rebecca exchange a smile. Malcolm doesn't allow them to leave it out. He says it'll go rancid in no time. They wonder what he'd make of Vivian and her "margareen." Of her breaking open a capsule over a big white block of fat. Of the yellow pus from the capsule seeping into…

"That's a long story," laughs Marion.

"Yeah, well, I don't like my bread ripped. You won't rip it, will you?"

While Randy struggles through his reading, Patsy Cline begins falling to pieces in the living room. It's five o'clock now and the "Country Show" has just begun. The kids don't think much of it, but it's all that's on.

"Hurry up, Randy. I'm bored."

"I'm going as fast as I can."

"Yeah, well, it's not…"

"Rebecca." Marion pushes at the little gauge on the stove. "If you're looking for something to do, you can always fill the oil jug."

"Sure." She scrapes her chair across the floor.

The stove is a pain. If it's not filled twice a day, it goes out. And it's never supposed to go out — not even in the summertime — or there won't be any hot water. But it's also a riot, since you can't fill it without getting your hands all covered with oil and there's always the possibility that something neat will happen — like the time Marion changed the jug, waited for the oil to seep into the line and then threw in a lit match and almost singed her eyebrows off.

Rebecca lifts the jug off its stand, flips it over as quickly as she can, then carries it across the room to the woodhouse, where the barrels of oil are kept. She's about to open the door when Randy groans.

"P-U! What's that smell?"

"Oil, dummy."

"No, not that. Something else. Coming from the fridge, I think." He gets up, opens the door and sniffs. "Nope. Not in there. It must be..."

"I know," laughs Rebecca.

"What?"

"A mouse."

"A mouse!" Marion rushes across the room. "Where?"

"It's OK, Marion," laughs Rebecca. "Not a live one, a dead one. In the wall, near where the clothes rack comes down."

"Let me smell."

"Me, too."

They push their faces right up to the boards.

"Dead all right."

"Hoo! You're telling me!"

"Gonna take a long time for the stink to go away."

The last pages of the datebook slip through Rebecca's fingers.

Gonna take a long time for the stink to go away.

She pushes herself up from the bed and drifts out of the room. As she floats down the stairs, her eyes are fixed on the chesterfield below. She'd left for Ontario by then, but she could still imagine Ruthie Sutherland's Samoyeds barking as her father stumbled home across the road. Still imagine her father lying unconscious on that chesterfield, quietly choking to death on his own vomit. Still imagine her mother sitting on the kitchen table, blubbering, asking everybody what happened, why they were there, if they wanted a drink.

Gonna take a long time for the stink to go away.

She's standing beside the chesterfield now, looking down at its soiled cushions. Only now it's 1965 again and her father isn't lying there anymore. It's her mother.

30

"Where the hell have you been?" snarls Vivian, as she struggles to sit up.

"I've been helping Ben in the garden. I told you."

"This late?"

"Here." Rebecca hands her a brown paper bag. "I brought you some peas."

"Never mind the damned peas." Vivian snatches the bag. "I need you to get me some beer." She holds out a brown paper bag of her own, this one tied round and round with string. "Well?"

"No."

"What did you say?"

"Get Cyril to do it."

"Cyril's over to Victoria Harbour."

"Well, then, Wally."

"Wally's sick."

"But I don't want to."

"Why not, for Christ's sake?"

"Because it's dark and..."

"Because it's dark and..." Vivian mimics her. "Jesus, you'd think it was one of those dens of *inequity* or something. Now here." She shoves the bag at Rebecca's chest. "You do what you're told."

"Ow! What's *in* here? Rocks?" She jiggles the bag. It sounds like coins — lots of them. "Wow! Where did you get them all?"

"I saved them."

"When? How? You never told me you were..."

"I saved it! OK? Now hurry, before Elsie gets here."

As Rebecca pedals through the moonlight down Old Post Road, her blouse comes untucked from her jeans and her eyes glisten with exertion. After every bump, there's a little chink, chink, as the bag of coins bounces up and down in the light blue, plastic parcel carrier. It isn't as noisy as it would be if the carrier were empty. Then it would go thwap, thwap, thwap every time she pedalled and every single person in Dogpatch would know she was coming down the road. As it is, there's just a little tinkle, like the sound of the jingle bells on Santa's sleigh. Or the tambourines in "Try to See It My Way."

Just before the Pierce Road turn-off, she notices her shadow. At first, she tries to catch it, then lose it, then ride right over it and squish it. But it's no use. Her eyes glisten with sorrow. Her parents used to have one or two really good binges a year, on weekends. Now her Dad paints for a month so they can buy enough booze to drink for a month. And then, when it's all gone, he goes back to painting again. Over and over and over, in an endless cycle of mirth stained with misery. She swoops around the corner into the darkness. Her shadow disappears.

If it were daytime, she'd take the shortcut to Bootlegger's Lane — up through the woods and past the slaughterhouse. But since it's nighttime, she takes the long way — right on Pierce Road, past McClare's and Stronach's and Frankie's old place, then right on Park Street, past her Uncle Charlie's house, then left on the narrow lane which leads to Dogpatch. It's hard to see the turns in the dark; hard to pedal through the sandy soil. When she reaches the narrow lane, she takes a deep breath and begins to coast.

In the daytime, it would be a sad place. Ramshackle houses, abandoned cars, piles of rusty bikes and fridges and lawnmowers. And lots of scrawny dogs. But there would be happy splashes of colour, too — a little white birdbath, a little yellow windmill, a chicken coop painted dark green and red. But at nighttime, it's just a scary place. No definition, no colour, just big dark shapes on either side of her. She peers at those shapes, trying to make out which one of them is Joey Shelton's house. She's been there once before, the last time the MacNair's were out of Tenpenny, but she can't remember how far along it is. And all she can hear is the scrawny dogs. Snoring, snarling, whimpering. They're everywhere. She tries not to make a sound. But she's going so slowly that she has to yank the wheel to keep from falling over. With that, the bag of coins chinks and the scrawny dogs begin to howl and she's so startled she veers off into a deep ditch.

"Oh, God." She picks herself up. "Don't be ripped. Please don't be ripped. Please." She reaches into the carrier and lifts out the bag of coins. "Oh, thank you, thank you, thank you." She kisses the bag of coins.

"Hey! Who's out there?"

The dogs are still howling.

"Joey?" She looks from side to side. "Is that you?"

"Yeah? What about it?"

"Joey, it's me. Rebecca."

"Who?"

"Rebecca. Rebecca Peterson. Remember? I was in the same classroom with you last…I was in grade five with your brother Howie, when you were in…"

"So?"

"So…" She hauls her bike out of the ditch. "I've come for my Mum's order."

"Tell the whole world, why don't you?"

Aylesford bootleggers don't lead very glamorous lives, thinks Rebecca, as she waits inside the Shelton's front door, in the lonely orange glow of a kerosene lamp. Unless you count living in a house with a pink garage as glamorous. Or maybe having two little black stableboys on your front lawn instead of one. But then, after all, they don't make the booze themselves. They simply buy it from the Liquor Commission in Middleton and then sell it for a huge profit to the first thirsty person who calls. Their busiest times for that are on Sundays and after ten at night on weekdays. Sometimes they deliver it; sometimes the person who needs it calls a taxi to get it; sometimes they keep people waiting for it.

Joey wasn't very happy about the bag of coins. He said "thanks a lot," sarcastically, when she handed it to him. And then went out back to count it.

"I wish he'd hurry," murmurs Rebecca, as she tries not to look around; tries not to notice that the place is full of flies, that there's a bucket of piss at the back door, that someone has scrawled obscene phrases on the unfinished gyprock.

"Psst." A face peeks out from the edge of the grubby orange curtain which divides the room. "What are you gawking at?"

"Nothing. I was just..." Rebecca shifts her feet. The floor beneath them is spongy.

"Would you like something to gawk at?"

"No."

"Oh, come on. It'd be fun." The grubby orange curtain draws back a little. There's a mattress on the floor and five or six bare legs and a big red stain.

"No, thank you."

"Hey!" hollers Joey, from the back room. "What the hell's this big brown thing? What the hell's your Mum trying to pull?"

A little while later, Rebecca skids to a stop by her own back steps. A little cloud of dust flies up and then sprinkles down, like stardust.

There's an old crate in the driveway — a '58 Plymouth Fury — and the door to the barn is open. She creeps over and peeks inside. Someone is standing in the dark, among the ladders and the cans of paint.

"Darrell? Is that...?"

"Jesus! You scared the shit out of me." He waves his bottle of beer at her.

"Sorry. I didn't mean to. How are you?"

"OK." Darrell limps to the door of the barn. "Jesus."

"You got a new car, eh?"

"Yeah," he laughs. "How do you like it?"

"It's great!" She gazes at the long, low, sleek car. It has bullet holes in the fins and four big black cavities where the headlights should be. "Way better than the last one! Remember? All the fancy chrome had come off the tailgate and the hardtop door didn't close properly and the shifter was all wobbly. It had neat windshields, though. All the way around. And real high taillights. Remember? Like a Cadillac. And headlights. Yeah! With those little hoods!"

Darrell is famous for his cars. He never buys them brand-new and he never keeps them very long. He just buys them and smashes them, buys them and smashes them. His record is seven cars in thirteen months.

"Ya want a ride?" he grins.

"No, I'd better not. Mum's still mad about the last time."

He laughs again — a wild, rough, mean laugh. The last time was when they raced his '55 Nomad up and down School Street, trying to hit all the potholes. Vivian wanted to go out into the middle of the road and try to stop him. But Harold said if she did that, Darrell would just gun his 265 cubic inch engine and run her over.

"She said I couldn't drive with you anymore."

"Yeah, well, what does she know?" He limps back into the darkness of the barn.

"Darrell, are you OK?"

"Yeah, why?"

"Is your leg bothering you or anything?"

"Look! It doesn't hurt, OK? It just doesn't work."

Darrell shattered his leg six years ago, when he dove off the top beam at Whitman Bridge. But he's twenty now — living with his wife Shirley in a cabin in the backwoods — and too tough to mention it, to notice it, to let anyone push him around. He hasn't let anyone push him around since he was thirteen and he stopped wetting his bed.

"What are you doing here anyway?"

"What does it look like?" He gulps down the last of his beer.

"I don't mean that. I mean…"

"I know what you mean." He sets his empty bottle on the counter. "I came to borrow a monkey wrench."

"Oh."

Rebecca likes her brother, but she's afraid of him. People still claim he's the one who shot that little white dog. She doesn't think so — she thinks he just uses his guns for shooting at icicles hanging from the cliffs at Morden — but she's still afraid.

Suddenly, there's a burst of laughter from the house.

"Who's here anyway?" sighs Rebecca.

"Same old drunks. Clary, Elsie, Ruthie." He makes them sound like characters from the *Looney Tunes*.

"Darrell?

"What?"

"Did they *always* drink? Did they drink when you were little?"

"No. I think they…"

"When the hell's the little brat getting back?" they hear Clary bellow. "There's no more friggin' booooooooze!"

Rebecca rolls her eyes. "He sounds like a sick cow."

"Yeah, well, you better get in there…before they start drinking the lighter fluid."

"Yeah, right." She turns away from him. "Bye, Darrell."

"Uh-huh."

When she reaches her bicycle, she discovers that the case of beer has poked through the plastic mesh on one side of the carrier. I guess that's how things get to be old crates, she sighs, as she lugs the case up the stairs and into the house.

Elsie Smeltzer is standing at the kitchen sink, watching cold water dribble from the tap.

"What the hell took you so long?" She lets a few drops fall into the mouth of an empty rye bottle, then swishes them around and drinks them.

"I *wasn't* long. You're just…Here." Rebecca hands her the case of Tenpenny.

"Thank you, my dear," grins Elsie. She has the rottenest teeth in the whole town. "I don't know what we'd do without you."

She leans over and tries to kiss her on the cheek, but Rebecca leaps away. She doesn't want those smelly teeth anywhere near her.

"You little brat," laughs Elsie, as she stumbles forward. "Wait till I…"

Rebecca darts into the west living room, where Clary Marshall is holding slides up to a dusty table lamp.

"Beautiful," he murmurs. "Just beautiful."

Rebecca wanders over to the table.

"Jesus in heaven. Would you look at this one!" He hands her a slide. "Isn't she a…?"

Rebecca squints at the transparency. "Yeah, Clary." She hands it back to him. "A real beauty."

"And then there's…"

"Where's Mum and Dad anyway?"

Rebecca hasn't got patience for the slides tonight. Clary's an electrician with the Coast Guard, mostly up north on an icebreaker.

Every time he comes home, he has slides. Hundreds of them. And always of the same thing — icebergs.

"With Ruthie, on the sun porch."

"Oh." She starts for there, then changes her mind and goes upstairs.

Within minutes, Rebecca's pounding down the stairs again.

"It's gone!" she shrieks, as she reaches the landing.

Vivian starts marching from room to room, thumping on a pillow. "Come on, everybody! Let's...aaach, aaach." She chokes on the dust. "Let's have a parade!"

"IT'S GONE!" Rebecca shrieks again. "Didn't you hear me? IT'S GOOOOOOONE!"

Harold sits up. "What's gone? What the hell's she screaming about?"

"How should I know?" wheezes Vivian. "Maybe she..."

"My coin collection! It's gone! Look!" Rebecca holds out a dark blue folder. All the holes are empty. "They're all like that!" She looks from face to face. "And my mint sets, too! Gone!"

"Gracious!" gasps Ruthie. "I wonder who..."

"You! That's who!" Rebecca points a finger at her mother's face. "You're the one who stole it!"

"I did not."

"Yes, you did. To buy your stupid beer."

"Ha! I've never heard anything so..."

"Vivian?" murmurs Harold.

"It must have been Peter or..."

"Vivian!"

"OK! Yes!" She swats at Rebecca's finger. "I took it! But what good was it doing her?" She, too, looks from face to face. "Sitting around in those friggin' blue books. Money's meant to be spent!"

Clary shakes his head.

"But it was *my* money, not *your* money! See?" Rebecca points to the inscription in the top left-hand corner of the folder. PROPERTY OF REBECCA PETERSON. "So I'm the one who..."

"OK! What's the big deal? I'll pay you back!"

"But you can't pay me back, stupid. You..."

Vivian smacks Rebecca across the arm. The empty folder flies across the room.

"Don't you talk to me like that! Don't you ever...!"
Rebecca scrambles back upstairs.

At first, it's deadly silent downstairs. But then there's the sound of breaking glass, followed by another hush, and then the sound of breaking glass again.

Rebecca peers through the balusters.

Clary's still in the west living room, staring at his icebergs. Harold's there, too, passed out on the chesterfield. But Vivian's edging slowly across the red wooden floor of the sun porch, doing her imitation of Marg Osborne's "Just a Closer Walk with Thee" and trying to balance an empty beer bottle on her head.

Rebecca tiptoes down the stairs.

"Oh-oh-oh..." Vivian makes it halfway across the room before the bottle teeters and slips and crashes to the floor. She plops down on the couch beside Ruthie. "It's not the same without Charlie," she sighs.

"Maybe we should get the cans next time."

"I can't work the tabs."

"Yes, well..." Ruthie pushes herself up from the couch. "I think they have rings now."

Ruthie gathers up her dress, so the folds make a kind of basket, and then begins picking up the pieces of broken brown glass. The slivers are too tiny. She just drops them into the folds of her dress. But the shards are big enough to lick first. Vivian, meanwhile, looks annoyed.

"It serves her right," whispers Rebecca. She can't help smirking. She's seen this before. She's seen the Tenpenny work its magic on everyone else but her Mum. Leave everyone else plastered and her Mum...wide awake.

"More. That's what we need. More." Vivian leaps up from the couch. "Rebecca! Get down here! Rebecca! Oh. You're here."

They stand face to face at the bottom of the staircase, with Elsie sprawled on the steps behind.

"What?" Rebecca's face is red and streaky.

"I want you to go get more beer."

"You're mental."

"What did you say?"

"I said *no*. Get your own."

"Look, you do what you're told or I'll..."

"What?"

"I'll give you a licking you'll never forget." Vivian pushes Rebecca into the kitchen.

"Yeah, right. That's what you always..."

Vivian grabs her shoulders and begins shaking her, hard.

"Ow-ow! Mu-um!" The words come out in little jerks. "You're hurt-ing me-e!"

Vivian keeps shaking.

"Mu-u-u-um!"

Suddenly, there's a shrill whistle.

"Hey! Leave her alone!"

Darrell is standing on the back landing.

"Hey! Did you hear what I said? Hey!" He comes banging through the screen door and yanks them apart. "Now stop it! Stop..."

Vivian shoves him in the chest. He smashes her in the face.

For a moment, all three of them just stand there, seething. Then Darrell pulls Rebecca out the door. "Come on. I'm taking you to Marion's."

There's a big, round woman in a fuzzy pink housecoat standing at the end of the driveway.

"It's OK, Irene!" calls Rebecca.

"Are you sure?" The woman jerks her hand up to her pale green curlers. "I wasn't spying or anything. I just heard all the shouting and...well, I couldn't see anything from the sun porch so I...well, as long as you're all right." She starts edging backwards. "I guess I'll be going home."

"Bye, Irene."

"Bye." She turns and waddles across the street.

"Did you see her hair?" giggles Rebecca, as Darrell yanks open the door. "Wait till I tell..."

"Just get in the car! Before...Oh, Jesus."

Vivian's finally followed them outside. She's standing on the back steps now.

"So what are you going to do, Mum?" Darrell pushes Rebecca inside the car. "Eh? Are you going to give us a licking now?"

Vivian sways for a moment, as if she's a cotton nightdress rippling on the line, and then lurches toward them.

"Stupid bitch." Darrell leaps into the car and slams the door.

As he starts the engine, Vivian bends over to grab a handful of sand, but she loses her balance and plops right down on her ass in the pit.

"God damn you kids!" she screams at them. "I wish you'd never been born! Do you hear me? I wish you'd never been born!" She flings a handful of sand at the idling car. It clatters against the side like sleet.

"Fuckin' whore. I'll show *you*." Darrell jams the car into gear and then floors it. There's a cloud of dust and a shower of stones.

Vivian puts her hands up to protect her face.

"Yeaaah!"

When he reaches the road, he turns back sharply into the other end of the driveway and guns it again.

"Darrell, don't!" pleads Rebecca. "That's enough!"

But he doesn't stop. He just keeps driving his Plymouth Fury around and around the sandpit, spinning its wheels and spraying stones at his mother.

"Darrell, please!"

After the fourth time, Vivian takes her hands away from her face and just sits there, letting the stones slash her skin.

"What's she doing anyway?" Darrell squints through the dust.

Rebecca presses her face against the window. "Smiling."

"Stupid bitch."

"I know, Darrell, but…"

"Stupid fuckin' bitch."

This time when he reaches the road, he straightens the wheel and squeals toward Marion's place.

31

There's a sigh and then a crunch, crunch. Another sigh and then a crunch, crunch, crunch, crunch.

Vivian is sprawled on the chesterfield in the east living room, watching *Search for Tomorrow* and stuffing her mouth with Hostess potato chips. There are scratches and bruises on her arms and face.

"Darrell's right," whispers Rebecca, as she peers at her through the sun porch window. "She is a stupid bitch."

Rebecca sneaked back in a little while ago, with Marion and Doris when they came to clean up last night's mess. But now that the two of them have gone to buy new bags for the Electrolux, she might as well enjoy herself spying on her Mum.

"Hey!" Vivian throws her slipper at the television. "Hey!"

Rebecca shades her eyes with her hands.

The reception on CHSJ isn't very good today. But then she's heard her Mum say a million times that she's going to write to those people in Saint John and complain.

"Oh-oh." Vivian shoves her hand deep into the bag of chips. The organ music swells. Her face contorts in horror.

"But she's lying!" she hollers at Joanne Barron. "She's lying! Can't you see the little bitch is lying? Jesus." She lifts the handful of chips to her mouth. But she's squeezed it so hard that it's nothing but crumbs.

"Ha!" She flings them back into the bag.

Rebecca shakes her head. Her Mum loves her "stories". She loves the excitement, the romance, the certainty that the bad guys will eventually get what they deserve. But they sure take a lot out of her. She can never watch the whole fifteen minutes without getting upset. Just when her favourite characters are on the verge of happiness, something terrible happens — a tragic accident, a stupid misunderstanding, a mistake from their past come back to haunt them. It's all so overwhelming to her, especially since she's the kind of person, she'll tell anyone who'll listen, who believes so fervently in the values of motherhood, of family, of loving, supportive relationships.

"My eye!"

Rebecca's about to shake her head again when her Mum leaps up from the chesterfield.

"Jesus Murphy! Jesus, Jesus..." Vivian seizes the rabbit ears and yanks them to the side, to the other side, to the back. But the snow on the screen remains.

"Dammit!" She swats at the long thin rods. "Now I'll never find out if Patti let him kiss her." She slumps to the floor. "Well, I could always call Wanda, but that's not the same."

The television crackles, like a giant Yule log. Rebecca squints through the window. Watches the thick white snow on the screen blow and drift into the shimmering past...Sees it heaped in two big piles at the end of the driveway. A pair of boobs, smaller than the ones at Marion's, perhaps, but only because the boys can't resist jumping on top of them. Sees it rolled into a snowman, tilted just a little to the left, with the big black buttons from Marion's best dress bursting from its chest. Sees it covering the trees, the wires, the cars, the slowly rotting steeple. Sees it showing up nicely against the sky, where the thick black smoke from the factory is billowing. Sees it dripping from her little axe. Sees it clinging to her white woollen pants and red woollen mitts and navy blue woollen coat. Sees it scraped aside by the lush green needles as she drags the Douglas fir from the woods towards the house.

Suddenly, there's a loud pop.

Rebecca blinks. Vivian scrambles back to the chesterfield.

"Dammit!" she suddenly screeches. "It's too late!"

Rebecca sniggers.

The search for success and security in the small Midwestern town of Henderson is over for today. Jo needn't worry about pinching pennies. Patti needn't worry about getting her period. Everyone is free from the clutches of death and divorce and drink.

"Never again," groans Vivian, as she cups her hand over her forehead.

"I was wondering when you were going to say that," murmurs Rebecca, as she stares at the bits of broken brown glass wedged between the planks on the floor of the sun porch.

Still, it's worse in the east living room, where, apart from the usual filth, there's vomit splattered all over the afghan and the distinctive smell of urine emanating from the thick brown rug.

"Yuck!" Vivian jerks her feet onto the chesterfield. "Who pissed in here?"

"Ha!" Rebecca claps her hand to her mouth. Her Mum smells it too.

"And how did that *jungle bunny* get in here?" Vivian points to a large grey puff on the floor by the TV. "The last time I looked, it was…" She tries to blow it across the carpet to the wall, but she can't muster the strength.

"Ow. Oh, Jesus." Vivian squeezes her head. "Never again. Never again. Never again."

"Oh, really?" Marion pokes her head through the doorway. "Where have I heard *that* before?"

Rebecca ducks.

"Jesus, Marion!" yelps Vivian. "You scared me half to death."

"Good! Now, come on, Doris. Before I change my mind."

"It's about time they got here." Rebecca sneaks from the sun porch into the west living room. "I was beginning to think…"

"Let me know if you need anything," calls Vivian, as she sprawls out on the chesterfield again.

"Don't push your luck," seethes Marion.

As Rebecca reaches the landing, she can hear Marion, in the kitchen, filling a pail with water. She can also hear her Mum muttering, "Copycats. Copycats. Copycats," as today's fifteen minutes of *Guiding Light* begins.

"Why the hell would I want to see amnesia in Springfield," Vivian continues, "when I saw it last week in Bay City?"

"Oh, brother!"

It's occurred to Rebecca that her Mum really believes that crap; really believes what the announcer told her last year, when *Another World* first aired : "*We do not live in this world alone but in a thousand other worlds.*" But her Mum doesn't always want to be reminded of it. She doesn't always want to hear the latest about war, assassination, abortion, civil rights. Things were better in the old days, her Mum's told her more than once, when strong women just sat around the kitchen table and talked about how they were going to endure things — ordinary, understandable things like a punch in the mouth or a two-timing slob of a husband.

"Can I do in here now, your Highness?" Doris drags the silver-grey Electrolux into the east living room.

Rebecca cranes her neck.

"Shsh. In a minute. It's almost over. Ha! I knew it! I knew it was him!" Vivian snaps off the TV.

"Did you?" sniffs Doris. She bends down to plug in the machine.

"Yes," Vivian sniffs back. "And I'll thank you not to suck up any socks or seagulls or…"

There's a tremendous roar. Vivian tries to shout above it.

"The kids were terrible to me last night, you know. You should have seen what…!"

When she sees that Doris intends to ignore her, Vivian wanders into the kitchen, where Marion is scouring the walls.

Rebecca cranes her neck the other way.

"How are you feeling an-y-wa-ay?" Marion rubs vigorously at a crusty blotch over the sink.

"Good!" Vivian holds her arm parallel to the floor. "See?"

Marion glances at her sister's hand, which is perfectly still. "Well, you deserve worse. That's all I can say-ay-ay-ay...Dammit!" She flings the rag into the pail of soapy water.

"Maybe you need more Spic and Span," goads Vivian, as she slips into a chair by the table.

"And maybe you need more...Forget it!" Marion flops down opposite her. "Well? What have you got to say for yourself?"

Vivian leans forward. "The kids were terrible to me last night, you know. You should have seen what..."

"Did you honestly expect them to act any differently?"

"Way to go, Marion," whispers Rebecca.

"What do you mean? I'm their mother. I expect them to treat me with..."

"Oh, please. I've heard it all before. All of it."

"You're not the only one." Rebecca leans against the banister.

"Yes, well, it's not my fault if..."

"Vivian!"

"What?"

"Rebecca says you stole her coin collection."

"So?"

"Edna's been giving her a mint set every Christmas for years."

"So? What good were they doing her? She wasn't using them for anything. She hardly even looked at them anymore."

"That's not the point and you know it."

"No, I don't know it. I don't know it one bit."

There's a brief, anguished pause.

"She came with you, I suppose," murmurs Vivian.

"Yes. But just to get her things."

Rebecca's in her bedroom now, stuffing clothes into brown paper bags. Lying on the top bunk is what's left of her coin collection — a metal piggy bank shaped like a globe, with pretty-coloured countries and a slit across the North Pole and a motto which proclaims: As You Save, So You Prosper. There's nothing much in this World Bank — just a few traders worth little more than face value. There wouldn't be anything at all except her mother wasn't able to twist the two hemispheres apart. Rebecca can tell she tried because the continents are cockeyed near the equator. Southern Africa is in the middle of the Atlantic ocean.

Suddenly she hears a familiar deep, rich baritone.

"*I could have slept all day. I could have slept all day. And still have begged for more.*"

"Dad!" She rushes to the bay window overlooking the driveway.

Her Dad's down below, carrying cans of black and white paint into the barn. She's glad to see him. She was worried he wouldn't wake up. Or that he'd wake up and fall off a ladder somewhere. She bounds down the stairs to greet him.

"*I could have waved my things and had a thousand flings I've never had be...*Whoa!" He pulls up his paint-spattered pants. "You should have knocked!"

"Sorry, Dad. Are you OK?"

"I will be when you turn around."

"Sorry." She does what she's told.

"How was school today, little one?"

"Good. Only I'm not little one anymore."

"Oh, yes." He grunts a little as he pulls his T-shirt over his head. "I forgot."

"Aren't you going to wash first?"

"I already did. At Marion's place. Which I take it is where you're going to live for a while."

She doesn't answer. She just stands there, listening to him change. It's what he does every single day of his life — get out of his paint clothes and into his night clothes, which happen to be identical except for the splotches of paint. Even in winter, he wears the white pants, the white T-shirt, the white cloth shoes, and perhaps some coveralls, if it's really freezing. And then, when the paint clothes wear out, he uses the night clothes for painting and goes up to McCarthy's for some brand-new night ones.

"There. You can turn around now."

"Dad, are you going to...?"

"Jesus. Before I forget..." He squats down and pries the lid off a gallon of paint. "What colour is that?"

She stares at the gooey white bubbles, as if they're part of a trick question.

"Well?"

"It's white."

"Ha!" He fits the lid back on the can. "That's what I said. But your Uncle Charlie said it was off-white and that it wouldn't go good with the rest of the house." He runs his hands through his greying hair. "The old bugger's going colour-blind. Here. Hand me that mallet."

As soon as she does, he begins to tap down the lid.

"Dad, are you going to...?"

"Yup!" He continues to tap. "I remember reading this article one time, in one of those encyclopedia yearbooks that Ben Kelly gets. It said that colour blindness mostly occurs in men over the age of...well, I forget how old. But it also said that..." He closes his eyes and begins to recite: "...in many animals, sexual selection appears to depend partly on colour."

"Da-ad!"

He opens his eyes. "What?"

"Are you going to go get the new ladder or not?"

He smiles as he struggles to his feet. "I thought you'd never ask."

"Da-ad!" She punches him in the arm.

"Ow!" he laughs. "That hurts!"

She slams her hands onto her hips.

Lesley Briggs runs a ladder business in Lake Paul. Rails from split spruce, rungs from ash. She loves the smell of the place; loves running her hands over the smooth brown skin of the wood; loves wondering whether the trees would actually have chosen to be ladders if they could have been sheets of paper instead.

"Well? Are you?"

"Damn right."

"Can I come with you?"

"Damn right."

"Yay!" She leaps up into his arms.

"Come on," he laughs, as he runs with her to the truck. "Before your Aunt Marion finds us something else to do."

Rebecca gives the datebook a vicious flip, flip, flip. But it's no use. She really isn't getting anywhere — just drifting in and out of memories, feeling happy one moment and crushed the next, and not a single memory closer to understanding why she came home or why Marion made such a point of leaving her the datebooks.

"Dammit!" She flings the one for 1965 into the closet. And then she laughs. At least one thing never changes, whether she's feeling happy or crushed. She's still always hungry.

A few minutes later, she's standing in front of a white wooden building wedged between Harriet's store and the ravine. It's supposed to be Caroline's restaurant. She has her heart set on a chickenburger, a coffee milk shake and a slice of strawberry pie with real whipped cream. But there's something strange about the...She leans forward and peers at the menu taped to the window.

"*Ku bo guy ding.*" She straightens up again.

It should be a tiny thing. After all, nothing stays the same and she remembers her Mum telling her the place changed hands several times over the years...from Caroline to Ellen to Gladys to some boat people from Vietnam who work long hours and always look harried and hot. But it isn't a tiny thing.

She peers up at the sign hanging over her head. THE NEW JOY INN.

The sense of loss is more annoying than profound — like a sorrow which never comes close enough to stab anyone; just stands back and flicks a wet towel at them — but it's driving her crazy. She can't bring herself to go inside. She can't even bring herself to peek through the two big plate-glass windows sitting on either side of the door. She doesn't want to see for sure that the arborite tables on the right are gone; that there are no more paper mats or chairs with chromium legs; that sleazy Ellen Connors isn't standing behind the counter on the left, serving floats to kids on stools, dreaming of the day she'll marry Reg Hodges and take over the restaurant — if she doesn't take over the hairdresser's from Reg's sister-in-law Gladys first — and worrying about her oldest son Barry, who's going to end up in the County Jail in Kentville if he doesn't watch it. And she doesn't want to see that Caroline Neily isn't at the rear, rushing back and forth from the cash register to the kitchen, checking on the bills and the food and the green and yellow budgie in the cage near the sinks, and wondering how long she'll be able to handle this place and the taxi business and her brother-in-law Wally, who's clumping from table to table on his wooden leg. And she doesn't want to see that Marion isn't sitting at the table at the front, near the jukebox, writing in her datebook, and that Frankie isn't slipping a dime into the slot, behind her back, and that…"*Try to see it my way. Do I have to keep on talking till I can't go on?*" She's not looking up. He's moving quietly away. "*While you see it your way, run the risk of knowing that our love will soon be…*" And she doesn't want to see that a tired little girl isn't hopping from stool to stool, slurping at leftover floats, making fun of Clary, who always orders a western sandwich because he's afraid to try anything new, and wondering why Marion and Frankie hardly talk to each other any more…"*We can work it out. We can work it out.*"

Suddenly, the sense of loss spreads, deepens, threatens to suffocate her sanity. "*Life is very short and there's no ti-i-i-ime.*" She misses them. She misses them so much. But she can hardly remember them. She shuts her eyes. Caroline. Medium tall. Quite hefty. Brown hair. Glasses. Marion. Medium tall. Quite hefty. Brown hair. Glasses. Frankie. "*We can work it out. We can work it out.*" Frankie. Frankie. Rebecca opens her eyes. Marion.

Her mind struggles to breathe. She drops the datebook to the pavement.

She's been ignoring this sorrow for a very long time. But now that it's gotten her attention, it isn't going to let her go. In fact, it's going to smother her in courtesy and high spirits. See? It smiles, as it picks up the datebook for her. And it's going to make a fool of itself in broad daylight, waving to her, waving to her, waving, waving…

"Hey! Hey! Is that you, Rebecca?"

"What?" She clutches the datebook.

"Ha! I thought it was you." Clary Marshall has seen her through the window. "But I wasn't sure, you know. I kept waving and waving but you didn't…Hey! Why don't you come inside and…?"

"Bean sprouts give me the runs."

"What? Oh. Ha! Ha! That's a good one. But you know they have regular food here, too. In fact, they make the best western sandwiches I ever…"

"Sorry, Clary. I can't."

"Oh. That's too bad. I know Alice would love to see you. Why don't you just come in for a minute and say…?"

"Clary, I can't. I have to go help Marion."

Suddenly, the datebook flips on its own and there they are, Marion and Rebecca, sitting in the den doing the payments.

"What are you getting this time? Apples? Potatoes?"

"No," laughs Marion. "This time I'm getting real money. Here." She pushes a mound of bills toward Rebecca, who snorts.

It isn't much, just a little pile of two-dollar, five-dollar, ten-dollar instalments. But it's a start. She copies the amounts into columns on the pale green sheets, then reaches for the receipt book.

"Rebecca?" Clary peers at her. "Are you OK? You don't look so...Who did you say you have to go help? Rebecca?"

"I have to go help Marion."

"What?" He pulls his napkin away from his neck. "What's that you said? Hey! Come back! Hey!"

She's running down the street toward Marion's.

The payments. She promised. The payments. She promised.

When she reaches the house, she flies up the stairs and into the back chamber.

32

Alan Rawding's barn is pretty spiffy on the outside — deep red with a glossy white trim — but on the inside, it's just a dark, smelly, dirty old barn. The kids love it. On this particular morning, there are four of them sprawled in the straw on the floor.

"OK, everybody. Pay up." Rebecca passes around a plastic container that once had candied fruits in it. There's a clunk, clunk, clunk as the pennies hit the bottom.

"What about me?" asks Eric Stedman.

"Not yet," answers Rebecca, as she copies the amounts into columns at the front of her scribbler.

"How much have we got?" Brenda cranes her neck.

"Wait a minute."

"Yeah, how much?" Alan leans over her shoulder.

"Look, you two." Rebecca lifts the orange stub from the page. "Do you want me to be treasurer or not?"

"OK, but hurry." Alan slumps back down into the straw.

It's the regular Saturday-morning meeting of the Yippy-Yappy Talking Club, which was formed at the beginning of the school year, after Mr. Armstrong kept bawling them out for talking too much. Rebecca, Brenda and Alan are the charter members. Eric is on probation. He's been their friend since grade three, when he was first bused in from the mountains with the other kids, but he's not much of a chatterbox.

"OK. Here's my report."

"About time!"

"Saturday, June 12, 1965. Collection 6¢. Spent 0¢. Altogether 22¢."

"Hey! I thought we had more than that!"

"Duhhh. We did, dummy, but we had to spend five cents on this." Rebecca holds up the scribbler.

It's a slim, green and white booklet with staples instead of spirals. On the front cover, there's a photo of a freckle-faced boy in a straw hat sinking his teeth into an enormous slice of watermelon. There's also Rebecca's latest rendition of the club's logo — a circle containing a stylized maze of crisses and crosses that has all the club's initials in it and which Marion helped her design. On the back cover, there's an arithmetic table containing some of life's stranger weights and measures. Four gills equal one pint. Twenty grains equal one scruple.

"OK, Brenda. It's your turn."

"What?"

"To read the minutes."

"Oh-oh. I forgot to bring them." ·

"Oh, brother."

"You're always forgetting."

"So? We didn't do anything anyway. We just played in the barn."

"And? What else?"

"I don't know. Nothing. We never...Oh, yeah! I remember! We talked about having a newspaper. Rebecca said it would be neat 'cause we could put in all the juicy gossip, about kissing and things. And Alan said he didn't want to 'cause the time they tried it at school, he got his hands all purple from the ink. And...and I said it was boring. So we voted and decided not to have it." She grins. "That's my report."

"Great!" Eric pushes at the bridge of his horn-rimmed glasses. "Now what about me?"

Alan looks serious. The club has only been going for a few months now, but already it's losing momentum. Rebecca has told him it needs fresh blood and it's his job as president to see that it gets it. "OK, Eric. Pay attention." He clears his throat. "We're letting you join…"

"Even though you don't talk much," giggles Brenda.

"Brenda! Don't interrupt! You're always interrupting!"

"Sorry." She claps her hand over her mouth.

Alan clears his throat again. "We're letting you join because you're not a twerp."

"Hey, thanks!"

"But there's no sticking gum in my hair," warns Rebecca.

"And no telling," adds Alan.

"I promise."

"OK, now you can give us your dime." Rebecca holds out the plastic container.

"A dime! You only put two pennies in!"

"Yeah, well, it's a dime to join. And then two pennies for dues."

"Oh. OK. But I don't have a dime. I only have…"

"Never mind. You can give it to us next week."

"Thanks. Now what do I do?"

"What do you mean?"

"You know…like…are you going to blindfold me or make me eat a worm or what?"

The others giggle. They've never thought of having an initiation ceremony.

"Hey, yeah!" blurts Brenda. "Like the Masons! My Dad says the Masons do all sorts of weird, mean things to each other!"

Eric looks frightened.

"The Eastern Stars don't, though," counters Rebecca. "They just make the new ones say the oath and then teach them some stupid signs and passwords."

"But we don't have any of those."

"I know. But we could always…Hey! I know! We'll make him go to the slaughterhouse with us!"

"Yeah! And cut the head off a chicken!"

"Yeah!"

"OK, then. When should we go?"

"How about next Saturday?"

"I thought we were going to the movie next Saturday."

"Oh, yeah. Well, then, the Saturday after that."

"Fine with me."

"Remember to write it in your book, Brenda."

"OK. Now." Alan tries to take control again. "Back to the main thing. We voted last week that we needed lots more new members. Does anyone know...?"

"Can I go with you to the movie?" interrupts Eric.

They think for a moment. After all, he hasn't been initiated yet.

"Sure. But you have to pay your own way."

"I will. How much does it cost anyway?'

"Thirty-five cents for the train."

"Each way."

"And twenty-five cents for the movie."

"OK."

It'll be the third time this year that the club members have taken the train to Middleton to see a movie at the Capitol Theatre. The first two times it was *Mary Poppins* and *Cat Ballou*. But they don't just go for the movie. They go for the trip itself. They love marching into the station and buying their tickets — even though they're only thin little paper ones, not cardboard, and the conductor ends up taking half of them. And they love sitting on the benches in the waiting room, eating their chips and pretending they're somebody important. And they love standing right up by the edge of the grimy tracks as the silver diesel car squeals to a stop beside them. But the most fun of all is racing down the sidewalk after they've actually reached Middleton. The movie always starts at two and the theatre's a ten-minute walk from the station. Since it's lucky if the train grinds to a halt by ten-to-two, there's plenty of ground to cover in a very short time, especially if they want to get popcorn or a box of Glossettes. After the movie, things are more tranquil. They usually just saunter across the road to Musgrave Motors, where Alan's father Harvey sells Chevies.

"Oh-oh," he always says, when he spots them strolling across the lot. "Here comes that girl whose friends sell Fords. We can't have that." And then they all laugh — even though Rebecca's always coveted that '57 Bel Air sitting in Harvey's lot. It's a two-tone Sports Coupe with a special "Gold Package," featuring gold grill and script, and a 283 cubic inch engine with a two-speed powerglide transmission.

"What's on anyway?" asks Eric.

"HELP!"

"Oh, good. I was hoping it wasn't anything too sad."

"Yeah. Like *Old Yeller*."

"Yeah."

"I saw that when I was a kid."

"Yeah."

They observe a moment of silence and then Alan brings them back to the morning's business. "What about Stanley Kaulback?"

"For what?"

"For a new member."

"Are you kidding?"

"No way!"

Stanley Kaulback is like a little bird, thinks Rebecca. He can't stay still for a second. He's always flitting around the schoolyard, pecking at people's hair. Rita Siggins especially hates it because she rolls her ringlets herself, using that handful of cracked pink cylinders she found in the trash outside Marilyn Addy's place. Stanley says he's going to be a missionary some day, but everyone thinks he'll probably just end up staying in Nicholsville, running a turkey farm.

"Why not? He can ride a horse and..."

"Hey, yeah! His Daddy's got an Appaloosa!"

"Neat!"

"And he knows lots of good fishing spots!"

"OK." Rebecca faces Brenda. "But if we do let him in, we don't want any mushy stuff."

Brenda turns beet red. "What are you looking at me for?"

"You know why!"

"No, I don't."

"OK, then, what's that?" Rebecca points to some faint, white chalk marks on the wall above their heads.

"Hey! I've never seen *that* before!"

"Yeah! What is it?"

The boys get up to take a closer look.

"Well?" asks Rebecca.

The boys look down at Brenda.

"I vote no," says Alan.

"So do I," agrees Eric.

"That's not fair!" squeals Brenda. "I don't even...!"

"*First, comes love,*" begins Rebecca. "*Then comes marriage.*" The boys join in. *"Then comes Brenda with a baby carriage."*

As Brenda gazes up at the faint, white chalk marks, however, Rebecca feels sorry for her. She can see that Brenda thought no one would notice them. Thought she traced them so gently, so lightly that you needed to be her in order to see the big white heart with BT + SK locked inside it.

"Not fair at all," murmurs Brenda.

The boys snicker.

Rebecca, meanwhile, has stopped feeling sorry for Brenda and is now feeling scared. It's all right if they find out about Brenda and Stanley. And maybe even about giggly Bonnie Fredericks, who has a huge crush on Leonard Jones, a soft-spoken loner with no hobbies, no interests and no friends. But she wouldn't like them to find out about her and Ricky MacNair. As a matter of fact, she's glad that *Ricky* doesn't know about it. Ricky's already one of Aylesford's bad apples — wild, rough, headed for juvenile reform school in Shelburne. Unlike the other Junior Hoods, however, there's a certain fascination to him. He isn't just naughty; he's something more desperate, more anti-social, more effective. He's also cute. And she just can't shake that image of him, standing in the field near St. Monica's Catholic Church, with his hands in the back pockets of his jeans and a cigarette hanging out of his lips. He's only thirteen, she marvels, and already he can do that.

"C'mon." Eric elbows Alan. "Let's go ride…"

"Shshsh." Rebecca grabs at their pantlegs. "Listen."

Alan's big black and white dog — a cross between Mona Spurr's German shepherd and one of Ruthie's Samoyeds — has started barking.

"Someone's coming."

"Hey! That reminds me!"

"Shshsh!"

Brenda lowers her voice. "Aren't you supposed to be at your…?"

"Rebecca? Rebecca! Are you in there, Rebecca?"

It's Alan's older sister Betsy. She's at West Kings now, trying to set a world record for joining things. She plays basketball and volleyball, sits on the Student Council, writes for the yearbook and the newspaper, is a Junior Librarian, a House Leader and a member of Allied Youth, which has just adopted a child from China.

"OK, you little brat. See if *I* care. But Marion's real mad." Betsy pauses to listen for rustling. "She says you're going to get it." She pauses again, then turns and strides back toward the house.

"What's going on?" whispers Eric.

Alan chuckles. "Same thing that goes on every week."

"Shshsh. It might be a trick."

They wait another ten seconds, then Rebecca hops to her feet. "I'm supposed to be at my piano lesson," she says casually, as she swats at the straw on her pants.

"Who's your teacher?" asks Eric.

Rebecca sticks her upper teeth over her lower lip, like a rabbit.

"Oh," laughs Eric. "Mrs. Haney. I take from Mrs. North."

"You're lucky."

Dorothy Haney lives a few houses down from the Rawdings, right next to Irene and Alvin Andrews. She isn't mean exactly, just organized, and, as far as Rebecca's concerned, that's almost the same thing as being mean. She makes sure her kids take exams, play at recitals and compete in the Kiwanis Music Festival.

Rebecca hates everything about the Kiwanis, which is held every June in Kentville. She hates the big auditorium. She hates how nervous she gets. She hates the terrible marks the adjudicator gives her. Last year, when she thought she and Chris Davidson played a perfect duo — Jean Williams's Fourth Piano Concerto in C Major — they only got in the high eighties. She can't understand why it's so much harder to get one hundred on a piano piece than it is on a science or arithmetic test.

"Are you going to get in trouble?" asks Brenda, as she struggles to her feet.

"No. I'll just pretend I forgot to go."

"Again?" laughs Alan. "That's what you pretended last Saturday. Come to think of it, you've been pretending that for years!"

Rebecca laughs, too. "Well, then, I'll think of something else! Come on. Let's go ride Duchess."

There are four horses in the Rawding's pasture today. A huge black Shire which belongs to Boyd MacIntyre. A big gold Belgian which Lindsay Nixon boards there. A small bay Morgan which Betsy owns. And Duchess, the little brown and white Shetland which Alan lets everyone ride.

As Rebecca swishes through the tall grass toward Alan's pony, something comes over her. She likes Duchess. She's nice and gentle and safe, like the sonatina by Clementi Rebecca learned to play last year. But Duchess isn't a real horse. Not like Northern Dancer. And not like that huge black one grazing by the fence.

Suddenly, the tall grass prickles her ankles.

"Hey! Where are you going?"

"You know you're not allowed to ride that one."

"Rebecca!"

She climbs up on the rail of the fence.

"Rebecca!"

She leans over and puts her arms around the huge black neck.

"OK, but don't blame us if…"

She slips onto the huge black back.

Pop, pop, chink. Pop, pop, chink.

Two weeks later, Alan, Eric and Rebecca are sitting in the lawn chairs at Marion's place, waiting for Brenda. Alan and Eric are lost in thought. Rebecca is tapping the head of her tambourine.

"Maybe she chickened out," she says at last.

"I guess." Alan stares down at his sneakers. The dew has already soaked right through them.

"What's the slaughterhouse like, anyway?" asks Eric.

Rebecca doesn't look up. "It's pretty yucky."

"Oh." Eric picks at the paint on the arms of his chair.

"My brother Donnie was going to work there one time but he went to work at the peat plant instead."

"Yeah? What's he do there?"

"I don't know. Dries the stuff, I guess. Then smushes it all down and packs it."

"Oh."

Pop, pop, chink. Pop, pop, chink.

Rebecca hasn't played her tambourine for years. But this morning, as she lay on the cot in the upstairs hall, she had an idea that it was the sort of thing you're supposed to take to initiations. And so she went to Frankie's cabin and lifted it off its nail by the door.

Pop, pop, chink. Pop, pop, chink.

The paint on it is cracked now, which makes the whole thing — the sand, the sea, the little white dog — look like a jigsaw puzzle. But the jingles are all there and the calfskin head is still stretched tightly over the rim.

"There she is!"

They leap up from the chairs.

"It's about time!"

"Where've you been, Brenda?"

"Sorry." Brenda comes puffing into the yard. "My mother made me eat breakfast."

"Well, goody for you."

"Now, come on. Let's get going."

The slaughterhouse is located on Old Factory Road, up near Bootlegger's Lane. The shortest way there is to cut through Alice's rosebushes, past Porter's barn, and then up the lane through the woods. But that means you have to go through the Field of Bones and that's pretty creepy.

"No, wait! I can't!" whispers Brenda, as they reach a dark brown doghouse.

"Why not?" Rebecca whispers back.

"'Cause I've only got my sandals on."

"So?"

Brenda hesitates. "So it'll hurt my feet."

Rebecca puts her hands on her hips. "Look, Brenda. This is the way we're going, OK? So either you…"

"You're always so bossy." Brenda puts her hands on her hips, too.

"Yeah? Well, you're always such a big baby."

"Oh-oh," whispers Eric.

"What?"

"Did you hear that?"

"What?"

"I think Sissy's…"

"Yow!"

There's a delirium of barking and squealing as Sissy bounds after them…Thud, chink. Thud, chink. Thud, chink…and then a stifled yelp. The kids stop running.

"Whew," pants Eric, as he leans against the side of Porter's barn. "We made it."

"Yeah," laughs Rebecca. "But it was way more fun when she was young. They didn't have her on a leash when she was young."

"Hey!" Alan looks around. "Where's Brenda?"

"Maybe Sissy got her," replies Eric. "Or maybe..."

"She's back there," drawls Rebecca. "By the lawn chairs. Now, come on. Let's get going."

"But what about Brenda?"

"What about her? It's not my fault she ran the other way. Come on."

Alan and Eric don't like the Field of Bones either. But they also wouldn't like Rebecca calling them big babies. They take a deep breath and follow her around the corner of the barn.

"Hey, look!" rasps Alan, when they reach the other side.

"Yeah!" marvels Eric. "They're gone!"

The boys exhale. The sun gleams down on the empty field.

Rebecca stares for a moment at the dirt and stubble, then turns and hollers up to the loft. "Carl! Hey, Carl! Carl!"

He pokes his head out the window. "Jesus," he laughs. "What are you trying to do? Wake the dead?"

"Where did they go, Carl?"

"What?"

"The bones." She slams her tambourine against her leg.

"Those old things? Ha! Some fellow from Berwick came and carted them away."

"What for?"

"He said he could use them."

"I know but what for?" She bangs her tambourine again. So far the initiation has been a bust. She doesn't know what she's going to do if there aren't any cows or chickens to kill later on.

"Well, let's see," muses Carl. "Lots of things. You can burn them outside, in some contraption or other, and get this white powder for making china. Or you can burn them inside...I don't know if it's the same contraption or not...and get a kind of black charcoal for making sugar. Or you can crush them all up and get bone meal. For food and fertilizer and such."

"Oh."

Rebecca is flabbergasted. She had no idea that the creepiness ever came to anything. She thought the bones were something for the pigs to suck on. She thought they'd pile up here forever.

Suddenly, a power mower starts up.

Rebecca gazes towards the Aylesford Memorial Cemetery. The lowbush blueberries on the east side are filling out now. A few more weeks and all the kids would be coming home with purple teeth and lips. And then Vivian would be making her famous wild blueberry pie, with just a touch of rum. And Grammie would be asking the whole neighbourhood to drop by for a taste of her blueberry grunt, which would probably have even more brown sugar in it than last year. And Harold would be standing in the kitchen on Sunday morning, dressed entirely in white, watching the deep blue berries bleed into his pancake batter.

"C'mon!" shouts Alan, over the roar of the Lawnboy. "This is boring!"

"Yeah!" agrees Eric. "Let's go!"

Rebecca peers past the wild tangle of bushes. Many of the graves are marked with red, white and blue ovals, just like the rubber ball she used to have. Others have plastic flowers poking out of them. All except the newest ones are covered with lush green grass. This morning Marvin Bennett is cutting it, pushing the mower right over the bodies lying below. He's pretty good at it — doesn't shred too many plastic petals or stems — but every once in a while the relentless rumble is interrupted by a screech, as the mower skins the top off a little mound of earth. Whenever that happens, Harley Rogers, who's been digging graves in the area for sixty years, looks up from his digging and chuckles.

"Yow!" Rebecca leaps back from the lane, as Carl's pick-up zooms by on its way to the slaughterhouse.

"Serves you right for daydreaming!" shouts Alan, through the cloud of dust. He and Eric are waiting for her up by Spinney's Bog. "Now come on or the two of us are gonna go do something else!"

"OK, OK," murmurs Rebecca, as she scuffs towards them.

When she finally gets there, she looks over at the bog and scowls. "We won't be able to skate here this year."

"Why not?" asks Eric.

"Too many reeds, dummy."

"Oh. Well, we can always go up to the bog on School Street, opposite Brenda's place. It's not overgrown yet."

"Hey!" Alan spins around. "Where *is* Brenda anyway? She should have gotten her shoes by *now*."

"Ha! I don't think she went to get her shoes. Ha! Ha!"

Rebecca's laughter joins the chorus of sounds which haunt Spinney's Bog. Joins the squeals of delight, as the little white dog scrambles madly across the ice — clumps of snow hanging from its whiskers and paws — slipping and sliding through the frozen stalks. Joins the squeals of pain, as the little black disk hits the goalie wearing the rubber boots — those awful brown ones with buckles and fuzz — right on the ankle bone. It's one of the last ghosts that will ever join that chorus, now that the cattails and cuckooflowers have taken over.

"I don't see what's so funny," whispers Alan to Eric. "Do you see what's so funny?"

In the slaughterhouse, death has many sounds and colours, but only one smell — a really bad smell, which seems to mock the scent of apple blossoms and French fries and "Magi," that Spanish perfume in the deep red and black box which Marion likes so much.

"P-U," gags Eric, as they reach the doorway of the big, grey wooden building.

Alan puts his hand up to his mouth. "Hoo! You can say *that* again!"

"Come on." Rebecca shakes her tambourine at them. "Let's go inside."

The first thing they see when they creep through the big, wide door is Calvin Loomer, hosing down the floors and walls. Somehow, they all know that he'll probably be able to get rid of the blood, but not the smell; that the smell will work its way into the unpainted wood and stay there forever, like Dustbane.

The kids look around the dingy room. Carl Porter's slaughterhouse is actually pretty empty inside. There are no fancy machines and contraptions; just a few ropes and pulleys and a big open area with stalls all around it.

"So this is what a *boudoir* looks like," remarks Eric.

Rebecca splutters. "It's not a boudoir, dummy. It's an abattoir."

"Oh, yeah. Ha! I knew that. Ha, ha!" He follows her up to the stall where Carl is standing with Murray Loomer.

"What are you killing today, Carl?" she asks.

Carl cracks open his pistol. "Cows and chickens."

"Oh."

Rebecca's a little disappointed. She doesn't come very often, but every time she does, it's cows and chickens, cows and chickens. She's still never seen a pig killed.

"Well, never mind. Come on, guys. Let's go stand over there."

"Why over there?"

Carl snaps his pistol shut. Murray eases a long gleaming blade out of his belt.

"You'll see."

Moments later, Alan is running back down the lane. It all happened so fast. First, a chink, chink, chink, hisssss. And then a shot...and the blood spurting from the cow's head into the air. And then a slice...and the blood splashing out of the cow's throat onto the floor. Rebecca thinks it was the spurt which got Alan; which made the big red splotches on his brand-new pants. But either way, his mother's going to kill him.

Back inside, there's so much steam that Eric and Rebecca can barely see the gore.

"Is it dead?" whispers Eric.

"It must be," murmurs Rebecca.

She runs her fingers over the calfskin head of her tambourine. It's so soft, so precious, so alive — much more alive than that gushing head on the floor. Of course, it's just as dead, too. Only here, in her hands, there's the promise of rhythmic beauty and there, on the floor, there's the promise of head cheese.

"I think if I had to be a cow, I'd rather be for milk than for meat," whispers Eric, as he turns away from the gore.

They can see it quite clearly, now that the steam has floated away.

"Yes," whispers Rebecca. "Only..."

"What?"

"Nothing."

She isn't mean enough to remind him that boy cows would have to be for something else besides milk if they wanted to live a long time.

"All set, Calvin?"

The men are preparing to hoist the carcass.

"Pretty near, Carl. I just have to get this hook through...I think she'll drain better if I...there!"

Rebecca, too, turns away from the gore. "Come on, Eric. Let's go."

"But what about the chickens? Don't I have to watch the chickens?"

Rebecca looks over at the coops. There are two big barrels standing nearby. "No. That's OK. You passed. You're in the club."

"Great! Thanks!"

"Now, come on." She chinks toward the big, wide door. "I'll race you back to Alan's place."

By the time they reach Spinney's Bog again, Eric is out of breath. "Wait! Wait!" he pants. "We don't want to get there too soon or his mother'll still be screaming at him."

"Yeah." Rebecca slows down. "You're right."

After the blood and the steam, the daylight seems very yellow, very clear. They walk the next hundred yards in silence — all the way back to Carl's barn, where there's a happy chorus of clucking and squealing.

"There's not much to the chickens anyway." Rebecca turns to face him. "They just chop their heads off on the bottom of one barrel, then push the heads onto the floor and throw the floppy bodies into the top of the other barrel."

"Oh."

"Not like when my Uncle Clifford used to kill them."

"What do you mean?"

"Well, Ben Kelly told me that when my Uncle Clifford was young, he was big and mean."

"So?"

"So when he got drunk, he used to twist the necks off chickens with his bare hands."

"What for?"

"How should *I* know?"

"Well, whose chickens were they?"

"I don't know. I only know he did it."

"Oh. Well, chickens have skinny necks anyway. I bet he couldn't twist the neck off a cow."

Rebecca laughs. "I bet he couldn't either. Now, come on. She must be finished screaming by now."

They race back through Alice's rosebushes.

33

The screen door bangs shut.

"It wasn't even my fault!" protests Rebecca, as she stomps into the dining room. "I was only..." She pulls open the middle drawer of the cabinet, clangs around in it for a few seconds and then flings four sets of silverware onto the mahogany table.

"You better not do that with the plates," calls Marion from the kitchen.

"Don't worry, I won't." She lifts four Spode's Tower plates from the shelf above the drawer, considers, for a moment, the consequences of turning them into flying saucers, and then sets them gently, mockingly on the crocheted place mats.

"Is it safe to come in?" asks Marion, as she edges into the room. She's carrying four glasses of ice water.

"Yes, it's safe," snorts Rebecca.

"Good." Marion begins circling the table, letting the glasses slip, one by one, out of her hands. "But what made you so late?"

"I had to stay in after school."

"Ha!" Marion lets go of the last glass. "That's a switch."

"It's not funny," sulks Rebecca.

"Sorry. Sorry." Marion wipes her hands on her apron — the one decorated with big ripe clusters of strawberries and a few shy little violets. "And what did you have to write *this* time?"

"What else? Lines!" Rebecca stomps into the kitchen.

"Well, I gathered that." Marion follows her. "But *what* exactly?"

Rebecca reaches into the red and yellow waxed bag on the counter. "Well, if you must know..." She flings four slices of enriched white bread on a plate. "I had to write: *It is unnecessary to talk unnecessarily during school hours.*"

Marion splutters.

"One hundred times! And it wasn't even my fault! I was only asking Alan if...!"

Marion bursts into laughter.

"Oh, skip it." Rebecca clumps to the fridge and yanks open the door. "What kind of pickles should we have? Mustard, bread and butter...?"

"Anything but the beets."

"Why? Are they mushy?"

"No, I think Ben forgot to put sugar in them."

"Again?"

There are four people sitting in the dining room now. There's no talking. There's no laughing. There's only the clink, clink, scrape of the silverware against the plates. Against the tower. Down the stream. Across the ornamental bridge.

Rebecca looks up from her red and white plate. Malcolm is sitting across from her — upright, scowling, pushing two or three peas at a time onto his fork. She bugs out her eyes at him, but he doesn't notice. Then she turns to her right, towards Ben, who's leaning on his forearm at the head of the table. She makes a face at him, too, but he's too busy shovelling stew into his mouth to see. Disappointed, she turns to her left and looks at Marion, who smiles and shrugs. The men are brothers, but they don't get along very well. In fact, they hardly ever communicate, except when there are stocks to buy or household bills to pay. Once again, she looks from one old man to the other. And then she shakes her head. What she *really* can't understand is how both of them have girlfriends.

Suddenly, there's a long, loud rumbling sound. Rebecca can't help giggling. Ben's stomach makes the biggest rumbles around.

"Good grub," he announces, as he flings his fork onto his plate. "What do you call it?"

"Stay-a-bed Stew," smiles Marion.

"Yuh." He breathes in as he says it. "Good grub." He leans back in his chair.

"It's not much, really. Just beef, onions, potatoes, carrots, parsnips and…"

"And the secret ingredients!" blurts Rebecca.

Malcolm glares at her.

She leans towards Ben. "A can of golden mushroom soup…" she whispers.

"Lovely."

"And a can of cream of chicken soup."

"Perfect."

Rebecca smiles. Ben's favourite food is gas station food — and anything else that has lots of salt in it, like dulse and kippered herring. Marion's preference is for starchy things, like scalloped potatoes and corn on the cob, and sweet things, like lemon meringue pie and butterscotch rice pudding. Rebecca, of course, will eat anything except lima beans, which she thinks taste like sawdust, and Brussels sprouts, which remind her of little farts.

"Yuh." Ben sucks in air again. "Good grub."

"OK," grumbles Malcolm. "How many times do you have to...?"

"Especially the peas."

Marion smiles at Rebecca, who spent all last evening on the front veranda, shelling them. She's getting pretty good at guessing how many there'll be in each pod — only two or three most of the time, but sometimes as many as ten.

"Great," growls Malcolm. "Now what else is there?"

That evening, as Rebecca tiptoes by the den, she hears Marion sighing. She wonders if it's about her or about Barry Connors. Her first choice is Barry. When Barry was younger, he cut the arms off Clary Marshall's wheelbarrow. Last night, he burnt down Ruthie Sutherland's barn.

Rebecca peeks through the doorway into the den. Marion is sitting at her big, old oaken desk, with the light gleaming off the golden rims of her reading glasses. Earlier, Rebecca had heard her promise to go over to Ellen's tonight. So they could think of a way to keep Barry out of the County Jail in Kentville. But then she'd had also promised to visit Ruthie, who's worried that the Apple Blossom Festival float that was stored inside her barn won't be covered by her insurance policy. And Walter Keddy, who needs a new glass eye. And Wanda Willoughby, who hurt her leg falling down the church steps. And Hugh Fancy, who wants to see if he can get anything for the hole in his ceiling made by last year's gigantic Christmas tree.

So it could be Barry Connors Marion's sighing about, thinks Rebecca. Or it could be her. And all because of last Sunday, when she couldn't wait to get over to Heather Kinsman's house on Maple Avenue. She told Marion it was to watch Heather's mother do the last word of her needlepoint. "She's gotten as far as *Goodliness is*...and I want to see what comes next." She didn't think Marion believed her, since she'd never shown even the slightest interest in embroidery — in silly little domestic scenes and mottos — but Marion let her go anyway. Later, after Marion had looked out the front window and seen the Kinsman's ditch on fire, she said Rebecca needed a good talking-to. But Rebecca protested that she and Heather hadn't intended to take a can of oil from the woodhouse, pour it onto the pile of leaves that had gathered in the ditch and then light it. It just happened. Anyway, there wasn't much flame — in fact, the leaves were so green that they just went out on their own — but Marion said it could have been serious. And she wasn't the least bit interested in Rebecca's reasons. "Mrs. Kinsman *was* sewing the word, but she was also crying and everything so…Well, Joan said we couldn't stay in the living room because she and Sammie Gates wanted to smooch. And Mr. Kinsman said we couldn't stay on the back veranda because he wanted to drink in peace. So we…so we were bored!"

Marion just said that Rebecca would have to learn that there's such a thing as consequences. And then find a way to make her life something greater than a tangle of those consequences.

"Whatever *that* means," whispers Rebecca, as she tiptoes away from the doorway.

There are six different lamps on in the living room. The light they cast by themselves, however — the glow, the glare, the sheen, the pool — is barely recognizable. There's no individuality here, only nameless illumination.

Malcolm is sitting in his aqua-coloured armchair, poring over the latest newsletter from Wood-Gundy. Ben is slumped on the burgundy-coloured chesterfield, probably wishing Malcolm would let him smoke his pipe in the house. Rebecca is leaning over the top of her rolltop desk, tracing a map of North America and peeking sideways at the latest episode of *The Beverly Hillbillies* on TV.

"Oh-oh. Watch this! Grannie's going to push that snotty Mrs. Drysdale into the *cee-ment* pond! Yeaaaaah!" She laughs and turns toward the men.

But the men are more interested in Diversified Securities and Amphora Brown tobacco than in the escapades of the Clampett family. She turns back to her homework.

She loves doing it here, at this old, reddish brown desk. A long time ago, it belonged to Grampy Newell, when he was Manager at United Fruit Company, but now it's hers. She smiles, as she draws the jagged shoreline of Lake Superior.

Jed, meanwhile, is telling Jethro and Miss Hathaway that, "*land o' mercy,*" he wishes he never set eyes on that "*black gold!*"

She turns to the men again. "Did you know there are *Beverly Hillbillies* colouring books out now?"

There's no response.

"Featuring all the characters?"

Nothing.

"Wonderful," she sighs, as she turns back to her map. It's the best she can do — leave a big, fat hint. If they can't guess that's what she wants for her birthday, then forget it.

"*I reckon I'll just rest a spell before…*"

"Oh! Ha! Look at Grannie's face! Have you ever seen her so…?"

Malcolm curses. Rebecca sticks her tongue out at him. And then pulls it right back in.

He usually spends his evenings muttering and scowling and changing the channel when her favourite shows are on. Tonight, she's been lucky. It looks like she's going to make it through an entire episode — unlike earlier in the week, with *Petticoat Junction, The Lucy Show* and *Voyage to the Bottom of the Sea.*

Suddenly, there's a loud ring. Marion leaps out of the darkness into the dining room.

"Malcolm, it's for you," she calls, a moment later. "Elva Trites."

"What does *she* want?" he barks at her. He's rotten to Marion, too.

"I don't know exactly. Something about her Royal Bank stocks."

"Hold on."

As she watches Malcolm push himself out of his armchair, Rebecca can't help chortling. She knows she shouldn't. She knows she should feel sorry he's got high blood pressure and poor circulation. But she can't help it. She thinks it serves him right — for taking so long in the bathroom, for one thing. And so she keeps chortling, as she watches him shuffle toward the dining room. It doesn't seem to bother him much. He seems to have his eyes fixed on the dial phone sitting on top of the sideboard, just over the place where they keep the honey wine.

When she thinks she's safe — when she's sure he's not going to veer to his right and change the channel — she turns back to her map and begins the outline of Great Slave Lake. On his way by, however, he surprises her.

"Take that, you little bitch!" He kicks at the leg of her chair.

Her pen scrapes across the page.

"Look what you've done!" she wails. "You've ruined it!"

Great Slave Lake now stretches from the North Pole to the Gulf of Mexico.

"Now I'll have to...Ooooo!" She crumples the page.

"Hello, Elva..." chuckles Malcolm. "Yes. What can I do for you?"

Rebecca leans through the doorway and fires her pen at him.

"Ow!" It hits him in the rear end. "God damn it!...What?...No, Elva. No trouble at all. See you then."

Malcolm flings down the receiver, then suddenly picks it up again and makes another call. Rebecca, meanwhile, folds her arms across her chest and sulks. Malcolm's ass will only hurt for a minute. Her map is ruined forever.

"What can I say, Avard?"

He must be talking to Avard MacIntyre, snorts Rebecca. The tall, rich man who sells men's clothing from door to door.

"Something's come up. You'll have to bring the suits over another night." With that, he flings down the receiver and slams out the screen door.

Rebecca leans through the doorway again. "At least I'm not afraid of bats!" she calls after him.

She doesn't like bats either, but she wouldn't scream. Not like Malcolm did last week, when he woke up screaming that there was a bat in his bedroom and then fled past her in his pajamas and shut himself in the kitchen. She would just hide under the covers. She thinks it's strange for someone so mean to be so chicken. She wonders how things about people get to be so mixed up.

"Well." Ben struggles up from the chesterfield. "Another pleasant evening at home, what?" He wanders out to the front veranda to smoke.

As soon as he's gone, Rebecca bolts out of her chair and over to the chesterfield. "I wonder if he's left any..." She lifts one of the burgundy cushions. "Damn!" And then the other. "Damn!"

Because Ben slumps so much, loose change often slides out of his pockets. And then slips through the cracks and underneath the cushions. But there isn't any there tonight.

"That's fine language for a young lady," remarks Marion, as she strolls into the living room.

Rebecca flounces down on the chesterfield. "I don't want to be a young lady."

"I can see that," sighs Marion, as she turns off the TV. "Well, come on."

"Where to?"

Marion still goes on her "rounds" every night, to make sure the town's all right. And every night, Rebecca goes with her.

"To Ellen Connors' place. To see about Barry."

"Oh. Do we *have* to?"

"No, we don't *have* to. Why don't you *want* to?"

"Well...Barry's a hood."

"So?"

"He steals things. He burns things. He's evil and mean."

Marion laughs. "Well? What about you? Are you evil and mean?"

"No."

"You set fire to the Kinsman's ditch, didn't you?"

"Oh."

"Rebecca?" asks Marion softly, as they pile into the car.

"What?"

"There's something I've been meaning to ask you?"

"What?"

"The needlepoint. You know, the one Margaret...Heather's mother was doing?"

"Yeah?"

"Did she finish it?"

"Yeah, she did. But it was dumb."

"Why? What did it say?"

"*Loneliness*," laughs Rebecca. "*Goodliness is Loneliness*. How stupid can you get?"

Marion drives slowly out of the yard.

34

Monday, June 21, 1965. Graduation Day. The ceremony is held at the
south end of the school, in the big open room that's created when the
wooden dividing wall between the grade-one and grade-two classrooms
is raised. This is where all the special events are held — concerts,
pageants, presentations. Once, the kids watched a film about how to
ride a bike safely. Another time, Christina Boucher, the only Apple
Blossom Princess from Aylesford ever chosen to be Queen Annapolisa,
came to show off her crown. None of the kids snickered that day, not
even at her goofy green gown and sash. They weren't about to act up
in front of royalty. And neither was Thorold Strum, the old hobo with
the long grey beard, who walked all the way to Wolfville to see
Christina's Coronation at Acadia. He tried to give her a bunch of lilacs
that time. This time, he just stood outside the classroom and peeked
in the window. Rebecca saw him!

Since graduation is a fairly solemn occasion, there isn't much
decoration on the walls — just the thirty-one flags Herbert Armstrong
made Rebecca's class draw last September, when the great flag debate
was raging across the country. Most of the designs are pretty flashy —
great gashes and swirls of colour — and some have unusual symbols.
Apples, seagulls and hearts are the favourites. There are even two
crushed skulls. But it's Rebecca's opinion that every one of them is
better than that "dumb old rag" Prime Minister Pearson finally picked.
There's nothing to that one. Not when you compare it with the three
red maple leaves and two blue bars that came in second. Or with the
crushed skulls.

As usual, today's ceremony is poorly attended. Other than teachers
and kids, there's only a handful of officials, a few mothers and Marion,
who's seated at the upright piano, scowling. Rebecca knows why she's
angry. It isn't about having to play for the assembly. She's played for
assemblies ever since word got out that she studied at the College of
Music while in Halifax attending the College of Business. It's about
the site for the new school. Marion wanted it to be built near the old
one, on School Street. She said she wasn't being sentimental. She
didn't care at all that no special note was being taken of today, when
Rebecca's class would be the very last to graduate from this decrepit

building. She said she was being practical. The new site was simply too close to busy Commercial Street. It wasn't sensible and it wasn't safe. Rebecca's never seen her so upset. So she wasn't surprised that Marion quit the Conservative Party — not after it ignored her recommendation and pushed through its own agenda instead. And she wasn't surprised that the Liberals immediately installed Marion as Second Vice-President in charge of organization for the Kings West riding association. They were pretty sure she'd work hard to see that Dr. Sutherland's nephew Dale became the next member of the legislature. Rebecca can't help smiling. Dale Sutherland runs the Berwick Bakery and attends all of his son's hockey games. He's a successful businessman and a devoted father. It's just that...well, she doesn't know exactly what a member of the legislature does, but she's pretty sure Dale's not going to hop onto a bulldozer and flatten the beams and girders which are already rising up on Commercial Street.

Marion is still scowling as she yanks at the salmon-coloured frames of her reading glasses and then bangs out the first few chords of "God Save the Queen." Startled, the assembly leaps to its feet and tries to catch up to her.

After the anthem, Mr. Armstrong booms out his usual greetings. Once again, Rebecca smiles. He's certainly not Our Miss Brooks, but he's not a tyrant either. In fact, he's really a bit of a pushover — especially with animals. He and his wife Kay are always adopting the poor kids' dogs and cats — taking them home, paying their vet bills, giving them the best food. Rebecca sometimes wishes she were one of the poor kids' pets.

When Mr. Armstrong finishes his remarks about the "meaning of achievement" — he tried the "meaning of life" last year, but it didn't go over very well — he turns down the volume on his hearing aid and sits down. Then comes a musical interlude, during which Mrs. Purdy's grade-three class rises to its feet and messes up the entire second verse of "Paper Roses." Rebecca's glad. Dorma Purdy divides the kids into groups, sitting the dumb ones with the bright ones, hoping that somehow something will rub off and in the right direction. But she can't even get the kids to sit still, never mind figure out what to do with the ones who are hungry or smell like sheep or have dyslexia, like Randy. He started a grade ahead of Rebecca, but he had more trouble than usual with his reading one year and Mrs. Purdy flunked him. Rebecca thinks it serves Mrs. Purdy right that her teeth are falling out and that her class sings even worse than Anita Bryant.

Next, it's Kevin Thomas's turn to give his sucky little report on this year's school trip to Haliburton House. And finally, it's time for the long list of marks to be read out. Almost everyone starts squirming. Mr. Armstrong, Rebecca notices, turns his hearing aid off completely.

Rebecca's class was the usual grade-six mixture of idiots, twerps, snots, goofs, bullies, wieners and brains. She's pretty sure that Mr. Armstrong did the best he could with them, but it probably won't amount to anything. It doesn't seem to matter much that he trained to be a minister and took extra classes at Acadia every summer. The kids are still going to do what they're going to do. Run skunk farms in Dempsey Corner, grow blueberries in Aylesford East, become missionaries.

Today, the lists of marks are like sirens. There's a loud wail…"Thirty-two!"…and then everyone knows that so-and-so is "real stupid." There's another loud wail…"Sixty-seven!"…and then everyone knows that so-and-so is "about average." Rebecca can't help thinking about Marsha Luddington. Almost everyone would agree that she's the dumbest. But Rebecca's not so sure. She doesn't judge people's dumbness on the marks they get. She judges it on their views. And at least Marsha didn't think that "racism" meant "running fast." Or that it was neat when a bunch of people sprayed another bunch of people with fire hoses. Or that it was strange that Rebecca and Frankie were friends. In any case, there's wailing for "fairly bright" and "brilliant," too, but not as much. Sometimes there's even a little moan or gasp from the back of the room, where the mothers are gathered. But not often. The few that are there already have a pretty good idea how many brains their kids have. Even Vivian, who wasn't able to get out of bed this morning, has an idea about that. That little gasp she made last year wasn't her display of surprise and delight. It was her attempt not to puke into her purse.

Rebecca tries to block it all out. But it's no use. The wailing goes on and on, through all the grades, until it reaches the end of the grade-six alphabet. It's time for the prizewinners.

"Eric Stedman…Ninety-eight!"

Eric leans over and pokes Rebecca. "Bet you won't beat that, you little twerp."

"Well, if I do…" Rebecca pokes him back. "Don't you dare put gum in my hair!"

They grin at one another.

Since grade three, Eric's done that more times than they can count. Still, he and Rebecca have actually taken turns getting the highest averages. Last year, when *she* won, the prize was *The Electronic Mind Reader*, a Rick Brant Science-Adventure story. The year before, when she finished second, she got Shirley Flight, Air Hostess, in a story called *Hawaiian Mystery*.

"Rebecca Peterson…"

She crosses her fingers.

"Ninety-nine!"

"Damn!" Eric slumps in his chair. "One mark, one lousy mark."

Rebecca uncrosses her fingers. "Better luck next year."

Unfortunately for Rebecca, her triumph is short-lived. First prize this year is *Cherry Ames, Student Nurse*.

"Trade you," she whispers to Eric, as she watches him leaf through *The Secret of Skull Mountain*.

"Are you kidding?" he whispers back. "No way!"

She sees his point. She wouldn't trade a Hardy Boys book for a book about a silly old nurse either. What she doesn't see is how a second prize gets to be so much better than a first prize.

"Hey, *I* know!" she blurts, as Marion yanks at her glasses again.

"What?"

"I'll give it to Sunny. She was going to be a Princess, you know. And then the wife of a Beatle. But now she just wants to be a nurse. In fact, she…"

"Yippy-yappy, yippy-yappy, yippy…"

While Mr. Armstrong booms out one last reprimand, Marion bangs out the first few chords of "O Canada."

"I'll tell you later," whispers Rebecca, as she leaps to her feet.

The Saturday after graduation, Marion's car speeds by the orchards along the road to Berwick.

"I know what that is," whispers Rebecca, as she watches the pickers gathering up tiny green apples. "It's the June Drop."

She learned about it in school this year. About how every June, apple trees thin themselves by dropping some of their young to the ground. They all learned about it, but no one else squished into the car is paying any attention.

A few minutes later, however, as the car pulls slowly into the parking lot, there are six kids pressing their faces against the windows.

"Are we here?"

"Of course we are, dummy. Can't you read?"

There's a yellow crescent over the entrance to the building. And big green letters which spell out BERWICK ARENA.

As soon as Marion stops the car, the kids spill through the doors.

"Hey, look! There's the tennis courts!"

"Yeah!"

"Remember Winifred?"

"Yeah!"

Last summer, they'd all come to watch Winifred play tennis in the annual Father-and-Daughter tournament. She didn't do badly, really; in fact, she made it as far as the "semis." But then her father double-faulted at match point and she stomped off the court to the car. It's what they'd all been waiting for.

"And over there. Isn't that where the ferris wheel was?"

"Yeah!"

"No, wait! That was the candy floss stand. The ferris wheel was further to the left."

"Yeah!"

They had all come to the annual carnival, too. Last fall. To stuff themselves with food and then see who'd be the first to get sick on the rides. Alan tried to hold Rebecca's hand that day.

"Who cares?" snorts Peter. "Now come on, you guys. Or we won't get good seats. Arrrrrrrgh." He charges toward the door of the arena.

As if the others suddenly remember how excited they are about Marion's graduation present, they let out a collective whoop and then scramble after him. They've all been inside once before. But that was only for Brenda's figure skating recital, which everybody agreed was really terrible. Today they're going to watch wrestling!

While Marion purchases the tickets, Peter rushes past the ushers toward the ring. He saves as many front row seats as he can — with his shoes and his socks and his shirt — but that still makes only five of them. He, Randy, Sunny, Brenda and Alan all get to sit right next to the action, but Marion and Rebecca have to settle for the row behind.

As the place fills up, Rebecca spots Dale Sutherland, shaking hands with his prospective constituents, and Gus Matheson, who's probably more excited than anyone. But then the lights are dimmed and a deathly pallor descends over the arena. The crowd begins murmuring in anticipation.

"I wonder if they have Dixie Cups," whispers Rebecca. "Last time we were here they had..."

Suddenly, the whole place goes dark, except for an eerie glow on the ring. Peter snuffles, Brenda gasps, Rebecca leans forward a little.

"There he is!"

"Oh, my gaaawd!"

"The Mummy!"

A tall figure wrapped in white gauze drifts slowly down the aisle. The crowd holds its breath. Randy reaches into the pocket of his shirt.

"Is he really dead?"

"Shshsh."

The tall figure climbs slowly through the ropes and into the ring. The light gleams off its bandages.

"He looks dead to me."

"Shshsh."

The tall figure drifts to the centre of the ring, begins to raise its arms toward the ceiling and then...flinches.

Rebecca giggles. Randy reaches into his pocket again.

"You got him in the leg that time, Randy. This time, try for the...oh-oh."

The tall figure peers through the darkness, turns slowly toward them, then past them, then...grabs at the back of its head.

"Yeah! That was a...!"

Suddenly, the crowd erupts in wild delight. It's Edouard Carpentier, doing back flips down the aisle toward the ring.

"Attaboy, Eddie!"

"You can do it!"

"Send the bastard back to Egypt!"

The last voice is Gus Matheson's.

When Edouard leaps into the ring, there's an excruciating cry of joy and hope. Anything seems possible. But then The Mummy turns slowly to face him and the bell clangs.

Today, as they invariably do, things go according to plan. Thus, the man who's acrobatic doesn't have a chance against the man who's embalmed and, by the end of the match, Edouard is lying in a heap on the canvas. As his handlers pull him to his feet, The Mummy kicks at the tiny green balls which litter the ring. Then he raises his arms in victory and twists from corner to corner.

"Boo! Boo!"

"Damn!" Randy turns to Rebecca. "I wish I had more peas!" He shoves his shooter back into his pocket.

"Never mind, Randy!" she shouts above the crowd. "You got him real good!"

"Yeah!" hollers Sunny, as the lights are raised to their normal levels. "And he never even figured out where they were coming from!"

There are four more preliminary bouts, featuring Wild Bill Curry, Little Beaver, Yukon Eric and The Beast, and then the lights come up full again. Peter snuffles, Alan blinks, Rebecca folds her arms across her chest.

"I'm starved!"

"Never mind," laughs Marion. "There's only one more bout."

"Yeah! A fight to the death between...!"

"Hey, Rebecca!" Brenda swivels to face her. "Isn't Wild Bill Curry the one we saw at the golf club?"

"Oh, yeah!" Rebecca unfolds her arms. "He was with a couple of other guys, right? Big, fat guys who couldn't hit the ball worth a bean."

Brenda knits her brow. "Do you think they were wrestlers, too?"

"Ha!" snorts Peter. "Wrestlers don't play golf. They bite the ears off people."

Everybody laughs.

The final match features Bulldog Brower against a local wrestler named Farmer Jim. At first, it's a fairly routine bout, with plenty of hammerlocks and half nelsons. But then the Bulldog starts fighting dirty.

"C'mon, ref!"

"Are you blind?"

"Watch the elbow smashes!"

Farmer Jim crumples in the far corner. The Bulldog prepares to pounce.

"Hey, Bulldog!" Unable to contain himself, Gus Matheson rises to his feet. "D'you know what we do with rabid dogs?"

The Bulldog turns and snarls at him.

"We shoot them!" Gus edges toward the ring. "Shoot them! That's what we do with them!"

The Bulldog claws at the air. An usher grabs Gus from behind.

"Oh, my gawd!" gasps Sunny. "Look!"

While the Bulldog is preoccupied with Gus, the Farmer struggles to his feet. There's a moment of pure sound without motion — all snarling and shouting — and then he leaps across the ring and lifts the Bulldog into the air.

"Way to go!"

"Flying camel!"

"Yeaaaaaaa!"

The crowd screams with delight, as the Farmer whirls round and around and around, with the Bulldog held high above his head. And then it shrieks — in utter, orgasmic disbelief — as he flings the him out of the ring.

Praise Him, praise Him, all ye little children.

Rebecca lifts her eyes from the page. It's all done with electric chimes now. The ones at the Baptist church have been ringing twice a day since 1974, the year the deacons finally decided to replace the badly cracked bell.

He is love. He is love.

She tries to find some meaning in those clean, crisp sounds, but they're too new. She needs to get back further than that. To the buzzer at school. To the bell at ringside. To the horn on Marion's car.

She looks down at the datebook again. July 1965. Places and times. Payments and promises. The horn on Marion's car.

35

"Why did you do that?" asks Rebecca.

"What?" Marion flings open the trunk of her car.

"Blow the horn."

"Oh, that. To scare the rats away." She lifts out a big bundle of newsletters. "Well? Are you just going to stand there? Or are you going to help?"

"Sure. But I still don't see why you…"

Marion trudges past her toward the dump. Rebecca pulls out a single newsletter.

"*She has sparkle and vitality,*" she begins to read aloud.

Marion heaves the bundle onto the pile of rubbish.

"*She is a community leader.*"

And then tramps back toward the car.

"*Her formula for success is…*"

"Move! You're in the way!"

"*Adjust to those around you and give accordingly.*"

Marion stumbles by with another big bundle. Rebecca raises her voice.

"*She is a good cook, an excellent home-maker, a sensitive friend…*"

Marion flings the second bundle onto the pile.

"*And a talented musician.*"

"Stop that!"

"Sorry. But I like it."

"Well, I don't!" Marion stomps back toward the car.

"Why? What's wrong with it?"

"Well, for one thing, it's not true."

"Oh." Rebecca peers at the page. "Which part?"

The *it* in question is an article about Marion in the latest issue of *Liberal Advance.* She assumed it would include a summary of her political efforts and a recipe for Stay-a-bed Stew. She'd no idea it would end up being a testimonial.

Not until Marion heaves a third and fourth bundle onto the pile does Rebecca look up from the newsletter. "Well, I like the picture. It's a pretty good picture, don't you…?"

"No!" Marion snatches it from her. "It makes me look fat!"

Rebecca giggles.

"I knew I shouldn't have worn that beige suit. I knew I…What are you laughing at? Eh? When you turn thirty, you'll have four or five chins, too!" She jams the newsletter into her pocket. "Now, come on." She slams shut the trunk. "Let's find some more."

They spend the morning scouring the town for newsletters. Drugstore, church, hairdresser's, bank. It's almost dinner-time when they turn onto North Park Street.

"If one more person congratulates me, I'm going to scream! Oh, hello, Sam. Nellie." She waves to them in her rear-view mirror.

Sam and Nellie Gates are digging weeds from their front lawn — which doesn't have a chance, jammed between the front lawns of the Warners and the Clems. But at least they don't see what Marion and Rebecca see as they pull into Grammie's driveway. Sammie Gates, who doesn't impress Rebecca as someone who's destined to follow in his father's clumpy footsteps and take up the collection at church, is making a pest of himself in Josephine Schwartz's backyard. She's trying to play croquet with Chris Davidson and Winston Forsyth, but Sammie keeps kicking over the hoops.

"Hey!" squeals Rebecca, as they pull around to the back. "It's Uncle Howard! Uncle Howard's here!"

There's a Mercury Monarch parked by the steps. Big, black, with one of those strange rear-window wedges which slants backwards and can be rolled down.

"And Tyrant, too!"

As Rebecca scrambles to pat the German shepherd tied to the door handle on the driver's side of the car, Marion smiles up at Grammie, who's peeking through the kitchen curtains. When at last they get inside, they discover Howard, eating his dinner at the kitchen table.

"Hi, Uncle Howard!" Rebecca flops down on the couch.

"Hi, kid! Want some cow juice?" He offers her his glass of milk.

"Howard! You needn't t'bother teaching her language like that!" Grammie smooths her housedress, then climbs the three steps to the landing and disappears into the bathroom.

"Too many baked beans," he whispers.

Rebecca giggles.

Like the rest of the Hendersons, Uncle Howard loves to eat and loves to laugh. He might not be the most intelligent of Grammie's kids. He doesn't sell insurance or teach at a fancy boys' school. But according to Rebecca, he's the most fun of all.

"How's Gail?" asks Marion, as she watches him shovel food into his mouth.

"She's good, good."

"Did she come down with you?"

"Yuh, she's here. Well, not right here, or I wouldn't be able to get a word in edgewise."

Rebecca giggles again.

"But she's here." He runs his hand through his thick black hair. "Yapped about my driving all the way down from Sudbury. 'You're going too fast.' 'You need some rest.' 'Shouldn't we stop for gas?' Jesus. Didn't shut up until I dropped her off over to Vivian's."

"What's she doing there?" asks Rebecca.

"Trying to buy your Mum's Electrolux, I think."

"And work?" Marion pours him another glass of milk. "How's work?"

"Well, now. I'm glad you asked." He lays down his knife and fork and leans toward Rebecca. "Last week I was down in the mine, working my ass off."

Rebecca giggles.

"Hey! What's so funny about that? Have you ever seen a man with his ass off? Pretty damned painful, I can tell you."

Marion laughs, too.

"Anyway, I drove my pick into a crack in the wall and...what do you think I found?"

"I don't know, Uncle Howard. What?"

"Nickels. Hundreds of nickels. Spilling out of the rock onto my feet."

"Wow! What did you do with them?"

"What do you think? Stuffed them into the pockets of my shirt and my pants. Stuffed them into my underwear even. Colder than hell, let me tell you."

They're all laughing now, even Grammie, who's nestling into the rocking chair. Laughing at his latest tall tale; following the nickels as they jingle out of the mine into registers, wishing wells, telephones, poor boxes, the handbags of whores.

And then, suddenly, Rebecca knits her brow. She can't see why everyone thinks Uncle Howard is a handful. A drunk, a liar and a thief is the way they always put it. She believes Auntie Florence when she says she once caught him selling cider from the canning factory to get money for booze. And she believes Uncle Donald when he says that the best twenty-five dollars Grampy Newell ever spent was for the taxi which took Uncle Howard to Bridgewater for the boat to Ontario. But there was also that time Grammie once told her about. That time

Grampy Newell was lying in the hospital, riddled with bone cancer, in so much pain he could barely stand having the latest grandchild placed next to his shoulder, and Uncle Howard came and sat on the edge of the bed and told stories. By the end of the evening, he had the man in the next bed to them convinced that Uncle Howard was a big-shot rancher, with fifteen thousand acres and five hundred head of cattle. So lies can be good things, too, reasons Rebecca, when she remembers that it was the last time Grammie saw Grampy Newell smile.

"What happened to the rest of the nickels, Uncle Howard?" asks Rebecca. "Do you have any left?"

"Well, I don't know. Let's see." He pretends to be digging in his underwear. "Yes, yes…" There's a tiny jingle. "Yes…What have we here? Yes…"

"Uncle How-aaard!"

"There!" He pulls out three shiny nickels. "The last ones!" He flings them onto the table. "Now, come on, Rebecca. Let's go unpack the car."

As soon as they reach the veranda, he turns and peers through the screen door. "Thanks for dinner, Mum. I left you a tip."

Howard and Rebecca make several trips back and forth from the car to the barn. There isn't much in the barn these days. In fact, except for Howard's suitcases and blankets and cases of beer, there isn't anything but an old brown barrel and a rusty hot-water tank.

"Percy Robar wants to buy it, Uncle Howard."

"What?"

"The barn. He told Grammie he wants to use it to fix up motorcycles. Oh, yeah! And that Volvo station wagon that belonged to the Corbetts. Before Clay died in that Argus crash and Maggie went off to marry the mayor of Fredericton."

"Well, he can't have it."

"Why not?"

"Because it's not for sale."

"OK, but…"

"Look." He runs his hand along the staves of the barrel. "Some places are just special, that's all."

"Is this place special? It doesn't look special."

"Ha! You got me there," he laughs. "But looks aren't everything, you know."

"Yes, but…"

"What?"

"Nothing. Except I don't see what use it is to anyone. I don't even see why we brought these dumb old things *in* here." She waves at his belongings. "We're just going to have to put them back in the car again when you go up to Gail's mother's place."

"True, true. But, in the meantime, until they get back from their holidays, the wife doesn't want to drive around…how did she put it?…in a moving pigpen. And your Grammie told me not to mess up the house. She's getting ready for her boarders."

"Already? But it's only July! They're not coming for at least…" Her voice trails off. She looks around the empty barn again.

"OK, listen. When me and your Uncle Donald were boys, we came out here every night to drink vanilla and talk politics with Uncle Filly. And every night, when your Grammie sent her detective Marion out to check on us, we'd stash the vanilla in here." He pats the barrel. "And slam the lid on it. Then we'd tell her we weren't up to anything; we were just trying to fix the hot-water tank."

"Oh." She doesn't quite get it. "So that makes it special?"

"Women!" he bellows. "I'm constantly under the thumb of women! How would you like to be under a thumb for a change?" He holds up one of his, ominously. "Eh? Eh?"

As soon as he makes the slightest move toward her, she squeals in horror and delight, and then runs out the door.

"Hey! Where are you going? Don't you want to take Tyrant for a walk?"

"No, thanks!"

She's still squealing when she reaches the kitchen.

"Now what's he done?" laughs Marion.

"Nothing." She tumbles onto the couch. "We were just playing."

"Well, here. Come and have some sandwiches."

"OK." She pops up again.

As Rebecca gobbles down her ham-and-cheese sandwich, Grammie scrubs vigorously at the top of the stove. Unlike Vivian, she's a meticulous housekeeper. No one would ever catch her place smelling like a "dirty mop," she makes a point of telling her daughter. When she's finished scrubbing, she opens a door to the dining room and disappears inside.

"What's she doing?" splutters Rebecca.

The dining room is so rarely used that its two doors — one to the living room and one to the kitchen — are always kept shut.

"I haven't a clue," murmurs Marion.

"There." When Grammie reappears, she's waving her cookbook. "I knew I'd left it somewhere."

She gets a pen from the counter, then sits down at the kitchen table and begins to write. Because she's left-handed, the letters lean a little backwards, as if lifting their faces to the sun.

"Who's coming this year, Grammie?"

"Well...Christina Boucher, for one."

"Really? The Apple Blossom Queen? Neat!"

"Her family's moving to Yarmouth. But Christina's staying here. She's got a teaching job at the new elementary school."

Grammie's cookbook isn't an ordinary one. Not only does she record her favourite recipes in it, she also copies out her favourite jokes and keeps a list of all her boarders — their names, their jobs, and one or two comments about the food they like, the hours they keep, whether they have a car or not.

"Which room are you giving her?" Marion takes a sip of her coffee. "The front one? On the left?"

"Of course."

It's the biggest and nicest.

"Well, make sure you give her lots of blankets."

"Yeah!" blurts Rebecca. "Sunny says that last winter it was so cold up there that her glass of water froze solid!"

Grammie laughs.

There's a big grate in the living room floor, just like the one at Fred Johnson's old store. In theory, heat from the furnace is supposed to come up through this vent and then keep going up the stairs. But it never works out that way. No matter what she does, it's always freezing upstairs in the winter.

"Maybe it would help if you didn't hang blankets in the stairway," offers Marion.

"No, then it would be freezing down here, too. Besides, sleeping in the cold never killed anyone."

"Not yet."

"It hasn't killed Sunny, has it?"

"No, Mum." Marion winks at Rebecca.

Grammie starts writing again.

"How much are you charging them anyway?" asks Rebecca.

Grammie purses her lips. "Never you mind."

Grammie doesn't take in boarders for the money. She takes them in for the company. She says she's had pretty good luck with them over the years — a few slobs, and one or two bores, and that wretched Jackie Kyle who drank a bottle of Black Leaf 40 in front of her lover and died on the spot, but mostly good honest people who liked to talk and to eat and didn't mind driving her places. She's also taken in kids, like Sharon Cragg and Rosalie Saunders, who have a rough home life, and her own grandchildren, whenever their parents are drunk or there's a lull between boarders, but she doesn't charge them.

"Who else is coming, Mum? Anyone I know?"

Grammie looks up from her cookbook. "Well, I was going to take in Mrs. Neufeld again." She crinkles her face. "But I got tired of hearing her stories about the boarding houses in Halifax; about how, before she came here, she never thought she'd see another white chest."

"What does that mean?" asks Rebecca.

"Never mind what it means…" Marion leans toward her. "She's not coming back."

"Oh. Well, then, who is?" She hopes it's someone neat — like Aileen Bezanson, who beat all Rebecca's uncles at arm wrestling.

"A nice young fellow from Cape Breton," says Grammie.

"What's his name?"

"Duncan McAlistair."

"What's he do?"

"Vice-principal at the new elementary school."

"Is he married?"

"No, but…"

"Great!"

"Why do you say that?"

"No reason." Rebecca winks at Marion.

Grammie shuts her cookbook. "But I think he's sweet on Cathy Harding."

"Oh. Nuts."

"Rebecca? Is that you?"

The voice is coming from the grate over the rocking chair.

"Sunny?" Rebecca leaps to her feet. "I didn't know you were here. Why didn't you tell me you were here?"

"Come on up, you little twerp."

Sunny and Rebecca are sitting, side by side, on the edge of the bed.

"Maybe if you brought over some of your Beatles pictures," sighs Rebecca, as she looks around the barren room.

"No. I don't think so."

"Why not?"

"I don't know. I don't feel like it. I might move back home."

"Are you crazy?"

"I thought I might try it."

"Well, *I'm* not going back."

"Never?"

"Well, maybe not never but..." She looks around the room again. "Is there anything to play with in here?"

Sunny smiles.

"Hey!" Rebecca jumps off the bed. "Maybe she still has those..." She starts rummaging around in the closet. "I knew it! I knew it! Remember these?" She holds up a plastic rail. "We used to play cowboys with them. We used to make them into a corral or a fort...you know, like in *F-Troop*...and then..."

"Yes, I remember."

"They look pretty much like wood, don't you think?"

"Yes."

"With the grains and everything."

"Yes."

Rebecca sinks to the floor. "There aren't many good cowboy shows left. There used to be *Maverick* and *The Rifleman* and *Wanted Dead or Alive* and..."

"Shshsh. Listen."

There are muffled sounds coming up from the kitchen.

"Is someone crying?"

"I don't know. It sounds like it."

"Let's find out."

They lie down on the floor by the grate, with their ears close to the metal bars.

"I wish they'd talk louder," whispers Sunny.

"Yeah, well, I'd settle for seeing better." Rebecca jams her eyes against the bars.

"What's wrong?" asks Grammie.

"This." Marion hands her the crumpled newsletter.

"Yes. Ha! I've seen it. It makes you sound like a saint."

"But I'm not a saint! I'm not! I wish people would...Jesus, if they only knew! If he only..."

"What? What is it?"

"Nothing. I can't explain."

I bet she means her Dad's gold watch, thinks Rebecca. She's never forgotten the time Marion first told her about it. And she's thought about it so much since that now she can actually picture Marion frantically searching for it. In the water. In everyone's pockets. In her pile of clothes. It would have been so much better for her if Cyril Neily had heaved it into the hawthorns. If George Best had smashed it with a beach rock. If she and Jack Hall had been playing catch with it and it fell into the brook. But it wasn't stolen or broken. It was just lost. There was no one to blame but herself. Except, of course, the poor cleaning lady, whom Grammie said was the biggest disappointment of her life; whom everyone agreed was the only one who could possibly have taken it.

Suddenly, Rebecca shakes her head. It was almost as if she'd turned into Marion for a minute. She isn't sure she's going to like understanding things if that's what it does to you.

"Well..." Grammie pulls a Kleenex out of her sleeve. "Maybe they should have interviewed *me*."

Marion takes it from her. "What do you mean?"

"I could have told them a few stories."

"Like what?" Marion blows her nose.

"Oh...like the time you almost burnt the barn down."

"I did not!"

"Yes, you did!"

"When?"

"When you were a little girl? When you stuffed your toy stove full of straw and then lit it?"

"Oh, God. Now I remember. God!"

They burst into laughter. Marion blows her nose again.

"Yes," sighs Grammie. "We all liked to laugh. We all had that in common."

"There's not much to laugh about now."

"Maybe not,…"

Marion buries her face in her hands.

"What? What is it?" Grammie leans toward her.

"I'm such a failure."

"Don't be silly."

"But I am!"

"Well, the Children's Aid doesn't think so. The Eastern Star doesn't think so. The Aylesford United Baptist Church doesn't…"

"But I am! They just don't know! *You* don't know!"

"I do," whispers Rebecca.

"Shshsh!" Sunny glares at her.

"Well, then, tell me," pleads Grammie.

"I can't."

"Fine!" Grammie sits up. "But you're notta gonna talk that way in front of me!" she says sternly. "You've always done more than your share — taken care of everyone; taken on all of their troubles — even when you were a little girl! When they should have been pushing *you* down the street in the carriage!"

"What do you mean?"

"Don't you remember? Your brothers and sisters. You may have been the youngest, but that didn't stop you from trying to fight their battles for them. Ha! Told George Best and Jack Hall that if they ever tried anything around Florence, you'd hit them with a beach rock."

"When?"

"When you all went swimming over to Kirk's Brook."

"Well, I…"

Rebecca can't help wondering if the guilt about the cleaning lady changed Marion's life for the better. Or if it just made her sad — and scared she was going to do something like that again.

"And then there was Vivian and her problems, and Donald and his problems, and…"

"Well, someone had to…"

"Why? Why did it have to be you? You spent so much time worrying about them that you didn't take time for yourself. No wonder you always vowed that you'd never have children."

"And I don't."

"None of your own, perhaps. Just everyone else's. And you try to take care of them all! So don't talk to me about being a failure." She holds out her palm. The crumpled ball rests gently in the centre. "You just can't solve everyone's problems!"

"I understand what you're saying, Mum. I do. But it's not that."

"Well, what, then? What?"

"Look! I'm a hypocrite, OK? A god-damned hypocrite!"

"Nonsense. You're just tired. You don't really mean that."

"Yes, I do. Jesus! Pretending to be so good, so caring, so *honest*..."

"But you are!"

"... all these years...ever since I...ever since he...God, it makes me puke!"

"Marion!" Grammie throws the crumpled ball at her.

Rebecca's eyes widen.

"And a coward. I'm the biggest bloody coward in the..."

Suddenly, there's a loud shriek.

"Ah! Ah! Get away from me! Get away from meeeeeee!"

Grammie leaps to the window.

"What is it, Mum? Mum?"

Grammie's laughing so hard she can barely speak. "It's Howard!" she splutters. "Running out of the...Oh!...Oh!" She crosses her legs. "He must have seen a...Oh, I'm going to piss myself!"

Sunny and Rebecca are laughing, too.

"Was it a monster, do you think?" asks Rebecca.

"No. Only a mouse," drawls Sunny. "You know how scared he is of mice. Like they were his own shadow or something."

"Yeah, it runs in the family," agrees Rebecca, when she remembers the time Marion jumped up on her desk in the den.

36

It's Sunday morning, just before ten. Eric and Rebecca are in the vestry, banging down the seats of chairs. The United Church kids just have ordinary, straight-backed chairs for *their* Sunday school. The Baptist Church kids have neat wooden ones, hooked together in rows, with flip-up seats that can make quite a racket if you want them to.

"Hey, Eric!"

"What?"

"Since no one's here yet, why don't we put them all up again?"

"What for?"

"Because, dummy. Then we can...Hey, where are you going?"

"It's Winifred!" He rushes to the front door. "She's brought her kaleidoscope!"

"Big hairy deal." She starts to flip up the seats.

"Oh, no, you don't," cautions Marion, as she places her *Big Book of Hymns* on the piano.

"Oh! Marion! You scared me! Where did you come from?"

"The back door. Now why don't you go see what the others are up to?"

"If I have to."

When Rebecca reaches the front lawn, Winifred is almost finished instructing Holly Stoddard on how to look through the kaleidoscope.

"Now, remember, Holly. Don't shake it, turn it."

"OK." Holly holds the long black tube up to her eye. "Gee. Look at that."

"OK, now Eric." Winifred takes it back again.

"But what about me?" whines Kevin Thomas. "I was here before he was."

Heather Kinsman pinches her nose and leans toward Rebecca. "I was here before he was," she mimics.

Rebecca elbows her.

Eric turns the kaleidoscope. There's a gentle chink, chink, as the loose bits of coloured glass fall into place.

"How does it do it?" he asks, as he squints into the tube.

Rebecca snatches it from him. "Mirrors, dummy."

"No!" Winifred tries to get it from her. "Not you, Rebecca!"

"Why not?"

"Give it back!"

"Come on, Winifred. I'm not going to wreck it or anything."

They hear the first few bars of "God Sees the Little Sparrow Fall." Rebecca joins in on the chorus. "*He loves me too, He loves me too, I know He loves me too.*"

"OK, but..."

"I promise!" exclaims Rebecca.

"OK!"

Rebecca peers into the long black tube. There's a stained-glass window at the end of it. She turns the tube a little and the window changes.

"That's enough." Winifred tries to grab back the kaleidoscope.

"Wait!" Rebecca wants to see what will happen if she turns the tube a little more...and then a little..."Huh." She lowers the kaleidoscope.

There were new patterns with every turn, but they were all basically the same — neat, pretty, obsessively symmetrical. Nice. But not magic.

She hands the kaleidoscope back to Winifred. "What's so great about that?"

The superintendent of the Sunday School is still Larry Swinnimer, the apple farmer, who now has three young children of his own. Today, he tells the kids stories about Lazarus and the Loaves and the Fishes. He tries to make it sound as if everyone there will always be healthy and have enough to eat, if only they believe in Jesus, but Rebecca's sceptical. After that, Marion sits down at the piano and leads them through every single verse of Hymn No. 594, "Praise Him, Praise Him, All Ye Little Children." Then they all go upstairs to their classrooms.

"Marion?" Rebecca has stayed behind to clear out the chairs.

"Yes?"

"What exactly is *ye*?"

Marion closes the *Big Book of Hymns*. "You."

"Oh." Rebecca flips up one of the seats. "Then why don't they say so?"

Marion drifts toward the staircase.

Rebecca flips up a few more of the seats. "Marion?"

"Yes!" She doesn't turn around.

"What exactly is a *hypocrite*?"

There's a brief pause.

"A hypocrite is someone who pretends to be better than he really is."

"Oh. OK. But..."

Marion begins to climb the stairs.

"Does being a hypocrite make you puke?"

Marion keeps climbing. "Sometimes."

There are five classrooms upstairs. Each of them holds ten to fifteen kids, divided according to age. The really young ones are taught by Agnes Salmon. She and her husband Mark are Davidians, who've come from the States on a "two-year mission." The next youngest get Colin Lutz, who's the grade-eight geography teacher at West Kings. Then comes Marion's bunch, where Rebecca is this year, and, after that, the older ones, who have Mr. Swinnimer's wife Jean.

Rebecca likes Mrs. Swinnimer. Apart from being nice — and not boring nice or square nice or creepy nice either — she's the only one who makes Thursday afternoon Canadian Girls in Training meetings bearable. She's the only one who laughs when Rebecca makes her endless plays on the group's initials. Conceited Girls in Training. Christian Goofs in Transit. Crazy Girls in Torment. And she's the only one who's taking the time to explain to them what being "on the rag" is all about. Penny Holland doesn't like it. Penny Holland doesn't think the vestry of the church is the place to discuss such things. She's OK with things that are in the Bible, like people starving to death or killing each other with slingshots, but she just can't face where she came from and what she's going to have to go through to make sure someone else comes from somewhere, too. Rebecca, however, thinks it's great. Otherwise, she might end up like her Mum, who was just given a dust cloth and two safety pins and told to tie it to her shirt and wait for it to stop.

As Rebecca climbs the stairs, she can't help wondering if all those grown-ups really believe in Jesus. Mr. and Mrs. Salmon probably do, she reasons, or they wouldn't send money back to their home church every month. And the Swinnimers probably do, too. That's why their orchards are the best in the county. But she isn't sure about the others. Maybe Marion and Mr. Lutz are just like her. Maybe they only go to church because someone makes them go. Maybe Jesus doesn't have anything to do with it.

When she reaches the top, she hears a jumble of recitations coming from the classrooms.

"*Our Father who art in…*"

"*Matthew, Mark, Luke, John…*"

"*Make a joyful noise unto the Lord all ye…*"

There's that word again, she smiles. And then she frowns.

She once memorized the One Hundredth Psalm, too; shouted it out the loudest and happiest of anyone. But all she got for a prize was a Rand McNally Junior Elf Book called *Friends of Jesus*. It wouldn't have been so bad if she hadn't seen the list of other books on the back cover. She'd rather have had No. 610. *Animal Stories We Can Read*. Or No. 691. *Mrs. Duck's Lovely Day*. Anything but that dumb old No. 687.

Suddenly, her frown disappears.

There'd been another psalm, too. The Twenty-third Psalm. It had been wintertime. The power had been off for two whole days.

She closes her eyes so she can remember better.

They'd all had to keep their coats on. They'd all been complaining…

"How come *you* never have to do it, Marion?"

"Yeah! I bet *you* can't do it."

Marion's hand brushes the little mink collar on her black, Persian lamb coat. She walks to the front of the class and begins to recite. *"The Lord is My Shepherd, I shall not want. He maketh me to lie…"*

At the sound of Marion's plaintive voice, Rebecca can feel the world change. The water is stagnant. The pasture is dry. There's a little black lamb cowering by the fence. It's so hungry. So lonely. There's no one there to pat it. The clouds overhead are billowy and white. But they have scary shadows. The little black lamb closes its eyes and makes a wish. *"Surely goodness and mercy shall follow me all the days of my…"*

Rebecca opens her eyes.

None of the kids had said a word. The power had stayed off for two more days.

She tiptoes into the classroom.

"Where've you been?" whispers Eric.

She slips into her seat. "Nowhere."

"Well, you've missed the best part." He holds up his drawing of Goliath.

She can't help chuckling. It looks like Uncle Howard.

"OK, everyone. Settle down." Marion gathers up the pencil crayons. "Today we're going to…"

"Psst! Eric!"

"What?"

"What are *they* doing here?" Rebecca points to Betsy, Holly, Penny and Winifred.

"Mrs. Swinnimer's sick today. So they had to be in with us."

"OK, now." Marion taps the back of a chair. "Who knows what a disciple is?"

"Someone who follows Jesus around," whines Kevin.

"Right. And how many disciples are there?"

"That's easy." Winifred hops up. "There are twelve disciples. Andrew, Simon Peter…"

"Thank you, Winifred." Marion interrupts her recitation. "But actually, there are…"

"Thirteen!"

"That's right, Rebecca! How did you know that?"

"I just…well, a couple of years ago I heard you and Reverend MacKay…Anyway, can I have my gum now?"

Marion sighs. "Yes, you can have your gum now."

"Teacher's pet!" Winifred sits down again.

"You can *all* have your gum now."

While the kids chomp on their Chiclets, Marion tells them the story of Matthias, the thirteenth disciple. She says his name means "Gift of God" and that he was chosen to take the place of the traitor Judas.

"Never heard of him."

"Me neither."

"Was he a fisherman?"

"No." Marion smiles at Craig Patterson. "He was a tax collector."

"Oh."

"What did they need him for anyway, when they already had eleven other guys?"

"They needed him to witness the resurrection."

"How come?"

"There had to be twelve witnesses, representing each of the twelve tribes of Israel."

"Who said?"

"God, dummy."

"Oh."

Eric cracks his gum.

"OK, but what made them choose *him*?"

"Yeah! What was so great about *him*?"

"Well, for one thing, he'd been a constant companion of Jesus throughout his ministry, all the way from his baptism to his crucifixion."

"Yuck! I wouldn't have wanted to watch *that*!"

"I would! I think it'd be neat!"

"And for another...well, the disciples didn't really have much say in the matter," continues Marion. "Their selection was divinely guided."

"What do you mean?"

"Didn't they take a vote?"

"Who's *they* anyway?"

"Wait a minute!" exclaims Marion. "One at a time." Her eyes are sparkling. "Yes, there was a vote, sort of. In the Upper Room, just before Pentecost. And the *they* who did the voting were the one hundred and twenty disciples who'd gathered there."

"One hundred and twenty!"

"I thought there were only twelve, I mean thirteen."

"Thirteen main ones, dummy. But all sorts of other guys, too."

"Like who, for instance."

"Well, like Mary's brother and Jesus' brother and..."

"I didn't know Jesus had a brother."

"Well, he did. Lots of them."

"Just like the McClares!"

The room erupts in laughter.

"You're making this up." Craig frowns at Rebecca.

"No, I'm not. Am I, Marion?"

Marion's laughing too hard to answer.

"Marion?" asks Holly, when they all calm down again. "What did you mean when you said there was *sort of* a vote?"

"Well, they didn't check off names on a ballot, like we do nowadays. They drew lots."

"What's that?"

"Eenie, meenie, minie...?"

"No, not that."

"Well, what, then?"

"First, they put two names in a vessel."

"You mean a ship?"

"No, a sort of jar. And then they prayed. And then they shook the vessel until one of the names leapt out."

"And so when you say the selection was divinely guided, you mean that God was the one who made it do the leaping?"

"That's right."

"Neat."

Mrs. Salmon pokes her head through the doorway. "OK, everyone. Time to go downstairs."

"Aaaaw."

"Just when we were getting to the good junk."

Marion smiles. "Go on, now."

The kids scramble to their feet.

"Oh, wait! For next week, I want you to read the Twenty-fourth Psalm."

"You mean the Twenty-third, don't you, Marion?"

"No. The Twenty-fourth."

"How does that one go?"

"You know. *The earth is the Lord's and the fullness…*"

"Never heard of it."

"Yes, you have," she insists. "*For he hath founded it upon the seas and…*you know the one."

Winifred opens her bluey green Bible — the one she got seven years ago for perfect attendance — and then tries to speak above the clamour. "*Who shall ascend unto the hill of the Lord?*"

The kids linger in the doorway.

"This oughta be good."

Winifred raises her voice a little more. "*Or who shall stand in his holy place?*"

"Well, not her, that's for sure."

Finally, Winifred is shouting. "*HE THAT HATH CLEAN HANDS, AND A PURE HEART; WHO HATH NOT LIFTED UP HIS SOUL UNTO VANITY, NOR SWORN…*" She closes her bluey green Bible. "*DECEITFULLY.*"

The kids hoot with delight and disbelief.

"What a moron!"

"You're telling me!"

"I wonder what makes *her* such an expert!"

"Thank you, Winifred," says Marion gently. "That was very nice. Now run along, everyone. And…"

The kids race each other to the stairs.

"And spit out your gum before you go in to church!"

Since today is White Gift Sunday, the sanctuary is decorated with baskets of flowers — tall, white wicker baskets which Randy once tried to hide inside. The other baskets are for the cans of food the congregation brings for the needy. Most people wrap their donations in white tissue paper. It makes the baskets look so much nicer, concedes Rebecca. As if everything inside them has poured out of one, clean, pure heart. But a few people, too drunk or too lazy to get to the drugstore in time, use paper left over from Christmas or their child's last birthday. This makes the baskets look too festive, in Rebecca's opinion. Although she's not sure why.

"What are *you* doing here?" whispers Rebecca, as she slips into a pew next to Uncle Howard.

"Oh, hi, kid. I thought I'd come see how things were going. You know, in the House of the Bored."

Rebecca giggles. Someone behind them clears his throat.

"A-hem to you, too," whispers Uncle Howard.

"Shshsh."

"Or is that A-men?"

Rebecca giggles again.

"Oops. Here we go." Howard points to Hattie North, who has raised her hands above the keyboard. "Time for the old organ grinder."

The introit today is "Leaning on the Everlasting Arms." It's also the cue for people to begin taking their gifts to the front of the sanctuary.

Rebecca put her gift in the basket before she set up the chairs for Sunday School. Marion had given her a choice between a can of lima beans and a can of asparagus. Rebecca had wanted to give away the lima beans, because they tasted like sawdust. But she didn't think it would count if she gave away something she didn't like. And besides, poor people probably didn't like sawdust either. So she gave away the asparagus; so the poor people could make her favourite "puke-on-toast," too.

It's easy to guess what most of the gifts are. Cans of soup and tuna and ham all have recognizable shapes. So do pork and beans, and Wanda Willoughby's Spam, if you look hard enough.

"God!" moans Uncle Howard. "It's making me hungry!"

But some of them are tricky — like prunes and cat food, which can disguise themselves as soup and tuna. And some of them are mysterious — like the one Waldo Neily is clutching as he clumps by on his wooden leg.

"What do you think that is, Uncle Howard?"

"Well, knowing Wally," he chuckles. "It's either a big bottle of ketchup he stole from the restaurant. Probably already opened, too. Or a…"

"What?"

"Or a forty-ouncer of booze. Oops."

"What?"

"Your Aunt Marion." He points behind the pulpit, where the choir is sitting. "She's giving us the evil eye."

"No, she isn't. She isn't even looking at us. She's…" Rebecca spins around.

The last person bearing gifts is strolling down the aisle. She's wearing a shocking pink mini-dress, black mesh stockings and light blue canvas sneakers, with dark blue Beatles heads stamped all over them.

"Would you look at that!"

"The nerve of some people."

"Oh my gaaawd!"

When she reaches the front, she kneels down and places her gifts, one by one, in the white wicker basket.

"Really, it's too much."

"I think I'm going to faint."

"Something has to be…"

The introit has begun to peter out as she strolls back down the aisle. At the last adventurous drone, she squeezes into the spot beside Rebecca.

"Hi, Sunny. I like your lip gloss."

"Me, too," chuckles Uncle Howard.

"Thanks."

As soon as they're called to worship, Rebecca starts squirming. Her brain tells her that she should listen — that there's probably some good junk to learn from the hymns and invocations, the scriptures and the prayers — but her legs just don't want to pay attention. She looks around. The grown-ups don't seem to be having trouble with *their* legs. Their legs aren't moving at all. Perhaps that's what being a grown-up is all about — having legs that do what they're told, no matter what.

After the prayer is over, four men stand up and begin singing Hymn No. 690. "Healer of Broken Hearts." One of them is Michael Ackroyd, the man with the mean and sneaky eyes, who's now a science teacher at West Kings District High School. She hopes she doesn't get him next year. The others are the Dempsey brothers — John, Robert and David, the doctor who usually directs the choir.

"Those that are broken in their hearts and grieved in their minds."

Rebecca looks around again. But she isn't looking for squirmy legs this time. She's looking for broken hearts. It's hard to tell about most of them. It's hard to decide whether cracks and chips actually count. But two of them are definitely busted.

"He healeth, and their painful wounds, He tenderly upbinds."

Edna Ogletree's heart has been busted for a long time, ever since she mysteriously started working as Dr. David Dempsey's secretary — even though she was so rich that she didn't have to work at all. When Rebecca was younger, she used to wonder how Edna could work in that office without holding her nose. There were so many dirty sick people, so many dirty poor people, so many dirty, disheartening smells. But now that she's older, she knows that love, besides poking people's eyes out, is also a kind of respirator. Edna probably doesn't even notice the smells — the sweat, the formaldehyde, the vaginal discharge. She's too busy handing swabs and slides and Tru-Touch examination gloves to her heart's desire. She loves her work, all right. But she also loves Dr. Dempsey. In fact, she can't take her eyes off him. Not there in the office, where he looks down raw, red, irritated throats all day. And not here in church, where he sings out to her like a ruby-throated thrush.

Rebecca might have leaned toward Edna and whispered "Shame, shame" — but love doesn't seem that funny right now.

The other busted heart belongs to Gloria Dempsey. But it's hard to tell whether her husband John has dropped it or whether it was just made that way. Gloria is the middle Marshall girl. Rebecca likes her because she has a poodle and a ping-pong table, but she can see how some people wouldn't. Ever since their wedding, when Gloria and John moved into half of the house next to Vivian's, Gloria's been complaining. In fact, now that her sister Sheila's moved away, Gloria and her mother take turns visiting each other and whining — about how they never go anywhere exciting; about how they married the wrong men. Sometimes, when Rebecca's over at Alice's, throwing the ball for Sissy, or Gloria's, giving Fifi her epilepsy pills, she sits down and listens to them grumble. She doesn't know whether they're right about Clary. But she's sure they're wrong about John.

"He counts the number of the stars. He names them everyone."

John has the sweetest voice of them all. He can't possibly be the wrong man. And if it's excitement they want, Rebecca doesn't know why they just don't go and visit him over at Berwick Hospital, where he's in charge of keeping the furnace going.

Rebecca looks up at the sanctuary.

Gloria is sitting with the rest of the choir, waiting for the men to finish singing. But she isn't looking lovingly at John. She's staring off into space. It's the same look she had last week, when Rebecca went over to borrow some vanilla. Gloria was sitting in the rocking chair, in the dark, listening to "The Sound of Silence," with the smoke from a Rothman's curling around her fingers. The song was pretty, but the stare was absolutely blank.

Rebecca sighs. She sure doesn't think much of this love junk. It never seems to make people very happy. But then, like the men just sang, Jesus is going to heal the broken hearts. Isn't He? She starts to squirm again.

Rebecca's legs wiggle through the announcements and the offering, the children's story and the hymn. They behave for a split-second, just before the sermon, when they wait to hear who will give it...but then start wiggling again when Reverend MacKay steps up to the pulpit.

Reverend MacKay is a nice man, but he doesn't speak very well. His sermons always touch on safe themes — like God's Goodness and Greatness — and his delivery is uninspiring. Perhaps that's why he often lets Mr. Armstrong take over the sermons. It doesn't really matter that the congregation sometimes has trouble following him because it's exciting when his voice thunders down on them, like the waves at Morden. Rebecca can't remember all the funny things Mr. Armstrong told them during English class one day, but she wonders whether he's ever found any of that "ecstasy" which his favourite poet John Donne once claimed "doth unperplex."

But it isn't Mr. Armstrong giving the sermon today. It's Reverend MacKay, who doesn't seem to have an ecstatic bone in his body — just gentle, weary, hesitant bones. His topic is "Mumbo-jumbo."

"Now in pagan times..."

Rebecca starts swinging her legs, rhythmically, back and forth.

"This was an idol or god which was supposed to protect the people from evil and terrorize the women into subjection."

"Fat chance," snorts Howard.

Reverend MacKay glances over at the stained-glass panels in the south side of the building. At the bottom of them are the names of his predecessors. Chipman, Tupper, Stronach, Read, Parry, Bancroft, Morgan. It's almost as if he's looking to them for guidance.

"But it's come to signify any meaningless ritual or..."

One of Rebecca's toes bangs into the pew in front. She winces.

"Or show of activity." He smiles at her.

There's something in his face she recognizes. He doesn't really want to be up there. Just like she didn't really want to be up there last Christmas, when they made her play a shepherd in the annual nativity scene. She feels sorry for him. But at least he gets to wear an interesting costume. She got stuck with a pair of Betsy Rawding's beige pants and the embroidered vest Edna Ogletree brought back from Mexico.

"Or perhaps some of you may know it better as gibberish."

Rebecca feels sorry for him all over again. She only had to say a few lines about the baby Jesus, but he has to stand up there, week after week, trying to make a million squeaks and squeals as intelligible as a single peek.

She looks past his face to the stained-glass window in the wall behind. Most of the bits of red, yellow, green and blue are arranged geometrically. It's almost as if someone has pasted a single turn of Winifred's kaleidoscope up there — so pretty, so abstract, so undemanding. But some of the bits are shaped into actual pictures, almost like paintings. There's a lily, a cross, a crown, an anchor and...She cranes her neck a little, so she can make out the inscription on the banner woven around the oak tree hidden behind Reverend MacKay's head. *Greater love hath no man than this — that a man lay down his life for his friends.*

"And so now," he continues. "We come to the Word of God which, far from being mumbo-jumbo, always serves to…"

She doesn't exactly understand why these pictures are there, but she knows it's not just for decoration. Like the Christmas tree. The red and gold balls are just ornaments. The star on top is something more. She turns to the window on her left.

Standing beneath the sparkling rosettes of red, yellow and blue are panels for Jesus and four of his apostles. Peter, who's holding a set of keys. John, who's not holding anything. James, who's holding a Bible. And Paul, who's holding a sword. She wonders if their long hair bothered them in the summertime. Or if anyone teased them for wearing dresses. She turns to the window on her right.

This is a memorial to some of the deacons who served the church during the last century. Each of the five tall, slender panels has a golden sunflower floating in a round red pool. And gleaming white beads which look like teeth. Or breasts. But they also have something distinctive. The one for West has a dove. The one for Harris has a cross and crown. The one for Whitman has a Holy Bible. The one for Graves has an anchor. And the one for Ben's grandfather Beriah Kelly has a sheaf of wheat.

As she turns to face the pulpit again, she suddenly feels hot. And then she smells something burning. She thinks it must be the windows, beginning to glow like precious gems. But then she's convinced it's her. Her skin! As if it's made up of tiny pieces of glass into which God is burning a pigment! She doesn't want Him to do it. He doesn't even know what her favourite colours are. Or whether she wants to be a pattern or a picture. But she can't run away. The pews and the people and her sense of propriety have turned into strips of lead. Holding her there. Beginning to define the shapes and the colours of her design.

Unable to escape, her eyes twirl from window to window until the entire room is one big, dark, rich stain. Then, as a last resort, they fly up past the burning sheaf of wheat to the window of the nursery overhead. There are smudges and scrapes on the pane of glass — from little boys pressing their contorted faces against it; from little girls beating their angry fists against it; from soundless expressions of their hunger and loneliness and fear. It's not a pretty sight. But at least the pane is clear.

"Boys, oh boys, it's hot in here," she whispers.

After the sermon, there's a special communion in honour of White Gift Sunday. While the deacons pass around the first set of trays, Hattie plays a largo version of "Bringing in the Sheaves." Someone mutters that, if she doesn't get a move on, they'll all be "withered in the fields" before she finishes. Ray Collins has just reached the end of Rebecca's row when Uncle Howard's stomach rumbles loudly.

"Oh, for heaven's sake!"

"Some people have no manners."

"Shshsh!"

Uncle Howard leans toward Rebecca. "Jesus, I'm hungry. I haven't eaten since last night."

Rebecca tries not to giggle, as she looks around her.

As far as the Body part's concerned, the congregation is divided into two main groups — the nibblers and the gobblers. And then there's Alice Marshall, who always sits there staring at her tiny cube of bread, as if it isn't actually what she ordered; as if she's asked for raisin bread and got cracked wheat instead.

"Jesus." Uncle Howard swallows his tiny cube. "It's not enough to feed a bird." He glances at Rebecca, who won't get a tiny cube until she's confirmed, and then looks around for Alice.

"Psst."

She's sitting in the row behind, two spaces over.

"Psst. Alice."

She looks up at him and smiles. "Oh, heeellooo, Hoooward. Hooow've you beeen?"

"Fair. Fair."

"I'm glaaad to heeear it."

He leans toward her. "Listen, Alice. I see you haven't…I mean, if you're not going to…" He points to her hunk of bread. "Can I have yours?"

"Ceeertainly, Hoooward." She hands it to him.

"Lovely." He pops it into his mouth and then turns back to the front. "Now all I need is something to wash it down with. Where the hell's the…?"

Ray Collins begins clinking down the aisle.

"Ha! About time."

As for the Blood part, which is really just grape juice, there are quite a few sippers. And just as many gulpers. But Rebecca suspects that some are caught in the middle, between their instincts and their manners. They can never get it all the way down without choking. And others make faces, as if it's really beet juice or Kool-Aid laced with cyanide.

"Aaah. There." Howard licks his lips. "Not quite the real thing, but it'll do."

Rebecca's legs make it through another hymn. And then the benediction. And then they're free.

"Come on, Sunny. I'll race you upstairs."

"What for?"

"For the books. Remember? We promised to help Marion fill out the cards."

"Oh, yeah. OK." She checks her black mesh stockings for runs. "Let's go."

The library is a narrow room at the top of the stairs, on the corner between a classroom and the hall. If you're working in there, Rebecca tells anyone who'll listen, it's a tight squeeze. You have to enter from the classroom and there's only enough space for two at a time. But if you're borrowing a book, it's fairly impressive. There are windows all down the side, so you can see the stacks from the hall. You just point to the book you want to borrow and then wait for someone to hand it to you out the casement window. Far less impressive to Rebecca are the actual titles. There are mostly Bibles and hymnals and pamphlets on how to be loving Christian parents. There are also a few on how to be good missionaries and several in the "God and…" series. "God and Your Fear." "God and Your Doubt." "God and Your Grief." There isn't one that's more popular than the other, since there's no telling what the grown-ups will want to check out after the service. The kids don't get a great choice either. But, at least, besides the usual *Bible Stories Made Easy…*or *Fun…*or *Familiar…*there are a few Hardy Boys and Nancy Drews and two new ones called *100 Pounds of Popcorn* and *Emily's Runaway Imagination*.

"Where's Marion anyway?" Rebecca pulls the two new books down from the stacks. She wants her name to be first on the cards.

"Still downstairs." Sunny leans against the shelves.

"Well, if she doesn't hurry, the people'll be here."

"So? We can handle it. Besides..." Sunny laughs. "She's probably down there making sure Uncle Howard doesn't poke holes in the tissue paper. Remember last year?"

"Oh, yeah." Rebecca laughs, too. "He said he wanted to see if his guesses were right. About what was inside."

Sunny crosses and uncrosses her ankles. Rebecca begins filling out her cards. Moments later, there's muffled clumping on the staircase.

"Sunny?"

"What?"

The clumping gets closer.

"What did you give anyway?"

"It's a secret."

"Come on, Sunny! Chocolates? Cigarettes? You had tons of packages!"

"I told you. It's a secret."

The clumping stops at the casement window.

"Good morning, Miss Ogletree," they sing out together.

37

Swish.

A tiny orange flower lies flattened in the grass. Rebecca glares at it.

"Try standing further away," suggests Ben, as he places his pipe on the arm of the lawn chair.

"I did that already."

"Well, try again."

Swish.

This time, a tiny orange flower pops into the air. Rebecca grins.

"That's better, what? Now..."

Swish. Swish. Swish. Swish.

There's a shower of ochre. Ben laughs. Malcolm shuffles into the yard.

"Little brat," he mutters, as he slumps into a chair.

"Yeah, well, I'd like to see *you* do it. You can't even..."

"C'mon, Rebecca." Ben intervenes. "Show us how it's done. Show us how the pros do it."

"OK, I will." She slings a shiny blue bag over her shoulder and stomps off toward the sidewalk.

Clink, clink, clink, clink.

She's hoping they won't notice how nervous she is. It's one thing to lop the heads off devil's paintbrushes with her brand-new Patty Berg golf clubs. It's quite another to hit a ball with them. And she hasn't done that yet. Marion only gave them to her this afternoon, after church.

When she reaches the oak trees near the sidewalk, she lets the bag slip off her shoulder and clatter to the ground. Then she turns and looks back across the yard. The evening's last light is dancing on the tips of things. On the tall grass, the peeling paint, the Brylcreem in Ben's hair.

"What's the holdup?" Malcolm shades his eyes.

"Nothing, you big fat twerp," she mutters, as she kneels down and unzips a pocket on her bag. It's filled with old cheap balls — stained ones, scuffed ones, ones with deep ugly cuts in them.

"Those are no good." She unzips another pocket and takes out a box of brand-new Spalding Star-Flites. There's a loud rustling as she unwraps it.

"Come on," needles Malcolm. "We haven't got all night."

She places a dimpled white ball on the grass, gently, carefully, with the two green dots facing straight up. Then she pulls the furry blue cover off her five-wood and slides it out of the bag.

"OK, you two." She's feeling brave again. "Watch this." She adjusts her stance and her grip and then...

Whoosh. Crack.

The ball soars over the lawn and the field, hangs for an instant at the summit of its aim and exultation, and then disappears into the woods.

The men are speechless. Rebecca flings her arms into the air.

"Yeaaaaa!"

"Boy, Rebecca. That was..."

She spins around. "God, Alan! You scared me!"

"Sorry. I didn't mean to." He scrapes at the sidewalk. "I was just..."

"Wanna hit some balls?" She walks toward her bag.

"Sure." He tumbles down the little slope to the lawn. "Only...I'm not very good."

"That's OK." She dumps the pocket of old cheap balls onto the ground. "You can't be as bad as Malcolm. You should see him practicing for his dumb old Wood-Gundy tournaments. And Ben..." She picks through the balls. "Ben once smashed one right through Alice's window."

"He did?"

"Yeah! And she wasn't even mad. Said it was the most exciting thing that's happened in that house since she was married. Here." She hands him a five-iron.

"Wow! Leather grips and everything. Are they new? Where did you get them? Maybe I shouldn't..."

Whoosh. Crack.

"Wow! Look at *that* one go. You'll *never* be able to find it."

"Who cares? Now come on." She kicks a ball to him. "It's your turn."

"OK." He steps up to it. "But don't say I didn't warn you." He takes his club back slowly, deliberately and then...

"Wait!"

"What! Am I doing something wrong?" He lets the club thump to the ground.

"No. Only you have to promise not to hit Tristan and Isolde, OK?"

"Oh. OK. Where are they?"

She points to a patch of tall grass near the dump. "There. See the screen?"

"Yeah?"

"Well, they're in there. In the sandpit."

"Do they have enough water?"

"I think so. I filled a little tub of it this morning. And made sure they had lots of dirt and grass, too."

"That's good."

The two of them gaze across the field. They caught the snapping turtles in Auburn, in a stream near the old Murphy house. Just put a stick in the water and waited for them to grab it with their mouths. Rebecca can't tell whether they're happy back there in the sandpit. They don't have very expressive faces. But at least there are two of them, so they won't get lonely.

"Come on." She steps up to her ball. "Or it'll be too dark."

For almost thirty minutes, there's a kind of starburst. They're only Rebecca's dull little Star-Flites, barely distinguishable as they shoot across the twilight. But they're still a welcome spectacle. Rebecca's face glows with pride as Alice Marshall sets up a lawn chair outside her back door and Herbert Armstrong comes all the way down to the end of his driveway — in that little brown Chevy Corvair he just bought from Harvey Rawding. Some of the stars on view are duds. They either squirt sideways into the hawthorns or dribble weakly across the lawn. But most of them fly high and far into the overshadowing sky. There are whoops and sighs and a few rounds of appreciative applause. When the bugs and the bats get bad, however, everyone goes inside. Everyone except Rebecca, who wants to collect as many balls as she can before it gets completely dark.

As she inches through the field toward the woods, she stops to say hello to Tristan and Isolde. Turtles aren't any good for patting, she muses. But they're still lots of fun — especially in the dark, when you can't see how close your fingers are getting to their mouths.

When she reaches the woods, she feels a shiver of excitement. It's almost like hunting for Easter eggs. Unfortunately, the first white thing she finds is a puffball. It disintegrates in her hand.

"Yow!" She wipes the brown powder on her pants. And then she laughs.

The woods may be damp and dark but they're always full of surprises. Rusty cans. An old black pot. And once, hundreds of tiny green and blue bottles. Randy said they used to contain a concentrate of something for the canning factory. But Rebecca voted for a special elixir which would make everyone happy and pretty and rich. At any rate, the tiny green and blue bottles were empty, and their corks were missing, and they had to hit them with rocks in order to break them. Rebecca cut her finger.

"Yuck." She plucks a dewy golf ball from a nest of needles. "Yuck." And another from the crook of an old dead branch. "My pockets are going to be…"

Suddenly, there's a little prickle of light and motion. She freezes. It's a little too early for fireflies. But not for skunks. Or racoons.

"Shoo!" she hollers into the darkness.

"Jesus." A shadow shivers behind a spruce tree. "You scared me half to…"

"Marion?"

The shadow drifts into the clearing.

"What are you doing here? Are you looking for…?"

The shadow has a face now. Stained with tears.

"Are you OK? Did you hurt yourself? Once I hurt myself. Once Randy and I found millions of…What's that?" She peers into the darkness. "I thought I saw…"

Another shadow slides from behind the spruce tree.

"Oh, it's you. Hi, Frankie. We were just…"

He reaches out his hand.

"What?" She extends hers, too. "Oh."

He drops a round white ball into it.

"Thanks."

38

Rebecca is standing alone on the beach at Morden, thinking. She's been doing a lot of that lately. Just drifting off into daydreams, right in the middle of something else. Today, she's thinking about Nature in general, which seems to do a lot of grumbling and murmuring and sighing. And about Morden in particular, which seems to do a lot of shouting.

"Ow! I wish we had sand!" Rebecca jams her feet into her moccasins and scrambles across the stones on the beach.

She has her eye on a big, black, slippery rock near the shore. When she reaches it, she climbs to the very top and then just stands there, with the wind whipping through her hair.

Suddenly, there's a shriek of delight. And then of scorn. And then of envy. She shades her eyes. The gulls are having fun today. Besides the usual fish and seaweed for them to eat, there are bits of hot dog bun left over from last night's corn boil. As she watches them soar and circle and swoop, she thinks it might be fun to be a gull; fun to make great arcs of grey and white in the sky; fun to dive down and snatch her snacks from the sea or the shore.

"Hey! That reminds me!" She stuffs her hand into the pocket of her blue jeans and pulls out a bag of dark purple seaweed.

Not many people can eat dulse — not even when it's been deep-fried to a crackly crispness, like potato chips. It's too salty for them. And maybe too strange. But Rebecca loves it. And so does Ben, who always keeps a bag of the cured stuff in the kitchen cupboard, next to his package of kippered herring. He's tried to get her to like the kippers, too, but there are just too many little slivery bones in them.

She rips open the bag with her teeth and then plucks a thick dark strand of purple out of the clump.

It feels OK, she thinks. A little slippery and cool, like a damp ribbon or an elastic band or a strip of burst balloon. But as soon as she pops it into her mouth, she spits it right back out again.

"Aaaugh."

When dulse is picked fresh and then properly cured, it melts in your mouth like chocolate truffles. But when it's old or sunburnt or soaked by rain, it doesn't matter about the curing. It just feels like rubber.

"Yuck." She flings the rest of it into the sea. "Wait till I tell Ben he got gypped!"

The seagulls begin to circle again.

"You won't like it either!" she shouts, as she scrambles down from the big, black, slippery rock.

The beach at Morden isn't great for exploring. Sometimes there are bits of broken glass hiding among the stones. And it's fun to guess how they got there; what kind of bottle they came from; what kind of mishap or reprisal or celebration there was. But there aren't any fossils or Indian arrowheads. That doesn't stop Rebecca from trying to find some, of course. She never quite gives up hope that somewhere, under a stone that hasn't been pushed around too much, she'll find a trace of the distant past. Micmacs. Mermaids. Dinosaurs.

"Rats!" Rebecca lets the stone clatter to the ground.

She's kept count this morning. One hundred and fifty-six stones and still no luck — not even a thirty-billion-year-old fern frond. And she'll have to give up trying soon. The tide is rushing in.

Out in the swells, there are heads bobbing up and down. In school, Rebecca's learned that the Bay of Fundy is the coldest body of water in the world that doesn't freeze. Even in the summer, a person can go numb in five minutes. But that never seems to bother her and the other kids. They just holler and squeal and forget to notice. They do take care to avoid the undertows, however. Sunny once rescued Winifred from one. And they do keep an eye on the shore. The Bay of Fundy has the biggest tides in the world. If they don't watch their little piles of sneakers and sweaters, the waves will swallow them up in no time.

"Hey, Rebecca!" shouts Randy. "Rebecca!"

"I don't think she hears us!" yells Sunny.

"Yes, she does. Rebecca! She's just ignoring us."

"Re-bec-caaaaa!" Peter has the loudest voice of all.

"What!" Rebecca lifts her head.

"Move our clothes for us, OK?"

She watches the water lap at Sunny's pink mohair sweater. "Why should I?"

"What?"

"What did you say?"

She cups her hands to her mouth. "I said why…Oh never mind." She picks up the little bundles and moves them back about ten feet. They won't last long there either.

"Thanks a lot, you little creep!"

She grins at them.

"Hey, Rebecca!" Randy pushes Peter's head under the water. "Why don't you come in?"

"No, thanks!"

"Chicken!" Peter pushes Randy's head under the water.

"I am not a chicken!"

"Are, too!"

"Am not!"

She throws a stone at them. Number one hundred and fifty-seven.

"Are, too!"

"I won yesterday, didn't I?"

The rules of the "dare game" aren't complicated. You just stand in the water while the tide comes in…to your waist and your armpits and your neck and your chin…as long as you can. Yesterday, everyone else dropped out around the mouth and the nose, but Rebecca let the water get right up to her eyeballs.

"So?"

"Maybe yesterday you weren't a chicken!"

"Yeah!"

She turns away from them. "Morons."

In front of her, towards the pier, the beach is a vast expanse of grey. So many stones. So many blank surfaces. And hundreds of ugly purple shells. Empty. Broken in half. Dead. She bends down to pick up one of the halves.

"Yuck!"

It's the hairiest mussel she's ever touched. She can't believe that anything good can come from it. That, as Grammie once told her, one of its ancestors kept the Acadians from starving to death. That one of its ancestors helped make the plaster walls for the Anglican Church in Auburn. But when she turns it over — when she gazes into the pearly pinks and greens of its gleaming inner surface — she sees that anything's possible. She drops it into the pocket of her red, white and black plaid shirt.

When she looks across the vast expanse of grey again, she sees she isn't alone. A man and a woman are stepping gingerly across the stones, towards one another. It's difficult to make out who they are for sure, but she thinks she recognizes the pale blue blouse and the pale green shirt.

"Hey, Marion! Frankie! Over here! Hey! Over...Oh!"

She sees Marion slip. And Frankie catch her. And Marion lurch out of his arms.

There's a brief flurry — a wild tangle of pleading and rejection — and then Marion turns away from him. It looks so unnatural, like the shore pulling backwards, away from the sea. And for a while, Frankie just stands there, letting it happen; letting Marion drift away from him. But then he rushes after her. And Marion looks back over her shoulder. And begins to run, too. Soon they are close enough for Rebecca to hear.

"No. Please. Please."

Frankie catches Marion from behind. "Why don't you believe me?"

"Let go of me."

"Why?" He tries to turn her toward him. "Why? Why?"

"Stop it. You're hurting me."

He wraps his pale green arms around her pale blue breast. The winds howl, the seagulls wail, the waves pound down on the desolate shore.

"Well, you're hurting me, too."

In the evening, away from the sea, the air is remarkably still. There's a constant rustle from the breeze sifting through the leaves. And an occasional cheep from the languishing birds. But, on the whole, it's quite serene. Until Uncle Donald and his gang arrive from Montreal, that is.

At the best of times, Wanda Willoughby's cottage isn't one of those candy-coloured delights which the guidebooks claim hug the curve of that spectacular coast. The kitchen's tiny. The veranda doesn't have a screen. There's no rug on the living room floor. And the outside walls are covered with fake brick siding — big, ugly green blocks which Wanda told Vivian looked much nicer than the fake red ones. But tonight it's a shambles. Empty bottles. Dirty ashtrays. Piles of cracked pink shells.

"Where did you say Marion was?" Uncle Donald takes a sip from his bottle of Alpine.

"She said she was going with Evelyn and Gene." Rebecca pokes at the piles of shells on the living room table. "Over to Evelyn's parents' place."

"And Florence?" He sprawls into an armchair. "Where the hell's *she* gone?"

"Over to Waterville." Rebecca thinks the tomalley is disgusting. Much too green and poopy to eat — no matter what her cousin Shelley says.

"Jesus. Don't tell me she still works at the nut house?"

"Only part-time now." She wonders if anything good will ever come of *this* pile of shells. "And it's not a nut house. It's a home for the mentally handicapped." She drops a jagged pink piece into her pocket, next to the empty mussel shell.

"Loonies. Retards. What's the difference?"

"Donald!" Aunt Joyce pushes herself up from the chesterfield.

"What? What? You think it matters to a retard that he isn't a loony?"

Aunt Joyce disappears into the kitchen.

Uncle Donald presses the dark brown bottle against his forehead. "Will she come over after work, do you think?"

"Who?"

Rebecca is staring at her uncle's face. It's always hot and red and sweaty, as if he hasn't come by train to Morden at all — as if he's still at Dosco Steel in Montreal, keeping the furnace going.

"Florence."

"No. She spends most of her time at her boring trailer."

"Or trying to get somebody to stay with her at her boring trailer." Vivian sashays into the room.

"Ha! Sounds like Mum." He pulls a pack of Player's out of his drenched shirt pocket.

Vivian flops down on the chesterfield. "Except that Mum isn't a bitch."

"Oh, come on, Vivian." He lights a cigarette. "Don't you think you're being a bit hard on Florence?"

Rebecca feels like a traitor. She should say something. She should tell them that Florence isn't just big and mean. That she lets Darrell and Donnie smoke dope in that tent outside her house. And that she...But sometimes it's hard to explain what you know about people; hard to explain that you've seen the very same thing they have — that life itself can be a crazy mixture of gaiety and gloom. Her Mum wouldn't understand this. But then her Mum never saw what Rebecca once saw. Never saw Florence playing Chopin's Nocturne No. 1 in G Minor with her eyes closed.

"And George?" wheezes Donald.

"What?" Vivian blinks.

"Will George come over?" He picks a bit of loose tobacco from his lower lip.

"When?"

"After he finishes teaching the droolers how to make their sleeve-boards?"

"No."

"Well, why the hell not? We can't get a party going without...Jesus! Where the hell is Marion anyway? She should be back by *now*!"

"He doesn't like the bugs."

"What?"

"George. He's not here much because he doesn't like the bugs."

Uncle Donald chuckles. "The old hypochondriac."

"Swells up something awful."

"I bet he does."

Rebecca titters. But her face is flushed with doubt as much as delight.

She likes her Uncle Donald. He's lots of fun. But he belongs to that group of Hendersons Grammie calls the "drunken liars," so she's never quite sure where she stands.

"Well, I don't care what anybody says," snorts Vivian. "The bitch doesn't deserve him."

Donald rolls his eyes. "Here we go again!"

"Oh, come on, Vivian," laughs Joyce, as she leans in the doorway to the kitchen. "Remember how much fun the two of you had when you were young?"

"I'll tell you what I remember. I remember her sitting at the top of the stairs..."

"Oh, Jesus. Not again. Not the apron."

"What apron?" asks Rebecca.

"Jesus. Don't tell me you've never heard about the famous apron!"

"No."

"It was my best one," murmurs Vivian. "The one I made in sewing class."

"*You* took *sewing*?" blurts Rebecca.

"And I came home to find her sitting at the top of the..."

"OK, Vivian! Get to the punch line!"

"She'd cut it to shreds! And she was just...sitting there...holding the scissors and the little torn bits of lace and..."

"And you've hated her ever since, right?"

"Yes!"

"Great. Now that we've decided that, for the one millionth time, maybe we could..."

"Donald!"

"Well, Jesus." He turns to Aunt Joyce. "I've never understood why she didn't just make another one."

"You wouldn't," she murmurs.

"What did you say?" Uncle Donald reaches for the unopened bottle of Five Star.

"I said you...Never mind. Come on, Rebecca. Time for bed."

"Aaaaaw. Just when we were getting to the good stuff!" She can't help wondering what her Mum did to make Florence so mad.

"Come on." Aunt Joyce pulls her toward the door. "Let's go find the others. Shelley! Melanie! Blaine!"

They pile onto the veranda.

"Speaking of others." Uncle Donald peers at his watch. "If Marion doesn't get here soon, we'll have to send out a search party."

39

It's their last morning in Morden. Marion and Rebecca are leaning on the faded grey railings of the pier, waiting for the tide to go out. Marooned at the nearby wharf are dozens of candy-coloured skiffs and dinghies and charter boats. But the real excitement is a little farther out, where there's a heart-shaped arrangement of white poles protruding from the water.

"What do you think we'll get today, Marion?"

"I don't know," she says wearily. "We'll have to see."

"I hope it's salmon." Rebecca leans her face into the breeze. "'Cause I'm getting sick of herring."

Marion smiles wanly. It's not salmon very often.

"Look! There's Lester!"

A stocky old man with thin white hair is slogging through the mud toward the weir. He's wearing his waders and carrying a burlap bag over his shoulder.

"And little Craig Patterson, too, by the looks of it."

"Where?" Rebecca peers along the mud flats. When she spots the small boy splashing up behind Lester Greaves, she frowns. "What's *he* doing there?"

"Practicing, I suppose."

"For what?"

"Well, he told me the other day that he was going to be a fisherman when he grew up. Said he was going to buy Lester's business from him when he'd saved up enough money from his allowance."

"Yeah, well, he'd be better off practicing his throwing." Rebecca folds her arms across her chest.

Two weeks ago, when Craig and Randy were playing catch on the back lawn at Marion's place, the ball squirted sideways out of Craig's hand and made a big dent in the door of Marion's car. Rebecca was furious.

"*You* should talk!" teases Marion.

"What do you mean?"

"I mean the time you drove your bicycle into the door of my car. Remember? When I was coming back from church?"

"Yeah, well...I was only learning. And it was way too big for me. And I got going so fast I couldn't steer or stop or...I just kept going."

"Yes, that's what you said at the time. 'I just kept going.'"

"Yeah, well..." Rebecca isn't furious at Craig anymore. But she is jealous.

For Rebecca, the weir is a magical place. Nothing but empty stretches of black nets hung between white poles, waiting for the water to cover them up, like an indigo-blue cloth. And then...presto! The cloth is ripped away again and there are hundreds of shimmering fish, either stranded on the tidal plain or trapped in the sodden mesh. They'd wanted to retreat with the ebb, but they got puzzled, confused, lost in the ghostly gossamer of the heart. On good days anyway. Because there can be practically nothing, too, like today, or Lester would have taken his wheelbarrow. But sometimes that's just as exciting, since the wishing is always more wonderful than whatever the tide chooses to deliver — whether it's abundance or slim pickings.

Rebecca wishes she could be down there, too, walking along the sea bottom, reaching up beyond the web of spindly spruce bows to that bit of cotton twine near the top of a yellow-birch stake, where right now there's a shimmering...

"Well..." Marion leans forward. "Looks like he's got a lot of shad today."

The nets sparkle with green and blue and silver.

"Yuck. Too many bones."

"Oh, and a flounder, too."

"Where?"

"There, in the tide pool."

They laugh as Lester stabs at it with a pitchfork. Little Craig leaps back.

"And maybe one or two..."

"Are they salmon, do you think?"

"It's hard to tell. They're certainly not crabs or shrimp. And they look too big to be alewives or pouts. Ha! Maybe we're actually going to get some..."

"Come on! Before someone else gets to them first!" Rebecca races down the pier to the shore.

In the late afternoon, Marion's car eases slowly up Wharf Road, past the Hayden cottage and the Dempsey cottage and the big grey pile of lobster pots in the front yard of Lester Greaves's place. These pots are worn and discoloured, from years of salt and sea and sun, and yet somehow, they're the most enduring things there. The Catholic church across the road is boarded up. The Methodist one down the way has a cross but no steeple. And the Anglican one on the edge of town has a stubby little tower which can't even attract lightning.

Rebecca begins arranging the stones and shells on her lap. She does look up once, with expectation, when they edge past Roger Tufts general store on Church Street. But they won't be stopping for popsicles today; not when the salmon is already smelling up the back seat. And then once more, with horror, when the car looks like it's going to turn into the driveway by Florence's trailer. But it's only Marion, playing a joke on her. They're soon speeding up and down the hills toward home, snaking away from the rugged coastline into the forested interior.

Suddenly, Rebecca leans forward. "Are you going to try it today?"

"If you like."

"Great!" Rebecca brushes the stones and shells to the floor. "But you'll have to wait until I..." She reaches into the back seat.

"What are you doing?"

"Getting my lupine."

"What for?"

"It'll be more fun." She examines the rows of purple flowers on the end of the long, slender green stalk. "It was all smushed down when I found it, but it's OK now."

The car zooms toward the crest of a hill.

"We're almost there," warns Marion.

"Wait! Wait! I have to tie the string on it!" Rebecca reaches into her shirt pocket.

"OK. But you'll have to hurry. It doesn't work if we haven't got up a good head of steam. Ready?"

"Almost."

"Ready?"

Rebecca rolls down the window. "Ready!"

At the very top of the long hill, Marion takes her foot off the gas and they begin to coast. The lupine trails behind them, like a purple ensign.

"Faster, faster!" Rebecca winds the string around her fingers. "Yeah!"

They're doing even better than last year, when they reached all the way to the railway tracks in Auburn.

"Yeaaaaaaah!"

He is Love. He is Love…

The electric chimes fade away. Rebecca peers at the datebook.

On the last day of July, there's another tiny black squiggle. *I am a sparrow in his arms.* She flips to the first week of August. There's one on that page, too. *They hold me above the torment.* And another just two pages later. *I cannot die this way every night.* She lifts her eyes from the book.

"Could it be she…?"

It's occurred to her that the tiny black squiggles aren't bits of poetry after all. They're confessions. About a secret lover. She flips quickly through the book, ignoring everything but the tiny black squiggles. At first, she's excited, as if any one of them might be the clue to his identity.

"Harry Robar, maybe. No. He was married. She'd never…And David Dempsey. Except that he was Edna Ogletree's special…Ha! Maybe it was Reverend MacKay!"

But then the tiny black squiggles begin to bubble and blister and peel and her excitement turns to envy. For her, love has always been a matter of pounding pegs into holes. She has no idea what it's like to be in this much pain; to be tortured by the very thing that replenishes you.

"Jesus."

She's in awe of the words — and of the secret yearning which made them necessary. She has to look away. But the words keep on scolding her, teasing her, daring her to wade into their ultimate misery and majesty and…madness. She takes them up on it.

And with that, Rebecca can see them. Can actually see the mystery man standing on the rocky point, with the waves crashing all around him. Promising to cleanse him. Threatening to beat him into submission. And then…And then she can't believe it! It looks like

Marion climbing up beside the mystery man, but it also looks like…"Like me," she murmurs, before deciding it had better be Marion.

And then she decides that, whoever they are, they've had a rough time of it. Perhaps there have been years and years of secrecy — of sneaky little pledges and denials — and the tide of nature, of public opinion, perhaps of their own belittling cowardice, has always been too strong for them. Perhaps they've never been brave enough to float on top of it or thrash around in it or let it get right up to their eyeballs.

At any rate, Rebecca can't believe it when they actually start speaking.

"What are you doing here?" she murmurs.

There are diamonds encircling the face of her watch. Perfect paragons. The only things now gleaming in the moonlight.

"I want to be with you."

"No. You can't. I've already…"

He reaches out and strokes her arm.

"Don't." She reels away from him. "Don't touch me."

His touch has always sent her whirling away from herself; has always ruined her perspective, threatened her consciousness, made her almost disappear. She doesn't want that now. It's madness to want it. And madness that will follow it.

She gazes out into the bay.

The ends of the earth are very far away. And without his touch, there is nothing in the world that can carry her there.

The waves spill out of her eyes.

If she could just be sure that the madness would be the same old madness…a disciplined little lunacy which made her secretly enthralled and secretly ashamed…but it seems larger this time, less manageable, as if it wants to ravish her out loud.

"I need you so much," she murmurs.

The waves come thundering down again.

"What can I do?"

"Just hold me."

He cups his hands around her grieving, adoring face. Time crashes headlong into space. They both disappear.

Lost at last in their wildest dream, they lead each other away from the rocky point, back toward the bluffs. There's a patch of tall grass there, waving faintly in the breeze.

"OK?" he asks, as they lie down in it.

"Yes."

They're desperate for each other's arms. For their glorious absurdity, their monstrous simplicity, their holiness. But they're also afraid.

For a few excruciating moments, they lie on their backs, staring up at the sky. There's something else gleaming in the moonlight now. Billions of stars. Beautiful, ominous, flushed with crimson, as if the hope at the centre of their brilliance has begun to hemorrhage.

"I'm sorry."

Their dream is fading. They're beginning to materialize. If they don't hold each other soon, they'll be flung back into ordinary time and space.

"I don't know if I can…"

"Shshsh." He reaches out and touches her shoulder.

She tumbles into his arms.

As the sea showers them with mercy, the lupines rise above their doubt and their fear, like multi-coloured steeples.

"Jesus. What was *that* nonsense all about?"

Rebecca doesn't know whether it was a scene for Marion or a dream for herself. She only knows that she's sorry she's coming to her senses again.

"Who the hell was he?" Her voice is soaked in sorrow. "And why on earth did they have to sneak around?"

Once again, she stares at the datebook.

The past is a connect-the-dots picture, except that the little black dots aren't numbered and she doesn't know where to draw the first line.

40

Rebecca slams her hands on her hips. "Come on, you two. If you don't hurry up, we won't get our right seats."

"It's not me." Vivian scurries toward her. "It's your Da-ad."

Harold grabs Vivian from behind, then starts crooning in her ear. *"Don't play bingo tonight, mother."*

"Stop that!" She scrunches her shoulders.

"*Stay home with Daddy and me.*"

"Harold! Let me..."

"*Don't play bingo tonight...*"

"Go!" She tears herself out of his grasp.

He flings out his arms and roars. "*We need your com-pa-nyyyy!*"

"Well, I don't need yours!" mutters Rebecca, as she stomps off down School Street. "I don't even see why you're coming."

"To see what all the fuss is about!" he hollers after her.

St. Monica's isn't an architectural wonder — just a neat little rectangle with a steeple in front — but it still holds the best bingo in town. Over the last few weeks, as the jackpot's risen higher and higher, the players have become increasingly testy. Now that it's Thursday, August 5 and four hundred dollars is on the line, they've turned into fiends. There was some pushing and shoving at the front door, when there weren't enough thick white cards to go around, and old Mrs. Graveline, who's usually so placid, actually hooted at the caller when he stumbled over the very first number.

They're well into the third game when Grammie looks up from her row of cards. "How are you now?" She leans across the table toward Marion. "The last time I saw..."

"Fine, Mum. Fine."

"You *look* better. Are you still...?"

"No, you were right. I must have been overtired or..."

"Shshsh. I can't concentrate," complains Clary.

"I bet you could if they were icebergs," mutters Rebecca. "If they were icebergs, you'd be..."

"G-49."

"Louder!"

"I-24."

"You're going too fast!"

"O-72."

"That's it! That's it!" yells Clary.

Everyone laughs.

"Whaaat do you meeean *thaaat's* iiit?" drawls Alice.

Clary's face is flushed with triumph. "I've got it! I've got a bingo!"

Everyone claps and cheers.

"One card in," announces the caller. "One shall be…"

"Wait!" cries a voice from the other side of the room. "That's it for me, too!"

"*Two* shall be recognized."

Everyone hoots and hollers.

All night long there are half-hearted cries of "Bingo!" followed by half-hearted cries of anguish. No one really cares about the single lines stitched across their cards. They're waiting for the ultimate upheaval — a blanket of chips. Everyone except Harold, that is, who sneaks out between the tenth and eleventh games.

"I'm set," whispers Gary Keddy, as things get under way again.

Vivian bites her lip.

"No, you're not, Tubby." Rebecca points to Gary's thick white card. "You've still got…"

"Oh, yeah." Gary adjusts his chips. "I didn't see that."

"Ha!" laughs Rebecca. "And I thought it was your *Dad* who only had one eye! Although you can't really tell, can you? Not when you watch him saw those dead cows right down the…"

"Yeah, well. They were covering two spaces instead of…"

Suddenly, there's a terrible commotion.

"Hey!"

"What's the big idea?"

"Bloody hell!"

The balls have gotten stuck in the chute.

Except at wrestling, Rebecca's never seen such an uproar. Almost everyone is screaming and cursing. Some of them are flinging the ends of their hot dog buns across the room. Old Mrs. Graveline is preparing to rush the platform.

"Son of a whore." Rebecca shakes her head in amazement.

"Rebecca!"

Vivian is hunched over her thick white card, protecting it from the jostling.

"What?"

"Your language!"

"What do you mean?"

"You know perfectly well what…Iyee!"

Someone has bumped into the back of her chair.

"No, I don't."

"Yes, you…"

Grammie intervenes. "Wherever did you learn *that* expression, Rebecca?"

"I don't know. I just picked it up, I guess."

Grammie sighs.

"Well, you can put it right back down again," insists Vivian.

"Why should I?"

"Because I said so."

"That's no reason."

"Well, it's the only reason you're going to get."

"Yeah, but I don't even…"

Rebecca can see that Marion's not going to be much help. She's too busy laughing.

"Forget it!" Rebecca shoves her chair away from the table.

"Hey! What about your card?" shouts Gary, as she stomps toward the door.

"Keep it!"

Rebecca is standing in the churchyard, staring up at the moon. It looks like a bingo ball that someone forgot to put in the cage. She wonders if it's the lucky one — the one that would've won the jackpot for her.

"Hey, Rebecca." Randy sneaks up behind her.

"What?" She doesn't turn around.

"Look what *I* got." He reaches into his pocket and pulls out a pack of Matinées. "See?" He holds it in front of her face.

"So?" She swats at it.

"Come on. Remember how much fun we had when we were little? You know…in the woods, when we smoked a whole…"

"Oh, yeah!" She spins around. "And we didn't even get sick!"

He hands her a cigarette. "They're a little bit squished but…"

"That's OK." She slips it between her lips. "Where did you get them anyway?"

"I stole them from Marion's purse. Here." He lights it for her.

"Thanks."

A cloud of white smoke drifts upward, toward the moon.

"I think she saw me." He lights his own. "But she didn't say anything."

There are a few moments of silence, while they puff on their cigarettes and pretend to ponder the universe. And then, from inside the church, comes a tremendous squeal.

"What's that?"

"I don't know. It sounded like a pig."

"Hey, you don't think…?"

There's lots of squealing now.

"Come on. Let's go find out."

They throw down their cigarettes and rush inside.

The place is a madhouse. Chairs are overturned. There are chips all over the floor. People are screaming and shouting and slapping each other on the back. It's difficult to know whether it's a victory party or a free-for-all.

Rebecca stands on her tippy-toes. "I can't see Mum and Marion. Can you?"

"No. And Grammie neither."

"Let's try to find them."

They begin to wade through the crowd. People on the fringes aren't screaming anymore, just shaking their heads and muttering.

"Jesus. I was so close."

"Me, too."

"What annoys *me* is…"

The people nearer the centre are openly hostile.

"How much did she win anyway?"

"You're kidding!"

"She could stay drunk for a month on that."

Randy and Rebecca exchange a glance, then elbow their way to their table. Vivian is slumped in a chair, with her eyes closed. There's a little protective throng of well-wishers around her.

"For she's a jolly good fellow. For she's a jolly good…"

"Wait!"

The singing and clapping stops abruptly.

"I think the shock may have…"

Vivian opens her eyes.

"Hurray!"

"What aaare you goooing to dooo with aaall that moooney?" drawls Alice, when the racket dies down.

"Wait a…minute," wheezes Vivian. "Let me catch…my breath. I

can't seem to..." She fans herself with a thick white card.

The kids spring toward her.

"Mum?"

"Are you OK?"

"I don't know. I think I am. Which do you want? A new stove and fridge or a..."

"Steaks!" they shout in unison.

While everyone laughs, Vivian reaches out and draws Rebecca to her side. *"I won't play bingo tonight, daughter."*

"Whaaat's thaaat she's siiinging?" asks Alice.

Clary is worried, too. "I don't know but..."

"I'll stay home with father and you."

Rebecca starts grinning.

"But maybe we better call Harold and have him..."

"Yeees, I thiiink she's..."

"I won't play bingo tonight, daughter."

"Come on, Vivian," urges Marion.

"Yes, it's time to go, Mum," adds Randy.

"Wait!" Rebecca joins in on the last line. *"I've something much better to doooo!"*

Rebecca and her Mum embrace.

It's Sunday evening now and the voice of Paul Robeson is drifting through the house. Rebecca's impressed. The record player is in the den, but Mr. Robeson's voice reaches all the way up to the bathroom, where she's holding a red rubber hose over her head. *"Swing low, sweet chariot. Coming for to carry me home."* As the water dribbles down the soapy strands of her hair, she wonders if Mr. Robeson will drive up to Aylesford sometime and sing a duet with her Dad. But then he's probably not singing just for her. His voice probably goes into the kitchen, too, where Marion's cleaning the top of the stove with vinegar and a wire brush. *"All my trials, Lord. Soon be over."* And then onto the front veranda, where Ben's sitting on a striped canvas deck chair, smoking his pipe. *"Dere's an ol' man called de Mississippi. Dat's de ol' man dat I'd like to be."* Ben loves Paul Robeson; he envies the pure, dark, rich sorrow that seems to hang inside his heart.

"Ol' Man River. Dat ol' Man River."

Rebecca pads into the kitchen. It smells like hot wax now.

"Did you have a nice bath?"

Marion is rubbing at the top of the stove with an old bit of pajama bottoms. In spite of Rebecca's pleading, she hasn't yet succumbed to Easy-Off, with its revolutionary dip-and-roll cotton ball.

"It was OK...if you don't mind no water pressure. Or the fact that the hose keeps coming off the faucet."

Marion laughs. "At least you didn't have to wait in line tonight."

"Yeah, but..."

"What?" Marion keeps rubbing.

"Nothing. I just wish..."

"What?" Marion looks up at her.

"I just wish I could have a shower sometime."

"Yes." Marion pushes the hair out of her eyes. "So do I. Now why don't you go and see what Ben's up to."

"OK." Rebecca turns and pads through the living room.

"Show me dat stream called de River Jordan. Dat's de ol' stream dat I long to cross."

When she reaches the front door, she stops and peeks around the corner. Ben is sitting the way he always sits. Stretched out. With his rear end on the seat of the fold-away deck chair and his feet up on the window ledge. He's wearing comfortable clothes, of course. A gold shirt that he's had for nine years, black shoes that Marion gave him four Christmases ago and suspenders, to hold up his dark brown pants. To Rebecca's delight, he's also blowing smoke rings.

Rebecca doesn't make a sound as she creeps out to the veranda. But when she eases onto the swinging chesterfield, it creaks.

"Sorry."

Ben doesn't answer. He's watching a perfect little circle of white smoke rise toward the ceiling. Just before it dissipates, he blows another and then another and another until soon there are dozens of them hanging in the air, each in a different stage of breaking up but always one...new, perfect, a little behind the others.

"Ah gits weary an' sick o' tryin'."

Rebecca is mesmerized. Lots of times, she's sat with Ben on the front veranda, not talking. Sometimes they shell peas or snip beans or listen to the whirr of propellers as the planes fly low on their approach to Greenwood. But the smoke rings are always the best thing of all not to talk about.

"*Ah'm tired of livin' an' skeered o' dyin'.*"

Suddenly, the pipe gurgles. There's only enough tobacco for one more ring. As it drifts upward, it looks like a chubby white halo. But it doesn't have any head to encircle and, like the others, it never quite reaches the ceiling before wavering, then tipping, then fading away.

"*But Ol' Man River, he jes keeps rollin' a-loooong.*"

"Aaagh." Ben knocks his pipe, hard, against the ashtray on the little, round, three-legged table.

Rebecca holds her breath. Once, he knocked it so hard against the grate of the fireplace that the bowl flew off.

"Aaagh," he complains again. "My tongue feels burnt."

"You always say that!"

"It's always true." He reaches into the drawer beneath the tabletop and pulls out a big green book.

"Are you still reading that?"

"Yes."

She recites to herself what he's told her about it so far. *White man. Mulatto maid. Illegitimate child. Flames.*

In Ben's opinion, *Raintree County* is the best selection he's ever made from the Book-of-the-Month Club lists. This will be his fifth time through since 1947, when the book was released. But his first since the writer — Ross Lockeridge Jr. — killed himself.

Haunted by the past, she adds to herself.

As Ben scans the first page, Rebecca leans back on a big, thick burgundy cushion and begins to swing...gently, so the heavy steel chesterfield only creaks a little. One by one, the cars stream by on Old Post Road. Countries. Cruisers. Classics. Larks. There are more from the west than from the east now, since it's Sunday evening and all the weekend visitors — the golfers, the campers, the restless relatives — are heading back to the city.

"Ben?"

"Yuh?" He makes that gasping sound he always makes when he speaks and breathes at the same time.

"Where do you think *they're* going?"

He looks up as a Ford Econoline van rumbles by.

"And what about them?"

It's a Chrysler Newport.

"And them? And them and...?"

Ben laughs. "I don't know but..." He points to the pale green Plymouth Valiant backing slowly out of the driveway next door. "I know where *she's* going."

Rebecca laughs, too.

It's only eight houses plus the church from Alice's place to Gloria's place, but Alice always drives now. And even with a cushion, she can barely see over the steering wheel. When she's driving with Clary, and the two of them have their heads crooked to one side, they look like dogs. Florence calls them "Laddie and Lassie".

"Clary says she's a terrible driver," comments Rebecca.

"I've seen worse."

"Like who?"

"Well...my sister Colleen, for one. She was the worst."

"She was?"

"Yuh. Ran into that oak tree once." He points to the end of the driveway.

"She did?"

"And into a wagon once, too. Damned near broke its wheel off."

"Neat! I wish I coulda seen it!"

Ben chuckles.

"What? What's so funny?"

"I believe she had more car accidents than romances."

"Yeah, well..." Rebecca doesn't see anything wrong with that. "What about your cars, Ben?"

"Well, I did my first dating in a 1928 Studebaker. Had more luck with the car than with the girls, as I recall. And then there was a 1928 Erskine. Had absolutely no luck with that. It had a lead engine which took three quarts of oil just to get it from here to Kentville. And then..." He closes his eyes. "My favourite was a 1935 Austin convertible. Dark grey."

"Wow! Did you smash it into something?"

"No. It pretty near smashed up on its own."

"What do you mean?"

Ben opens his eyes. "I can't say it ever had much power anyway, but this one time, when I was driving back from Digby, the connecting rod broke. Yuh. Went clanging and clattering all the way home. Must have heard it for miles around."

Ben's chuckling as he returns to his book. But Rebecca, who still loves cars, who's just sent away for the seventh edition of the *Observer's Book of Automobiles* — to go along with her Observer's books of *Larger Moths, Common Fungi, Horses and Ponies, Flags and Pond Life* — has something else on her mind.

"How many cars do you think go by in a whole year?"

Ben doesn't look up. "It's hard to say."

"Well, take a guess then. You can always…"

"Here." He thumps shut the big green book. "I'll tell you what. Let's see if we can count how many go by in a single night. That would be a good start, what?"

And one more thing, Rebecca reminds herself. *Of threaded bones of lovers in the earth.* She adds that to the list of things she knows about the big green book. It's on the very last page.

"Rebecca? Don't you want to count the cars?"

"What? Oh, yeah! Great!" She leaps to her feet. "And we can have a contest, OK?" She disappears into the hall. "You can be the east side and I'll be the west side. Or…wait!" She comes back with pencils and a bridge pad. "I mean…"

Ben is chuckling again.

"Don't worry, Rebecca. You can choose whichever side you like."

"OK, then." She sits back down on the chesterfield. "I pick the ones *going* east, back toward Halifax."

"Lovely."

"And you can be the…Oh, here." She hands him a pencil and a slip of paper. "Put the date at the top, OK? And then the time. Great. Now no cheating."

Ben laughs.

"Promise?"

Their pencils are poised.

"Go!"

Between 9:25 and 9:55, Rebecca makes seventy-one scratches and Ben makes forty-three. She doesn't have time to savour the victory, however. There are only five minutes left before *Bonanza*.

"It's the only good cowboy show left," she insists, as she collects the pencils and papers. "Hey! You haven't signed yours!" She hands them back to him. "*Gilligan's Island* and *Bewitched* are OK. Way

better than that stupid *Green Acres*, with that stupid pig. And I like
The Fugitive and *The Ed Sullivan Show*, too, especially when he has
jugglers on. And singers, like The Animals and the Singing Nun. And
Judy Garland, when she's drunker than Mum. And Red Skelton, too!
Ha! Remember last week when he sneezed and his hair flew all over
the place? Even Malcolm laughed at that!"

Ben offers back his pencil and paper.

"Thanks. But cowboy shows are best, don't you think?"

Ben opens the big green book again. Rebecca turns and races into
the house.

It's late now. Rebecca is lying on the swinging chesterfield, watching
the millers beat against the tall, damp screens on the front veranda.
They're trying to get at the rusty lamp on the three-legged table.

She studied moths in school this year. She learned everything there
is to learn about their structure and development — including some
funny things, like how the males can find the females from more than
a mile away because their antennas are sensitive to the odours the
females spread around with those little brushes they keep in their
secret pockets. But what she can't understand is why they fly towards
the light. It isn't something they can eat. In fact, it usually makes
them blind. And if they get too close, it burns the powder off their
wings.

"Silly things." She reaches up past her head and switches off the
lamp.

On the really hot and sticky nights, Rebecca sleeps on the front
veranda. Sometimes, if Sunny or Randy are staying over, they move a
cot out there, but tonight she's all alone. She hates the waterproof
plastic coverings on the cushions of the swinging chesterfield. They
crinkle and squeak whenever she moves. But she loves the view. In
the moonlight, you can see quite a distance down the street, in either
direction, and right into the living room of the Armstrong's across the
way — although there's never any juicy stuff going on over there.

"Aaaah-uh!"

Rebecca stretches and yawns. The chesterfield crinkles. She reaches
for something on the grey wooden floor.

Things haven't taken turns being the best present in the whole wide
world for several years now. But, right this minute, if she had to vote,

her best present would be the tiny transistor radio she got from Marion last Christmas, as a sort of substitute for Dick Tracy's wrist radio. She wishes she had his Junior Detective Kit, too, with its Secret Symbol Decoder and its *Junior Detective Manual*, which has chapters entitled "How to Act in Emergencies," "How To Shadow Suspects" and "How to Tie Up Saboteurs." But that came out in 1945 and nobody in town kept it.

She holds the little black and silver radio up to her ear. There's a click and then a rush of static.

"Yow!" She quickly turns down the volume.

"*Meanwhile, rioting continues for a second straight day in the Los Angeles district of Watts. Nobel Peace Prize Winner, Dr. Martin Luther King, in…tonight to…*"

She shakes the radio.

"*… voting rights, desegregation, the settlement of the Vietnam…has appealed to…sides…calm.*"

Rebecca frowns. She knows all sorts of things about moths but she doesn't have a clue about this. Once, when she asked her Mum what *integration* was, she was told that it didn't matter; that there was nothing in Aylesford to integrate.

"*The National Guard has been ordered…*"

She shakes the radio again.

But it must matter to some people or else why are they being so mean to each other about it? She wishes she knew what the clubs and tear gas and fire hoses are for. She wishes she knew why that man with the letter for his last name was shot or what Reverend Beeb did to make Governor Wallace so mad or why President Johnson hadn't fixed it so Jimmie Lee Jackson could walk down the street without getting killed.

"*Estimates of the damage have ranged as high as…*"

The reception is bad tonight. No matter how hard she shakes the radio, it still isn't going to tell her what she wants to know. Selma. Montgomery. Marion. Watts. They're still just names. Too far away to be places.

"*The number of confirmed dead now stands at…*"

Her head's swimming with ignorance. *Poll tax. Night march. Conspiracy. Indictment.* She slams the radio down on the chesterfield. But she can still see the flames, the tears, the blood, the bodies dangling from trees. She fumbles at the dials.

"There must be a station that..." She holds it up to her ear again. "Great! The Beatles!"

"*Everywhere people stare. Each and every day. Chink.*"

She closes her eyes.

Their voices aren't as resonant as Paul Robeson's, but they aren't as sad either. And this song is especially good because...

Her eyes pop open.

She can't tell whether the jingling has come from the radio, where John is tapping on a tambourine, or from someplace else.

"*How can I even try? I can never win. Chink.*"

It can't have been the cicadas, she thinks. She's studied those in school, too, and they only vibrate the special organs on their undersurface in the daytime. And it can't have been the crickets. Her eyelids flutter. Their forelegs only chirp, not...

"Ha...ha..." She's almost too drowsy to laugh. "It must have been Fred."

"*How could she say to me Love will find a way? Chink.*"

"Putting out the milk bottles...ha...on the front porch...ha...beneath the light of the...ha, ha, ha, ha..."

Her head is swimming with familiarity now. It's the end of *The Flintstones*. The credits are rolling. Dino, the pet dinosaur...No, it's the cat who's locking Fred out of the house. And Fred who's pounding on the door and shouting. *Wilma!* Selma. *Wilma!* Selma. *Wilma! Wilma! Wilma! Wilma!*

"*Chink. You've got to hide your love away. Chink. You've got to hide your love away. Chink. You've got to...*"

Chink, chink, chink, chink...

She hears Frankie's door open. And her tambourine jingle gently in the breeze. And then, for some strange reason, the X at the end of Malcolm becomes a kiss. It's safe enough to fall asleep now.

41

"Come on! I'll race ya!" Randy drapes his towel around his neck, then hops onto the seat of his bike.

"Hey! That's no fair!" shouts Rebecca. "You've got a head start!"

She stuffs her towel into her carrier and clatters after him.

Clink, clink, clink, clink, zzzzzzz.

Soon they're pedalling furiously down Old Post Road. Randy's bike is an old crate — a warped and rusty hand-me-down from Darrell and then Donnie and then Peter. He's clipped an Allan Stanley hockey card to the spokes. But Rebecca's is the big, blue and white CCM she's had since she was six. It has a few dents in the fenders, a few scratches on the frame — and it's missing its handle grips — but other than that, it's as good as new. Maybe even better, since she can finally reach the pedals without standing up.

"Yabba dabba dooooo!" Randy veers down Maple Avenue.

"Yeaaaaa!" Rebecca swoops after him.

They're headed for Whitman Bridge, where they go swimming almost every day, but it isn't the destination which matters. It's the motion. It's their aching legs, their spinning brains, the increasing possibility of a smashup. They can't understand how some kids can just sit at home, hour after hour, reading boring books or, worse, playing with those two dumb dolls that are so popular now. In *their* opinion, Barbie and Ken are just skinny little twerps — even if they do have all the accessories, like miniature towels and sunglasses and bathing suits.

Rebecca tugs at her straps. "I'm catching up to you, Randy!"

"Wanna bet?"

They tear past Graves Pond, a little bulge in the Annapolis River behind Ruthie Sutherland's house, where Ben Kelly went swimming when he was a boy. And then past Vellinga's Nursery, where Randy and Rebecca used to play with the chickens and sheep before old Gert Vellinga decided there was more money to be made from bedding plants and shrubs. And then past the tiny grey shack where Deborah Grant lives. Deborah is a Jehovah's Witness. Which means she's the only kid in class who doesn't tape a tiny, handmade packet to the side of her desk on February 14; the only one who doesn't get to count her little red hearts or wonder who her secret admirers are — doesn't even get the chance not to have any. And December 25 probably isn't much better. Rebecca's never been inside Deborah's house at Christmas, but she bets it doesn't have millions of cards like Marion's does — perched on the mantelpiece, taped up around the doors, sitting on every available flat surface in every single room.

"Hey, Rebecca!" Randy glances over his shoulder. "Am I going too fast for you?"

"Ha!" She lowers her head and pedals even harder.

When Rebecca looks up again, the world is a glorious blur. Exuberant browns. Extravagant greens. And air that feels sensuous, superior, unique. But then comes a little flash of yellow and red. And then another and another…and her joy is smeared with memory.

"Damn!" Her foot slips off the pedal.

The houses she's now coasting past all have yellow cards propped in their living room windows — yellow with a big red MBC printed on them. That means they all have dirty clothes for Alfred Jollymore to pick up.

Mr. Jollymore owns Moon-Beam Cleaners. Once a week he drives his van around town, collecting dirty clothes from houses with cards in their windows. The next week, after he's cleaned and pressed the clothes, he brings them all back. Rebecca has to admit that he's a pleasant man — tall, soft-spoken, a pretty fair golfer — but she doesn't like him. It's *his* fault, she insists, that she had to get rid of her squirrels; *his* fault that her little red squirrels both died.

"See ya later, slowpoke!" Randy swerves off Maple Avenue onto Whitman Road.

"If you're lucky!" Rebecca pedals slowly through the swirl of dust.

Rickie and Reddie were the best pets she ever had. Last spring, after they chased each other down the telephone pole and across the driveway and up the steps into the big screened porch by Marion's back veranda, Rebecca felt a little funny about just shutting the door on them. But they didn't seem to mind. In fact, they lived in there for months — happily eating and pooping and chattering and scrambling up and down the tall, bug-spattered screens. But then Alfred Jollymore came by and *accidentally* let them out. They eventually came back, but by then Marion was convinced they should have a proper home. Rebecca reluctantly found them one with Taylor Wade, who's four years older than she is and lives on a farm. But Taylor put them in a tiny cage, just like all the other animals he'd collected, and they were miserable. Finally, one day in the fall, Rickie escaped…only to have Taylor's cat pounce on him and eat him. Reddie was so lonely without his pal that he went crazy — just kept running over and over into the sides of the cage until he killed himself. Marion tried to tell her that these things happen; that it was nobody's fault; that she'd have kicked them out by Christmas anyway, so she could slide the huge turkey pan and vegetable dishes out the window of the dining room into the big screened porch. But Rebecca didn't listen. And now she hates Alfred and Taylor and the cat, in that order. And General Electric, for making fridges too small to store leftovers. And Ricky MacNair, for being so cute that she named one of her squirrels after him. She wonders if anyone guessed. She did change the spelling, after all. And she wonders if anyone realized that she named the other squirrel after the main character in one of her favourite Thornton Burgess books. *The Adventures of Chatterer the Red Squirrel.* Which was really her.

The swirl of dust finally settles.

Whitman Bridge is a simple span of turquoise steel about one and a half miles from Vivian's place. Down below, on a gentle curve in the South Annapolis River, there are maple trees bending gracefully over the rippling water and daisies waving saucily from the red clay banks. The kids don't actually swim there, not since the day Rebecca's brother Darrell dove off the top beam and shattered his leg. It's too shallow — nothing but eel grass and sand bars. But they do leave their bikes there.

When Rebecca spots the bridge, she puts on a final, mad spurt and then skids to a stop. Stones clatter against the metal struts.

"Yeaaa! Even better than yesterday! Wait till I tell Randy!"

She peers through the turquoise diamonds which form the truss. There's a twisted pile of metal on the bank, at the foot of the abutment. Randy's bike. Peter's bike. Heather's bike. Holly's bike. Craig's and Brenda's bikes, too. She can tell from the colours and scratches and dents. Just as she can tell that the shiny, pink, spotless one, off by itself, is Winifred's.

"Damn! I'm the last one here." She slithers off the road and down the bank.

Winifred's bike is brand-new — with a silver light and a silver bell and sparkling pink and white streamers on the end of its handle grips. Rebecca flings her bike on top of it.

Being the last one there means she'll have to walk through the pasture by herself. It's pretty scary when the bulls are out, but it's a lot quicker than the path through the trees and at least Mr. Pettipas hasn't put an electric fence up yet.

"Jackknife!"

"Ha! You call that a...?"

"Swan dive!"

"Watch out! You're...!"

"CANNONBALL!"

She can hear the squealing and splashing as she creeps through the johnny-jump-ups toward the pond.

"Oh-oh."

She glances down at her bathing suit. It's red. Sunny's old ruffled one. If the bulls are there; if they even get a glimpse of it...Suddenly, she can see the crowd, the colours, the little pile of spears. And then the men in black hats and white, sequined coats, trying to wave her through the air — as if she were a red cape. She prepares herself for an orgy of sound and slaughter. She takes a swig of tequila from the ad on the facing of the bull ring. She waits.

But today, there's no passion, no frenzy, no blood — not even in her fantasy. There's just a slow, stately execution and a tired old bull, slumping sideways, like a hippopotamus. There's just an empty field.

"Huh!"

There aren't any bulls out today; just blueberries.

"OK, kids. Kids?"

She can hear Barb Slauenwhite's voice now.

"Can I have your attention? Thank you. Now, as I started to tell you before..."

Rebecca shoves a handful of blueberries into her mouth and swishes toward the pond.

Barb and her husband Dennis, who's the son of the new bank manager, recently moved into an apartment near the woods; near where the kids always go to play "Free the Bunch." Today is their first day giving swimming lessons.

"The best way to learn how to swim is..."

"But I already know how to swim." Peter has his arms folded across his chest. "I'm the best swimmer here."

"Yes, well..." Barb fiddles with the Red Cross Instructor's badge on her emerald-green bathing suit.

Dennis takes over. "The best way to learn how to swim is to..."

"I know! I know!" Rebecca flings away her towel and wades into the water.

"Hey! Look who's here!"

"Did ya get lost or something?"

"What's that all over your face?"

Rebecca grins. Her lips and teeth are a deep purple.

"The best way to learn how to swim is to get my Aunt Marion and Uncle Clifford to throw you from a bridge!"

"Neat!"

"Let's try it!"

"That's sooo dumb."

"No, it isn't, you twit." Rebecca splashes water at Winifred. "That's how they taught my Uncle Howard. They just…"

Winifred splashes back. "Watch it!"

"OK, everyone." Dennis claps his hands. "Settle down."

"Try and make us."

"You'd think it was school or something."

"Well, I suppose we have to get our fifty-cents worth."

"Shshshshshshsh."

"Thank you." Dennis tries again. "Now, today, we're going to learn the breast stroke."

Holly giggles.

"You start by…"

"Oh, here, Dennis." Barb yanks a bathing cap over her thick, sandy-coloured hair. "I'll show them." Her athletic body begins to glide through the water. "See my arms? Out and to the side. Out and to the side. And now my…?"

"Ha! Look at her legs!"

"Just like a frog's legs!"

"Let me try." Peter hops around in the water.

"Not like that, silly. Like…EEEEEEEE!"

"What's wrong, Winifred?"

"I don't know. I felt something. Something brush against my leg."

Randy glances at Rebecca. "Lamprey eels!" he shouts. "Quick! Run for your lives!"

There's a tumult of squealing and splashing, as every single one of them scramble out of the water.

"What do you want to do now?" pants Rebecca, when they reach their bikes again.

"I don't know." Randy bends down to adjust his Allan Stanley card. "What *is* there to do?"

"Well, we could always go over to Grammie's and watch her..."

"Naw. I went there already."

"OK. Well, then, we could..."

"Hey, Randy!" Craig's caught up to them. "Me and Brenda are gonna go mess around on our bikes. Wanna come?"

"Sure."

"What about you, Rebecca?"

"Naw." She wheels her bike up the bank.

"Why not?"

"'Cause I've got better things to do, that's why."

It's late morning when she coasts up Grammie's driveway.

"I haven't seen *you* for a while." Grammie pins a dripping housedress to the clothesline.

"I've had things to do." Rebecca leans her bike against the porch.

"Well, I have things to do right now," smiles Grammie, "so you can go inside and keep your Uncle Donald company."

"OK." Rebecca trudges up the steps.

Uncle Donald is hunched over the kitchen table. His face is purple from the heat; from the exertion of eating and smoking at the same time. There are tiny transparent beads dangling from the thick black hairs on his chest — like miniature Christmas ornaments.

"Hi." Rebecca slumps down on the couch.

Uncle Donald picks a bit of dried tobacco off his tongue. "Hi, yourself," he wheezes. "What have you been up to?"

"Swimming lesson."

He raises his enormous eyebrows. "Well?"

"We said there were eels. Well, Randy actually said it. But it was really just boring."

"Ha!" He takes a puff of his cigarette and then tears at the steak on his plate.

"Where is everyone anyway? Uncle Donald?"

When he finally looks up, his eyes are twinkling. "They failed to return last night."

"Oh."

"Here." He jabs his fork into the steak and holds it aloft. "Want some?"

"OK." Rebecca hops up from the couch.

Uncle Donald reaches behind him, to the porcelain drain-board where a pile of cutlery is drying. "Hand me those scissors, will you?"

"Sure. Here."

He cuts the steak in two and offers her a piece.

"What about knives?"

"Ha! Who needs knives?" He tears off a bit with his teeth.

For the next few minutes, they gnaw at their steaks and talk about baseball. Rebecca tries to be serious. She wants to know what he *really* thinks about the Orioles's chances of winning the pennant this year. But all he wants to do is make fun of her.

"Ha! So you're the little expert now, are you?"

"I didn't *say* that! I only said…"

"Ha! I remember the time, not too long ago, when you couldn't even pronounce Mickey Mantle."

"That's when I was little!"

"Oh, I see. So you're not little anymore. You're…"

"Donald!" Grammie strides through the back door. "You needn't t'bother teasing her like that." She tosses her empty clothes basket onto the couch.

"Yes, Mum."

"And clean up that mess when you're finished."

"Yes, Mum."

She disappears into the living room.

Uncle Donald's eyes are twinkling again. He leans toward Rebecca and whispers, "Minnie Mackerel. Minnie Mackerel. Minnie Mackerel."

"Quit it!" She leaps up from her chair.

"Hey! That reminds me. I'm going trout fishing this afternoon. Do you want to come?"

"No!" She flops down on the couch, beside the empty clothes basket.

"Why not?" he chuckles.

"I don't feel like it."

"Oh, I see. You'd rather sit here and sulk."

"No, I wouldn't. It's just that…well…the only time I went fishing, other than the fishpond at the church supper, was at that bridge near Holly Stoddard's place. Victoria Bridge? Anyway, Ben took me. And the only thing I caught was an eel. A real eel."

Uncle Donald laughs.

"It's not funny! It was the ugliest, slipperiest, slimiest thing I ever saw. I hated it."

He turns and slides the dirty plates into the porcelain sink. "Well, you won't catch any of those if you come with me. You'll catch big, juicy trout, every time you throw in your line."

Rebecca's face softens. It's true. Her Uncle Donald is the best trout fisherman around. It's as if he knows their secret hiding places.

"Where're you going anyway? Auburn? Morden? Mattinson's?"

Uncle Donald pushes himself up from his chair. "No. I thought I'd try that little brook a mile or so up from town, near Arthur North's corner." He snatches his shirt from the counter.

"I don't remember any brook there."

Uncle Donald laughs. "Well, it's not a brook, really. Just a little trickle of water through a farmer's field."

"Arthur North's field?"

"I'm not sure. You have to turn right at Arthur North's place, I remember that." He slips into his shirt. "And then go down a dirt road until you...Oh, hell! Cyril'll be able to find it. He's taken me there before." He shuffles into the living room.

Grammie is sitting in the big green armchair next to the telephone table. The light from the window is streaming over her.

"What about you, Mum?" Donald begins to dial. "Do you want to come fishing?"

She doesn't answer.

"I hear they're biting pretty good these...Hello, Cyril?...It's Don...Don Henderson...Fine. Fine. How's business?"

Cyril Neily still runs a taxi service out of his house on Park Street, near the Fire Hall.

"Great. Great. And Wally? How's old...?"

Cyril's brother Waldo still drives, too, but only in an emergency, since his diet of candy and chips has made him fatter than ever. He spends most of his time, when he isn't helping out at Caroline's restaurant, washing and waxing the snow-white body of the Bubbletop or teasing its Black Jack engine with gas from the pump in the side yard.

"Great. Great. Now listen, Cyril. I need you to drive me up to...Ha!

Of course, I'll pay you! I'll give you a dozen trout!...Right. Right. OK, see you then. And Cyril, don't forget that other little...You'll bring some? Great!"

Uncle Donald hangs up the phone.

"Cyril tells me that Wally's a volunteer with the fire department. Can you believe it? I would've thought he was too...Mum?"

Grammie is staring straight ahead, into the deep grey soul of the television screen.

"You needn't t'bother thinking you're fooling me."

"What do you mean?"

"You're going over there to drink. To drown your sorrows."

"Shows how much you know." He stuffs his shirt into his pants. "Sorrows can't be drowned, Mum. They have gills."

Grammie and Rebecca are alone at the kitchen table. There's a faint breeze sifting through the south window — just strong enough to make the plastic curtains bulge a little; to make their lacy orange and white flowers bend into the room. But not nearly enough to sway the pot of English ivy which is hanging next to their folds. The only sound is the loud ticktock of the miniature grandfather clock on the dark brown shelf above the sink.

Rebecca leans her arms on the cool arborite table. "Have you done it yet?"

"Done what?" Grammie drops a dollop of orange-blossom honey onto the last mouthful of home-made tea biscuit.

"You know." Rebecca looks up at the shelf.

On one side of the miniature grandfather clock, there's a row of greeting cards — warped, discoloured birthday wishes and Mother's Day tributes and thank-you notes from last year's boarders. Any more breeze and they'd topple off the shelf into the sink. On the other side, there's a row of Grammie's "remedies" — bottles and tins of olive oil, Wampole's Emulsion, Milk of Magnesia tablets, oil of wintergreen and Rexall's Asthma Powder. Grammie takes a little bit of everything, everyday, as a matter of prevention. Most of this ritual isn't worth seeing. Just a little sip here, a little rub there and a bit of crushing, since she doesn't believe in swallowing pills whole. And a bit of twisting open and dumping out, since she's sure those gelatin capsules are bad for your stomach. But the Rexall's Asthma Powder is a real production. Rebecca often comes over just to watch it.

"Yes." Grammie pushes herself up from the table. "I know."

She rinses her plate and her spoon and then places them carefully on the drain-board. Rivulets of water seep down the ridges towards the sink.

"How come you have so many remedies, Grammie? Do you want to live a long time or something?"

There's a long pause, during which Rebecca wonders whether Grammie's going to tell her again about that first remedy — those sulphur poultices they put on her back after World War One, when she caught the "bad flu." They left some hideous scars, she always sighs, but they did the trick. She wasn't one of the many who died.

"Not a real long time," Grammie answers at last. "Not longer than my kids. I wouldn't want to go through that. Now. Let me just…" She reaches up to the shelf and takes down the clock.

"You and I are the only left-handed ones in the whole family," brags Rebecca, as she watches Grammie wind it.

"Yes." Grammie slides the clock back onto the shelf. "And look where it's gotten us."

Rebecca knits her brow.

"OK." Grammie takes down a large tin. "Is this what…?"

"Yay!"

Rexall's Asthma Powder comes in two sizes. Grammie always buys the large tin — a big cardboard cylinder with a metal lid and bottom.

"Right." Grammie pries up the lid. "Now we need a dry spoon."

Rebecca leaps up. "I'll get one!"

While Rebecca rummages through the silverware drawer, Grammie sits down at the table again.

"What about this one?" Rebecca holds up a tarnished Princess Margaret spoon.

"Oh, my soul!" laughs Grammie. "I haven't seen that one for years!"

"Is it OK?"

"Lovely."

Rebecca scurries back to her chair. "Here." She hands Grammie the spoon. "No, wait!" She snatches it back again. "Can I do it this time? Please!"

Grammie laughs. "I don't see why not." She pushes the tin toward Rebecca. "But remember, you only have to take a..."

"I know. I've watched you do it a million times. You take the ass end of the..."

"Rebecca!"

"What? What else do you call it?" She scoops a little of the pale green powder onto the spoon handle. "Pretty gritty, isn't it?" Then flips down the lid and dumps the powder on top of it. "There." She taps the spoon on the lid. "Now all I..."

Grammie reaches into the pocket of her apron and pulls out a box of wooden matches.

"Thanks."

"Now, don't forget. You have to be..."

"I know." Rebecca takes out one of the matches. "You have to be quick." She leans toward the tin. "Ready?"

Grammie leans forward, too. "Ready."

Rebecca strikes the match on the side of the box, then holds the flame over the pale green powder. "Oo-oo! It smells funny, doesn't it? Just like that stuff Barry and Darrell were smoking in the barn last...Oops. I forgot. I wasn't supposed to tell. They said if I told, they'd..."

Grammie takes a long, luxurious drag. Rebecca watches the thin wisp of smoke zigzag into her nostrils.

"Well?" Grammie peeks at her over her glasses. "Aren't you going to try some?"

"Can I? Thanks!" Rebecca sniffs a little bit, too. "Aach, aach. It's not like cigarettes, is it?"

Grammie takes another turn. And then so does Rebecca. In a matter of seconds, it's over. A cloud of smoke crawls along the ceiling. They lean back in their chairs.

"Hey, Grammie?" Rebecca is staring at the blackened lid.

"Hmmm?"

"How come you have asthma and Mum has asthma, but nobody else in the family has asthma?"

Grammie pauses before answering. "We can't always help what we pass down to our children."

42

"Weeeeeee! Look at meeeeeee!"

Rebecca is coasting down the sidewalk near the church, with her feet on the seat of her bike.

"Not bad!" shouts Craig, as she sails toward him. "But watch this! Me and Brenda are going to have a race! Without using our..."

"Weeeeeee!"

"Hey!" Craig hollers at Rebecca. "Didn't you hear me? I said we were..."

"Who cares?" drawls Brenda. "Now, come on. On your mark, get set..."

"Wait, Brenda! I haven't...!"

"GO!"

As Craig and Brenda barrel toward her, with their hands clasped behind their backs, Rebecca slips off her bike and into the church. She's greeted by peals of laughter.

"Would you look at this one!" Marion holds up a brown woollen skirt. "The zipper is crooked. The facings are puckered."

"Yes," agrees Vivian. "It's not fit for a dog to wear."

"Ladies. Ladies." Reverend MacKay sounds stern. "We have to remember the spirit in which these things were given and not worry about...Oh, hi, Rebecca." He can't help spluttering. "And not worry about whether they're unwearable or not."

"Yes, Andrew. You're right, of course." Marion gazes at the large mound of clothes on the floor of the vestry. "And we're not the ones to talk, are we, Vivian? We can't do much more than sew on a button!"

"I'll say," agrees Rebecca.

"Ha!" Vivian snorts. "Harold's always complaining...How does that joke go?...That I can't even menstruate. That's it! That I can't even..."

Marion snickers.

"Ladies!"

Rebecca can't help laughing. She can see that Reverend MacKay approves of Marion, but isn't quite sure what to make of Vivian. Perhaps it's because she hasn't been volunteering long and her breath always smells like booze. "High spirits but no reverence," Rebecca can almost hear him saying.

"OK." Marion is the first to settle down again. "So we'll divide them into three piles. One for Acceptable." She plucks a blue and white gingham apron from the mound of clothes and tosses it onto the floor a few yards away. "And one for Needs Mending. Whew! And washing, too." She starts another pile with a grubby green cotton dress.

"Janet Pine'll take care of those," interjects Rebecca.

"And one for..." Marion flings the brown woollen skirt toward the kitchen. "Unwearable."

She and Vivian burst into laughter again.

Rebecca examines the large mound of clothes. It's part of the annual Red Cross drive to provide for the less fortunate in the community. It's usually a fairly tame exercise, but this year it's turned into an obsession. That's because the Order of the Eastern Star, which customarily holds rummage sales to help maintain its homes for the needy, the elderly and the orphaned, has decided to collect clothing as well. The competition between the two groups to see which can gather and distribute the most is fierce.

"Who do you think's ahead?" she finally asks, when the large mound of clothes begins to diminish.

"I have no idea," smiles Marion.

"Well, you should. You're collecting for them as well as for the Red Cross, aren't you?"

"Yes. That's true. But it wouldn't be fair for me to..."

"Oh, come on," pleads Vivian. "Give us a hint."

Marion laughs. "Well, I'll tell you one thing. If that pile keeps getting bigger..." She points to the one near the kitchen. "Then the Red Cross hasn't got a prayer."

The women burst into laughter again.

"So, Vivian." Reverend MacKay tries to calm them all down again. "Vivian!"

"Yes," she sputters.

"How do you like collecting for the Red Cross?"

Vivian flings another apron onto the Acceptable pile. "I like it fine. Except for all the ignorant people I meet."

Marion laughs.

"It's not funny! Last night, Jerry Veinotte practically slammed the door in my face!"

"Hmm," muses Reverend MacKay. "Jerry Veinotte. Jerry Veinotte. He's not one of ours, is he?"

Marion smiles at him. "Well, he is and he isn't. He doesn't attend services here. But he's the man we get to plough the parking lot in the winter. Lives across from the old schoolhouse."

"Oh. Yes. Goodness. The one they say…"

"Murdered James Henry!" blurts Rebecca.

"Rebecca! That'll be enough!" scolds Marion.

"What do you mean? Why can you say what you want to say and I can't say what I want to say?"

She might not know much about "endless articulated steel bands," but she knows what she's heard about Jerry Veinotte squishing James Henry with a road grader, when they were up fixing that bad section of Route 221 last year.

"Yes, well. He said he had nothing to give," continues Vivian. "Ha! He must make a mint driving that ugly yellow bulldozer of his. Probably spends it all on special tutors for that stupid kid he's got."

"Vivian!"

"Well, I can't help it. He's an arsehole. Oh, sorry. I guess I shouldn't…" She glances into the sanctuary. "Anyway, I don't mind putting up with one or two ignorant people, if it's for a good cause."

Rebecca rolls her eyes and slips outside again.

On the sidewalk in front of the church, Craig and Brenda are comparing notes.

"That was fun!"

"Yeah! You whooshed right by me!"

"Just like in the circus!"

"Yeah!"

"Let's do it again!"

"OK. Only this time, let's start further back."

"Yeah!"

"You go to your house and I'll go to…Ya wanna do it, too, Rebecca?"

"OK." She hops onto her bike.

"And then we'll…Well, you know."

Within moments, there's a blur of metal.

"Faster! Faster!"

"Watch out! You're…!"

"Whoa-oa-oa-oa…!"

And then Craig's pedal clips the front fender of Rebecca's big, blue and white CCM. And Rebecca tumbles to the ground.

"Help!" yells Brenda. "Come quick! Rebecca's cut her lip!"

Marion appears in the doorway of the church. "Tell her to put a Band-Aid on it."

"Ha!" Vivian appears beside her. "Or maybe we could get Mum to make up one of her bread and mustard poultices."

"No! You don't understand! It's real bad! Look! There's blood...all...over..." Brenda starts blubbering.

"OK, now. Slow down." Reverend MacKay strolls down to the sidewalk. "And tell us what happened."

"We...were just..." Brenda glances at Rebecca. "We didn't do anything. She just fell."

"Yes?"

"And cut her lip on her handlebar. I told her she should get new grips."

"Jesus." Vivian claps her hands to her breast. She finally sees what Brenda means by "real bad."

Rebecca is now kneeling on the sidewalk beside her bike. There's blood streaming from her mouth.

"It's OK, Vivian." Marion leads her down the stairs toward the sidewalk. "It's OK."

"Will she need a *transformation*?"

"What? No. She'll be fine. We just have to..."

"Stupid idiot!" Rebecca suddenly hollers at Craig, who's pedalled away so furiously that he's now well past the cemetery.

"Shsh, Rebecca." Marion lifts her to her feet. "I think it's best if you don't talk right now."

"I don't care!" She spits out some blood. "Look what he's done to my bike!"

"Yes. And your blouse," murmurs Marion. "There's another one for the Unwearables."

43

It's early Saturday morning. Vivian and Rebecca are in the east living room, watching cartoons. Rebecca is sitting cross-legged on the floor, close to the screen. Big garish gobs of colour are flashing across her smiling face — including her swollen lower lip, which has seventeen stitches on the outside and seventeen on the inside. Vivian is further back, sprawled on the chesterfield. Only the brightest gobs can reach her there.

"Ha! Look at that! Did you see that? Barney didn't even…"

"Rebecca." Vivian adjusts her pin curls. "I don't think you should talk. Remember what Dr. Dempsey said about your stitches?"

"Yeah, but I can't help it. It's funny."

Vivian has to agree.

In the old days, she's just been telling Rebecca, they only had an hour of *Merrie Melodies*. Silent little pictures of silent little animals, running around, getting into trouble, finding silent little sweethearts. But now they have *Mighty Mouse* and *Caspar the Friendly Ghost* and her favourite *The Flintstones*. She loves Wilma's eyes, she says. They don't have any whites to them. And Fred's lawnmower. It's just a tyrannosaurus on wheels. And Pebbles, who's the first baby ever born to a TV cartoon couple. Even with the animal-skin clothing and the bare feet, it's so much more realistic than the *Merrie Melodies* had been. In her opinion. And so much more fulfilling than her "stories," which all took turns for the worse lately.

"Are Fred and Wilma getting a divorce?" asks Rebecca, during the commercial for Frosted Flakes.

"Ha!" Vivian yanks out one of her pin curls. "What makes you say that?"

"Well…" Rebecca looks over her shoulder. "You know how they're always fighting? Well, last week was the first time they never kissed and made up. Last week was the first time they just forgot all about it. And so I thought…Oh, hi, Sunny."

Vivian looks over her shoulder, too. "Ha! Have I missed something? Is it Halloween?"

Sunny is leaning in the doorway to the dining room. She's wearing a bright orange mini-skirt and blouse — with big black polka dots on them — and shiny, black thigh-high boots.

"You're such a cretin."

"Ha! You're probably right, Sonja. But you're still not going to Halifax dressed like that."

"Why not? What's wrong with it?"

"It's not decent. Not what a proper young lady should…"

"Me! What about Rebecca? What about what she's wearing? She

looks like a..."

"What?" Rebecca examines her clothing.

"A hobo."

"I do not!"

"Yes, you do. Like Thorold Strum. Look at your shoes!"

They're navy blue sneakers with no laces.

"Yeah, well, they broke. And anyway, that's the way all the kids are wearing them."

"And your jeans?"

Rebecca fingers the frayed patch in the left knee of her burgundy pants. "So?"

"And your blouse?"

"My blouse is brand-new! Marion gave it to me! To replace the one that got blood on it when that stupid..."

"Ha! Ha! Look at Barney! Oooooo! I think I'm going to..."

Vivian is rolling around on the chesterfield, cackling, wheezing, squeezing her thighs together.

"Yeah? Well, go ahead," drawls Sunny. "Piss yourself."

"Oo. Oo. Aauch, aauch, aauch!"

"You should be locked up, you know. Just like...Thank God!" Sunny straightens up.

"What?" Rebecca's still angry. She really likes her new madras blouse.

"I hear a car."

"Oooo. Aauch. Oooo. Oooo."

"Yeah!" Rebecca scrambles to her feet. "But it doesn't sound like Marion's." She rushes into the west living room and peers through the window.

The driveway is shrouded in fog. There's a big, grey unfamiliar shape in it.

She rushes outside. "Marion? Is that you? Is that...? Wow!" She stops just short of the big grey shape. "A brand-new one."

"Yes." Marion smiles at her. "What do you think?"

"I think it's..." She reaches out her hand, then quickly pulls it back.

"It's OK," laughs Marion. "You can touch it."

Rebecca runs her hand over the silver-grey fender. "It's so smooth. It's...so smooth."

"Yes."

Rebecca steps back to examine the body. "And four doors. That's good. And…"

"And I bet you can tell us exactly what kind it…"

"Hey! Who's that?" Rebecca peers into the plush red interior. "Oh, hi, Irene. Are you coming with us?"

Marion's best friend is sitting in the front seat.

"Yes, if it's OK with you."

"It's great with me. Marion says we're going to shop and eat at restaurants. And take showers! Do you like to take…?"

Suddenly, the screen door slams and Sunny struggles down the steps with their overnight bags.

"Look, Sunny! Look!" Rebecca runs to help her. "A brand-new Ford Falcon Futura. With bench seats and everything!"

"It's very nice, Marion."

"Thank you, Sonja." Marion opens the trunk. "And you look very nice this morning, too."

"Ha!" Sunny flings her bag inside. "Tell that to Mum!"

"Giving you a hard time, is she?"

"Doesn't she always?"

"Yeah, well…" Rebecca flings her bag inside, too. "You were giving me a hard time and I didn't even…"

"Look! I like your blouse, OK? I was just trying to get Mum off my case." Sunny glares at her. "OK?"

"Sure."

Marion shuts the trunk. "Now." She tugs at her girdle. "Are we ready?"

"*I* am!" shouts Rebecca, as she clambers into the back seat.

Two-tone red. She sizes up the interior. Like pictures with frames around them. Artificial cloth. But not totally vinyl. And no plastic covers, like the last one had because some of them still peed.

She bounces up and down a few times, to test the springs, then settles back into the cushions. All she can see is the back of Irene's curly blonde head. It isn't moving. Just like that time a couple of years ago, on Sunny's birthday, when Rebecca sat behind Irene and Marion in Irene's living room and watched that President Kennedy get shot on TV. Irene's head didn't move then either. Not for hours.

"Oh, no!" Rebecca suddenly wails. "I forgot my camera!"

"Whose camera?" drawls Sunny, as Rebecca scrambles past her.

"I'm coming with you," says Marion softly. "I have to see your Mum about something."

When Marion and Rebecca reach the kitchen, Vivian is resting her palms on the cool, white enamel surface of the stove. It's part of her bingo winnings.

"Bloody Goody-Two-Shoes," she seethes. "Bloody Miss Perfect. *Miss* Perfect, mind you. Well, my girls are back home with me now. You'll never take my girls..."

"What?" Rebecca snatches her camera from the arborite table. "Are you talking to me or to..."

"That skirt makes you look fat," Vivian snarls at Marion.

"Yes, well." Marion pulls her yellow jersey down over the waist of her straight blue skirt. "I haven't come to discuss wardrobe with you. I've come to..."

"What? To ask me to go to Halifax with you?"

"No. Not that."

"Ha! Why not? Are you afraid I might embarrass you?"

"No," says Marion softly. "But you wouldn't have a good time. I have clients to see and some papers to sign for the Eastern Star and Sharon Cragg's mother asked me to..."

"And you don't want an old drunk tagging along, is that it?"

Marion sighs.

Like the wind through a dying spruce, thinks Rebecca, at the same time as she wonders why things like this come to her.

"OK, Vivian. Can you honestly tell me you'd last an hour without drinking? Can you? God! I haven't got time for this. I'll take you shopping in Greenwood next week, OK? Come on, Rebecca." She bundles Rebecca out the screen door to the concrete steps.

"It's not the same thing." Vivian follows them as far as the door.

Marion glares at Vivian through the mesh.

"Yes, well, it'll have to do. Now. Where's Donnie?"

Vivian shrugs. "How should I know?"

"Someone broke into Hal's last night."

"It was probably him," says Vivian calmly, before slamming the heavy wooden door in their faces.

"What are *these* things?" asks Rebecca, as the car pulls slowly into Hal Jackson's Fina station. She holds up a black nylon strap.

Marion glances in the rear-view mirror. "Seat belts."

"Do we have to wear them?"

"You should."

"Well, *I'm* not going to. It wouldn't be any fun."

As soon as Marion turns off the ignition, Sunny pushes open her door.

"And where are *you* going?"

"I won't be long, Marion." Sunny's halfway out of the car. Her shiny black boots are rising out of the gravel like columns of tar. "I told Jim I'd give Sharon a message from him."

Jim is Hal Jackson's eldest son. He's a tall, good-looking boy who's keen on basketball. Keen on Sharon Cragg, too, if what Rebecca's been hearing from Sunny is true. But even if it isn't, Sharon is Sunny's best friend now. When her father was manager of the bank, she lived uptown in a big white house next to Walter Keddy's place. But now that her father's died, and her mother's moved to Dartmouth, Sharon boards with Grammie during the school year and then stays in the city during the summer.

"OK. But make it quick."

"Thanks!"

Rebecca watches Sunny glide through the fog toward the service area, where there's a gentle hissing and clinking, and then suddenly throws open her door.

"Hey! Stop right there!" commands Marion.

"What?"

"I'm sure Sunny and Jim don't want..."

"I'm not going there! I'm going to help Hal fill the tank!"

"Oh, no, you're not!" Marion pushes open her door, too. "Hal and I have something private to discuss."

"Well, then, I'm going to go look at the bus!" She races into the fog.

The cement building at the back of Hal's place used to be another service station, but now it's where Philip Harding stores his bus — a big blue and white one with MARITIME BUS SERVICE stencilled on the sides. He tried doing ACADIAN in red, by hand, but he made a mess of it. Right now, the bus isn't getting much business, but it still makes daily runs between Aylesford and Kentville. Which it must be doing right now, sulks Rebecca, when she discovers that the cement building is empty.

As she scuffs back to the car, she can hear that Marion and Irene are talking about her.

"She sure likes things with engines," chuckles Irene.

"Yes," agrees Marion. "Anything that goes fast and makes a lot of..."

"Marion?"

When Rebecca hears this new voice, she peers through the fog. She can just make out Hal's wife, who's drifting toward the car.

"Oh, hi, Lonette." Marion turns to greet her. "I'm sorry about the trouble last night." The two of them disappear into the fog. "If there's anything I can do for you or Hal, just..."

Rebecca isn't listening anymore. She's too busy noticing. Something she's been doing a lot of lately. Near the pumps, everything is still. There's no clinking, no whispering, no mad scurrying after passion or adventure or the right thing to do. Only Marion's brand-new car, waiting calmly in the mist, with three of its silver-grey doors wide open.

"Wow!" she whispers, although she doesn't know why.

For a moment, Marion gazes through the windshield at the fog. Then she grips the steering wheel tightly, with both hands, and pulls out onto Old Post Road.

For about seven miles, the car moves in strange little surges. Rebecca gets the idea that it isn't the fog that's making it move that way. It's Marion. She seems to have something on her mind. Something she's going to do and then isn't going to do. And then, across from the peat plant, just a little past Floyd Taylor's cranberry bog — where Rebecca knows there'd be red-winged blackbirds and fireweed and damselflies, if she could see anything — the car almost trickles to a stop.

Rebecca leans forward. "Why are we slowing down?"

"I can't see the road."

Marion's right foot is hovering over the brake pedal.

"But you've been down it millions of times!"

"I know, but..."

There's a tall, lean shadow by the side of the road.

"Hey! What's that?"

"I don't know."

The car tilts toward the right shoulder.

"Look out, Marion! You're going to...!" Irene clasps her hands to her mouth.

Marion's right foot squeezes the brake.

The tall, lean shadow is opposite the rear door now. It's clutching a tiny bag.

"Hey! It's Frankie!" Rebecca rolls down her window. "Hi, Frankie! We almost didn't..."

"Where are you going?" asks Marion softly.

She's staring straight ahead, with both hands on the steering wheel.

"To Halifax," he answers, still looking at Rebecca.

"Hey! That's where we're going!" Rebecca swivels to face Marion. "Can Frankie come with us? Please, Marion! Sunny and I can always squish..."

"Yes." Marion's voice is still soft.

"Yay!" Rebecca shifts toward Sunny.

But even as she shouts, there's something else she thinks she hears. A reluctance in Marion's voice. An urgency in Marion's voice. As if she's decided that she has to do what she doesn't want to do. As if she'll die if she doesn't do it.

"Thanks." Frankie eases into the car. "I wasn't sure how I was going to...I wasn't sure if anybody would be..."

But there's something else Rebecca thinks she sees, too. She peers past Frankie into the fog.

Standing a little back from the road, next to an enormous mound of peat moss, are two more shadows, — look like Barry and Drew to her. She'd be sure they were if one of them spit and the other one lit a cigarette, but they don't. They just stand there, staring.

I'm sure glad they don't need a ride, she thinks, as Frankie finally shuts the door.

When Marion pulls the car into the road again, it surges faster — as if somehow she's adjusted to that damp grey cloud enveloping the asthmatic earth. She takes her left hand off the steering wheel. Irene gives her a quick glance.

44

"It's quiet, isn't it?"

Rebecca is resting her head on the back of the plush red seat.

"For once," sighs Sunny, as she arranges the scrap of orange and black fabric on her thigh.

"Not me, dummy." Rebecca elbows her. "The car. Almost as quiet as that big expensive thing Edna Ogletree has. Hey, Marion!" She bolts upright again. "Remember the time we drove Edna's big, pink Chrysler New Yorker down to Halifax?"

Marion doesn't answer.

"Ha!" Rebecca turns to Frankie. "It looked like a giant powder puff, Frankie! Only with fins! Anyway, Marion had never driven a car with an automatic transmission before. Or power brakes. So when she went to stop at this light on Jubilee Road, she put both feet on the brake by mistake and the three of us nearly went through the windshield!"

"Gracious."

"No! It was really neat! You should have seen us! Edna was on the floor — she just slid right underneath the glove compartment — and I was...!"

"You should have been wearing one of these." Frankie pats the silver buckle lying between them.

"I guess." She stares at the empty silver clasp. "But we had a good time, though. In Halifax. We always have a good time when we go there. Marion usually gets a big suite at the Lord Nelson Hotel, with a shower and everything. Have you ever been to the...? Ha!" She turns to Sunny again. "Remember that time Irene was staying with us and she...?"

"Shshsh." Sunny gestures toward the front seat.

Rebecca lowers her voice. "Remember? She was having trouble with her gall bladder or something. And she ate all those cream puffs from that bakery on Quinpool Road and then..." She slaps at Sunny. "She shit herself!"

"Quit it!" Sunny slaps her back.

"No! You quit it! I was only..."

"Juvenile!"

"I am not!"

"Well, what do you call somebody who still wets her..."

"I don't! I haven't done that since...Don't!"

Sunny is holding her nose.

"I said don't or I'll..." Rebecca leaps at her.

"Ow! Ow!"

"Watch my stitches!"

"Girls!"

The two of them freeze. There's a pair of eyes glaring at them from the rear-view mirror. If you don't stop that, they seem to be saying, then one of you will have to sit up here, in the front.

"I didn't start it, you know." Rebecca pleads with the eyes. "I was only..."

"She did, too, start it." Sunny takes her turn with the eyes. "She always starts it."

"That's what you think, you big..."

Marion takes her foot off the accelerator.

Rebecca slumps back in her seat. "OK, but it's not fair."

"It's not fair," mimics Sunny, as she smooths out the folds of her mini-skirt.

The car speeds up again.

"Hey, you two!" Irene calls out brightly. "Why don't you play I Spy?"

"It's too foggy," answers Sunny.

"Yeah." Rebecca folds her arms. "We're not even going to be able to see our gypsum."

"Your what?" laughs Irene.

"Our gypsum. That big cliff of it near Hantsport. We always have a contest to see who remembers to look for it."

"Oh. Well..." Irene thinks for a moment. "Then why don't you sing?"

"Yeah!" Rebecca bolts upright again. "Only we have to pick a song that everybody..."

"*Hey! Mr. Tambourine Man, play a song for...*"

"Not that one, Sunny."

"*I'm not sleepy and there is no place I'm...*"

"No! I don't know all the words!"

"Yeah, well, if that's what we're going by, we'll be stuck with 'Three Blind Mice' or something."

Frankie laughs softly. "What about a tune by Gladys Knight and the Pips?"

"Who?"

"I was just teasing. How about 'What's New Pussycat?'"

"Yeah! That's a good one!"

"Yeah!" Even Sunny's excited.

Soon they're careening through the fog, with Frankie singing the pertinent questions of the song and everyone but Marion joining in on the *Wo-oh-OH-ohs*. But Rebecca gets bored after a while, not knowing anything but the chorus — no matter how raucously she bawls it out — and her merriment soon fades away.

"Now what?" she grumbles.

"Oh, come on," urges Frankie. "There must be something."

"How about a hymn?" asks Irene, with a twinkle in her eye.

"No way!" pleads Sunny.

"Well..." Rebecca has an idea. "We *could* do a hymn. But if we do one of those, we have to do one of my Dad's songs, too. One of the ones my Mum always says are irrelevant."

Irene hoots.

"What?" Rebecca jiggles her shoulder. "Isn't that a word?"

"Yes, it's a word but I don't think she actually means..."

"Well, that's what she calls them. Irrelevant. Says my Dad doesn't have a hope in hell of going to heaven because he's always being so irrelevant."

Frankie's laughing now, too.

"Well, I for one wouldn't mind hearing one of those *irrelevant* songs. Do you know any of them?"

"Yeah! My favourite's the one about the elephant with the big ears. Only he changes the words around so it goes..." She lowers her voice and sings. "*Does your dink hang low? Does it dangle to and fro? Can you tie it in a knot? Can you tie it in a bow? Can you throw it over your shoulder like a...*"

The eyes are in the rear-view mirror again.

"Sorry, Marion. I was only..."

"*I think I'm gonna be sad. I think it's toda-ay.*"

Sunny is crooning softly, slowly, as if the words are a moving staircase and her voice isn't sure where they're leading. Once again, everyone but Marion joins in.

"*Yeaaa.*"

They could lead up to a castle, where everyone is rich and pretty and safe.

380 ❖ SUSAN BOWES

"She's got a ticket to ri-ide."

Or they could lead down to a dungeon, where everyone is scrawny and scabby and afraid.

"She's got a ticket to ri-i-ide."

Just like Snakes and Ladders, thinks Rebecca, as two bars of sunlight slash through the fog, defining the obscurity, imprisoning the view. Sunny continues riding.

"She said that living with me is bringing her dow-own."

The others offer their encouragement.

"Yeaaa.

For she would never be free when I was arou-ound."

Rebecca notices that the eyes are in the rear-view mirror again. But they don't seem to be looking for her this time. They seem to be looking for...She turns her head. But Frankie's eyes are closed. She turns back in time to see the eyes disappear from the rear-view mirror.

"My baby don't care. My baby don't care. My baby don't..."

"Hey!" Rebecca leaps to the edge of her seat and peers out the windshield. "We've missed it! The gypsum! We went right by it and didn't even...Damn!" She leans her arms on the back of the front seat, as the car speeds farther away from that magical wall, with its chalky white hints of Dover...Paris...the Pyramids. "Marion?"

There's no answer.

"Marion!" Rebecca pokes her in the shoulder.

"Yes?" Her voice is distant.

"What *is* gypsum anyway?"

Marion pauses. "Well...it's a kind of calcium."

"You mean like teeth?"

"Not exactly, more like..."

"Is it good for anything?"

"Oh, lots of things."

"Like what?"

"Well...like a filler in paint, for one thing."

"Oh."

Rebecca thinks for a moment. She has this image of gypsum as a kind of bread crumb or cracker that you add to the colourful mixture you're stirring in order to hold it together, make it go farther. She wonders what paint would be like without it. Maybe the colours would

be brighter, but they'd probably just slide right off the walls you were
trying to cover.
"Marion?"
"Now what?"
"How much farther?"

According to the guidebook Sunny's been reading aloud to them, the
lobby of the Lord Nelson Hotel has a "sophisticated elegance." There's
an impressive row of arched windows at the front, dark wood panelling
on the pillars and trim, black iron grillwork on the railings of the
balcony and two large, green and brown carpets. Sailing in the circles
at their centres are identical schooners, rocked by identically choppy
seas, with identically rowdy seagulls swooping past their identical
mastheads. There's also an imposing grandfather clock leaning stoically
against a pillar and two paintings — one of the famous Admiral Nelson
and the other of his mistress. But what Sunny likes best, she's just
told everyone, is the gold. There's golden marble on the floors, golden
plaster on the walls, golden plaster on the ceiling, too, except that it's
also arrayed with hundreds of amber discs and octagons depicting
oak leaves and fish, lions and ships. Even the leather armchairs and
the standing ashtrays are golden, as are the tiny shades of the sixteen
little lamps which form the chandeliers. But the most golden of all,
and the shiniest, too, is the brass. The elevator doors. The balustrades.
The enormous mailbox. Their uses cannot hope to compete with their
lustre.
    While Marion and Irene make arrangements with the desk clerk for
extra towels and picking up messages, Sunny just stands there, soaking
in every opulent detail. Rebecca, who's slumped in one of the golden
armchairs, scowls at her. She can see that Sunny thinks the Lord
Nelson is the next best thing to Versailles, that golden palace of her
extravagant fantasies. But she wonders if she's forgotten there are
places like Dogpatch in the world, too.
    "It's gorgeous," whispers Sunny, as her eyes scan the room, slowly,
carefully, so they won't smudge anything.
    "If you say so," snorts Rebecca, as she sinks further into the golden
armchair.
    She thinks the chair's neat because it squeaks whenever she moves,

even the tiniest bit, but other than that, she doesn't have much use for it. For any of it. It's all sort of pretty, but it does dumb things to people — makes them whisper, makes them walk slowly, makes them wear their good clothes. She likes the rooms better. The walls may be that same ugly yellow colour — like mustard that's sat too long with the top off — but at least you're allowed to laugh and jump on your bed and run around in your drawers in there.

Her face crinkles.

Frankie didn't come in with them; not even into the lobby. There would have been plenty of room for him to stay, since they took a big suite again, but when she asked him, he just smiled strangely and said, "Thanks. But I can't."

"Hey! Wake up!" Sunny shoves Rebecca's elbow off the golden leather armrest. "We're waiting for you."

"Me!" Rebecca leaps to her feet. "I've been ready for ages!"

"OK, girls." Irene slings a large canvas bag over her shoulder. "Which do you want to do first, shop or eat?"

"Shop!" Sunny calls out eagerly, then claps her hand over her mouth when she remembers the opulence.

"Nooo! Eeeat!" whines Rebecca. "I'm starving!"

"OK, then, we'll vote," whispers Sunny. "Or better still…Eenie, meenie, minie, mo." She points her finger back and forth at Rebecca's chest and then her own. "Catch a tiger by the…"

"Nooo! That's no fair! It always turns out the same!"

"I don't know what you mean."

"Yes, you do, you cheater! When you start with the other person, you always end up with…!"

"Stop that, you two!" Marion's face is flushed. "Or I'm never taking you anywhere with me again!"

Rebecca giggles. "You always say that."

"Yes, well, this time I mean it. Now, come on. We'll shop for…" She glances at her watch. "For half an hour. Next door. In the Lord Nelson Arcade. And then we'll eat. OK, Sunny?"

Sunny sticks her tongue out at Rebecca. "Fine with me."

"Rebecca?"

"OK, but then I get to pick the place."

"Ha!" snorts Sunny. "Let me guess. The Gag and Spew, right?" This time she forgets to clap her hand over her mouth.

Forty-five minutes later, as they're piling through the front door of The Garden View restaurant on Spring Garden Road, Rebecca grabs Marion's sleeve. "Wait! I want to…"

Marion turns to her. "What is it? I thought you were starving."

"I am but…" The others have already slid into a booth. "I want to ask you…"

"What? You look so serious."

Rebecca narrows her eyes, as if trying to remember the exact look of that strange smile. "How come Frankie can't stay with us?"

"Frankie?" Marion looks flustered. "Ha! Frankie has better things to do than stay with a bunch of yapping women."

"Are you sure?"

Marion narrows her eyes, too. "Yes, I'm sure," she answers softly.

"Oh."

"Now, come on or the others will have…"

"Hey!" hollers Rebecca, as she scrambles down the aisle. "Don't you dare order anything with bean sprouts, Sunny! They give me the runs!"

After lunch, they hold a conference on the sidewalk outside the hotel. Irene, it's finally decided, will take the girls for a stroll around the Public Gardens and then on a bus up to the Bayers Road Shopping Centre. Marion will spend the afternoon working, so they can all spend the evening visiting.

"Hey, look, Sunny!" shouts Rebecca, as they tumble across South Park Street. "The green man's got red lips today!" She points to the bronze bust of Sir Walter Scott which rests atop the pedestal at the entrance to the Public Gardens. Someone has smeared paint on his mouth.

Sunny smiles. "Probably been smooching with the Lady of the Lake."

"Who's she?" asks Rebecca, as she skips toward the monument.

Sunny chuckles. "No one *you* know."

"Me neither," murmurs Irene, as she stops to gaze at the statue's pale green patina.

"What's that, Irene?"

Rebecca is standing beside her now.

"Nothing. It's just that…well, I wish I'd seen him without it. You know, before he aged; before he added all that…that green stuff."

"Yeah, well, I hear it's to protect things. I don't know what from. Anyway, come on. Let's go!"

"Have a good time!" calls Marion, as she watches them push through the big, black wrought-iron gates.

Rebecca spins and waves. "You, too!" she hollers back, from beneath the ornate clumps and swirls of the archway.

She's expecting Marion to turn away now. But she doesn't. She just stands there, on the top step, with her hand suspended in the air…so long, so still, that Rebecca's afraid it might start getting covered with a pale green patina.

The guidebook Irene's using describes the Public Gardens as a sixteen-acre floral haven. Roses. Rhododendrons. Dahlias. Daffodils. Shy, little violet wisps from a thistle poking out of a rockery. Great, big showy gobs of red from a begonia lounging on a carpet bed. And a statue to the Roman Goddess Flora, looking down on it all from her spot near the hyacinths. But there are lots of green things, too — to keep the statues of Demeter and Artemis happy. Over eighty species of trees. Almost two hundred varieties of shrubs. The weeping beech. The ornamental plane. The exotic maiden hair. Along with the brooks and the bridges and the overfed ducks. And the fountains. The one commemorating the Boer War is appropriately austere, but the one honouring Queen Victoria's Diamond Jubilee is a surprisingly energetic tangle of nymphs and cherubs and leaping fish.

"My goodness," sighs Irene, as she plops down on a wooden bench facing the frolicking figures.

"Hey!" Rebecca leaps in front of her, blocking her view. "I thought we were going to the canteen!"

Irene laughs. "You can't still be hungry! You can't be!"

"No, but we need something to drink. And *those* ugly things…" She whirls to face the fountain, "…are useless. You can't get a drink from *those*."

"Yes, well, you two go ahead without me."

"Really?"

"Yes. I'll catch up to you by Griffin's Pond."

"OK, see ya." Rebecca hops out of the way.

Irene can see her nymphs again.

A little while later, after they gulp down their Mountain Dews, Sunny and Rebecca begin swishing through the floating flower beds toward the bandstand. Sunny is enthralled by the sumptuous symmetry of it all. True to her Versailles fixation, she says she prefers the French formal to the English romantic — geometric arrangements being much more dependably gorgeous than random plantings and curving paths. Rebecca, on the other hand, is getting bored. To her, it's all very neat and pretty, but it isn't beautiful. There's something missing. Something wild and spontaneous that she only gets a glimpse of when she comes upon a quince that has fallen to the grass or a bunch of bread crumbs that are bobbing on the surface of the reflecting pool. Apart from those disorderly touches, it all reminds her of Winifred's kaleidoscope.

"Have you ever seen anything like it?" marvels Sunny, as she leans against the white wooden railing of the octagonal bandstand.

"Yes."

"When?" Sunny turns to her.

"The last time we were here!" hoots Rebecca.

Sunny turns away again. "Sometimes you're so...God! Look at that! I've never seen that before!" She points to a tree with snow-white flowers and heart-shaped leaves. "What do you think it is?"

"Who cares!"

Sunny pushes herself away from the railing. "I thought you liked flowers."

"They're OK. But not nearly as neat as vegetables. Vegetables are pretty and..."

"Ha!" snorts Sunny.

"Well, they are!"

"If you say so."

"And you can eat them, too!"

Sunny bursts into laughter. "I should have known!"

"What? What did I say?"

Sunny spins toward the steps of the bandstand. "Come on. Let's go find Irene."

On the way to Griffin's Pond, they check out the nameplate beneath the flowering tree. Sunny was hoping it would be something amorous like Lover's Lace or Heart's Sweet Dream. Rebecca just didn't want it to be something in Greek. She isn't nearly as disappointed as Sunny, then, when the two of them bend down and read: Indian Bean Tree.

By the time they reach Griffin's Pond, Irene is pacing back and forth along the bank.

"What's the matter?" asks Sunny. "We're not late are we?"

"No, it's not that. It's...Ooooo! I wish I'd brought my camera."

"What for?"

Irene points toward the pond.

"My God!" gasps Sunny. "The black one. I've never seen the black one before."

In 1877, Irene's already informed them, one of Queen Victoria's grandsons donated two pairs of Royal Swans to the Public Gardens. One white and one black. Over the years, the white ones flourished — meeting, mating, growing fat on scraps and crumbs. But the black ones didn't. Some of them died from exposure; others from malnutrition. Others swallowed bottle caps or were shot with BB guns. A few were stuffed into plastic bags and taken home for supper. The one that remains usually keeps to itself. But today it's slipped out into the open water and is swimming gracefully with one of its white compatriots.

Suddenly, the black swan rises a little from the surface of the pool and extends its wings.

Sunny holds her breath.

It waves those black satin capes once, twice, as if casting a spell over its own sorrow and yearning, and then settles back into the water.

"God!" Sunny begins to breathe again.

"Yes." Irene stares at the ripples.

"I'll be right back!" exclaims Rebecca.

"Hey!" Irene snaps out of it. "Where are you going? Hey!"

Rebecca is zigging and zagging down the path, back toward the entrance to the Gardens.

"To get my camera!" she shouts, without turning around. "I left it in the...!"

"And it's really *my* camera," yells Sunny, as Rebecca's words grow faint.

As Rebecca races up the front steps of the hotel, she swears she feels something brush against her cheek. It's as if Marion's hand is still there, suspended in the air, telling her to stop. For a split-second, she shudders. But then she just runs right through it. When she reaches the door of their room, however, she puts on the brakes. She wants the camera badly, so Sunny and Irene can have their little memento of the black swan, but she doesn't want to disturb Marion. If Marion's disturbed, she won't finish her work, and if she doesn't finish her work, they won't be going visiting tonight. She gently turns the handle of the door and creeps into the room.

"Oh, brother," she snorts, as soon as she gets inside.

There's the sound of rushing water coming from the bathroom. Marion isn't working at all. She's taking a shower.

Rebecca tiptoes toward the open door. She can never understand why grown-ups have to be so clean all the time — at the funniest times, if you ask her. She pokes her head through the opening and then...freezes.

She can see through the steam, through the sliding pane of translucent glass, that there are two big grey shapes in the shower. Before she can back away, however, the two shapes move together. And then they sink to the floor, like a stocking full of kittens about to be drowned.

That evening, while Marion and Irene discuss grown-up things with Sharon Cragg's mother, Sunny and Rebecca ride back and forth on the Halifax-Dartmouth Ferry. Sharon would have come, too, but she says she's too upset over her message from Jim.

After the fifth crossing, Sunny turns to Rebecca. "What's the matter with you? Are you sick? You haven't said a word since we left."

Rebecca doesn't answer.

"Are your stitches bothering you? Thirty-four stitches would bother *me*."

Sunny waits a few seconds, then sighs and takes out her tube of lip gloss. While she applies the latest layer of Apricot Smile to the edges of her mouth, Rebecca stares down into the water. So deep, so dark, so calm. She wonders how many secrets it can hold.

"Sunny?"

"What?" Sunny presses the cap back onto the tube.

But Rebecca has heard that other water again — that noisy, impetuous, frightening cascade inside the shower stall.

"Nothing."

45

"OK, everyone." For what seems to Rebecca like the twentieth time since they arrived, Irene slings her large canvas bag over her shoulder. "Who's coming with me?"

"I am!" Sunny leaps out of the armchair.

"Great! And what about you, Rebecca?"

"That depends on where you're going." She jams her feet into her sneakers.

"Well...I thought we'd start with Citadel Hill and then..."

"Count me out." Rebecca sits down on the edge of the bed.

"Oh, come on, Rebecca," laughs Irene. "It'll be fun."

"No, it won't."

"Okaaaay..." Irene glances at Marion. "Well, then, you might learn something."

Rebecca folds her arms. "I don't want to learn something."

"Just this morning?" Marion slams her comb down on the dresser. "Or never?"

Rebecca looks down at her feet. "How should I know?"

There's a brief pause and then Irene tries again. "We won't stay long, you know. Just take a quick look at the maps and badges and...Hey! Wouldn't you like to see a Victoria Cross? Sunny told me there's a..."

"No!"

"You're such a brat, Rebecca," drawls Sunny, from the doorway.

"Yeah, well, just because you're interested in that history junk doesn't mean..."

"That's enough!" Marion swivels to face her. "Jesus."

Rebecca looks down at her feet again. "You don't have to yell."

"And you don't have to be such a...Oh, I give up! Irene. Sunny. Have a good time. We'll see you after we get back from..." She leans toward Rebecca. "Church."

"Church?" Rebecca gapes at her. "No way! Church? Is that where you're going?"

"Wow! Ever neat!" Rebecca races past a row of rickety wooden houses, towards a big yellow bulldozer. It's one of several City of Halifax vehicles lying silent amidst the growing mounds of debris along the shore of the Bedford Basin.

"Rebecca! Don't you dare...!"

But it's too late. She's already clambered up to the seat.

"Wee! Look at me! Vroom. Vroom. Vrooooom. I'm going to bash down that..."

Suddenly, the sun glints off the tailgate of a big yellow dump truck. Rebecca shifts into neutral. It's the same colour as that dinky toy she stole when she was four. She turns off the ignition and looks down at Marion and Frankie. "What is this place anyway?"

"Africville," answers Frankie. "The place where I grew up."

"Oh."

He points past some rubble to the basin. "That's where I went swimming."

"Yeah?"

"And up there's where I picked blueberries."

"Yeah?"

"And, well...up until recently, that..." He waves at a heap of rotting red shingles, "...was the schoolhouse and that..." He waves at the rotting blue heap next to it, "...was the post office."

Rebecca slips from the seat to the tread, stands there for a moment, with her brow knit, looking out over the colourful ruins, and then hops to the ground. "But what's happening, Frankie? What are they doing to it? I mean, I can see what they're *doing* to it, but *why*?"

"They say it's been designated for industrial use. Anyway, they're clearing us out. Relocation is the official word for it. Those with no legal title to their house — and that's most of us — get five hundred dollars. And then the house is flattened, before we can change our minds. That's what the dump trucks are for, to cart away our belongings, as if they were just another load of..."

Marion puts her hand on his arm.

"But *where* are they moving you, Frankie?"

"To a new public housing project. With sewers and running water."

"Oh." Rebecca thinks those are pretty stupid reasons to have to move. "I still don't get it, Frankie. I still don't see why they're making you move."

"Well, they say that after one hundred and fifty years of abuse and neglect, they want to improve housing standards. *To integrate us into the life of the city* is one of their fancy phrases. But I think they're just embarrassed by..." He waves at the piles of rotting boards.

"Yeah, well." Rebecca gazes at a cluster of patchwork tin shacks, up past the railway tracks. "You have to admit some of it *is* kind of ugly. But was it a nice place to live, Frankie? Did you like living here?"

Frankie laughs. "Well, you're right there. It wasn't always pretty — although most houses were painted the colour of gum drops and weren't too bad on the *inside*. And it wasn't always what you'd call nice either. The city didn't bother to extend its water and sewage services out here. They said they couldn't bore through the rock. But I don't know what their excuse was for no police, no garbage pick-up, no paved roads, no insurance. And then there was the dust from the stone-crushing plant and the smell from the cesspools. At any rate, we had to boil our water. And use kerosene lamps."

Rebecca knits her brow again. You can't run a TV on a kerosene lamp.

"And sometimes burn old batteries in the stove to keep warm. We had a few cases of lead poisoning from that. And pray that the wood we got from the dump to build with didn't already have bedbugs in it."

"Yuck."

Once again, Frankie laughs. "But there was still something about it that..." He closes his eyes. "Even now I can hear a wailing saxophone. And feel a crab shell slice into my finger. And see a small boy skittering down a snowy hill on a cardboard box. And I can smell things. The dump, my Dad's boxing gloves, the sewage pit, my Mum's biscuits, the slaughterhouse." He opens his eyes. "Oh, I don't know. It's hard to explain. It was..."

"Home." Marion's voice rings out over the rubble.

Frankie looks at her. "Yes. One, big, happy family. Four hundred or so poor, stupid niggers who didn't..."

"Frankie!" gasps Rebecca.

"What?" His eyes seem filled with a crazy mixture of pride and self-hatred.

"Don't say that word! You're not allowed to say that word!"

He smiles at her. "*You're* not allowed to say it. It's OK if I say it."

"What do you mean? I don't get it. I thought..."

"Never mind. Let's go around the turn. I just have time to show you our old house. Or rather, what's left of it."

"Frankie," murmurs Marion. "Maybe we shouldn't. Maybe it's better if we…"

"Come on."

Marion and Rebecca stumble after him.

A few minutes later, they're staring across another expanse of rubble. Rebecca thinks it looks exactly like the rest of them but Frankie obviously recognizes something familiar in the various piles of tar paper and tin.

"Yes." He smiles. "Yes. We lived here. Right here."

He's ankle deep in debris. Marion looks away.

"And there." He points to a pile of sticks and stones a few yards away. "That was Leroy's place."

"Who was Leroy?" asks Rebecca.

"Ha! Leroy Steed was the best damn horn player I every heard. Would pretty near blow the roof off whenever he played at church."

"Wow!"

"Didn't get much regular work, though. Just odd jobs as a stevedore and such. Had to make ends meet salvaging scrap metal and old auto parts from the dump like everyone else. Ha! Married his cousin Billie, who ran a penny store, and had seven of his own kids and two others they just picked up along the way."

"Does that mean I can marry Blaine?" Rebecca whispers to Marion.

"No," Marion whispers back.

"Shared a party line — and a contaminated well, come to think of it — with Jasper Carvery over there. And Bessie Dixon. Yes. Jasper was a railway porter and Bessie a cleaning lady — after they both stopped working in the bone-meal plant, that is. When I was a boy, they were always drinking and fighting and carrying on together — all day and all night. I remember the time Bessie persuaded everybody to pitch in and get a wringer washer. Didn't *that* cause a stink! Jasper said if the Good Lord had wanted…"

"Frankie?" interrupts Rebecca. "What did your Dad do?"

"My Dad was a truckman."

"What's that?"

"Someone who carts the effluent away."

"The what?"

"The shit."

"Yu-uck! And your Mum? Did your Mum have a yucky job, too?"

Frankie laughs. "That depends on how you look at it. To folks out here she was a sort of doctor. Which can be pretty yucky, I guess, especially when the babies are being born. But mostly she just prescribed things. Prescribed the exact same things, come to think of it, whether you were suffering from pneumonia or a cut lip." He smiles at her. "Half an aspirin, a teaspoonful of castor oil and a hot bath."

"Just like my Grammie! She's got her remedies, too!"

"Yes, well..." He turns away. "Come on. Let's go see if the others have arrived."

"Frankie?" murmurs Marion. "Are you sure they want us?"

He keeps walking.

"Frankie, wait!" Rebecca grabs at his sleeve. "Slow down! I want to ask you something."

"What is it, little one?"

"What would happen if...well...there's still some houses left, right? So what would happen if the people just decided they didn't want to move? If the people got together and said that no one could make them move, that it wasn't fair, that it..."

"Rebecca." He smiles at her. "It's too late."

"Yeah, well...I think it stinks!" She picks up a stone and flings it at a big yellow bulldozer. It strikes the blade with a resounding clang.

The place has come alive now. There are hundreds of people picking their way through the devastation down to the shore, wearing their Sunday best and carrying enormous hampers and pots.

Rebecca's eyes are wide with delight. "What's happening, Frankie?"

"We're having a baptism."

"Oh." She thought it was a picnic.

"Folks have come from Preston, Beechville, Waterville, as far away as Weymouth Falls."

"That's nice. But..."

"What?"

"Where's the church?"

"Ha! Where do you think?" He waves up the road.

"Oh. But, then, how can you...?"

"It's not the church that saves you, little one — not the building and not the people who run the building. It's your belief."

"But what if you don't have a belief? I don't think I have a belief."

Frankie laughs. "Well, then, you better find one pretty quick!"

"But Jesus is so...well, dumb."

"Then it doesn't have to be Jesus! It can be...well, a whole series of little beliefs, starting with..." His eyes twinkle. "Hot dogs, for instance."

There's a pause while Rebecca tries to digest this latest information...and then she remembers the hampers and pots.

"Oh, I get it! I get it! You mean that, in those baskets over there, there could be...?" Her eyes twinkle, too.

"Yes! That's right! Of course, there could also be sixty-five cans of lima beans, but then you just have to take your chances."

"Frankie!" She punches him in the arm.

All afternoon, there's a procession of candidates wading waist high into the cold seawater. Rebecca doesn't think much of their long white gowns, which pull and sag as soon as they get wet. And she doesn't think much of the preacher, who says the very same words to each of them before practically drowning them. But she likes the tambourine, which chinks in time to each stately step. And she likes the makeshift choir. Not their first hymn. Not that forlorn rendition of "Deep River" which accompanied the first few immersions. But the hymns which come after. The hymns which everyone shouts because they're just too happy to be quiet.

"Yeaaah!"

Rebecca loves the racket. But she's glad it's only shouting and dancing, clapping and singing; glad that no one rolls his eyes or has a fit or starts speaking in tongues. She's heard those things sometimes happen when Baptists get too worked up.

"Marion!" she hollers, over another rousing chorus of "Get On Board, Little Children."

Marion is clapping as loudly as anyone. "Yes?" she hollers back.

"This is the most fun I've ever had at..." She leans toward her. "Church!"

Marion tweaks her nose. "Me, too!"

When the ceremony's over, those who are soaked go to change their clothes, while the others set up tables and lay out the food. Rebecca's delirious. Not only are there hot dogs but pop and chips and ice cream, too. And she hasn't even had a belief about *those*.

46

On the way to Peggy's Cove, Sunny told them all about it. Read straight from the guidebook about how the quaint little fishing village, with its lighthouse and its massive granite boulders, was a photographer's delight. The subject of countless picture books and calendars. Especially when the waves crashed down on it. She even dropped in a few extra tidbits that weren't in the guidebook. Like how these ancient rocks were picked up and dumped next to the sea by the last of the retreating glaciers.

Of course, by the time Sunny and Rebecca are actually scrambling over those smooth white rocks, they aren't concerned with something that happened ten thousand years ago. They just want to see how close they can get to the pounding sea before Marion and Irene, who are standing up above, with their arms folded over their breasts, freezing, will bawl them out.

"Who the hell was Peggy anyway?" asks Rebecca, as she slithers down what Sunny says is a four-hundred-and-fifteen-million-year-old slab of granite.

Sunny is fondling a clump of sea lettuce.

"How should *I* know? Maybe the woman who used to own the place. I'll have to look it up."

"Yeah, well, while you're doing that..." Rebecca has reached the edge, the place where the smooth white rocks turn slippery and dark. "I'm just going to..."

"Rebecca!"

Marion has read the guidebooks, too. And she's told Rebecca, over and over, to watch out for that reindeer moss which covers many of the underwater surfaces and makes them so slippery.

Rebecca looks over her shoulder. "What!"

"Don't you dare go any further!"

"Why not?"

"Because if you do, I'm..."

Rebecca grins. It isn't going to do Marion much good to threaten to leave her home from now on. She's done that for years.

"What?" teases Rebecca. "I can't hear you!"

There's a tremendous crash, and then a burst of white spray.

Marion cups her hands to her mouth. "Because if you do go any further..." she hollers, "you're not getting any lobster!" She lowers her hands. "Come on, Irene. Sunny." They turn toward the Sou'wester Restaurant and Gift Shop. "If that doesn't do it, I don't know what..."

"Wait for me!" screams Rebecca, as she clambers up the face of the rock. "Wait!"

She doesn't know why they have to be so stuck up about it and call it bisque, but she sure does like that lobster chowder they serve up there on the hill.

"Ha!" Marion turns to greet her. "I thought that might get your...attention. Jesus." She claps her hand to her chest.

Standing all alone, on that massive white boulder, Frankie looks like a black steeple.

Rebecca's face crumples. "Yeah, well, I don't suppose he's eating with us this time either."

Rebecca lifts her eyes from the datebook.

He didn't come in with us. He just stood there, with his back to us. From the time we started to the time we finished.

"God! I wish I knew what was going on. What *is* going on. What *will be*...God!"

Her tenses are as muddled as time itself. She doesn't have a clue when to pick up the threads of her own story, never mind separate the strands of anyone else's. And now that the wind has whipped up and is threatening to tangle them, she needs to hurry.

47

According to Sunny, who takes a keen interest in these things, the best invention of 1965 is flour which doesn't need to be sifted. Of all the things designed to cut down on the amount of time spent in the kitchen — like Pop Tarts and frozen pizzas and instant omelets —

this is the one she predicts will have the most profound effect on her own life, when at last that life actually begins. But it's hard to convince Vivian. She's more excited by the new margarine, which stays soft even when cold, than she is by the new flour — which she just doesn't trust.

"Come on, Mum." Sunny holds out a brand-new bag of Swan's Down flour. "It won't bite."

Vivian waves at it. "It won't work either."

"Well…" Sunny plops it down on the table. "You're welcome to think that. But if you expect to make a cake tonight, you're going to have to try it. We've run out of the regular stuff."

Vivian thinks for a moment, then snatches at the bag. "OK! I'll try it!" She tears at the top, then peeks inside. "But I'm still going to sift it first."

"Great," sighs Sunny.

"I'll get the bowls!" cries Rebecca.

When she isn't half-tight, and there's money around for ingredients, Vivian's a wonderful cook. In fact, according to the girls, her white cake is the best around. Sunny once tried to convince her to give it a name. Cake so moist, so soft, so tasty deserves to be called something special. But all Vivian could come up with was "Delicious White Cake" so Sunny gave up.

"What kind of icing are we going to have?" asks Rebecca, as she cranks the sifter. It's always been her job to do the sifting so she isn't really sorry that her Mum doesn't trust the new bag of flour.

"What kind would you like?" Vivian wipes her brow with her apron.

"I don't really care." She taps the side of the canister. "Chocolate is good. Or orange." She taps it a few more times. "Just as long as you don't put on too much of it, OK? I like the cake way better than the…Marion!" She leaps up from the table. "When did *you* get here?"

"Just now. Hi, Sonja. Vivian. Here. Help me with…" She hands Rebecca one of the two bags she's carrying.

"What is it?"

"Corn on the cob."

"Yay!"

"And a few apples."

"Double yay!"

They set their bags on the counter.

"Well, it looks like the three of you are busy."

"Yes, we are," snaps Vivian. "So if you want tea, you'll have to get it yourself."

Marion smiles. "No, thanks. I can't stay. I've just dropped by to…"

"I'll get you some." Sunny saunters over to the stove.

"Thanks, Sonja, but really, I have to…"

"There's cake, too!" exclaims Rebecca. "Left over from the last time we…"

"OK!" Marion sits down. "You've convinced me! But just one piece. I promised Mum I'd talk to Rosalie Saunders tonight."

Vivian clatters her wooden spoon against the side of the bowl. "What's *she* done?"

"Nothing. She's just having a rough time at home, that's all. And I thought I'd…"

"So what else is new?" Vivian flings the spoon into the sink.

Rosalie Saunders comes from one of those poor families with lots of kids that Grammie and Marion are always taking under their wings. Her brother Drew is a hood, but Rosalie's just full of hell.

"Sorry about the napkin," drawls Sunny, as she hands Marion a slice of cake. "It's all I could find."

Marion smiles at the poinsettias which are decorating the napkin. "Thanks."

Vivian slams the pan down on the table and begins to pour in the batter.

For the next minute or so, there's an awkward silence. Rebecca wonders what Marion's thinking about. It could be Rosalie. Or it could be the poinsettias. They remind Rebecca of the ones she and Marion snuck into Frankie's cabin, years ago, while he was working on that woodlot in Millville. There was also a tin of shortbread, a few sprigs of holly and a little tree, with little silver balls and bells. But the best thing was that gigantic pot of exuberantly red blooms. Not only were they pretty, but they made Marion happy. She even joined Randy and Rebecca on their forty-fifth time through the "Chipmunks' Christmas Song" that evening.

Suddenly, Rebecca frowns.

But then something came along and spoiled it. Late that night, the hoods came and threw snowballs at Frankie's cabin. Rebecca can still hear the terrible thud, thud, thud, thud…

"More cake?" Vivian lets the oven door thump shut. "Oh, no, I forgot. You have to be going."

The girls peer through the oven's tiny pane of amber glass.

"Yes." Marion buries her lips in the poinsettias. "But first, I have to tell you what..."

"What you and Gene have decided, right?" She wipes her hands on her apron. "Well, go ahead. Tell me and then get on your way. I'm sure you've got people to save."

"Vivian," says Marion softly. "It's not that we've decided anything. It's only a suggestion."

The girls shift a little, so they can see the reflections of the adults in the tiny window.

"OK, OK. Just say it."

"OK. You know that Donnie's been getting into an awful lot of trouble lately."

"So?"

"This business up at Hal's place was only the latest..."

"Yes, yes."

"Anyway, we think it's best if he goes away for a while, to that private school we were telling you about in Granby."

"No."

"Oh, come on, Vivian."

"It's too far away."

"I know it seems that way. But Clifford lives nearby and he can always..."

"No!"

"And you wouldn't have to worry about the tuition because Gene and I have worked it out between..."

"No." Vivian is crying now. "No."

The girls glance at one another.

Marion crumples her napkin. "Vivian, it's either Feller College..."

Vivian sniffles.

"... or juvenile reform school in Shelburne."

The girls straighten up. They've heard what happens to kids at those places.

A few minutes later, Rebecca is scurrying around, trying to find her sneakers.

"Wait! Wait for me! I just have to...!"

She loves going with Marion on her rounds. There's always lots of neat gossip — and sometimes food.

"Ready!" She springs toward the door.

"Ha!" laughs Sunny, as she watches the two of them traipse toward the silver-grey car. "Just like a pair of detectives. Risking their lives to solve the mysteries of the universe. Forsaking their own happiness so that...so that Rosalie Saunders can be restored to her rightful..."

"You're crazy!" laughs Rebecca, as she opens the car door.

"Yeah, well, the same can be said of..." Sunny points to Marion. "Eliot Ness. And..." She waves at Rebecca. "Dick Tracy."

"No! No way I'm Dick Tracy!"

"Why not?"

"Because he's just a dumb old guy in the comics. I want to be someone real."

"Yeah? Like who?"

"Well...one of the Hardy Boys maybe. Or even Nancy Drew, 'cause *she* always gets a really neat car. What?"

Sunny is doubled over with laughter.

"What'd I say? What?"

"Come on, Rebecca," pleads Marion. "Or..."

"But I want to know what's so funny; why Sunny's laughing so...books are *realer* than comics, aren't they?"

"... or Rosalie'll think we've abandoned her."

Rebecca knits her brow. "Yeah, OK." She ducks into the car and pulls the door shut. "I wouldn't want her to think that. I like Rosalie. She's the best in the whole class at spitballs."

"Is that right?" Marion can't help smiling.

"Yeah! This one time we were shooting at the Queen...well, not the Queen exactly, but that picture of the Queen over Mr. Armstrong's desk...you should've seen Rosalie! She put it right through the old bag's eyeball!"

The next morning, there are four of them hovering around the silver-grey car. Grammie and Vivian, who've never learned to drive. Alice, who cherishes her trips to Greenwood with the "giiirls she's knooown foreeever." And Marion, who always gets stuck with being the chauffeur. Rebecca's there, too, but she isn't hovering. She's perched on the plush red seat, behind the shiny red steering wheel, pretending to drive.

"Vroom! Vroom!"

"We've got a nice day for it, I'll say that," remarks Grammie, as she scans the sky.

"Yeees," drawls Alice. "We haaave."

"Vroom!"

"We couldn't have aaasked for a beeetter…"

"Vroom! Vroom!"

"Rebecca!" Grammie pokes her head in the window. "We can't hear ourselves think!"

"Yeah, well, I can't…"

"Rebecca?" Marion pokes her head in the other window.

"Sorry, it's just that…" She twists from one to the other. Grammie and Marion don't look like they'd understand that it's way more fun when you make the noises. "Never mind." Her hands slide off the wheel and thump onto her lap. She shifts to the centre of the seat.

"OK, everyone. Time to go." Marion reaches into her pocket and pulls out the hard, red, leather key case Rebecca gave her for Christmas — the one with the cute little flashlight inside. "Alice, I thought you and Vivian could sit together in the back seat." She presses a little button. The key case pops open. "And Mum, you could…"

"Ha!" Rebecca swivels around. "As long as you promise not to fight."

Vivian and Alice look at one another. Last week they had a terrible argument over how many times Alice underbid her hand at bridge. Vivian eventually stomped off, leaving Rebecca to complete the second table. Alice was going to stomp off, too, but she thought better of it. For one thing, there was really no place for her to stomp off to, even if she were an experienced stomper. And for another, there were all those gooey squares still left on the plate.

"OK?" Rebecca persists.

They break into tiny, tentative smiles.

"Yeees," drawls Alice.

"We promise," sniffs Vivian.

"Great." Rebecca bounces back to the front. "We can go now."

"Not quite," says Marion mysteriously.

"What do you mean? Oh. You mean seat belts."

"Nooooo." She jangles the keys in front of Rebecca's face.

"You mean me? You mean I can drive?" She hops onto Marion's lap.

As they swoop by Florence's place in Auburn, Rebecca smiles. She knows she isn't really driving. Her feet don't come anywhere near the pedals. But there's something about steering which lets her imagine things; makes it easy to pretend that she's in charge; gives an extra edge to the adventure. Still smiling, she slides her hands around the wheel to the bottom, where she's seen people put them when they feel confident, relaxed, in perfect tune with...

"Hey!" Her hands have run into Marion's. "No fair! You're not supposed to have your hand on the wheel!"

"Oh, yes, she is," says Grammie firmly.

"But I thought I was the one who...Wow! Look at that!" Her hands leap off the wheel.

Up ahead, by the side of the road, there's a huge black crow, pecking at the carcass of a porcupine. As the car speeds by, she swivels her head. "Did you see it, Grammie?"

"Yes, I saw it."

"It was two feet long!"

"Yes."

Vivian begins reciting the familiar verse. "*One crow sorrow, two crows joy.*"

Alice joins in. "*Threeee crooows weeedding, fooour crooows boooy.*"

"At least two feet long."

"*Five crows silver, six crows gold, seven crows a little story that's never been told.*"

"Boys, oh, boys," marvels Rebecca, as she turns to face the front again. "I've never seen one so...Oh, no! I forgot!" Her hands snatch at the wheel again.

"Too late," murmurs Marion. "We've all been killed."

"Sorry."

Sometimes Grammie can't wait until after they've been to the IGA Foodliner. Sometimes she just has to have her butterscotch sundae before they drive an inch further.

"What about you, Alice?" asks Marion, as she pulls into the Tasty

Twirl Drive-In. "What are you going to have?"

"Oooh. I don't knooow. A cooone, I gueeess."

"Grape nut, for me," blurts Vivian.

Marion laughs. "Not here, Vivian. Remember? They only have soft vanilla ice cream here. With toppings, of course."

"Oh."

"And you, Rebecca?"

"Well...I've narrowed it down to two choices. I'm either going to have a pineapple sundae..."

"So what else is new?"

"I know. It's my favourite. If I can't have orange-pineapple ice cream, that is."

Grammie smiles. It's one of her favourites, too.

"Or I'm going to have a banana split. It's not my favourite but it's bigger."

A little while later, they're standing by the side of the road, licking at their spoons and cones.

"*Five crows silver*," chuckles Grammie, as she picks at the nuts caught in her false teeth.

"Hey!" Rebecca swallows a lump of banana. "That reminds me!"

"Oh, no!" laughs Marion. "She's remembered they have French fries here!"

"No! The crows! I wanted to ask you something about..."

"And hot dogs!" shouts Vivian.

"And haaamburgers!" cries Alice.

"And..."

"Quit it!"

"Oh, come on, Rebecca," laughs Marion. "We're only teasing." She tries to put an arm around Rebecca's shoulder, but she spins away. "Sorry. Sorry. So what about the crows?"

"Well, for one thing..." Rebecca's spoon is overflowing with syrupy chunks of pineapple. "I wanted to ask you who made up the verse."

"I don't know. Why?"

"Because it's dumb, that's..." She catches the drip on the bottom of the spoon. "That's why."

Vivian wipes her fingers with the thin little tissue that was wrapped around her cone. "What makes you say that?"

"Well, there's never more than one crow, is there?"

"Yeees, there iiis," drawls Alice.

"OK, maybe two. Sometimes. At the most."

"Yes, I know, but it's only a…"

"She's right, you know." Grammie has given up on her teeth. "In all my years, I've never once seen three crows, never mind seven crows, all together in one spot."

"Yes, well, stick around, Mum." Marion's eyes are twinkling. "Stranger things have happened. Ha! Cows have even jumped over the moon!"

"What do you mean?"

"I mean it's only a verse."

"Yes, that's true. But every once in a while, whoever writes those verses should have to get them right. If there's only one crow, there's only one crow."

"I agree," says Rebecca, as she tosses her gooey tub into a rusty oil drum. "Haw! Haw!" She dances around the drumful of garbage. "Haw! Haw! Haw! Haw! Haaaaaw!"

"Jesus," moans Marion, as she struggles out of the car. "Remind me not to eat so much next time." She puts her hand up to her mouth and belches quietly.

"Yeees." Alice is marvelling at the number of cars in the parking lot. "Ice creeeam is so faaattening."

Marion smiles. Alice has always been petite. It isn't likely she's ever going to have to worry about her "calves turning into cows," as Harold once put it.

"What is it, Vivian?"

"I don't know, Mum." She's squinting at the pavement a few yards away. "It looks like a penny. Let me just…" She bends down to pick it up but then, at the last moment, snatches her hand away.

"What's wrong, Vivian?"

She straightens up. "Nothing's wrong."

"Then why didn't you get it?"

"Because it wasn't a penny." She smooths her dress.

"What was it, then?"

"A nickel."

"But that's even better, isn't it?"

"Oh, no! You're never supposed to pick up nickels! It's pennies that bring good luck!"

"I see," smiles Marion. "So you're just going to leave it there?"

"I certainly am. Now, come on." She strides forward. "Or they'll have run out of Fluffs."

Rebecca lags behind for a few seconds, until they're too far away to notice, then pounces on the nickel. It isn't luck she cares about. It's five cents worth of Chickenbones.

The IGA Foodliner is just a bigger, gaudier version of the corner grocery store. Marion says it's the size which keeps the prices down; which allows Richard Lowe, the manager, to stock the more exotic items, like Carnation Instant Breakfast and pizza-flavoured ketchup. But it's the gaudiness — mostly streamers and fluorescent lighting — which Rebecca loves.

As they make their way across the parking lot, Mr. Lowe positions himself at the main entrance. It's the best spot for shaking hands and exchanging small talk.

"Yow!"

He manages to corner the grown-ups all right, but Rebecca's too quick for him. She slips beneath the pat he tries to give her on the head and bounds inside.

"Now, Rebecca," warns Grammie. "You needn't t'bother…"

She's headed for the aisle where the baked goods are displayed; where Irene's husband Alvin is in charge.

Alvin Andrews is a stubby young man with thick, wavy brown hair. Rebecca's heard people whisper that he's "kind of fruity," but they said the same thing about Marty Grainger and he was the best shortstop she's ever seen. Anyway, she thinks Alvin's nice and she's got her fingers crossed that he'll get that service manager's job down at the new Canadian Tire. She won't mind if she doesn't actually find him, however. If he isn't there, stacking the boxes of cupcakes, she'll find some other neat place to be. At the coffee grinder, perhaps, watching people spill beans all over the floor. Or at the electric elephant, waiting to see which kids start crying when it jerks them up and down. Anywhere except walking beside Grammie. She may be the best Grammie ever, but she does such embarrassing things sometimes —

like checking to see if the Perfection Butter is fresh by peeling back its wrapper and scraping off a bit with her thumbnail. And like farting out loud as she saunters down the aisles.

"Any broken ones today, Alvin?" Rebecca sidles up to him.

"Not that I've come across." He places another box of cupcakes on the shelf. "Of course, I expect there will be."

She hangs around Alvin and the cupcakes for a long time, talking about tires and fixing up his cottage at Morden and how some of the offering boxes have been going missing lately. But mostly she just waits…to see if his thumb will *accidentally* break through any plastic today.

"Oh-oh," she murmurs, when she sees that the others are already at the checkout. "I guess I have to go."

"Gracious!" Alvin peers at a box of cupcakes. "Would you look at that! I swear they're making it thinner and thinner these days. Well!" He puts his hands on his hips. "They're obviously no good to anyone now. Not with a big hole in the wrapping. I guess I'll have to throw them…"

"Al-viiiiin!"

As they make their way back across the parking lot, all five of them are laughing and chattering.

"You should've seen her, Rebecca. I wish you'd seen her."

"Yeah! So do I!" She stuffs the last bite of cupcake into her mouth.

"She had the dog riding in the cart; you know, up where you put your purse."

"Neat!"

"And she was…she was feeding it potato chips from a big bag she'd…"

"Feeding her own face, if you ask me."

"I just hope she pays for them."

"Ha! Florence wouldn't, I can…"

"Oooh, my gaaaaawd!" Alice stops dead.

The others cluster around her.

"What is it?" wheezes Vivian. "You look like you've seen a ghost."

"Loooook!" Alice points at the silver-grey car.

"Jesus," rasps Vivian.

There's a long, ugly scratch running down its side.

"Now who would have done that?" Grammie creeps forward. "Who on earth would have…?"

"Well, come on, everybody." Marion strides toward the car. "Nothing we can do about it now." She flings open the trunk.

"But Marion! Don't you think we should tell someone? Call the police or something?"

They place their bags inside.

"What could *they* do?"

"I don't know but…well, Richard Lowe, then. I'm sure he'd be interested in knowing what kind of things go on in his parking lot while he's busy…"

"I'll talk to him! I will! But not right now, OK? Now. Are we all set? Watch your fingers!" She slams down the lid of the trunk.

As Marion walks around to the driver's side of the car, she flinches. Rebecca runs over to see why. There's a long, ugly scratch on that side, too. Rebecca backs away.

"It's no big deal," Marion calls out brightly. "The insurance will cover it. Now. I think we deserve another ice cream, don't you?"

Grammie eases onto the front seat. Alice and Vivian flop down heavily onto the back.

"Oh, come on, everybody. It's not *that* bad. Ha! It's only a scratch, as they…Rebecca? Are you coming?"

Rebecca's backed up so far that she's now standing at the spot where Alice first stopped dead. She shakes her head.

"If she knows what's good for her, she is," wheezes Vivian.

Marion closes her eyes for a moment, then turns and strolls toward Rebecca. "Not very pretty, is it?" she murmurs, when she reaches her.

Rebecca shakes her head again.

"But they can fix it, you know. A little sanding. Some new paint. Hey! You can come and help me pick out a new colour, OK? Grey was never really my favourite anyway. And now that…"

"It's my fault," whispers Rebecca.

"What is?"

"The car."

"Don't be silly," Marion says softly. "How can it be your fault?"

"Because of the nickel."

"What?"

"The nickel." She reaches into her pocket and pulls out a silver coin. "I picked it up."

"Oh. I see."

"Come on, you two," complains Vivian. "It's hot in here."

"Well, I don't think it was really your fault," says Marion soothingly. "I don't think luck works that way."

"It doesn't?"

"No. But if it'll make you feel better, why don't you change your luck? Why don't you throw it back on the ground?"

Rebecca thinks for a moment. Then she winds up slowly, deliberately, like Warren Spahn always did, and flings the nickel as far away as she can — so far away that they can't even hear the clink when it hits the pavement.

48

The Valley Drive-In Theatre is located in Cambridge, about ten miles east of Aylesford. In the daylight, it's a scruffy place, overgrown with weeds and strewn with rusty bottle caps. Randy once found five dented Eric Nesterenkos in one hour! But in the darkness, especially if you get a good speaker, it can be magic.

"Oh, my God!"

"Jesus!" Without taking her eyes from the screen, Marion passes back the giant bag of popcorn.

"It's about time." Rebecca takes it from her.

"Shsh," pleads Irene, who's sitting up front with Marion. "We're getting to the good part."

"Yeah?" Rebecca stuffs her mouth with fluffy white kernels. "Well, that's about time, too."

"Shsh."

Rebecca thumps against the backrest. She likes going places with Marion and Irene, but not the drive-in — not even when they sneak her into the Restricted ones under a heavy woollen blanket. They always stick her in the back seat, where she can't see, and then gush and giggle and whisper about things she can't understand. About things they can't understand either, judging from their reaction to the first movie in tonight's double feature.

"What I want to know," sighs Irene, as the credits for *The Collector* roll by, "is why he put her in there in the first place."

"I don't know." Marion's eyes are still glued to the screen. "I honestly don't know."

"Yeah, well, I do!" Rebecca leans forward. "Because he was mental, that's why. He thought she was...like a sort of butterfly or something and he wanted..."

"Yes, I know. But why? What made him do those terrible things to her?"

"Ha!" laughs Rebecca. "At least he didn't squish her head. Not like you do to real butterflies when you collect them."

"I suppose. Anyway..." Irene turns to Marion. "They sure don't make movies like they used to. God! Remember *The Long Hot Summer*? And *Desire under The Elms*? And..."

"*The Blob!*" blurts Rebecca.

During the intermission, Rebecca plays on the swings at the front, close to the screen. As she sways gently through the late-summer night air, a preview for the Coming Attraction flickers overhead. When it gets too bright to ignore, she gazes up at the gigantic screen. Mountains. Nuns. Soldiers. Lots of kids. The same lady with the short blonde hair who played Mary Poppins. It looks like it might be a good one — at least way better than *The Collector* just was. In her opinion, it isn't fair for a movie to be scary *and* sad. There should be a rule that says it can only be one of those. She isn't sure which one's the best. She isn't sure which she'd choose if she were told she could either be scared or sad. She just hopes the next movie's funny.

"Oh, no!" She leaps off the swing.

The snack bar is at the rear, in the projection building. If she wants to get some chips before *The Pawnbroker* starts, she'll have to hurry. Unfortunately, as she's scrambling over one of those little mounds where people put their front tires, she stumbles.

"Iyeeeeeee..."

To break her fall, she grabs onto one of those little white poles where people plug their speakers.

"Phew! Good thing..." She gazes out over the darkened lot.

There are hundreds of these little white poles and her Dad has painted every single one of them; has even added a little black cap to them — "to give them character," as he put it.

Filled with pride, she throws back her head and shouts. "Yeaaaaa!"

It's too late to get anything to eat now — even if she had decided which of the two long lines to join — so she dances through the darkness toward the car. As soon as its body has definition, however, her pride dissolves into anger. Not even the strains of "Woolly Bully" coming from a few hundred crackly speakers can stop that slow and steady fade.

"Stupid idiots," she mutters, as she stares at the car.

It's painted beige now. And looks as good as new. But *as good as new* isn't the same as new. Nothing is the very same as anything else. A sofa isn't a chesterfield. Crying isn't weeping. And new is something special that nothing else can really be.

Sam the Sham and the Pharaohs are still wailing as she reaches for the door handle.

"What are you going to do?"

Startled by the sound of Irene's voice, Rebecca pulls her hand away. "About what?"

"You know."

"Oh, that. Nothing."

"But you have to do something."

"Why? It was just kids fooling around."

"Are you sure? Marion?"

"Look. What do you want me to do? Take out an ad in the *Berwick Register* telling everyone they're imagining things?"

"Are they?"

"Don't be silly. Of course, they are."

49

Rebecca usually lounges in bed until 8:00 or 8:30 now — too late to wander over to Porter's to help with the milking — and she never eats breakfast. Sometimes, when she's lying on the top bunk, gazing up at Paul McCartney's chubby pink cheeks, she misses the cows. But she never misses the Fluffs.

This morning, she's intending to race her bike right up to the warehouse, to check on how Ben's doing in the tractor-selling contest. On her way by the old school, however, she spots Peter, polishing the big brass bed which stands in the front yard.

"Is Bobby here?" She skids to a stop.

Peter keeps rubbing. "No, he isn't."

Bobby Smeltzer has taken over the old school. Vivian likes him because he's good for as many drunken laughs as his wife Elsie. And Peter likes him because he lets him hang around and help. But Rebecca thinks Bobby's crazy. And scummy, too. The scummiest man she's ever met. If she absolutely has to talk to him, she never stands too close, since he can't make it through a single sentence without hacking and honking and spitting. Still, the worst thing about him is what he's done to the school.

Rebecca frowns as she surveys the yard.

He said he was going to turn it into a tourist attraction; that people would come from miles around to browse through the antiques in his "Aylesford Museum of Canadiana." But all he's done is wreck it. The buildings don't look too bad yet, although no one's actually peeked inside to see what he's done to the basement he's remodelling as a home for his family. But the yard's a shambles. Everywhere she looks there's junk. And not neat junk, like old clocks and weather vanes and crystal bowls. But rusty, useless, broken junk. Old scales that are missing a dish. Old buggies that are missing a wheel. Old telephones and toasters that have no knobs on the ends of their frayed and filthy cords. And hundreds of things that are too new to count, even if they weren't busted. Only the big brass bed seems to have any real value. And only when it gleams.

She hopes Peter's doing a good job. She hopes Bobby isn't taking advantage of him.

"See ya later!" she hollers, as she hops back onto the seat of her bike. "And make sure he *pays* you, OK?"

Peter doesn't look up.

In an effort to keep up with the times, Ben replaced the old, wooden K.S. Bowlby and Co. sign with a brand-new glass one. For exactly one day, it hung over the entrance to the warehouse, looking impressive — as clean and sharp and bright as the times could possibly be. But it also made an inviting target for the Junior Hoods — boys like Stevie

Cleveland and Ricky MacNair who were going through the rock-throwing stage. That night, it got the first of its holes. And last night, it got some more.

"Hey, Ben!" yells Rebecca, as she leaps up the steps. "I see the Juniors have...Oh, no! Am I too late?"

Ben is standing next to the Massey-Harris Ferguson chart on the wall in his office.

"No." He turns to her and smiles. "You're not too late."

"Oh. You mean you didn't sell one?"

"Yes," he laughs. "I sold one. But I've been waiting for you to get here before I...Gracious! I swear that dimple of yours gets bigger and bigger every day."

"Be-en!" She snaps her hand up to her left cheek.

"Sorry, sorry. I wouldn't want to...Are you ready?"

She races up to him. "Ready!"

"OK, then." He reaches up to the chart, which is really just a big block of paper with a separate number on each page for each tractor sold. "On your mark. Get set..."

Ben pauses dramatically...and then, with a tremendous flourish, he rips a page off the chart.

"Yaaaaay!"

"Gracious," laughs Ben, as he slumps into his chair. "You'd think I'd just won the World Series."

"No, well, almost as good."

He smiles and reaches for his Dublin pipe.

"Do you think you will, Ben?"

"What's that?" He opens his pouch of tobacco.

"Sell enough tractors to win that trip to Mexico."

"Hmmm. That's hard to say."

"Well, I bet you will. I bet you'll sell enough for *two* trips!"

"Ha!" He lights a match. "And then take you along, I suppose."

"No, not me. I've got school in January. But your girlfriend, maybe. The one with the bad wrist. And then the two of you could wear sombreros and go to a bullfight and..."

Ben blows a smoke ring.

"Well, get me a present, maybe."

"Ha! And what would you like? A taco? A burrito?"

"Nooo! Not food!"

"Well, then, how about a donkey? I hear there are lots of donkeys in…"

"Nooooo!"

After the third phone call about insurance and the second about perpetual care, Rebecca starts to fidget. She usually doesn't mind listening in on Ben's business calls. She can pick up some really neat junk that way — like how long mashed fingers take to heal or how long plastic flowers last in those pointy little tubes before someone comes and steals them. But today, she's more interested in hearing about Mexico and the tractors. She knows there'll be parades and exhibits — long lines of industrial yellow, great patches of agricultural red; living proof of the Rugged New Breed, as they're calling it this year — but there'll also be competitions of strength and agility and she wants to know if Ben will be putting on a white coat and a hard hat and driving in any of those this year. Of course, she's never actually seen him *drive* a tractor, only sell them, but he knows all the parts and stuff and she's pretty sure he'd be able to do it if he had to.

"Maybe not the obstacle race," she murmurs, as she slides off the bench. "He doesn't have very good depth perception. But the pulls." She drifts out of the office. "He'd be OK at those."

Rebecca is standing all alone, amidst the radios and the wood-stoves, when something calls to her. Not out loud, so anyone else can hear, but privately — like God with Samuel in that Sunday School story. She turns and gazes through the sliding doors.

The entire back room is filled with red tractors, gleaming in the sunlight. The warehouse has seventeen windows on the north side and fifteen on the south, so anything stored in there usually gleams. Today, however, the tractors look particularly shiny. If they didn't, if they just looked brand-new, then she might race right up to them. As it is, she creeps beneath the clock and into the room. She isn't afraid of the tractors. She's been on red tractors lots of times, sometimes even when they were moving — like when the superintendent of the golf course let her ride beside him while he dragged his cutter over the greens and fairways. No. She's afraid of the shininess. It's prettier than usual. She wants to run her hands over it more than ever. But it's also scarier. She wouldn't touch it for a million bucks.

Stupid, she tells herself, as the sunlight streams through the rows of windows. Stupid to be so chicken. Stupid not to have fun.

Suddenly, a huge shadow edges across the room.

Quickly, while everything is safe and drab, she hops up onto the black vinyl seat of the nearest tractor. It's a small all-purpose vehicle — a utility model built close to the ground, with a low overhead clearance.

"Useful in orchards," she once heard Ben telling Cousin Herman. "Yuh. Yuh. And great for mounting tools."

"And no oversized bicycle seat," she murmurs, as she leans forward to grip the wheel. "God, they used to hurt my...!"

Suddenly, the tractors are gleaming again.

She closes her eyes. The walls creak. There's another shadow. Her mind goes blank.

"Rebecca? Rebecca!"

She opens her eyes. "Yes, Ben?"

He's standing in the doorway. "You better go home now."

"Why?" She blinks at him through the gloom. "What's happened?"

"Nothing. But it's about to. Listen."

The walls are creaking fiercely now.

"So? It's only a storm. I've been in lots of..."

"Not like this one. Come on." He turns back to the office. "I'm going to close up."

"You are?" She hops off the tractor. "Wow!"

It's only 10:30. Ben never closes the warehouse before six o'clock on weekdays, not even in the summertime. He used to keep it open until six on Saturdays, too, but that was before he took up golf and decided that noon was late enough.

"It must be a really bad one!" she exclaims, when she reaches the office.

"Got everything?" he asks.

"What do you mean? I just brought me."

He smiles, then leads her out the door.

They stand for a moment on the landing, squinting out at the gathering fury. The telephone wires are swinging like skipping ropes. The gigantic maple tree across the street is nearly bent in two. But it wouldn't be anything without the sounds — without the wailing and swishing and banging.

"OK, see ya!" Rebecca bounds down the steps to her bike.

Ben ducks his head. "Yes." He pulls shut the outer door and turns the key. "And maybe tomorrow it'll be...Hey! Where're you going?"

"To Grammie's!" she shouts, as she wobbles down the road. "To make sure she's...!" Her voice is lost in the growing tumult.

The wind is swirling now. It brings her snatches of colour and sensation — a flying carpet of green and yellow, a belligerent shower of gravel, the smell of roast chicken — as she pulls herself up the back steps. She can't help smiling.

"Boy, Grammie!" Rebecca stumbles through the back door. "It sure is...! Grammie?"

The kitchen is deserted.

"Hey, Grammie! Where are you?" She opens the oven door and takes a deep breath. "It's me, Grammie! Rebecca! I've come to see if...!"

It's no use. The wind is too boisterous now. She can't hear her own strenuous shouts, let alone the sizzle of the drippings.

"OK, Grammie!" She lets the oven door slam shut. "Here I come! Ready or...! Gee. I wonder what happened to *them*."

Her old pair of puddlers is standing by the back door. The elastic looped around the top button still looks pretty resilient but the translucent plastic has all turned yellow.

"Okaaaaaaay!" She spins toward the living room. "Ready or not you must be...! Oh. You're in here. I thought at least I'd have to..."

God moves in a mysterious way his wonders to perform.

Grammie is seated at the Palmer upright, playing hymns. At least, it sounds like hymns. In between the whines and shrieks of the wind, there's a series of urgent twangs which resembles Hymn No. 40. Rebecca flops into the big green armchair and tries to listen.

He plants his footsteps in the sea and rides upon the storm.

Grammie plays hymns a lot. In fact, the hymn-book is the only piece of music she keeps inside the piano bench. But she never goes to church. As far as anyone can tell, she has a real grudge against it — especially St. Mary's Anglican Church in Auburn. She used to go there as a young woman, after she made her way east from Bridgetown. When she suddenly stopped, the local gossip put it down to everything from the inept minister to the snooty lady's auxiliary. All Grammie ever said was: "I didn't like the walls."

His purposes will ripen fast, unfolding every hour.

Grammie adjusts her bifocals. They're a brand-new pair with "far-out frames," as Sunny calls them — dove-grey plastic on top and silver-grey steel on the bottom.

The bud may have a bitter taste but...

Grammie wiggles her glasses a little more and then squints at the hymn-book. Rebecca, meanwhile, tries to figure out what Grammie meant by her "walls" comment. She's learned at school that St. Mary's was founded by Charles Inglis, who was both the first Anglican Bishop of Nova Scotia and the one to introduce Bishop Pippin apple trees to the area. It's also the church that has those plaster walls made from the thousands of powdered mussel shells left behind by the Acadians. But Grammie sometimes acts like she left them behind; like she, too, was once huddled on the cliffs at Morden, with the Acadians, waiting for spring to make her escape. Like the sea crashed toward her. Like the wind whipped her hair against her face. Like the empty purple shells clattered over the rocks at her feet. Rebecca thinks this might be what it means to "sympathize" with things, but she's not sure. It might be something more.

Naked, come to Thee for dress. Helpless, look to Thee for grace.

"Pardon?" Rebecca leans forward.

But Grammie hasn't called out to her. She's simply moved on to another series of urgent twangs — this one sounding quite a bit like Hymn No. 267.

Rebecca settles back into the big green armchair. There's a lonely entreaty in each note, but the wind is too noisy for her to hear very well. Her attention wanders. She looks around the room.

The wallpaper is light cream and beige, with what the catalogue described as a "slight fleck."

She smiles.

They had a tough time matching up those slight flecks. In fact, Grammie almost pissed herself laughing when those flecks went cockeyed or ripped or curled obstinately away from one another. But, then, it doesn't take much to make Grammie piss herself.

Her smile fades.

The wallpapering turned out OK. There aren't any big gaps or anything. But something's happened to Grammie. She isn't as much fun as she used to be and it's been weeks since she copied a joke into her cookbook.

A single, sad, beseeching note squeezes through the howling. Rebecca gazes toward the piano.

There's a shiny golden trophy sitting on top — the one presented to Sunny for being the "outstanding performer" at the provincial track and field meet in the spring. The local papers made a big deal out of her record-setting victories in the 100- and 220-yard dashes; out of her solid anchoring of the winning 440- and 880-yard relay teams. In fact, the *Berwick Register* proudly proclaimed that she could "outrun all males east of the New Brunswick border." But something's happened to Sunny, too. She's crabby all the time now and has lots of secrets and wants everyone to call her Sonja. That might not be as bad as what's happened to Arch Ballou, the old Meat Man, who hooked up a tube to the exhaust pipe on his panel truck last fall and gassed himself to death. Or to Laura Nunn, who's only fifteen and already has gnarled fingers and a lumpy face and is almost bald. But it's still something.

Rebecca wrinkles her eyebrows.

Propped up next to the trophy are Grampy Newell's first military insignia. Eighty-fifth Battalion. Nova Scotia Highlanders. It occurs to her that, sooner or later, something happens to everybody. It certainly happened to Grampy Newell. He came back from Hill 145 at Vimy Ridge to find his little sister hiding under the bed because she thought he was a German. And then he got fired from his job as manager of the United Fruit Company after twenty-five years because they thought he was an old drunk. And then…

Foul, I to the fountain fly. Wash me, Saviour, or I die.

Rebecca purses her lips.

What she really wants to know is whether, once something's happened to people, they have to stay that way forever. But she doesn't even remember enough about Grampy Newell to know whether he actually acted like a German or an old drunk, never mind whether he had to stay those things. He had a sister named Beatrice, who wore her braids wrapped all the way around her head. She remembers that. And she remembers that the thick black smoke which always billowed across the sky came from his factory. And that he had a big brown birthmark on the outside of his left knee. But none of that tells her anything. She wishes she remembers the part about his cancer. Sometimes she thinks she remembers, but it's just things her Mum's told her, not things she's seen for herself. After all, she was only a little baby, perched on his bloated stomach. She couldn't possibly have seen that he was smiling with pride and suffering "something awful" at the same time.

Rebecca closes her eyes. The insignia begin twinkling on the back of her lids. She can't help wondering when something's going to happen to her, just like it happened to Grammie and Sunny and...

Craaaaack...Boom!

"Heavens!" Grammie leaps up from the piano. "I'd better go get...Oh! Rebecca! You scared me half to death! When did...?"

Boom!

"Oh, come on! Hurry!" She pulls Rebecca out of the armchair and pushes her towards the dining room. "You have to...Sunny! Sunny, get down here!" She flings open the dining room door. "Quick! Under the...Sunny!"

"Yeah? You called?"

Grammie darts over to the stairs, grabs Sunny by the arm and drags her over to the dining room.

"Ow!" laughs Sunny. "Ow! You're hurting me!"

Craaaaack...Boom!

According to Grammie, the only safe place in a thunderstorm is under the dining room table. She's so convinced of this that she won't even let the kids sleep through one. At the first ominous signs from the heavens, she wakes them all up and bustles them downstairs. And then, while the wind howls and the trees cringe and the sky flashes and bangs, she keeps watch over them.

"What's she doing now?" giggles Rebecca, as the rain thrashes the window panes.

Sunny pops her head out and back. "Guess," she smirks.

"Same as usual, I bet." Rebecca's face is contorted with glee.

Boom! Boom!

"God!" Sunny shifts her leg. "I hope it's over soon."

"Not me! I think it's fun!"

"Yes, well, I don't like being so scrunched up."

"Oh. Well, at least we don't have the boarders under here with us. Remember the time she tried to…?"

BOOOOOOOM!

"Boy! That was a big one!"

Rebecca peeks out at Grammie, who's walking around and around the table, with her eyes closed and her hands over her ears. "Yup." She huddles close to Sunny again. "Same as usual."

Fifteen minutes later, it's sunny and calm.

Sunny drifts back upstairs. Grammie goes to check on her chicken. Rebecca finds a spot on the kitchen couch, between the piles of folded sheets and housedresses, and tries to jam her feet into her old pair of puddlers.

"Damn! I knew they wouldn't fit. I guess I'll just have to get wet." She tosses them onto the floor by the back door.

"Where are you going anyway?" Grammie pours a spoonful of sizzling fat over the breasts of the chicken.

"Nowhere in particular." Rebecca hops up from the couch. "Just around. To see if anything got wrecked."

The world is so sparkling and bright, with the sunlight glittering on all the damp tips and edges of things, that at first nothing seems wrecked. But gradually, as she pedals slowly down School Street, the damage becomes apparent. There are several flattened trees, a few crumpled chimneys and a whole yard full of tangled junk.

"Hey, Peter!"

He's pacing back and forth in the ditch across from the old school. "Are you OK?"

He looks up at her with glistening eyes. "*Your mules, also, are unharmed*," he mumbles.

"What?"

She knows it's a line from a Hardy Boys book. He's always quoting those. But she doesn't have a clue what he means by it. She pedals up to him.

"Sorry, Peter. What did you…? Wow!" She peers down into the ditch. "How did *that* get here?"

It's the set of springs from the bed he's been polishing.

"Eh?"

Peter's too distraught to answer.

"Well, never mind." She lets her bike clatter to the ground. "Come on. I'll help you carry it."

No sooner have they lugged the springs back across the road than a swarm of kids on bikes comes flying toward them.

"There she is!"

"Rebecca!"

"You should see Porter's barn!"

"What about it?" she asks mildly, as they skid to a stop.

"It hasn't got a roof anymore!"

"Yeah!"

"It blew right off!"

She and Peter exchange a glance.

"Gee, I hope the animals...Come on, Peter. Let's go see."

He hesitates.

"You can ride with me, on the handlebars."

As they streak down Old Post Road, toward what's left of Porter's barn, Peter sits very tall and still, like an overgrown hood ornament.

"I hope you're right," she whispers into his ear, just before they veer up the path. "You know. About the mules and everything."

50

It's a Thursday afternoon in late September. A soft breeze grazes Rebecca's cheek as she poses in front of the garage at Marion's place. She's wearing a baggy, dusty-green cardigan, with the bottom button done up, and she's doing her best to display the gigantic Musgrave Motors Trophy which Harvey Rawding presented her for winning this year's Junior Championship at the golf club.

"Hurry up, Ben! My arms are falling off!"

"OK, OK. Just one more second and I'll be..."

Ben is standing a few feet down the driveway, trying to focus his brand-new Super-8 Kodak.

"There. I think I've got it. Are you ready?"

Rebecca glares at him. "I've been ready for ages!"

"OK. Now a little more to the left."

Rebecca tilts the trophy. The sunlight glints off the tiny golden golfer at the foot of the tower where Winged Victory is perched. She's been caught at the apex of her swing, before she's had the chance to begin her follow through.

"No, the left, the left."

Rebecca purses her lips.

"*My* left."

"Be-en!"

"OK, great. Now smile."

"You're not going to be able to see the nameplates anyway," she grumbles. "Not from way back there. So I don't see what difference it makes if..."

"Smile!"

For the next few moments, the only sound is the gentle clicking of Ben's movie camera. Rebecca's mind begins to wander through the blur of the last few weeks. First, there was school and then her birthday and now this. The trophy sags a little as she tries to sort things out; tries not to let them end up in a jumble at her feet — like Ben's film usually does when he's trying to work his projector.

So far, Grade Seven at West Kings District High School has been "OK, I guess." It's her standard answer. She hates wearing dresses, of course. And she hates trying to make them. There's never enough time. There are never enough machines. She can never make them go flat in the back, no matter how much Chantal Fougère yells at her about her facings.

"Haw! Haw!"

She glances down at the trophy. Even Winged Victory seems to be laughing at her.

In any case, she's not allowed to keep this gigantic trophy. Harvey told her that right away — that she'd have to give it back to the club in the spring. But she's allowed to keep the little one. It doesn't have a lady wearing wings on it, just a lady frozen at the apex of her tiny, perfect, golden swing. But that's fine with her. Her mind slips back into the blur — which it seems is becoming a jumble after all.

At first, she's back at Rathburn's, that fancy store in Middleton across from the movie theatre, where she has to walk up three steps to get to the dressing rooms. She's not coveting the dresses, of course; she's coveting the kneesocks. They come in packages of two — a navy pair with white squiggles and a scarlet pair with black squiggles — and are just like the ones Pauline Mitchell has. And Pauline's already on the rag! But then, suddenly, Rebecca's not at Rathburn's. She's at Rawding's, waiting for Winifred so they can all catch the bus. And then at school, where Sunny is punching a girl in the mouth in intramural basketball. And Nelson Riddle's brother is thinking seriously about forming a band. And Rebecca is failing her cooking test — for the third day in a row! — because she refuses to put water in the scrambled eggs to make them fluffier.

She tries to blinks away the blur.

Life at West Kings improved during School Spirit Week, when people started signing up for things. She met a plaid skirt, with navy, green and black crossbars, when they both joined the Newspaper Committee, and a deep red corduroy jumper, with a zipper that goes all the way down the front, when she peeked in to see how volleyball practice was coming along. She was going to join the Yearbook Committee, too, and maybe one of the Science Clubs, but she thought she better save enough time for golf.

The screen door creaks.

"Are you two still at it?" Marion comes out to the back veranda. "I thought you'd be through by now."

"It's all Rebecca's fault," chuckles Ben.

"*My* fault! What do you mean, *my* fault? You're the one who can't work the stupid..."

"If she hadn't won that big shiny trophy, we wouldn't be out here in the first place."

"Oh, I see." Marion chuckles too. "That makes sense."

"Does not." Rebecca glances down at the trophy again. The tiny golden plaques look like headstones. She can't help shuddering.

Some of the neatest kids are right in her class. The navy blue woollen jumper with golden chains and buttons looks exactly like a horse. But she's smart, she's a good field hockey player and, best of all, she was born on Coronation Day — and has a silver spoon from the Queen to prove it! The burgundy mini-dress with the paisley scarf has tons of brothers and sisters. She says she wants to be a psychiatrist and her mother is their grade-seven history teacher. The baggy, canary-yellow cardigan is the one who's trying out for the golf team. She's smart, she's nice, she's athletic and she's already going steady — with the son of the greenskeeper, no less. Rebecca used to envy her, but that was before she got her very own dusty-green cardigan, a match for the canary-yellow one.

"How's *your* golf game been lately, Ben?" Marion strolls toward him.

"Not bad, not bad." He peers through the view finder. "As a matter of fact, I only have one problem."

"What's that?"

He looks up at her. "I can't hit the ball with the club."

Marion roars with laughter.

"Be-en!" complains Rebecca. "You're pointing up at the sky!"

"Oh, sorry," he chuckles. "Sorry."

She gazes down at the pearly-white buttons on her cardigan. "How much longer anyway?"

"Not long. I just have to make sure that..."

"Good."

She got the cardigan a few weeks ago, for her twelfth birthday. The tag on the wrapping paper said: "Love, Mum." But it was Marion who'd been with her in the pro shop; Marion who'd watched her finger the dusty-green nubbly material; Marion who'd told her that she'd be lucky to get a swift kick in the rear end for her birthday. As it turned out, she got everything she wanted — a leather wallet, for the peso Ben was bringing back from Mexico after he won the tractor-selling contest; a copy of the fifty-fifth edition of *Official Rules of Card Games*, so she and Sunny wouldn't fight so much over Fish and Crazy Eights; and that *Beverly Hillbillies* colouring book she wanted for three straight years. She's really too old for it now. But she doesn't have to let anyone actually see her colouring and nothing can be as dumb as that book of cut-outs Winifred gave her. She's never understood how anyone can have fun putting flat, paper clothes on flat, paper people, especially when the tabs always rip. She played with that present "for about two seconds," she huffed, when Marion asked what became of it.

Suddenly, the wind swells. Strands of her hair brush across her eyes. The cuffs of her pants caress her ankles. But the skirt on the tiny golden golfer stays absolutely still.

"OK, Marion." Ben turns off the camera. "Your turn."

"Oh, no!" she laughs. "You're not going to take *my* picture!"

"Oh, yes, we are!" Rebecca places her trophy on the hood of Marion's car and then races toward the back steps. "You keep her there, Ben! I'll get her trophy!"

A few minutes later, Marion is standing in front of the garage, holding the Tyro trophy. It's the one presented annually to the best of the thirty-six handicappers — to the "Best of the Worst," as the winner is affectionately called.

"I'm going to get you for this."

"No, you won't!"

"Keep still, Marion."

"All right, look. I'll make you a deal. If you let me go now, I'll make you…"

"What?"

"Well…how about blender shakes?"

"Banana?"

"If you like."

"Great!" Rebecca puts her hand in front of the lens.

"After you get back from CGIT."

Rebecca takes it away again.

Because of choir practice and bingo, Thursday evenings still have the potential for magic and melodrama. Tonight, however, there doesn't seem to be much of anything in the air except Rebecca.

"Son of a whore!" she complains, as she scuffs down the walk from her place to Marion's. "Son of a bloody whoooooore!" She tears at the collar of her blue and white middy.

To her, CGIT is just a bunch of prissy little snots, sitting around, trying to get a Christian education. And she doesn't think she really needs a Christian education. Joan of Arc had a Christian education and look where it got her — although she does concede that being burnt to death is probably yuckier than being bored to death. But the worst thing is the uniform. A sailor blouse that's three sizes too big and a slippery blue tie that needs four tricky little manoeuvres before it looks like anything but a big, fat lump. She wishes she could wear her new cardigan. And she wishes she could have her milkshake. First, Marion made her wait until after CGIT. Then her Mum made her wait until after supper — if you can call grainy white lumps of potato with "margareen" on them *supper*. And now she'll have to wait until after choir practice — maybe even bingo. She hates waiting.

As Rebecca stomps by the Baptist Church, there doesn't seem much hope for this particular Thursday evening. At the front entrance, however, she slows down. She doesn't mean to but there's something about the notes wafting through those open doors which mesmerizes her.

"*Long lay the world in sin and error pi-i-i-ning.*"

The spell is quickly broken.

"Way to go, Thelma," she giggles. "Still the wobbliest voice in the whole choir."

But her laughter is as much out of dread as pleasure. It's the wrong time for Christmas carols. There's something creepy about having to practice them so far ahead.

"*A thrill of hope, the weary world rejoices. For yonder breaks...*"

"OK, everyone."

"*A new and...*"

"People, people!" Dr. Dempsey claps his hands.

"*Glorious...*"

"Thank you, Marion. We know it's your favourite."

Everyone titters.

"Now what we need here..."

Rebecca strains to catch his instructions.

"... is clear, crisp enunciation. *Breaks. Breaks. For yonder breaks.* We don't want to slur the phrase. OK, now. From the top. Three, four..."

"*O holy night, the stars are brightly shining.*"

Rebecca peers up at the sky.

It's not dark enough for stars. And the moon looks like the clipping from Malcolm's big toenail. There isn't much evidence of holiness up there. Down below, however, there's something which comes pretty close.

She gazes at the stained-glass window on the west wall of the building.

An hour ago, the sun would have shone directly at it, obscuring its colours and patterns and symbols. It wouldn't have looked special at all. But now that the sun has dipped below the tree tops and the window is backlit by the gentle glow from the sanctuary, it looks almost hallowed.

"Gee. It's pretty."

So pretty, in fact, that, for a split second, she forgets to wonder what it means.

"*Chains He shall break, for the slave is our brother.*"

For a split second, it seems enough just to gawk at the back of the golden lily, the golden anchor, the golden banner woven around the golden oak tree without feeling the need to get right inside them — inside their glamour and serenity; inside their burning pigments. That golden crown, too. The one with the golden cross sticking out of it. She doesn't care whether it really means the Kingdom of God, like Reverend MacKay says it does, or whether it has more to do with the tiny, golden golfer on her trophy.

But then the air is filled with shrieking...and Dr. Dempsey is asking his sister Constance not to sing during the "fall on your knees" section this year either. The split second is over. Rebecca turns and races toward Marion's place.

Rebecca is standing alone in the gathering gloom.

"*Fall on your knees. O hear the angel...*"

"Angel voices, my ass!" She stomps off into the garage.

When she emerges, she's carrying her sand wedge. She hates her sand wedge. It either makes the ball go two inches...or fifty feet past the pin.

"*Fall on your knees. O hear the angel...*"

"Alright, already! How many times do you have to sing it?" She wades into the sandy soil of the garden, steps up to the first half-rotten tomato she sees and takes a mighty swing.

Thwap!

The tomato explodes. Half its pulp flies upwards into her face.

"Yuck!" She wipes her mouth with the sleeve of her middy. And then steps up to another squishy tomato.

The voices have subsided, she thinks. They must have finally got it right.

Thwap!

The tomato splatters against the side of the garage.

"What a sand save, ladies and gentlemen! Never in my life have I witnessed such skill, such nerve, such...Hey!" She peers down at the sandy soil.

Lying amongst the dying vines and vegetables is a tiny, dark brown sphere.

"My Superball!" She bends down to pick it up. "I was wondering where it went."

Superballs are the latest rage — as popular now as hula hoops were in 1958. They're a little bigger than a golf ball and made of highly compressed rubber, which causes them to bounce wildly and high. She got hers about a month ago, after her bicycle accident.

"*Long lay the world…*"

"God! Not that part again!" She brushes the sand off the ball.

"*In sin and error…*"

She places the ball on a little mound and then lines up her feet so they're pointing slightly left of Craig Patterson's back door.

"*In sin and error…*"

The choir is like a needle, stuck on a deep scratch.

Whoosh, whoosh.

She takes two practice swings and then steps up and addresses the ball.

"*In sin and error…*"

Whump!

The Superball soars into the sky.

"Wow! Look at it go!" she marvels. "I've never seen it go so…Oh-oh." She scrunches up her face.

It's heading straight for the stained-glass window on the west side of the church.

"I think I've had the biscuit."

"*Till He appeared and the soul felt its…*"

CRACK!

The enunciation is perfectly crisp and clear. The ball breaks right through the golden anchor.

"Jesus. I have had the biscuit."

As Rebecca bounds up the back steps and into the house, there's a tumult of squealing and shouting.

"And then what?" groans Rebecca. "What the hell happened after that? I always get this far and then…Forget it!" She clumps straight down the stairs to the front veranda.

As far as she's concerned, she's no longer resisting. She's completely at the mercy of her memories. But that's the problem. They're her memories. They can't possibly tell her things she doesn't already know. And only if she wants to know them.

She flops down on the swinging chesterfield.

She wishes she'd been there to see their faces when that crazy Superball bounced all over the...

Suddenly, she sits up again.

She did go to the church that night. Afterwards. To see if she could find her ball. But what she found instead was...? What did she find? What did she see? What?

She squeezes her eyes shut.

At first, she just sees a strange little pile of broken glass. But then she sees Marion sweeping. Marion talking to Frankie. Marion following Frankie up to the...

"Come. Where? Come. Yes."

"Dammit!" She glances at the datebook which has fallen beside her. "It's not in there," she hisses. "It's in here!" She smacks herself on the head.

If only she could see what made Marion stop sweeping. If only she could see where Marion and Frankie went after she stopped sweeping. She thinks she knows. She thinks she's seen it...once.

She closes her eyes again.

It's hard being Nancy Drew now; hard slipping through that little pile of glass into someone else's past; hard making yourself come out of hiding. Not in the sanctuary, but at the top of the stairs...where she once got an eerie feeling that none of them were alone and so raced outside and...

Her eyes pop open.

And ran smack into Barry Connors!

Barry always stayed out late, but she'd never seen him hanging around the church before. He said he was waiting for someone. He told her to beat it. And then they both looked up, thinking they heard laughter.

"Oh, God!"

Rebecca stares through the screen into the darkness.

It isn't what she wants — wandering through the ruins, picking up bits of other people's agony. Shards of their bewilderment. Cut-glass reminders of their defeat. But at least she's found something to push her through the little pile of broken glass. At least she's found the laughter. Crazy. Filled with sorrow. All there is.

She opens Marion's datebook to that fateful Thursday in September. CHOIR PRACTICE. In big, bold letters. Bingo? With the question mark a little darker than the rest. And...She scans the page, looking for a tiny black squiggle.

"*His sea washes through my sands*," she reads aloud. And then she stares through the screen again. It's a mild, still, almost voluptuous night. She can't hear a thing, except the gentle croaking of the frogs on Spinney's Bog.

51

It's a Saturday afternoon in late October. According to Rebecca's transistor radio, President Johnson is busy having his gall bladder out, dropping stuffed animals and school supplies on North Vietnam, claiming to be using non-poisonous gas, and turning a blind eye to the Quakers immolating themselves in front of the White House. Vivian and Harold, meanwhile, are lounging in their glassed-in sun porch, watching the world go by. Rebecca is in there, too, squatting in the corner by the bookcase, sifting through a jumble of paperbacks and toys. A little while ago, it was a family gathering, with the six kids sprawled on the red wooden floorboards, reading Spiderman comics and making rude comments about everyone who passed. But then Darrell and Donnie, who are only visiting, went outside to sit on the little hill overlooking the sidewalk, and Sunny and Randy went to swing on a rope over the brook at the back of the house, and Peter decided it was time to practice walking on his stilts again. That left Vivian and Harold, who don't have enough money to go on a binge this weekend, and Rebecca, who's been grounded for a few weeks now.

"Weeeeeee!"

"Yeaaaaah!"

At the squeals of glee coming from the brook at the back of the house, Vivian begins to tell Rebecca about the time her brother Clifford jumped from the branch of a willow tree near the bank. The water was only a foot deep in that part of the brook and he got his head stuck in the mud.

"Damned near broke his neck," Vivian murmurs.

"Yeah, well..." Rebecca fires a dog-eared *Peyton Place* into the bookcase. "Probably served him right." She's heard the story a million times.

"Hey!" Harold reaches down and pulls a brand-new Bible out of the jumble on the floor. "Where did this come from?"

Vivian chuckles. "From those two nice Mormon boys who came by last week. Ha! They marked three passages for me and said they'd be back to..."

Harold cracks open the book and begins to recite. *"And the slain of the Lord shall be at that day from one end of the earth even unto the other end of the earth: they shall not be lamented, neither gathered, nor buried, they shall be dung upon the ground."* "Ha!" He slams the book shut. "Cheerful stuff."

Rebecca whoops.

Vivian looks solemn. "I don't think that's one of the passages they wanted to discuss. I think..."

"It might as well be. Here. Catch." He tosses the book toward Rebecca.

"No way!" She pulls her hands away. "I don't want it!"

It lands with a thud on top of the pile.

"Good girl," laughs Harold. "Now let's see if we can find something more suitable for tender ears."

"What about this?" Rebecca hands him a picture-book with the cover torn off.

"Did the Mormons leave this one, too?" he teases.

"Nooooo! I got it when I was born! From Marion, I think."

It's a book for infants called *Baby Animals*. According to her Baby Book, she was "turning its pages with interest" by eight months.

Harold gingerly looks inside. *"Baby Racoon washes his apple. He never eats anything until he has washed it first. He even washes a fish."*

They all laugh.

"I like books about animals a lot," announces Rebecca, as she shuffles through the pile again. "Like Beatrix Potter and Thornton

Burgess." She holds up *The Adventures of Mr. Mocker*, one of his Bedtime Stories. She used to have the adventures of Grandfather Frog and Bobby Coon, too, but Peter hid them. "But what I really like are books about families that have happy endings. And TV shows, too. Like *The Andy Griffith Show* and *Leave It to Beaver*, where everybody is nice and everything always…"

"I didn't know you liked reading at all," interrupts Harold. "You never touch those books Ben's sister Colleen sends you from Ottawa."

"Yeah, well…" She still thinks it'd be way neater to eat lunch with Colleen in the middle of Sparks Street than to read a book about the Great Plains.

Harold's eyes twinkle. "But I suppose it's better than some of the other things you like doing, like breaking windows."

Rebecca looks down at the pile. "I suppose."

She's never really *hated* reading. In fact, she's always been pretty good at it. It's just that reading is boring compared to playing outside, where the best junk always happens. Even breaking the church window was a neat thing to do. It's going to be a costly one, too, after the replacement pieces arrive, but for now there's a sheet of newspaper taped over the hole. One side of it has an editorial claiming that President Kennedy would have pulled out of Vietnam after the 1964 election. The other side has an article warning of the imminent Chinese crackdown on tight trousers, jazz records, religious objects, mahjong sets, antiques, pets, girl babies and the playing of Chopin.

"Ha!" interjects Vivian. "You just be glad you're *allowed* to read. If I had my way, you'd be…Oh!" She peers through the smudgy pane of glass facing the driveway.

"What's the matter, Mum?" asks Rebecca. "Has he fallen again?"

"Yes," sighs Vivian, as she watches Peter struggle back onto his stilts. "But he doesn't seem to have hurt himself."

"Never does," crows Harold. "Not once in seven years. Now come on, Rebecca. Enough of baby racoons. Tell us what you're reading these days."

"Well, two books, actually." She holds up a thin red one and a thin pink one. "*100 Pounds of Popcorn* and *Emily's Runaway Imagination*."

"Hmmm." Harold looks from the exploding pots of popcorn on one cover to the girl in the flashy pink convertible on the other. "Are they any good?"

"Yeah! Real good. The best books I ever got out of the church library."

"Which doesn't say much."

"I know but...Well, I like them anyway."

"Don't tell me," laughs Harold. "Because they're about nice, thoughtful, ordinary people who do funny, exciting things together and love each other with all their hearts."

"Are you making fun of me?"

"No, not fun, exactly. It's just that things don't always turn out that way; happily ever after, I mean."

"I know that."

"And books don't often show the real..."

"OK, but this one..." She holds up *Emily's Runaway Imagination* again. "Is *fairly* real. I mean, the town in it looks a lot like Aylesford. There's large, white wooden houses and fields where they have bulls and johnny-jump-ups. And there's a large, white wooden church where they sit at long tables and have pot-luck suppers. And there's a Masonic Hall and a warehouse and a drugstore and a post office and..."

"OK, OK!" laughs Harold. "We get the point!"

"And the girl's a lot like me, too. She wears brown oxfords and makes Valentines and likes riding in cars and tractors and hates to be teased. And there's a grandmother who's a good seamstress and always smells like violets. And another woman — Oh, I couldn't believe it when I read it! — who plays bridge and sings 'I'm Forever Blowing Bubbles.' Just like Marion! There's an old Chinese man, too, that nobody seems to like. But the mother, when she's cooking one of her chickens, says that people should accept those who are different, that there's lots of sameness in them."

Vivian and Harold exchange a glance.

"I understood that a lot better than some of the other things she said, like *fortune means different things to different people* and *this world's goods are never evenly divided*. I thought those were a little..."

Suddenly, there's a loud clanging and then an impressive cloud of dust.

Rebecca leaps to her feet. "The fire truck! Wow! Look at it go!"

In a matter of seconds, the kids are chasing it down the street — Darrell and Donnie in Darrell's latest crate, Sunny and Randy on Randy's bike, and Peter, for a few feet at least, on his stilts.

Rebecca swivels around. "Can I go? Please! I promise to be good for ever and ever if you just let me…"

"No." Vivian reaches for her cigarettes.

Rebecca glares at her. "OK, but what about Halloween? Will I get to go out for Halloween?"

"We'll see. After all, I'm the *matahark* around here."

Harold's eyes wander next door. "Look, you two! There's Head and Shoulders!"

Rebecca scrambles across the porch.

The lady who shares the Dempsey house with John and Gloria is staring out her side door window. Vivian says her name is Charlotte Schofield and that she and her skinny little husband and the two, fat, curly-haired sissies they have for sons have moved here from Hantsport. They've never even seen her whole body, since the side door is solid all the way up to the window and she never leaves the house.

"Yoohoo! Head and Shoulders!" Vivian slips a cigarette out of the pack. "Are you having a nice…?"

"Shshsh, Vivian. She'll hear you."

"Not through the glass, she won't. And besides, I don't really care. She gives me the creeps. Ha! You should've seen her last May. You know, when the floats went by on their way to Kentville? Everyone else went right out to the sidewalk to see them." She pauses to light her cigarette. "But old Head and Shoulders just…aaach…stood there, with her…aaaaach."

"You shouldn't smoke, Vivian. Not when your asthma's been acting up."

"The doctor told me…aaach…that it was OK as long as I didn't…aaach…inhale."

Rebecca rolls her eyes.

Harold tries again. "Yes, well, it doesn't sound all right to me and if you don't watch it, you'll end up in hospital again."

Vivian takes another drag. "So?"

Over the years, she's been to Berwick Hospital quite a few times — for babies and broken bones and kidney stones and one or two bad asthma attacks and that operation to remove her uterus which she insists the doctor called "The Wreck of the Hesperus." But all that was nothing compared to how she started out. A seven-month *preemie*, she's told anyone who'll listen. Born blue, without fingernails. Wrapped in a blanket and placed in the warming oven of Grammie's big black wood-stove. So it's not Vivian who goes deathly pale at the thought of hospitals. It's Harold.

"Ha! Remember when Darrell was born? Remember when you crept into the room? 'Is that him?' you said. 'Is that him?' And I said, 'Well, what do you think?' Ha! He was the only baby in the room! The only baby in the...aaach, aaach." She stuffs her cigarette into the ashtray. "And now look how he's turned out. Look how they've all turned out."

"Oh, brother," mutters Rebecca, as she opens her book to the page where Emily is scraping the burnt parts off her toast.

"One of them's a murderer."

"Oh, now wait a minute, Vivian. I think that's going a little too..."

"Ha! Then what do you call a person who takes his rifle one night and...just because he feels like it...shoots a poor, helpless little dog?"

Vivian waits for Harold to answer, but he doesn't. He just stares straight ahead, through the bug-spattered glass.

"And one of them's a thief."

This time, Harold doesn't object. It was Donnie who broke into Hal Jackson's Fina station all right.

"And one of them's a retard. And a whore. And a bugger. And..." She pauses for a moment, unsure of what to call a little girl who breaks stained-glass windows. "And one of them still wets her bed."

"Not any more!" protests Rebecca.

"Vivian! That's enough!"

"But it's true! Can't you see it's...?"

"Of course, it's true. But you can't blame the kids. How did you expect them to turn out, with a couple of drunks for parents?"

"Yes, well..." Vivian pats her pin curls.

"You have to admit we were always carrying on, scrounging for money, letting the kids run wild."

Rebecca stares down at the page where Emily is eating baked beans and brown bread at the town's Hard Times Party.

"Yes, well...I still think I wouldn't have had so many worries if I hadn't had so many kids."

"And I still think it would've been better if we'd paid more attention to them, disciplined them, made them do chores or something. You know, I've never seen them wash a dish or fill the woodbox or...God damn it! The stew! I forgot about the stew!" Harold stumbles into the house.

Rebecca looks up at Vivian. "Don't tell me," she grimaces. "Cabbage, right?"

"Right. And about eight quarts of it, judging by the pot he's using."

"Of course, it's the only thing he can make, really. Except for breakfast. And it won't last long." Vivian snaps open the *Berwick Register*. "Not if Peter gets to it first."

Rebecca glances at the pile of newspapers and magazines on the floor of the sun porch.

The ones on top are copies of *National Enquirer* that Gloria Dempsey brought over. Vivian said she was going to browse through them this afternoon, but she was scared away by the picture of the two-headed baby on the first one. She says she can stand the claims that The Beatles are Martians, that Bing Crosby beats his kids with a seven-iron, that a West Coast gymnast has just discovered a foolproof method of dissolving gallstones in one day. But she draws the line at two-headed babies.

"Here." Harold hands them each a bowl of cabbage stew. "I thought you might like to have it out here."

"Great." Rebecca clunks her bowl on the floor.

"Thanks." Vivian lays the *Berwick Register* across her lap, then places her bowl on top.

"Well...?" Harold flops down beside Vivian. "Anything new in the world?"

"No, not much." She peeks beneath the rim of the bowl. "On October 13, Helen Ogilvie and Phyllis Lutz were supper guests of Dorothy Ogilvie of Morden."

Harold blows on his spoonful of stew.

"And on October 17." She tilts the bowl a little. "Marlene and Gerald Wolsley of Berwick, and Nancy and Rae Hagerty of Auburn were visitors of Maida and Frank Reynolds of Aylesford East."

"Hmmm. Some exciting."

"Yes, well, they were probably over to Maida's to discuss Nancy's *mongolian* baby."

"Her what?" splutters Harold.

"Her *mongolian* baby. You know, the ones with the big heads."

"Oh, those!" chuckles Harold, as he wipes his chin.

"And at least..." She lowers her voice. "At least there's nothing in here about Marion and that coon friend of hers. Honestly, I don't know what gets into her sometimes."

"Mu-um!" Rebecca nearly chokes on her stew.

"Well, maybe it's just like you," muses Harold.

"What do you mean?" asks Vivian indignantly.

"Well, people don't know what gets into you sometimes either; having Wanda Willoughby for a friend. You said yourself they're always asking you how you can get along with someone who bounces her ass around the room, picking fights with...!" He points his spoon across the street. "Speak of the devil!"

Wanda is pulling her big, blue Bonneville into her driveway.

Vivian knits her brow. "It's not the same thing, you know. Wanda may be hard but at least her skin's in the right place. I mean..."

"Whoa! Look out, Wanda! Or you'll tip over!"

"Harold!" Vivian takes a swipe at him.

"I can't help it, Vivian." He watches Wanda teeter out of the car. "They're huge. Absolutely..."

"Oh!" Vivian clasps her hands to her mouth.

"What? What is it? Oh, my gawd!"

Rebecca scrambles to her feet.

The big, blue Bonneville has been left in neutral. Before Wanda is completely clear of it, it slides forward, dragging her along the gravel and smashing headlong into the garage door.

"Eeee! Eeee!" wheezes Vivian. "Serves her right, the old...aaach, aaach...whooooore!"

"Come on, Dad! Let's go see!" Rebecca leaps over the pile of *National Enquirer* and out the door.

52

Whenever Halloween falls on a Sunday, as it does in 1965, it's bumped back to Saturday. Rebecca doesn't understand this. She thinks women who turn into pillars of salt and men who show up at banquets after they've been crucified have quite a bit to do with ghosts and goblins. In any case, late Saturday afternoon, barely fifteen minutes after she gets permission to go out that day, Rebecca and Alan put a firecracker under the front steps of Stuart Hiltz's barbershop. Marion, who's next door at Marilyn Addy's, trying to decide between a fluff and a feathercut, leaps to her feet when she hears the bang. Stuart, unfortunately, stabs Emerson Hill in the back of the neck with his scissors. For a while, there's quite a commotion, with everyone there either doubled over with laughter or madder than a wet hen. But then Marion diffuses the situation by promising that, although no one actually saw who did it, she'll take the prime suspects out to eat at the White Spot restaurant in New Minas that night — away from further temptation; from the eerie appeal of devilry and disguise.

Later, as they coast down Old Post Road in Marion's car, Rebecca can't help noticing the hoods hanging around the pool hall. She wonders what they'll be getting up to tonight. Stevie Cleveland and Ricky MacNair are still Junior Hoods, who haven't yet made the transition from naughty to evil and mean. They'll probably just steal UNICEF boxes from the younger kids or break into the Baptist Church and tear up the hymn-books. But Barry Connors, whom Marion saved from a stint in County Jail after he burnt down Ruthie Sutherland's barn, is another story. There aren't many transitions left for Barry to make. He and Drew Saunders are already the greasiest, scariest people in town — a perfect match for the evening's undercurrents of menace and monstrosity.

As they pull away from the intersection, Rebecca sees Barry spit in their direction. She's not sure whether he's showing his contempt for them or for the blue and white police car from the Kingston RCMP which is passing by in the other direction. But she can't believe it would be for them — not after Marion went to the Kings County Courthouse and gave him a character reference and paid his fine.

"Ugh," groans Marion, as they make their way through the darkness back to Aylesford. "I'm so stuffed I can hardly breathe."

Alan rubs his stomach. "Me, too."

"Not me!" blurts Rebecca. "I could eat another whole lobster!"

"Ha! And another slice of banana cream pie, I bet." Marion swings the car around a bend. "Why am I not surprised?"

"Yeah, well, we don't go there very often, so I like to eat as much as I can."

Marion laughs.

Alan keeps rubbing his stomach. "I think I might be allergic to scallops," he whimpers.

"Or lime Jell-O," snickers Rebecca. She still can't believe that's all he wanted for dessert.

"Never mind, Alan. We'll be home soon. And then you can...Ha! All quiet at the pool hall, I see." Marion peers up through the windshield. "And no sign of smoke or flames. It must have been a calm night, after all."

Rebecca leans forward, too. "Looks like it."

"Of course, the trouble-makers..." Marion glances sideways at her. "...were busy doing something else, weren't they?"

"I guess."

"OK, Alan," announces Marion, as they turn left into his driveway. "Here we are."

"Thank you, Marion." He forces open the door. "I had a wonderful time. It was very nice of you to include me."

"You're welcome, Alan." She laughs at his well-mannered groaning. "We'll have to do it again some time."

"Yeah!" blurts Rebecca. "It's way classier than Caroline's! With lots more choices! And maybe next time we can stay at the motel!"

"Can you walk?" calls Marion, as she watches Alan mince toward the house.

"I think so," he moans.

"Ha! I might as well get out here, too," splutters Rebecca. She slides across the seat and out the door.

"Are you sure?"

"Yeah." She presses the door shut. "It's just across the road."

"OK. See you in church, then."

Rebecca leans through the window and beams. "Unless I get allergic to something before then."

For the next few moments, the air tingles with laughter. It's not just their laughter, but the laughter of the evening — of its terrors and pranks and allusions. It's still there as Rebecca skips across the road; still there as Marion waits to see a tiny glow coming from inside Rebecca's house; still there as Rebecca waves for Marion to come and pick her up again. By the time the car has eased along the pavement to Thelma Peel's house, however, the laughter's begun to wobble. And by the time they reach the Baptist Church, it's died out completely. There's hardly any sound, then — at least no prickly traces of mockery or merriment or nervous apprehension — as they pull into Marion's driveway.

As the car bounces gently along the gravel, their eyes widen. The headlights have picked up something dangling over the driveway. As they coast nearer, they keep their eyes fixed on two tiny, round, metallic glows which somehow seem to be pulling a prank on them — one last trick before turning into slits and darting away. But the tiny round glows don't move. Marion and Rebecca look up through the windshield.

Hanging by its tail, from a limb of the Bishop Pippin apple tree, is a disembowelled black cat.

Rebecca stares at the page. WHITE SPOT RESTAURANT. It's the last fun she ever had.

She never got a close look at that poor black cat. Ben and Marion took it down and buried it before daylight. But she got a close look at Frankie's body. She saw it lying on the ground near the front door of the church, all twisted up and covered in blood.

"We warned you about him, Marion."

"Yes."

"We told you time and time again that he was no good."

"Yes."

"We only hope that now we can all put this…unpleasant business…behind us and move onto…"

Rebecca closes the datebook. And feels like she's felt for twenty-six years now — ever since her mind went quiet and dark.

"Come on, now. You can't sit in here all day."

"Why not?"

"Because it's not healthy."

"So?"

"So it would be better if you went out and saw people."

"What for? People are no good."

She stopped taking piano lessons, quit the golf team, told Alan and Brenda and Eric that their stupid Yippy-Yappy Talking Club was for retards. It was as if she were frozen in time; caught at some horrible moment of insight between dead calm and delirium.

"Look! If you won't tell me what's bothering you, maybe you'll tell…Why don't we give Marion a call and see if she'll…?"

"Nooooo!"

"OK, but I thought you…"

"Marion's a liar! A coward! A big, fat hypocrite! I hope she never stops puking!"

Rebecca runs her hand over the cover of the datebook.

Her mind is still dark, but it's not very quiet. Her hydra is hissing more loudly than ever.

"I don't think I can do this," she whispers.

And yet somehow she realizes that the hissing will be less scary if she sees which head it's coming from. As lightly as she can, as if it's important not to disturb the memories too much, she opens the datebook to Sunday, November 7, 1965.

The box is blank.

Frankie's body caused quite a stir that day. It wasn't usually what greeted people when they arrived for Sunday services. And no one was more surprised than Rebecca. The first rumour which rippled up and down the pews was that he'd been murdered. Barry and Drew even bragged that they did it. The next was that he'd been hit by a car. Barry and Drew bragged about that, too, only neither of them had a car that worked. When there wasn't enough evidence to support either of these theories, they decided he'd fallen trying to break into the church. Through the bell tower. To steal the offering boxes. The deacons decided, that is — "being what he was, after all" — and everyone went along with them.

"Marion! Didn't you tell them?"

"Yes, but they didn't listen."

"Then you have to make them listen!"

"There's nothing I can do."

"Yes, there is! You can tell them again! I'll tell them! I'll march right over there and…!"

Rebecca's eyes bore through the page.

"He didn't do it, Mr. Collins. He couldn't have. Frankie was the nicest, kindest, most…You just ask Marion. She'll tell you."

"I don't know what she's talking about."

She thinks if she bores deep enough, she'll get to the other side of that terrible blank.

"Yes, you do, Marion. And besides, you were there."

"Don't be silly."

"But I saw you. I saw her, Mr. Collins. And I talked to her. And she told me the hoods...well...that they killed him."

"Honestly, Ray, I don't know what she's talking about."

"So they probably took those stupid offering boxes, too."

"Don't be silly."

"Stop saying that! I'm not silly! I'm telling the truth!"

"Sorry about this, Ray. She's always been a bit...inventive...but this is..."

"Were you there, Marion?"

"No, of course not. She's just...You know how kids are."

"Yes. Especially the Petersons."

"But she was there! I saw her! I saw her! I saw herrrrrrr!"

The next day, Rebecca was sent to Dr. Dempsey for a checkup. The deacons said it probably wasn't anything serious. In fact, they put it down to her Runaway Imagination — "being what she was, after all" — and no one disagreed. The day after that, she spent a long time hanging over the edge of the top bunk, staring down at the pile of records on the floor. Bill Hailey and the Comets. Diana Ross and the Supremes. The Beach Boys. The Temptations. The Grateful Dead. Finally, she leapt down to the floor, scooped up as many of them as she could and stumbled over to the window overlooking the driveway. She could have just pried it open and pitched the whole armload to the gravel below. Instead, she threw them, one by one, like flying saucers, against the red-shingled roof of the barn. Most of them exploded, just like the Ranger when it crashed into the Sea of Tranquillity, but one of them — "Little Brave Sambo," she thinks — floated serenely toward the roof, hovered for a moment over the rusty-red shingles, as if it were the Mariner, hovering over the lifeless, crater-pocked surface of Mars, and then disappeared on the other side.

She got through all the little yellow records — and all the black ones with little holes, too. She was just starting on the black ones with big holes, however, when her Mum came in and caught her.

"Look! I'm asking you for the last time! What is the matter with you?"

"Nothing."

"Nothing! Then perhaps you can tell me why you did this."

"No reason."

"Ha! I'd like to see you explain that to your sister. She's going to be heart-broken."

"So? What do *I* care?"

"Why you little...Jesus! I don't know what's got into you."

They sent her to Dr. Dempsey again. But it was too late. Something had got into her — something she'd seen; something so tender and terrible that she pretended she hadn't seen it. And then blotted it out altogether. Dr. Dempsey, who'd sent for some books from the Victoria General in Halifax, suggested that she was suffering from the pre-teen jitters — the double pull of awareness and repression; of her period and her desire to stay a child forever. He said not to worry; that it was only a matter of time before she grew out of it.

She hasn't grown out of it yet.

"God!" She stares into the blank again. "There must be something I'm missing."

For a moment, she thinks she sees Frankie in there. With a gash near his eye. And Marion, too. With her tiny, silk, apple-blossom handkerchief dabbing at his...But then they're gone and she's left with a mound of gooey red rags.

It's Sunday morning again.

Frankie's body caused quite a stir that day, but not enough to cancel the service — since, of course, it was only Frankie. In fact, they all seemed more concerned about the black and white sign which used to stand on the manicured lawn, before Frankie landed right on it and ruined it. They couldn't believe their eyes. And now Rebecca can't believe her ears. The choir is wobbling through its latest rendition of "Healer of Broken Hearts" and Marion is doing the solo.

"How sweet the Name of Jesus sounds in a believer's ear. It soothes his sorrows, heals his wounds and drives away his fear."

Rebecca's shocked by how well Marion does it — especially for someone who should be puking her guts out instead of singing.

"How could she?" Rebecca whispers into the blank.

But all she hears is a flat and lifeless refrain. *"There's nothing I can do. There's nothing I can do. There's…"*

Suddenly, there's a face to go with the words. It's a pale face; a face with the gaiety drained out of it. Rebecca didn't see Marion very often after that. But every time she did, Marion had that same face. It was in the window of Irene's car as they drifted by on their way to the doctor's. That was right after it happened and Rebecca thought it served Marion right if she were sick, since she was such a liar. And then it was on the podium for the annual meeting of the Kings West Liberal Association, behind the counter for the annual pot-luck supper at the Baptist Church, at the head table for meetings of the Cancer Society, the Red Cross Society, the Children's Aid Society.

"God! She was busier than ever! Bridge, choir, those countless meetings. How could she do it? How in hell could she…?"

Suddenly, Rebecca sees that face again. Sees it in the window of the back chamber when they turn Frankie's cabin into a storage shed; when they cut a hole in one side and call it a dog house; when they cut an even bigger hole and drive a ski-doo inside; when they tear it down altogether and the grass grows over the spot so fast that you'd never even know something had been there. And then she sees her own face, in that year's school picture. A whole sheet of wallet-sized faces. Just as pale as Marion's, with the same gaiety drained out of them.

And then suddenly, Rebecca shudders.

It isn't Sunday morning anymore. It's Saturday night. There's a crash and a blood-curdling scream…and another face. It's Frankie's face and it's resting against the bare, wet ground. And Marion is bending over it to…

"Oh, my God!"

His eyes are my sky. He fills my sands with his sea. I cannot die this way every night.

"It was Frankie!"

Rebecca snatches 1965 from the swinging chesterfield and rushes upstairs to the back chamber. When she gets there, she dumps the box of keepsakes onto the floor and begins to thrash through the other datebooks.

"There's one. And another. And…yes!"

The tiny black squiggles start in 1958, just after Princess Margaret went by on the train, and end...She flips back and forth through 1965 again...on Saturday, November 6.

"It was Frankie she loved!"

Rebecca closes her eyes.

She isn't going to be as lucky as Nancy Drew. She isn't going to get that one, big moment of truth when the relationships become clear and the perpetrators of evil are exposed. In fact, there *are* no perpetrators of evil, unless perhaps fear and ignorance and cowardice can be called that. There are only Frankie and Marion. And the love they shared. And the love they were forced to keep hidden.

"It was Frankie. Jesus. It was Frankie. How could I be so stupid?"

She remembers the times she saw them together — at the ball park, on the beach, in the woods. Now that she's older, she can see there was always something sad about those times — as if the hope never really had a chance against the havoc. And she can hear Grammie's boarder Mrs. Neufeld saying that coons were lazy; that their pricks were bigger than cucumbers; that if she ever caught one even *looking* at her daughter, she'd rip his guts out. And she can hear the snowballs beating against Frankie's cabin and see the scratches on Marion's car. And she can even see...

"Oh, my God!"

She and the past take each other's hands. Together, they duck behind a pew in the church.

Marion thinks she's alone in the sanctuary. She's stopped her sweeping to gaze at the stars shining through the hole in the anchor.

"What happened in here?"

Marion turns and squints through the darkness. "Frankie?"

"Yes."

He's leaning in the doorway to the vestry.

"It was funny, really. The ball came right through there." She points with the broom to the stained-glass window over the organ. "And then hit the floor behind the pulpit." She uses the broom as a pointer again. "And then bounced over...Oh, I don't know." She twirls around. "It was bouncing crazily, all over the place, and everyone was ducking and screaming and..." She stops twirling. "What?"

"You look pretty tonight," he says softly.

There's a heartbeat of silence.

"No, I don't." Marion begins to sweep up the shards of golden glass. There's a gentle tinkling, as he drifts towards her down the aisle.

"I have a pretty good idea who did this, you know. And when I get my hands on the little bugger, she'll wish she'd..."

He clasps the broom.

"Oh, Jesus," Marion whispers. "I don't know whether I can do this. I..." She brushes the hair from her face. There's a little, yellow plastic ring on one of her fingers.

From the Cracker Jack box, Rebecca's about to say, before the past puts a hand over her mouth.

"Come." Without taking his eyes off Marion, Frankie reaches out and lays the broom on top of the organ.

At last, she looks at him. "Where?" she whispers.

Their eyes can see the edge of gladness. It isn't very far away. But they can also see the brink of doom, standing even closer, wearing the guise of the edge of gladness, daring them to leap over its rocky cliff into the sublime and terrible waves.

"Come." He leads her toward the anteroom. They leave behind a little pile of broken glass.

On their way by the choir racks, Frankie lifts two black and white gowns off their metal hangers. Then he leads her up the stairs and into the bell tower.

Rebecca stares at the past.

"*Come. Where? Come. Yes.*"

"Now?"

Rebecca lets the past take her hand again. Together, they creep up to the very top of the...At last, they're sharing a pair of eyes as well as ears.

There's no trembling, no wild urgency, as Marion and Frankie begin to undress each other. It's almost as if the waves have sucked themselves out to sea.

"OK?" he whispers, as he spreads out one of the black and white gowns.

"Yes."

They sink to the floor.

Overhead, the steeple has turned into a lighthouse — to warn them of their uncharted ocean's might, complexity and utter contempt for safe havens.

"Oh, God."

Riding a great crescendo of inescapability, the waves come crashing toward them. They're frightened at first by the power, the passion, the promise of obliteration. They don't know whether to loosen their grip on the slippery rocks of their self-possession or not. But then the waves promise to swamp their doubts, their denials, their lingering disgust. They leap over the cliff into the sea.

As soon as they hit the water, they disappear. There's no more time, no more sorrow, no more traces of cunning or conscience. There's only the current racing through the cave.

Unfortunately, their sea always gives up its dead. A few minutes later, they begin to materialize.

"Cold?"

Frankie stares up through the cracks in the steeple. "A little."

She draws the other black and white gown around them. "What are you looking at?"

"The stars."

"Where?"

He points upward.

It's not a gleaming benediction — only one or two jewels, twinkling between the boards. But suddenly, she's afraid they'll become flares, showing the whole world where they are.

"Oh God, Frankie! What if someone comes in?"

He laughs. *"Here's the church. Here's the steeple. Open the doors*...there's both the people."

"Don't!" She punches at him. "It's not funny."

"Isn't it?" He wraps his arms around her.

"No."

Those arms are usually their salvation; the place where their sorrows are healed. But tonight she's too practical for that.

"Don't!" She wriggles out of his grasp. "Don't hold me."

"Why not?" He looks down at her with those grieving, adoring eyes.

"And don't look at me like that."

"Like what?"

She punches him again. "You know what I mean."

"But I love you!"

"Well, I don't want you to love me." She turns away from him.

"Oh, God! Not this again."

But it is this. It's always this. This exhilarating melody and then this bittersweet dissonance. Over and over, as if consciousness is their one true enemy.

He looks up at the stars again. "So what do you think they'd do if they caught us? Skin me alive? String me up by the balls?"

She turns and makes him look down at her. In each other's eyes, they can see their infinity. And their infinite infirmity. "Yes," she answers softly.

The giant green frog on the weather vane starts spinning, madly, around and around…as if it hears something, as if it sees something, as if it…

The present grabs Rebecca's hand and yanks her down the stairs.

"What are you doing here, Barry?"

"Nothing, you little twerp. Now, beat it, or I'll…"

"What? I'm not afraid of you."

"Well, you should be. And so should…"

Rebecca opens her eyes — so she doesn't have to see Barry squint toward the bell tower.

"Jesus."

So there were reasons why Marion and Frankie kept their love a secret. She can see that. She can even see why Marion threw herself into those countless meetings and projects. So no one could tell how much she'd lost. So she might not be able to tell it herself. But it doesn't explain why she let them think such terrible things about him.

"Marion! You have to tell them!"

"I tried to tell them."

"No, you didn't! I heard you! You just said yes, yes. Every time they said anything, you just…"

"There's nothing I can do."

She closes her eyes again.

Marion's pale face is darting from brightness to brightness, trying its hardest to be everywhere.

"Oh, my God!" she rasps.

All those years she tried to live without him; without the comfort that blurting out the truth about them might have given her. But she couldn't escape the consequences of her silence — the sorrow, the guilt, the self-loathing. She hated herself even more than Rebecca did. There was something she couldn't undo. There was something unbearable that wouldn't go away. There was that telephone pole across from the peat plant.

I cannot die this way every night.

It wasn't suicide, since not wanting to live is different than not being able to live. It was an inevitable accident.

As soon as Rebecca solves the mystery of Marion's death, she spots her own pale face, hiding in the darkness, trying its hardest to be nowhere. But Marion won't let it. She left her the datebooks, after all — not just because her old pal Dick Tracy is the only one who can decipher those maddening squiggles and blanks, but because the unbearable moment wasn't Eliot Ness's alone. It was Dick's, too. And only *she* can make it go away.

Her eyes pop open.

"You have to."

"But first I have to remember!" she cries, as she reaches for 1965 again. "What the hell were they doing that night?"

She turns back a few days to Sunday, October 31. DEACON'S MEETING. The words had been written with such fury that they'd torn the page.

"Why on earth would she go to that?"

The only pressing matter was fixing the rotting steeple and Marion wouldn't have known about that — especially since it was really the deacons' big secret and Rebecca only knew because she overheard Ray Collins telling her Dad about it when they were having clams and chips up at Caroline's restaurant. It was more likely that the deacons had summoned Marion there. For giving out Chiclets again in Sunday School. Or telling the kids that story about Matthias, the thirteenth disciple, who went to spread the gospel in the land of the meat-eaters. Or putting too much food on the plates at the church supper.

"Dammit!" Rebecca snaps forward through the pages.

She still doesn't know what the two of them were doing that night.

And there isn't a single clue in these endless lists of meetings and appointments.

"Dammit! Dammit! Dammit!"

She looks down at the page; at the rotting remains of Saturday, November 6. *Black paint*. It's the last squiggle. The only one that doesn't make any sense now.

Chink, chink, chink.

She lifts her eyes.

Gleaming down at her, from a nail on the wall above her head, is the tambourine Frankie made for her.

She shudders.

There's not even the hint of a breeze. It couldn't possibly have sounded on its own. And yet it seems to have. It seems to have jingled with the hopes and sorrows and ceremonies of another lifetime.

She reaches up and lifts it off the nail.

The face of the little white dog is chipped and peeled. But it's not alone now. It's been joined by other faces. Frankie's. Marion's. Her own.

Chink, chink, chink.

She shudders again.

The faces are being called back. She doesn't want to go with them. She doesn't want to see that wicked sparkle in the eyes of infinity. Or hear that arrogant cackle in the voice of eternity. She doesn't want the faces to die all over again.

Pop, chink.

She taps the rim of the tambourine.

But she has to go.

Pop, chink. Pop, chink.

She has to go before it's too late.

Pop, chink. Pop, chink. Pop, chink. Hisssssss.

53

"What's that?" Rebecca sits up in bed. "Sunny? Sunny!"

"Whaaaaat?"

"Did you hear it? It sounded like my tambourine."

"Great. Now go back to sleep." Sunny pulls the covers over her face.

Rebecca slips off the top bunk to the floor.

Hisssssss. Hisssssss.

Once outside, she doesn't know which way to turn. It's so dark and still. But then she just follows the sound of the jingles — as if they're the charmers and she's the snake.

Suddenly, there's a crash and a blood-curdling scream. She ducks behind the hawthorn bush at the east corner of the church.

Pop, chink. Pop, chink. Pop, chink. Pop, chink.

She waits for the sounds to die away, then leans forward and peeks through the branches. She can't see anything at first. The branches are too thick with shrivelled leaves and berries. But gradually, she picks out her tambourine, lying all alone on the bare, wet ground, like the moon might lie if it had fallen all that way from the sky.

"I thought I heard it," she whispers.

And then she spots Frankie, lying a few feet away, in a drift of splintered white boards and shingles.

Her eyes widen.

And then Marion, who's sunk to her knees beside him and is frantically kissing his face.

She backs up into the shadows, where she can just make out the little white dog on the head of her tambourine. And the rifle, which someone is pointing at its trusting little face. And the...

"Noooooooo!"

She tries to run away. But she steps on the bottom of one of her pajama legs and stumbles a little.

"Who's there?" Marion lifts her face. There's blood on her lips.

"Just me, Marion." She creeps forward a little.

The black and white sign has disintegrated. There are white plastic letters scattered over the lawn.

Marion springs to her feet. "Here! Hide this!" She hands Rebecca a silver pail.

"But..."

It jerks her arm toward the ground.

"Hurry!"

"But what happened?"

"Please! Do what I say!"

"Is he dead? What happened? Have they killed him?"

"No." Marion wipes her lips with the sleeve of her jacket. "I mean, yes. Yes! Now hide that!"

"OK, but where?"

"Oh, God. Let me think." She looks down at Frankie. "In the cabin!"

"But I can't carry it all that way! It's too heavy!"

"Yes, you can. You have to."

"OK, but you have to call somebody."

The white plastic letters are hopelessly jumbled.

"Marion? Promise you'll…?"

"Yes."

"We can't just leave him…"

"Yes. I know. I will."

"What if he's still…?"

Hisssssss. Hisssssss.

"You have to. You have to. You have to."

As she struggles down the street, the metal loop pinches the skin on her fingers. She tries changing hands and then using both hands and then finally gives a mighty heave and clutches the pail to her chest.

Chink. Chink. Chink. Hisssssss.

When she hears the tambourine again, she looks back over her shoulder.

Marion is playing it over Frankie now, as softly and slowly and mournfully as if she were leading his funeral procession. Rebecca wonders why she's wasting time on that kind of junk; why she's not running for help or screaming. And then, suddenly, the chinking stops.

And there's that big blank again.

"Dammit!" Rebecca slams the tambourine against the floor.

The blank must be one of those "clues in the diary" she's been looking for. There's no other explanation for why all three of them are stuck inside it. But what exactly does it mean? And why exactly is it there, at that particular…?

Suddenly, it's that awful Sunday morning again and no one is more surprised than Rebecca. She can't understand why Frankie is still lying there. She can't understand how Marion's heart has mended so quickly that she can sing that stupid hymn.

"What the hell was she thinking?"

She tries to arrange the white plastic letters into an explanation. But all she gets is her own sarcasm.

"Poor Marion. So confused, so scared, so senseless with grief. Ha! Her pitch was perfect. Her vibrato completely under control."

Rebecca once thought Marion was the nicest, kindest, bravest, prettiest person in the whole wide world. And then she hated Marion — with all her dark and silent heart. Now she wishes there were some middle ground; some place between reverence and loathing where she can find Marion again.

"Dammit! Dammit! Dammit!" She scrubs her face with her hands.

Marion should have guessed what everyone would think if they found him outside the front door of the church, with no witnesses and no explanations. She should have guessed what they'd accuse him of if...She must have had a plan. She must have had a plan. She must have had...And then suddenly, she does.

"Have they killed him?"

"No...I mean, yes. Yes!"

It's a miracle. Rebecca has scrubbed her face so hard that the blank has disappeared. She can see Marion quite clearly now, rummaging around in the pile of splintered white boards and shingles — no longer senseless with grief, but alert, inventive, devious, alive. "If I clear away the rubble..." Rebecca can even imagine Marion's reasoning. "And then place a single white board beside his bashed and bleeding face...then I don't see why the police won't come and blame Barry Connors. Or Drew Saunders. Or some of the other hoods who are always hanging around." It's a great plan, agrees Rebecca. And who can really blame her for hatching it? After all she's done for those boys over the years — giving character references, paying fines, making sure their mothers have enough money to put decent clothes on their backs — she's finally fed up. The cat has done it. The cat has brought them all here, to this — to a lifeless body and a splintered white board. She hopes they'll all get charged with murder. Then thrown into jail and rot!

"Dammit!"

When Rebecca stops scrubbing her face, the rotting boards and shingles are still there on the ground. And all she has to show for her own rummaging is a handful of white plastic letters. It's what their lives have come to. It's all they ever meant to each other. It's…a handful of nonsense.

"Oh, my God!" Rebecca slides her hands off her face.

Most people can't avoid their hydras in the light either. They usually step on their heads anyway, because they're born klutzes or meanies or morons.

"Have they killed him?"

"No. I mean, yes. Yes!"

For twenty-six years, she's wanted that to be the whole conversation, but it wasn't.

"Is he dead? What happened? Have they killed him?"

"No. I mean, yes. Yes! Now hide that!"

It wasn't Marion who had a devious plan. She was only answering the question of whether Frankie was dead or not. It was Rebecca. Rebecca who heard what she wanted to hear. Rebecca who started the rumours rippling up and down the pews. Rebecca who needed there to be blame, longed for someone to pay for her misery, couldn't bear to see who Marion really was. According to her storybooks, it should have been the hoods who were responsible for killing Frankie, for ruining Frankie, for killing and ruining them all. Every one of them should have been caught and punished. But it was only Marion. Who did guess what everyone would think if they found him outside the front door of the church, with no witnesses and no explanations. Who guessed and still couldn't do anything about it. Who finally caught and punished herself.

"Dammit! I have to go back!"

Chink. Chink. Chink. Hisssssss. Chink. Chink. Chink. Hisssssss.

As she struggles down the street, the metal loop pinches the skin on her fingers. She tries changing hands and then using both hands and then finally gives a mighty heave and clutches the pail to her chest.

Chink. Chink. Chink. Hisssssss.

When she hears the tambourine again, she looks back over her shoulder.

Marion is tapping it against her leg. It's not conscious. It's not part of an ancient ritual. Even at age twelve, Rebecca knows as much about

Rituals as she does about Larger Moths and Pond Life. It's just the mechanical chinking of time, as Marion tries to think of what to do.

The pail is so heavy. Rebecca wants to run away. But the anguish on Marion's face is just too entrancing.

Chink...chink...chink...chink...

Marion taps the tambourine slowly, faintly, as if time itself is winding down. And then, suddenly, she stops. Her face is still flushed with self-loathing as she sinks to her knees beside Frankie.

Rebecca's arms are aching. But the darkness is so mad, so manipulative. The stillness is so ecstatic. She just can't move.

There is a moment, when Marion seems about to kiss Frankie again...Her lips are almost brushing his...But she doesn't. She just crawls through the rubble, on her hands and knees, gathering up all traces that she was ever there. The key case, the tambourine...

When at last Marion rises, Rebecca tries to scream. But she has a mouthful of white plastic letters.

Chink, chink, chink, chink, chink, chink, chink, chink.
"I would have gone for help," sobs Rebecca. "I would have. Only I thought she was going to do it. I thought..."

She hugs the pail as tightly as she can and then...But it's too late. Before she can spin away, she sees. She sees Marion turn away from him. And save her skin instead of her soul.

"How could you?" she wails. "How could you leave him...? Aaaaach!"
Rebecca finally spits out that mouthful of white plastic letters. A shortage of vowels, still no punctuation. They could have landed on a table with the steamed bottle caps, the dented lobsters, the dismantled lists of upcoming events back at work. But they clatter against that cockeyed sign on the lawn of the church, in a shape resembling ELERLASTIN VOVEG.

"How could you?"
Right now, Rebecca hates Marion as much as she ever has. It's not for keeping quiet — for never saying a word to defend them; for letting the whole town think that Rebecca was a liar and Frankie was a thief. It's not even for refusing to admit that she knew him very well, let

alone that his eyes were her sky. It's for leaving him lying there, all alone, on that bare, wet ground all night. He should have been her Tristan. He deserved to be wounded in a dual and die in her arms. Instead, she treated him as if he were *dung upon the ground*. If Marion had had a plan — even a dumb plan — she'd have forgiven her. But Marion was never that devious. She was just a coward. Such a coward, in fact, that she never even wrote a tiny black squiggle about it in her...

"Oh, my God! That's it!"

Once again, Rebecca stares into the blank on Sunday, November 7, 1965. Only this time, she understands.

"Were you there, Marion?"

"No, of course not."

And in a way, she wasn't. Not there or anywhere, ever again.

"I will always voveg you," murmurs Rebecca. "You are the voveg of my life. My one and only..."

Suddenly she hears the cry of a loon. A lone loon, drifting sadly away from life's shouting and squealing and splashing. It's a widow's cry, filled with the ghosts of her ecstasy, with the enduring echoes of her astonished sorrow. She will never find another mate.

As soon as the tambourine stopped chinking, Frankie was dead and Marion was doomed. She could sing that stupid hymn all right — not because her heart had healed, but because it had stopped beating. And afterwards, when who she was became too much for her to bear, her mind disappeared, too; went darker and quieter than Rebecca's ever was. Through all those years of relentless activity, then, she was really just a blank. With no more inner life. Dead already. Like that box in her datebook. Or perhaps one of Grammie's Apples of Sodom — pretty good to look at on the outside, but just ashes on the inside.

Rebecca has finally found that "essential clue" she's been searching for since she first dumped the datebooks onto the floor of the back chamber. Not where she thought she'd find it — among the many lists and squiggles — but in the void. She's not interested in any of the fancy metaphysics involved in that. She's just interested in what happened to Marion. Without that blank, Marion might have gone mad, right there, on the front lawn of the church. It probably kept her from dying when Frankie did. It definitely kept her going all those years between the splintered white boards and the telephone pole.

But it's also what finally killed her. Marion's blank wasn't impenetrable. It had little cracks, little soft spots. At first, there was just seepage — little damp stains of deceit and disgust. But finally, the whole thing filled up again with memories and she was lost.

Rebecca has finally found her middle ground, too. Halfway up a ladder. Halfway down a snake. Somewhere in that jumbo-sized box of 101 Games in One, on the trickiest board of all. Marion probably *was* the nicest, kindest, bravest, prettiest person in the whole wide world. Just not perfect. She'd tried to tell Rebecca that. She'd tried to tell her with that story about the gold watch and the cleaning lady. But it's only now that Rebecca can look back and imagine how horrified Marion must have been to see that her old self was still there. After all those years of trying so hard to be good, she hadn't changed at all. Only now, the cleaning lady was Frankie.

Rebecca would have to forgive Marion for that. And feel sorry for her, too. Even as she was turning away from Frankie, the multi-headed evil was turning into the multi-headed sorrow. Her hydra was about to grow so many heads that she'd never again be able to think, to see, to find her beloved's face amongst its writhing, conniving ones. Let alone pick which one to decapitate.

One last time, Rebecca looks back over her shoulder. There's a big black crow there now, munching on the carcass of her childhood. She picks up the tambourine and joins Marion in the funeral procession.

Chink. *Chink*. Chink. *Chink*. Chink. *Chink*. Chink. *Chink*.

There's no *Observer's Book* for things like this, but it seems their duet is an ancient lament for dead lovers, for desperate measures, for plans that go astray. And for a while, it's right that they play it together. But Marion has to keep on playing it. Her memory and her fate have collapsed into one another and she can't get out of the rubble. Rebecca, however, has to stop.

She places the tambourine back on the nail.

It's not over for her yet. She still hasn't found out what they were doing that night. And Marion's final entreaty keeps going over and over in her head.

"*You have to. You have to. You have to.*"

Suddenly, she's stumbling down the road again. And the metal hoop is cutting through the skin on her fingers.

"Oh, my God!" She stares at her hands. "I HAVE TO!"

She glances around the dark and dingy room.

Lying at the back, near the dusty window, is an old apple crate — with a glint of silver peeking through its slats. She pounces on it.

"My God!" She uses Marion's shoehorn to pry off the lid. "It is! Black paint!"

It's the last "essential clue." The last thing she needs to connect the dots — hers and everyone else's. It's no longer hard for her to imagine what she never actually knew. Her world and Marion's world and the world the world always kept to itself have come together.

54

"Look!" Ray Collins slaps his hands on his thighs. "This is the third time we've met to discuss this! The big storm was in August! We have to make a decision!"

Amongst the deacons gathered in the vestry, there's a long and sullen silence. Most of them were up late last night, giving out candy kisses and waiting for the fire alarm to sound. They aren't in the mood for debate; for much of anything, in fact, except sitting down to Sunday dinner.

"Today?" Marvin Bennett asks timidly.

"Yes, today. Did you know that Harold Peterson refuses to go up there anymore? He says it's getting too dangerous."

"See? I told you," sniffs Emerson Hill. "We'll have to repair it first."

"Ha! That's not what you said last week!" bellows Herbert Armstrong. "Last week you said we should just paint it."

"I did not."

"Yes, you did. You said there were better things to spend the money on."

"Like what?"

"How should *I* know? You were the one who said it."

"Gentlemen." Reverend MacKay clears his throat. "Maybe we should try to be practical."

"Yeah!" interjects Gordon Rogers. "Maybe we should just tear the wretched thing down!"

With that, Marion storms into the vestry. "I'm sorry to break up your cosy little meeting, but there's something I have to discuss with you. I've tried to be..."

"Yes, well, can't it wait, Marion?" Ray is exasperated. "I mean, we're in the middle of something important here."

"Important? You call sitting around on your asses playing eenie meenie minie mo about who will go to Bible College next summer important?"

"Honestly, Marion." Emerson glares at her. "I don't think it's necessary for you to use language like that."

Herbert chuckles. He can see that she's surprised herself.

"In fact..." Emerson is still in a huff. "I'm sure the Reverend will agree that the vestry is no place for..."

They all look to Reverend MacKay. But he's lost in a private quest, searching for a hint of that exotic perfume she always wears. Sometimes he thinks he's the only one who smells it. Sometimes he wishes he were the only one who smells it.

"Reverend!"

"Well, yes. Your language, Marion." He sheepishly averts his eyes. "It does seem a bit excessive. Perhaps you can..."

"Language? You're worried about language when Barry Connors and his friends have been hanging dead cats from my tree? I should think your time would be better spent worrying about how to improve the spiritual well-being of the community."

"And for your information," sighs Ray. "We weren't talking about Bible College. We were talking about the steeple. About whether we should..."

"Shsh. We're not supposed to tell anyone."

"Oh, who cares what you were talking about? I'm talking about a dead cat. Dead, with its guts all..."

"Goodness." Alvin Andrews leans toward her. "I didn't hear about that. Was it your cat, Marion?"

"No."

"Well, good." He sits back up. "That's a blessing anyway."

"Is it?"

"Speaking of which..." Emerson kicks Reverend MacKay's chair.

"What?" He's been searching for the Magi again. "What is it?"

"The spiritual well-being of the community. You know..."

"Yes, all right. I suppose now's as good a time as any." He runs his hand through his thin blonde hair. But he doesn't look at her. "It's come to our attention, Marion, that you've been...how should I put it?...embellishing the truth again."

"What do you mean?"

"I mean that matter of the Loaves and the Fishes. Little Winifred said you told them it was really brown bread and lobster."

"So?" It's a story she borrowed from Rebecca. "What's wrong with that? Do you think Jesus was allergic to shellfish?"

"Marion!"

"Shame on you!"

"Don't you know it's a sin to blaspheme?"

"She knows it. She just doesn't care."

"Well, she *should* care. Or she shouldn't be allowed to teach our children in Sunday School."

"Right."

"I agree."

"Who knows what else she tells them when we aren't...?"

"Ha! I *should* tell them that you're all about as much use as a piss-hole in the snow!"

In the ensuing uproar, Marion pauses...partly to marvel at her vehemence and partly to give Reverend MacKay one last chance to stick up for her. She keeps hearing Rebecca, as a lippy little five-year-old, declaring that "sticking up for people is the most important thing in the whole wide world." But it's no use. Reverend MacKay is having trouble even looking at her. He tries to tell himself that it's complicated. His posting is up for reconsideration; his wife Naomi says he's spending too much time at clothing drives; he's never been able to understand what Marion sees in that Frankie Lewis fellow...But the fact is he's a coward. Even if he *could* look at her, all that look would say is: "There's nothing I can do."

"Great!" Marion gives up on him. "I came here to discuss a serious matter; to ask you to have a talk with those boys before their ugliness gets out of hand. And all I get is a reprimand, for trying to add some spice to a stupid little story about...Why should it be mackerel? Is there some reason why everything in this god-damned world has to be mackerel?"

"Gracious!"

"Marion!"

"I told you she wasn't fit to…"

Herbert Armstrong leaps to his feet. "That's enough!" he booms. "Everyone! If we can't be civil to one another, there's no point in going on!"

He scowls at each of them in turn. They shift in their chairs, like naughty school children.

"Now. Ray?"

"Yes. Well. We're sorry to hear about the cat, Marion. And, although we don't know for sure who did it, we'll certainly bring it up at our next meeting. Gordon, perhaps you can put that on the agenda, please."

"Before or after the offering boxes?"

"What about them?"

"They've gone missing again."

"How many times is that?"

"Two or three. I don't know how they're getting in but…"

"*Before* the offering boxes."

"Thank you, Ray," roars Herbert. "Now. Marion?"

But Marion doesn't play along. Instead, she just stands there, with her hands on her hips, glaring at them.

Alvin picks at his fingernails. Ray shuffles his papers. Gordon and Emerson glare back.

"Jesus. Jesus. Jesus." She suddenly whirls and stomps out of the vestry.

"Well!"

"I've never seen *her* so worked up before."

Herbert turns down his hearing aids.

"Homely sort of thing, isn't she?"

"You think so?"

Reverend MacKay goes blank.

"Well, she never married."

"I know, but…"

"Why do you think they did it anyway? The boys."

"Who knows!"

"They must have had *some* reason."

"Yeah. And I think I know what it is. My wife says she's been carrying on with that…"

"OK, everyone." Ray slaps his hands on his thighs again. "Order, order."

"Yes." Marvin imitates him. "Where were we?"

The steeple was once the pride of Aylesford — an elegant, pyramid-shaped tower with a tall, tapering spire. But years of wind and wet have taken their toll and now it's in serious disrepair. The white wooden shingles are cracked and the boards underneath are rotten. The deacons are embarrassed by it. "Never mind the rain getting in," Harold mused, when they asked him, all hush-hush and everything, about painting it again. "I'd be more concerned about the friggin' frog. There'd be real hell to pay if that came crashing down on someone."

"Uh…" Alvin looks at his watch. "I think Gordon has just suggested that we tear the whole thing down."

"Oh, no!" Marvin is agitated. "We can't do that! There wouldn't be any room for the bell!"

"True. But we've never actually agreed that we need a bell. It's sounded awful bad for years now, ever since it got that big crack in it, and I hear those new electric chimes don't take up much space at all."

"But don't you think that…?" Reverend MacKay has come to his senses again, "…that apart from these considerations, which, of course, are all very important, we should take a moment to think about the spiritual effect? I don't know about the rest of you but I've never found short, squat towers very inspiring."

"Yeah, you're right."

"They're some ugly."

"I agree."

"Well, then…" Ray's stomach gurgles. "Where does that leave us? Are we going to table this question or…?"

"No!"

"Let's decide now."

"We can't leave it any longer."

"OK, then. Paint or repair. That's the…"

"And then paint."

"Right. That's the question before us. So let's see a show of hands. Who's for just painting?"

Emerson jabs his hand into the air. Herbert snickers. Ray makes a notation.

"Right. And who's for repairing first and then painting."

The rest of them raise their hands.

"OK, OK," snorts Emerson. "But let's at least get rid of that God-awful frog!"

55

Chink, chink, chink, chink, chink, chink, chink, chink.

When Marion bursts into Frankie's cabin, the tambourine nearly falls off its nail by the door.

"Something wrong?" he asks softly.

"Yes, something's wrong! Oooooooo! The nerve of those tiny, little, narrow-minded..." She tears off her coat and flings it onto the end of the cot. "And Andrew MacKay's the worst! I expected better of him. I expected...Oh, I'm so mad I could spit!"

"Yes, I can see that."

"But I'll tell you one thing. I'm not going to stand by and..."

"Whoa! Whoa! Slow down a minute." He guides her onto a wooden chair. "There. Now tell me what happened."

"Nothing happened! That's the trouble! I told them about the cat and all they did was change the subject. Ha! Gave me some crap about my language and my teaching methods and then promised to look into it later. It was unbelievable. Absolutely unbelievable."

"Was it?" he murmurs, as he drifts to the window.

The sky is immense this afternoon — bigger than their love and their guilt and their secrecy.

"Yes!" She's irritated by his calmness, which to her is less like serenity than surrender. "So what do you think I should do?"

"Maybe there's nothing you *can* do."

"Frankie! You sound just like...Well, Andrew didn't exactly say that, but he...Oh, I don't know. It's hard to explain. Anyway, I'll tell you what I'd like to do. I'd like to smash someone in the face!"

"That doesn't sound like you."

"Well, maybe *me* is changing. *Goodliness is Loneliness*, you know."

His eyes widen. "And it doesn't sound like that passive resistance stuff you were going on about the other day."

"OK. But maybe I was wrong. Maybe the meek don't inherit the earth. Maybe they just get sand kicked in their face."

"Do you really want to inherit the earth?"

"Frankie, if you don't stop teasing me I might just smash you in the face."

"Now you sound exactly like Rebecca."

"Yes, well, at least...at least she...So you think I'm being childish?"

"No, no. It's just that...Do you have to do anything?"

"Yes. I have to. Don't you understand? I *have* to."

"Why?"

"Ha! The real question is why you don't want to. It's *you* who should be trying some of that civil disobedience stuff."

"Is it?"

"Yes!" Her irritation has turned to anger. "You're the one who's always going on and on about how we should tell everyone. You know, about us. For years you've tried to convince me that we should let the whole town know how we really feel about each other."

"OK, I admit that. But this is different. I don't have a good feeling about this."

"Oh, don't be such a chicken!"

"Is that what I am? Sorry." He turns back to the window.

"No, of course not. I didn't..." She joins him there.

"It's just that I don't know what you *can* do, short of...how did you put it?...smashing someone in the face?"

"Well, no. It has to be some sort of non-violent protest. I don't want to be a quiet little mouse anymore. But I'm..."

"I thought you were afraid of mice."

"But I'm not ready to go on a bloody rampage either."

"Good. I'm glad to hear it."

"And I'm not sure I want to get caught."

"Oh, I see. You want to play a prank. Like putting a firecracker under the barbershop steps? Well, I'm sorry, but that's just not like you."

"Isn't it?" Marion grins at him. "I'm not so sure. And anyway, what if I don't want to be like me? What if I'm sick and tired of being like me? Look where being me has gotten me? Why should the little buggers of this world have all the fun? Or the little punks and creeps, for that matter?"

"OK, but..."

He's still the reluctant activist, just as she's always been the reluctant lover.

"Oh, come on, Frankie. Please. For meeeee."

"Oh, all right. But I hope you realize it won't amount to anything."

"Except put a stick up someone's ass."

"I mean anything significant. Jesus, they were right about your language."

"Well, I'm not out to change the world, you know. I just want to have a bit of fun. And I don't see what harm it can really do."

Frankie stares up at sky again. "OK, then. But first, tell me. Are you angrier at Barry or at the deacons?"

"The deacons."

"OK. Then they're the ones you have to get."

For a few moments, they stare up at the sky together. But there's little inspiration in its stern immensity. Down on the ground, however, there are impertinent weeds, with naked stalks and flaming orange heads. Suddenly, as if the devil's paintbrushes have chosen their lots for them, they have a plan. They will strike the deacons where it really hurts — at the source of their enormous pride.

"Next Saturday night, then. OK?"

"Yes. OK." He bundles her into her coat again. "If you're sure that's what you really..." He turns her toward him. "As long as you realize that you're making me do this. And that you have no one to blame but yourself if..."

"Yes." She kisses him on the cheek. "About two. I'll meet you there."

"With the paint?" He kisses her back.

"Yes. With the paint. God, I can't wait to see their faces the next morning when they...oooo!" She shivers with excitement.

"Yes. Too bad *I* can't be there."

"Yes. It'll be quite a sight. Of course, if we did it in polka-dots, it would really..."

"Marion!"

56

Late Saturday night, Rebecca turns off her headlights and coasts into the churchyard. As she passes the scaffolding that Rafuse Roofing and Siding has erected, she leans forward and peers through the windshield. The intricate pattern of poles and planks is gleaming in the starlight. It looks sturdy enough. But she doesn't care. As soon as she pried the lid off that can of paint, she was overcome with purpose. It was as if the fumes were her holy spirit and the bubbles her inheritance. She's finally figured out what Frankie and Marion had been trying to do that night; what she must do, too — before she can go home again.

"Yeah, well, that's what I'm going to do when I grow up," she can hear herself proclaiming all those years ago.

"You're mental," she can hear Brenda answering.

When she opens the door of her car, the dull little lights under the dashboard illuminate the can of paint, which is resting on the floor. She pats the back pocket of her jeans, to make sure there's still a brush sticking out of it, then hoists up the can and staggers out of the car. When she reaches the base of the scaffolding, she gazes up through the crisscross of metal and wood. The sky overhead is radiant. Its stars are glittering, like diamonds on a black velvet cloth. As she makes her way toward them, the can of paint clangs against the poles. She grimaces, but keeps going. When at last she reaches the steeple, however, she pauses…just for a moment…to marvel at life. It can be so silly, so hideous, so spiteful and so dull. But it can also be so death-defying.

Chink, chink, chink.

"Shsh." Frankie waves at her.

"Sorry." Marion clutches the tambourine to her chest. "But it's hard to…God, that's heavy!" She lets the can of paint drop to the ground. "It's hard to keep the bloody thing quiet!"

Frankie smiles at her. "I don't know why you brought it."

"I don't know either," she shrugs. "I thought maybe I could signal with it or something. In case anyone came."

"Oh." He inhales, deeply, to catch a hint of Magi, and then gazes up at the steeple.

The bell tower isn't as magnificent as that eight-sided domed cupola they have at the Anglican Church in Bridgetown. In fact, it looks a little like a dunce cap. But it's topped with a higher spire and there's nothing to compare with its final touch — that copper finial, with that big, fat bullfrog sitting on top.

"Are you sure we should be doing this?" shivers Frankie, as he stares up past the weather vane.

"Honestly, Frankie. I never realized you were such a...Jesus." She, too, is overwhelmed by the sky.

They certainly won't be needing the little flashlight in her hard, red, leather key case. There are billions and billions of stars out tonight. It's as if someone has turned on all the lights in the Houses of Heaven.

"*O holy night, the stars are...*" He starts to sing.

"Frankie!" She slaps him on the arm with the tambourine.

Chink, chink, chink, chink, chink, chink, chink, chink.

"What?"

"You *know* what. Now let's get going. Or do you think...?" She squints up at the steeple. "Do you think I should go get one of Harold's ladders?"

"No, I think I can get there from the inside. It's not usually locked, is it? Anyway, you wait here, while I go check."

A minute later, there's a sustained jingling.

"What?" Frankie pushes open the slatted window of the bell tower.

Marion peers up at him. "I thought I heard something."

"Probably just me. It's hard to get around up here in the dark, you know."

"Sorry."

"Anyway." He squeezes out through the window. "The tower's OK. But if you want the spire done, too, you'll need a ladder."

"Oh. OK." She lays the tambourine on the ground. "I'll be back in a..."

There's a tiny creak. And then a sigh.

"Frankie! What are you doing?"

"Well, you keep calling me a chicken. So I thought maybe I could..." He starts to shinny up the white wooden shingles.

"No! It's too dangerous!"

"OK, OK." He slides down to the little ledge again. "Whatever you say. But hurry up with that ladder. It's cold up...What? What are you looking at?"

Above his head, the pale green copper frog looks like it's about to snatch at a firefly. Only it can't make up its mind. There are just too many of them.

"The stars. They're gorgeous."

Frankie doesn't look up. He can already see a sparkling beauty and joy. In fact, he can't take his eyes off it.

"And so are you," he murmurs.

"*I'm forever blowing bubbles,*" sings Rebecca, as she slaps on a coat of thick black paint. "*Pretty bubbles in the...*Dammit! I can't reach from here!" She leans back against the scaffolding and inspects her handiwork.

Many of the shingles on the steeple are black now. And still wet. So they have little glints of impudence as well as virtue.

"Right." She flings the brush into the can.

If she's going to get the overlapping rows further up, nearer the point, she's going to have to climb even higher.

"Whoa!"

As soon as she steps onto the last platform, the scaffolding sways a little. She looks down at the stained and dented plank beneath her feet.

"*You have to.*"

She's been doing the steeple in basic black. That's as far as Marion and Frankie would have gone, since they were only Junior Hoods. But that old, scored plank seems to have an even better idea.

During the next few minutes, there's a flurry of brush strokes and a spatter of memories...of initials, gouged in the table behind the chesterfield, carved on the drooping limb of a sugar maple bush, traced in a faint, white, chalk heart on the wall of a barn. When at last she's finished, she leans back against the railing and smiles.

At last. The one thing they could never tell anybody. The one thing she had to blurt out for them. On the highest part of the steeple. In huge, black, shimmering letters.

MARION LOVES FRANKIE.

Rebecca glances over at the big, fat bullfrog sitting on top of the steeple — as if it might be getting ready to warn her, entice her, share some juicy bit of heresy with her. But it's not doing much croaking these days. It's just sitting there, with its sex cells and its poop coming out of the same hole. Not quite Winged Victory, perhaps. And probably not what Thornton Burgess had in mind. But a survivor. Something else besides her sanity which didn't come crashing down with Frankie and the boards and the moon.

"Ha!" She flicks her brush at it. "Won't have to paint you!"

The big, fat heretic has oxidized so much over the years that its patina has gone from pale green to black. But it could use a new skin or at least a new layer of mucous — something to match the gleam on that huge declaration she's just painted on the steeple.

"Or maybe just a touch," she snickers, as she plunges her brush into the thick black paint again. "To give you character." She stretches as far as she can out over the railing.

"They fly so high, nearly reach the..."

Suddenly, there's a sickening crack and then a shower of boards and shingles. And Frankie, diving towards Marion. He looks so graceful, so proud, with his arms stretched out to his sides, that there's a split second when their eyes aren't filled with desolation and disbelief. He's the black swan. She's the water. But then he flings his arms together. And there's a blood-curdling scream. And the split second crashes into eternity.

57

"Yow!"

The bright red Miata skitters over the soft and sandy shoulder. Rebecca yanks it back onto the pavement.

Her heart is pounding so hard that she can barely concentrate on the road. She's played a game of leapfrog with sorrow and ruin and death. Near the end, they tried to cheat. They waited until she was about to jump over them and then lifted up their backs. But she just landed right on top of them and squished them. Or spread out her legs even wider and vaulted past them.

"God! I must be crazy!"

She pulls the car into the little laneway near the French Cross. She'd been heading to Digby to catch the ferry. But something welled up inside her; filled her with the desire to feel the fury of Morden one last time. As soon as she opens the door, the wind whips her hair across her face. She smiles. It's just as she remembers it. The darkness, the delirium, the deafening roar of the sea.

She edges her way down the hill by the little brook, then scrambles happily over the stones on the beach.

"Ow! God, that hurts!"

She picks her way towards the roar; towards the waves which are thundering against the slippery rocks. When she reaches the very edge of their rage, she stops and gazes up at the stars. There are billions and billions of them, each one immune to explanation, to exaggeration, to acts of renewal or revenge. She takes a deep breath, then plunges her hands into the sea.

"Oh! God! Oh! That's freezing!"

She tries to scrub the black paint off her hands and arms and face, but it's no use. The water is just too cold. When she springs to her feet again, she still looks like a timbrel — one of those wild, white African doves which has black tips on its wings and tail.

"Brrrrrrr."

She folds her arms over her chest and begins to hop from foot to foot. And then, suddenly, she's dancing. It's as if substance and shadow have overlapped, and time has passed away. Nothing can bless her or belittle her now. She isn't cold anymore. She isn't sad anymore. She's simply there, spinning and reeling on that desolate shore, by that thundering sea, beneath those billions and billions of sparkling stars.

"Yeah! Yeah! Yeeaaaaaaaaah!"

Susan Bowes's passions include literature, music and sports. She obtained her doctorate in English from Dalhousie University, Halifax, and currently resides in Hamilton, Ontario. *Crazy Sorrow* — in which she explores her conviction that "there are many ways for life to dance circles around death" — is her first, published novel. The sign over her writing desk reads "Prose Begins at 40."

POLESTAR FIRST FICTION

The Polestar First Fiction series celebrates the first published book of fiction — short stories or novel — of a Canadian writer. Polestar is committed to supporting new writers, and contributing to North America's dynamic and diverse cultural fabric.

ANNIE
Luanne Armstrong • 1-896095-00-3 • $16.95 CAN / $12.95 USA

••

BROKEN WINDOWS
Patricia Nolan • 1-896095-20-8 • $16.95 CAN / $14.95 USA

••

THE CADILLAC KIND
Maureen Foss • 1-896095-10-0 • $16.95 CAN / $14.95 USA

••

CRAZY SORROW
Susan Bowes • 1-896095-19-4 • $16.95 CAN / $14.95 USA

••

DISTURBING THE PEACE
Caroline Woodward • 0-919591-53-1 • $14.95 CAN / $12.95 USA

••

HEAD COOK AT WEDDINGS AND FUNERALS
Vi Plotnikoff • 0-919591-75-2 • $14.95 CAN / $12.95 USA

••

A HOME IN HASTIE HOLLOW
Robert Sheward • 1-896095-11-9 • $16.95 CAN / $14.95 USA

••

IF HOME IS A PLACE
K.Linda Kivi • 1-896095-02-X • $16.95 CAN / $12.95 USA

••

RAPID TRANSITS AND OTHER STORIES
Holley Rubinsky • 0-919591-56-6 • $12.95 CAN / $10.95 USA

Polestar Book Publishers takes pride in creating books that enrich our understanding and enjoyment of the world, and in introducing discriminating readers to exciting new writers. Whether in prose or poetry, these independent voices illuminate our history, stretch our imaginations, engage our sympathies and evoke the universal through narrations of everyday life.

Polestar titles are available from your local bookseller. For a copy of our complete catalogue — featuring poetry, fiction, fiction for young readers, sports books and provocative non-fiction — please contact us at:

POLESTAR BOOK PUBLISHERS
1011 Commercial Drive, Second Floor
Vancouver, British Columbia
CANADA   V5L 3X1
phone (604) 251-9718 • fax (604) 251-9738